THREADS OF SUSPICION

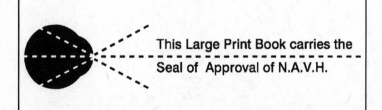

This Large Print Book carries the
Seal of Approval of N.A.V.H.

AN EVIE BLACKWELL COLD CASE

THREADS OF SUSPICION

DEE HENDERSON

THORNDIKE PRESS
A part of Gale, Cengage Learning

GALE
CENGAGE Learning·

Farmington Hills, Mich • San Francisco • New York • Waterville, Maine
Meriden, Conn • Mason, Ohio • Chicago

GALE
CENGAGE Learning®

LIBRARY OF CONGRESS CATALOGING-IN-PUBLICATION DATA

Names: Henderson, Dee, author.
Title: Threads of suspicion / by Dee Henderson.
Description: Large print edition. | Waterville, Maine : Thorndike Press, a part of Gale, Cengage Learning, 2017. | Series: Thorndike Press large print Christian fiction | Series: An Evie Blackwell cold case ; #2
Identifiers: LCCN 2017008957 | ISBN 9781410499639 (hardcover) | ISBN 1410499634 (hardcover)
Subjects: LCSH: Cold cases (Criminal investigation)—Fiction. | Large type books. | GSAFD: Christian fiction. | Mystery fiction.
Classification: LCC PS3558.E4829 T48 2017b | DDC 813/.54—dc23
LC record available at https://lccn.loc.gov/2017008957

Published in 2017 by arrangement with Bethany House Publishers, a division of Baker Publishing Group

Printed in the United States of America
1 2 3 4 5 6 7 21 20 19 18 17

THREADS OF SUSPICION

ONE

Evie Blackwell

As Governor Bliss came to the podium, Lieutenant Evie Blackwell dug her hands into her coat pockets, grateful the January cold would keep this press announcement on schedule and limited to twenty minutes. His inauguration just the day before had been sunnier and a few degrees warmer. She did her best to ignore the television cameras trained on the podium, knowing she and the other officers on the stage were now in their view frame, and that this clip would run on the local evening newscast.

The governor, at ease with the crowd, spoke without notes. "Thank you all for coming this afternoon. As one of my first acts as governor, I am pleased to announce the creation of the Missing Persons Task Force.

"Led by Lieutenant Noble of the Riverside Police Department," he said, motioning toward her in the row behind him, "these detectives will take a fresh look at cold cases across the state of Illinois, where a loved one has gone missing, bringing new insights, questions, and ideas to the table. Working with local police, they will endeavor to find answers and bring needed closure.

"I know when you are waiting for news, any wait is too long. My sister, Shannon, was missing for eleven years. I never stopped searching, I never gave up hope, and through God's grace and Shannon's courage, she is home again. We need more miracles that will get similar news to many families. And for those whose missing father, mother, daughter, or son will not be coming home again, so that they will be able to lay their loved one to rest. This is a first step, a good step, toward helping find answers.

"I would like now to introduce the man who leads the Illinois State Police, Commander Frank Foster, for a few brief remarks."

It was official. For the next two years she would be time-sharing between her current job with the Illinois State Police's Bureau of Investigations and the new Missing Persons Task Force. Evie caught the eye of her boyfriend, Rob Turney, in the audience behind the press corps and shared a smile. It had been nice of him to take a day off work, fly down to Springfield from Chicago, to be part of her day and this announcement.

The commander's remarks concluded, Evie in turn shook hands with the governor, stood for photos with the other taskforce members, and the event was completed.

Evie maneuvered through the crowd to join Rob. "Would you like to say hello to the governor? I can get us a minute with him before he slips away, if you like," she offered, sliding her hand into his. Rob had met then-Governor-elect Bliss at the Christmas party of her friends, Ann and Paul Falcon, and had spoken about the encounter many times since. Ann had gotten Evie her job on the task force, as their friendship covered more than years.

Rob considered the crowd around the governor. "I appreciate the thought, Evie, but there will be future occasions when your cases are successfully solved. This signature piece of his administration is going to have his considerable attention. I'll get to talk with him another time."

Her hand tightened on his as she smiled. "I love the optimism. Can you stay for a meal?"

He replied by leaning down, kissing her softly. "Thanks," he said, his voice full of regret, "but I need to be getting back for a late meeting. You'll be getting organized with the new group and I'd just be in the way. I'll catch a return flight with Ann and Paul. Call me tonight. Let me know where you're heading tomorrow. If it's anywhere north, we'll meet up for dinner this week."

She hugged him, and his arms held her close as she whispered, "Thank you." It conveyed a wealth of unspoken realities. Her present job took her back and forth across the state, and she'd just committed to twenty-four months of even more relentless travel.

"You'll do great work, Evie, and make us both proud."

She let him go. She had a marriage proposal from him waiting, an offer that he would make if and when she was ready to say yes. He wanted the permanence of being married to her, and she simply wasn't there yet. But she was thinking more and more about it. As she had scanned across the faces familiar to her at the event, she realized again that his presence mattered a great deal more than any of the others.

As Rob headed over to Paul and Ann Falcon, Evie looked around to see where her group was gathering. David Marshal was the only one not presently in conversation with someone from the press. She moved to join him — a solid guy, comfortable with the attention, and taking it all in stride more easily than she was. She was sure she was going to enjoy working with him, as his reputation as a New York City cop preceded him. He had come back to his Chicago roots just for this new venture.

"Your guy?" David asked, nodding at Rob's receding back.

"Yeah."

"Nice. I'm glad he was here to see this."

Evie smiled. "You have a girl?"

David returned the smile and said easily, "I do. We've been dating a number of years now. She's still in New York, but is moving back to Chicago soon." He nodded an acknowledgment to a person in the crowd. "I hear you're hosting tonight."

"I hope you like your chili hot and your jambalaya spicy," she replied with a smile. She was the only one in the group who actually lived in the Illinois capital of Springfield. She had volunteered her home and a meal for their first gathering as a team.

"It sounds perfect for a cold day."

The others joined them as they got clear of the press. She would have the honor of

11

working alongside some of the best detectives in the state. Sharon Noble in charge, Theodore Lincoln out of Chicago, Taylor Aims from St. Louis, David Marshal back from New York. She hoped to keep up, to pull her weight, to do solid, effective work representing the Illinois State Police.

"How about directions, Evie, and we'll reassemble at your place?" Sharon suggested. "Besides a nice meal, we're going to be able to get some actual work done today. This is exciting," she said, rubbing her cold hands together. They all laughed at her enthusiasm.

Evie gave directions, then added, "The dogs are Apollo and Zeus and love nothing more than to have a rumble with guys. You want to make a friend for life, toss a tennis ball and watch them smash into snowdrifts for the catch. Neighbors on both sides are in Florida for the season, so park wherever the snowplows have cut a path." She glanced at her new boss. "Sharon, why don't you bring John? Since your Riverside PD will be doing task-force paperwork, shouldn't he be in on the opening round of decisions? There's plenty of food."

"He's got to meet up with Commander Foster first, but I'll suggest he come by after that," Sharon agreed. John Graham, deputy chief of the Riverside PD, would be involved even if not formally. Sharon presently wore John's ring, and wedding plans were in the works. Evie was hoping to have a few minutes to ask John for wedding-shower gift ideas.

Plans settled, the group dispersed toward the parking lot.

"Evie, I think your dogs are stalking me."

She set down the pitcher of iced tea and turned, saw that David was right. The German shepherds were about four feet behind him, both in a hunting stance, intently creeping up on him. She grinned. They'd attack his shoelaces if they could get close enough. "They get bored during the winter." She walked over and interrupted their hunt, leaned down and scratched behind their ears. "Relax, guys. He's too big for a decent quarry. Go play with your rope or find your ducks."

David laughed as they reluctantly headed out of the kitchen. "You've got to give them credit for working together." He dipped himself another bowl of chili, added grated cheese and crackers. "It's great chili, by the way."

"Thanks — my grandmother's recipe. Throw it in a crock-pot, it's ready any time."

She dipped out a bowl of the jambalaya and carried it with her iced tea over to the table, glancing at Sharon, who gave a nod to her questioning look.

"I vote we head to the most heartbreaking counties first," Evie said, responding to the question at hand. "Douglas County has three missing seven-year-olds, plus a school principal and a grandmother."

"That county needs to be on our short list," Theo agreed, writing it on the large whiteboard she'd brought in for their convenience. They had already determined to work county by county, taking a fresh look at cold cases five to fifteen years old. Evie had done a test run of the strategy in Carin County over her vacation last November, and it had worked well. Which county to head to first was the question on the table.

"We will have extra media interest in the initial months," Taylor said. "We can use that to get the public's help with certain cases. Those missing in Briar County, for example, cover the gamut," he added, reviewing a summary sheet. "A wife and two daughters. A college student. A businessman in his fifties. A teenage boy. A private investigator. That's a lot of human interest in one place, helping keep appeals for information prominent in the news."

"Not to be too political, but do we want to factor in the likelihood of *solving* the cases into our decision?" David asked, setting down the second bowl of chili and pulling out a chair beside Evie. "Some cases have already had more media exposure, more manpower hours, than others. Clark County has two missing women, both with a history of prostitution. The reality is they likely wouldn't have been worked as aggressively as the missing seven-year-olds. And if we could solve those two cases, we likely would be able to do the same in adjacent counties, since those kinds of missing persons tend to be part of a larger pattern."

"Working those could lead to a major arrest," Sharon said. "Add that county to the short list, Theo. I like the idea of going where there is the suggestion of a larger pattern. What's the consensus? Do we want to try for a home run our first time at bat? Or do we play softball while we jell as a group?"

"Attempting a home run first time at bat, you mostly hit air," Theo cautioned.

"What's the mood of the locals?" Taylor asked. "Some of these counties' law enforcement will want our help, while others will be less than welcoming. We're going to need homegrown assistance. They know the area, the people, and we need that kind of knowl-

15

edge to run down leads. I'd say we go first where we know we're wanted."

Murmurs of agreement came from around the table.

"All three of these counties would welcome our involvement," Sharon told them. "David, you've traveled the farthest to join the task force, so I'll make this your choice. Which county do we work first? And which case there do you want?"

"Let's head to Briar County. For full disclosure, I still need to get settled housewise, and that's close to where I'll be buying. And I like the idea of looking for that missing PI. It suggests some interesting work."

Sharon nodded and continued around the table. "Evie, which case would you like?"

Evie scanned the summary sheet, and it was an easy choice. "The college student."

"Theo?"

"The teenage boy."

"Taylor?"

"The businessman."

She wrote their selections down. "Okay, I'll take the missing wife and two daughters. Good. We've got our opening salvo. We'll work them both individually and as a group. As we solve one, we'll double up on the others." She sorted maps in her briefcase and pulled out Briar County, unfolded it on the table. The locations where the individuals had gone missing were already circled. "We're going to be spread out across this county. Evie and David, why don't you base in Ellis, help each other out? Theo and I will head to Park Heights. Taylor's in Juno. Let's plan to meet as a group in Juno on —" she pulled out her calendar — "Wednesday, the twenty-eighth of January, to talk through our progress."

"Drive or fly?" David asked, glancing at Evie.

"I'd rather have my own car than a rental," she said. "Roads are snowy, but we could make it there by, say, one a.m. if you want to go up tonight, travel in tandem."

"I'm for getting there, sleeping in," he agreed.

Sharon folded the map. "The travel budget is going to accommodate what we need, along with decent hotels. I plan to fly north with John and Theo in the morning. It's faster to make your own reservations and put in for reimbursement, or you can let the State Police travel staff make your bookings — the number is in your packets. It's taking about ninety days to get repaid right now."

"Some things never change," Taylor remarked with a shrug. "I'll plan to drive up tomorrow."

"Good. With the exception of David, we've all got current jobs that are going to demand attention too. You get called away, be sure to leave your notes. David, can you handle covering interviews if someone needs to step out?"

"Not a problem."

Evie rose to cut the pies — she'd bought apple, cherry, and lemon meringue. "The case files, Sharon," she said over her shoulder, "should we call tonight to get evidence boxes pulled?"

"Briar County is one of a handful that has already retrieved their case files from the archives. The boxes will be with the officers who most recently worked the cases, waiting for pickup. I'll make some calls tonight and locate workspace for us at these various locations — probably a conference room at the local PD or empty office space. I'll text you specifics as I get them. I don't want us having to work a case out of our hotel room unless that's your choice." Sharon looked around the table. "What else am I forgetting?"

"You'll handle the press?"

"Only if I can't get a volunteer."

"We unanimously vote that one's yours," Theo replied for the group with a smile.

18

"I was afraid of that. What else?"

"We're good. Come have pie," Evie suggested after a moment, getting plates out. "We'll celebrate the start of the task force in style."

Sharon Noble

Sharon looked around the room at the cops eating pie, getting better acquainted with each other, and felt a deep satisfaction. The Illinois Missing Persons Task Force would do good work over the next two years. In her opinion, the depth of talent in the room was unrivaled. This was her team now, and for the next two years, professionals all. They would get it done.

She had been working missing-persons cases for the last eight years with the Riverside PD and loved the job. She was an optimist — missing persons could be found, or at least closure could be had. Being asked by the governor to lead this task force was a gift, one she was going to enjoy.

John Graham, the deputy chief of police for the Riverside Police Department, and the man whose ring sparkled on her left hand, had arrived and was in earnest conversation with Theo. She'd be juggling wedding plans with her task-force work, but she'd handled more difficult complications

19

in the past. John had encouraged her to take this on. Everything needed for success was here. Now they just had to deliver on the promise, find some people.

"Sharon, when's the wedding?" Evie asked, coming over to join her.

"We've decided on the twenty-seventh of April."

"A spring wedding. Nice."

"John wants three weeks away for a honeymoon, and I'm considering that idea. I'd rather have two and spend a week of that getting settled into his home. Travel isn't my thing, and for every day away, the piles on both our desks just grow that much higher."

Evie laughed. "A minor negotiation between the romantic and a pragmatic."

"Governor Bliss asked me to pass on his thanks again for your willingness to serve on the team. I don't need to tell you how personal our success is for him."

"I know. I'm going to like the work."

"So am I. The idea of solving what has happened to a mother and two daughters has me itching to get those files open," Sharon admitted with a smile. "Ann said to get in touch with her if you need anything. She's now officially on the FBI payroll as a retired homicide cop consultant, so we can draw her in on whatever investigative work we want while the task force gets established."

"Good. For starters, I plan to ask if she wants to walk around a college campus with me."

"She'll be useful to all of us. Your dogs will be okay with your extended absence?"

Evie turned and saw the two German shepherds watching her guests from a perch on the stairwell landing. "Recently retired military guys on this block take care of them while I'm traveling — basically wear them out with an army version of daily PT. I'm the mom who babies them when I'm home. My dogs get the best of all worlds when I travel." She'd given them a bath the day before, and for tonight they looked like gentlemen. "I'm clearing out perishables since I don't know when I'll be home next. You want oranges, bagels to take to the hotel for the morning?"

"Sure."

"How about a piece or two of pie?"

Sharon looked over to see what John had chosen. "He's favoring the cherry if there's extra of it. He'll view it as fruit and have it for breakfast." They laughed, and Evie went to box it up.

An hour to wrap up here, Sharon thought,

mentally listing immediate tasks, *let Evie and David get on the road, make calls to find workspaces, and then a quick text to the governor — keep him in the loop as requested.* John glanced over, shared a smile with her. He was her biggest supporter in this new endeavor. *God, you really favored me with a good man,* she mentioned to Him in gratitude.

Balancing work and a personal life when you were a cop took unusual wisdom, and Sharon knew Evie was in the process of sorting it all out for her own life. A young, gifted detective, destined to be Ann's replacement on sensitive matters for the governor. One of the reasons Evie was on the task force was so Sharon could help get her ready for that role; she was going to enjoy that mentoring role. Teaming Evie with David had been the first step toward that end. David was a great guy. He'd been in a solid relationship for a while, and the dynamics of juggling the job and dating would be another point of common ground and possibly helpful discussions.

Theo was single, but older than the others here. He dated interesting women but had no plans to settle down to married life in the immediate future. A solid cop with a calm demeanor, he'd spent his career focusing on cold cases, and she was fortunate to have him. She thought he would become the natural linchpin of their group, and others would key off him when their cases were stuck. She knew she would.

Taylor, married with two sons in college, didn't fit any particular law-enforcement pattern, had loved patrol, worked undercover, served in administration, become a detective. Everywhere he went, the departments improved — better morale, quicker response times, fewer citizen complaints, falling crime stats. Sharon had realized after meeting him a few times that he was praying for people around him — simply part of how he operated, doing it with such consistency that he left peace and justice in his wake.

Sharon smiled as she realized they all loved this work. Solving real-life puzzles mattered, and they weren't the kind of cops to give up easily when a case hit a brick wall. They brought a wealth of experience to finding answers. It was going to be a good two years.

TWO

Evie Blackwell

It was even colder in Ellis than it had been in Springfield. Evie, glad to be getting out of the wind, held glass doors open for David as he pushed a flat cart loaded with boxes into the building. "I'm curious," she asked, "how do you prefer to begin a case?"

He wrestled against a stiff wheel that wanted to drift left. "I like talking to people. Once I've seen the facts I've got to work with, I like to get out and start asking questions, see where those answers lead. People point you different directions. The majority of the time they're being honest and trying to be helpful. When I come across someone lying to me, I know I'm getting close to the answer."

"You're looking for the person who shades the truth, lies to you."

"Pretty much. How about you, Evie?"

"I like to get inside the world of my

victim, see what they were doing, where they were going, how they crossed with someone who did them harm."

"Re-create the day of the crime."

"The best I can."

"A good approach."

Evie used keys the security guard had provided to unlock the main doors for office suite 5, then flicked on lights. The space had recently been refurbished for new tenants — a design firm was moving in late next month — and it still smelled of fresh paint and new carpet. Having expected a small room at the police station, this was luxury.

David scanned the area. "You've got four boxes, I've got seventeen, so I call dibs on the conference room through there. I need the long table and even longer whiteboard."

"A couple of desks and the rolling whiteboards will serve my case," Evie agreed.

"An hour to sort through boxes and see what we've got, then bring in an early lunch, update where we are?"

"Sounds good." Evie set an alarm on her phone. "It's going to be fun — if I'm allowed to describe it that way."

David grinned. "I like this job, though I'm careful how often I admit that. I'm sorry my PI is missing, but it makes for a fascinating puzzle, considering what he did for a living. I get paid to do work I love. Everyone should be so fortunate."

"Ditto." Evie lifted her boxes off the cart and over to a desk, and David pushed the remaining ones into the conference room.

The detectives who'd had these cases had been cordial, polite, but not enthusiastic about offering further help. They told them, "It's all in the files," without saying, *Good luck with finding anything else.* There were still two map tubes in transit from the archives for her case, but the bulk of the case materials were before her.

The lack of assistance from the locals was probably for the best, at least for now. The facts were in the reports. The theories of what happened . . . well, Evie would rather formulate her own, as would David.

In her experience, solving a cold case came down to looking at the existing facts in a different way, asking new questions, searching intently for a thread that would yield information overlooked in the past. Not an easy thing to do when a case had been worked aggressively, but inevitably overlooked items came to light if she kept digging. If the new evidence didn't yield an answer, her second course of action was to dig deeper into the lives of the people

26

involved with the missing person, and then push out to find more names beyond the family and friends in the record.

The passage of time nearly always brought out undiscovered truths about people. The "good man" with a terrible secret had been found out and was now in jail, the thief who never got caught had committed one too many burglaries and finally been arrested, and the woman who drank too much now had the DUIs to prove she had a drinking problem. *Life reveals truth.* That was what Evie depended on when it came to a cold case like her missing student.

Time changed circumstances. Close friends were no longer speaking to each other, families split apart, alliances shifted, people would now talk to authorities about things they'd seen or wondered about when past loyalties had kept them silent. The same interviews done today could yield a treasure trove of new information. Whichever approach worked — looking at facts a new way or finding new insights about those people involved — she'd push until this case yielded an answer.

This missing Brighton College student was her choice off a single line on a summary sheet. Now came the moment of truth. Would it turn out to be an interesting choice? Evie lifted the top off the first box, eager to dig in. "Okay, Jenna Greenhill, what have the cops already found for me?"

The folders were thicker than she had expected. From the dates, it looked like detectives had come back to this case many times. She thumbed through the folders, found lab reports, witness statements, daily updates, phone call lists, credit-card statements, even police reports on five possible related cases. There was a lot of reading ahead of her, but when she was done, she would know how the detectives had approached the case, what they had discovered. *Good, the foundation is here.*

Thankfully, the detectives had included flash drives with electronic archives of their reports. She'd have searchable information at her fingertips, which would speed up her investigation considerably.

She lifted the lid on the second box and found a treasure trove of Jenna's personal items. Purse, wallet, keys, desk calendar, journals, cellphone. Evie opened the evidence bag holding the phone, slid the battery back in, and wasn't surprised when the device didn't light up. The battery was dead. She'd pick up a replacement as one of her first errands. Jenna's laptop was sealed in an evidence bag, along with a technician's note providing a neatly printed password. The last significant item was an accordion folder stuffed with bills, menus, flyers, handwritten notes with phone numbers, names, lists — likely Jenna's desk and kitchen-counter clutter swept together and kept, since what would matter might be anything here. *Good — the cops had paid attention to the small things that could be key to solving this case.*

The third box was more of Jenna's papers, stored in folders with the girl's handwriting on the tabs — college class schedules, financial aid, class notes, medical records, bank statements, utility bills. One titled FAMILY AND FRIENDS was mostly saved birthday cards and a few personal letters. Jenna had liked her world organized. Her life was here, at least the structure of it.

Evie opened the fourth box and nearly laughed out loud. Jenna had created scrapbooks and photo albums — eight of them, neatly stacked. "Thank you, Jenna. You're going to make my job easier."

Four file boxes . . . enough material to build a solid foundation, but not so much Evie couldn't properly get her arms around it. She was already having a good run of luck with this case.

Evie stepped to the conference room door.

"I hit a gold mine."

David looked up from the box he was unpacking.

"Scrapbooks and photo albums."

"Girls do like photos and fluff."

She laughed softly at the kind way he said it. His case boxes were now lined up against the far wall, their lids tucked behind each one. "Having any luck with your discoveries?"

"My PI is Saul Morris — he looks to be an interesting man. I have what may be the contents of his office spread across ten boxes. Two are personal items from his home. A box of police reports and witness statements. And finally, a good assortment of electronics — two laptops, four phones, three cameras, a shoebox full of backup CDs and flash drives. There's a stack of handwritten notebooks in this one, not unlike a cop would make. I'm very optimistic."

"I'm glad for you. I'm going to start putting together my board and timeline. Unless you would like some help?"

David considered what was around him. "I'm good for now. Thanks for the offer."

Evie took the now-empty cart to get it out of his way, checked the supply cabinets, found colored markers for the whiteboards, magnetic clips to hang items. There were a dozen mobile whiteboards stored in the auxiliary space beside the conference room — the design firm had organized this office for doing a lot of visual work. Evie rolled one over to her desk, drew a horizontal line, marked the middle with *October 17, 2007,* the date Jenna Greenhill had gone missing.

Sometimes determining what was going on before a crime pointed at the solution, but most of the time with cold cases, the answer was discovered in how people acted after the disappearance — guilt stained a person, criminal conduct continued — so there were as many clues, if not more, after a crime as before it. She would work both sides of the timeline with equal intensity.

Perspective first, then details of the disappearance, Evie decided. She looked through the boxes again for facts that would define Jenna's life.

Jenna Greenhill.
Last seen: October 17, 2007
DOB: 11-12-85, age 21 when last seen
Parents: Rachel and Luke Greenhill
Siblings: sister, Marla, 3 years older

She found a casual photo of Jenna with her mother in an early album — *Mom and me, Saturday morning tea and talk of college plans.* Jenna wore stylish glasses, shoulder-length auburn hair — she didn't have a classic beauty, but she looked attractive. Her smile looked a touch self-conscious. No jeans and a casual top, but a summer dress, nice necklace, earrings, no rings. The mother looked much more relaxed than Jenna. Evie posted the photo.

She added a family photo: parents and two girls with snowcapped mountains behind them — Yellowstone, 2003, according to the caption. Luke was nearly a foot taller than his wife and daughters. There were no obvious signs of stress in the family photo, such as one of the girls avoiding being too close or resisting a parent's touch, and the smiles seemed genuine.

A helpful cop had added Post-it notes to Jenna's albums. Evie reviewed images, chose several that seemed the most relevant, and added them to the case board.

Current boyfriend: Steve Hamilton
Former boyfriend: Spence Spinner
Best friend: Robin Landis
Study group friend: Amy Bertram
College friend: Tiffany Wallace

Her first interviews would be with family and friends. Evie reached for the phone and called her preferred researcher at the State Police, gave him the names to track down. Jenna's college friends would have dispersed across the nation after graduation, but hopefully some were still in the area. The rest she'd re-interview by video. She would wait to contact the parents until the detective assigned to the case spoke with them and conveyed the news the task force was once more taking up the search.

"Will music bother you?"

Evie turned to look at David. It *was* quiet in here. "Try it. I'll tell you if it does."

At another desk he pulled up a playlist of songs on a website, and music filled the office suite at a comfortable volume. She didn't know a lot about popular music, but she recognized the song currently climbing to the top of the charts. "You like her music. You had that band, Triple M, playing on our drive to pick up the case boxes."

He dug out his wallet and slipped out a photo, showed it to her.

Evie stared. "Margaret May McDonald? She's *your girl*? Are you kidding me?"

David laughed. "She prefers just Maggie. There are dozens more photos on my phone, but this is my favorite." He slid the photo back into his wallet. "She's scheduled to be the special guest a week from Friday at Chicago's charity benefit sponsored by the mayor. She'll be singing a couple of songs. If you'd like to go, I'll introduce you."

"I'd love that," Evie replied, stunned at the news. "Wow. At our first break here, you owe me the story of you two, how that came to be."

"It's more dinner-hour fare, as it's long, with ripples folding back on each other. But it's a good one to tell."

"You're on."

"I'm going to find the break room and start some coffee. How do you take yours?"

"Black is fine."

David headed down the hall. Evie added more notes about Jenna to the whiteboard.

Brighton College
Biology major
Chemistry minor
Junior year by credit count
4.4 out of 5.0 GPA

Her thoughts were no longer fully focused on her case. *Her working partner was a celebrity's boyfriend.* How had she missed *that*? It couldn't be that tight a secret in the music world. Cops were notoriously low-key about celebrities in their midst, but when the significant other happens to be this famous and *dating a cop*? Evie was struck by how many comments must have drifted by her and not registered.

No wonder David had smiled at her question about a girl. Oh, yeah, he had a girl. Only one of the most famous singing sensations in the country!

Deal with it, Evie whispered to herself, forcing her attention back on task. She posted a copy of Jenna's class schedule. She searched out names of Jenna's professors, TAs, her academic advisor, listed them under the class schedule.

She'd been a bit intimidated to work with David Marshal before this, knowing his official reputation, but now it was on a whole new level. He'd probably been backstage at numerous concerts, met any number of other celebrities in New York. She was going to have to brush up on her music knowledge. She knew what kind of music she liked to listen to, but could rarely remember the title of a song, let alone name the singer or the band.

Something similar happened when Rob would introduce her to someone at a party. She'd say hi and have no clue how important the person was in the greater world of finance and business. People probably thought she was rather self-assured, not intimidated to meet important people, when most of the time she simply didn't know who they were. Ann did the same, introducing Evie to the governor-elect, to the former vice-president. Ann's world seemed normal and yet was filled with areas that were anything but common. Ann was comfortable there, but Evie struggled to figure out how to do that. She never wanted to be personally famous. If she had a single goal in life, she just wanted to be a good detective.

The alarm on her phone interrupted her introspection. Evie found the stack of area menus the security guard had provided and scanned through them. "What sounds good to you for lunch?" she asked David as he came through the door with two mugs of coffee.

"A sandwich is fine. I'm thinking Italian would be nice for dinner tonight. A good spaghetti or lasagna."

"I'm game." She called in a delivery order for soup and sandwiches, considering David. He didn't look like the boyfriend of a famous singer. He looked like a cop. She'd just think *cop* and hopefully forget, or at least adjust quickly to, the unexpected fact of his girlfriend's status in the music world.

She drank the coffee he had brought her

and once again shook off the distraction. She scanned over the collection of data. *There's enough to give me a basic sense of Jenna's life,* she thought. Time to look at the specifics of what had happened. She pulled out the first police report. It had been called in by Jenna's best friend, Robin Landis, on Monday afternoon, October 20. Jenna had last been seen Friday night. *A rather long gap . . .*

Once the timeline was filled in with details pulled from police reports and witness statements, Evie settled back in a desk chair to study the information and unwrapped a roll of sweet-tarts. A bag of them had showed up at her home, gift-wrapped, with a *Have fun on the task force* note from Gabriel Thane. The sheriff of Carin County was a good friend who knew her well. She'd tossed the entire bag in her suitcase, figuring it might last the first week.

Okay, Jenna. I'm looking for you now, and I'm going to dig in until I find you. What's here to see? The items on the board showed a typical college student going about her life. Classes. Friends. Boyfriend.

Jenna had gone out with a group of friends on that last Friday night, dinner first and then a concert. She had parted from the group just after 11 p.m. on the block where she lived. At 11:42, Jenna sent a text message to her mother — *Back in apartment, received your message, will call you in the morning.* After that . . . nothing. Jenna hadn't been heard from or seen again.

The missing-persons report had been filed on Monday afternoon. Jenna hadn't been answering texts or calls, she missed church where she was a semi-regular, missed her classes on Monday morning, including a chemistry test worth twenty percent of the semester grade. The building manager had opened the apartment door for a worried friend, and her friend had then called the police. Jenna's purse was there with her phone and keys. Her car was in its assigned parking spot. No sign of a struggle. Just no Jenna. . . .

It was fairly typical for a missing-persons case landing on a detective's desk. A few days of delay, friends and family getting worried, the realization they couldn't locate her, so call the cops.

On the surface, the case seemed straight-forward. But it hadn't been solved in the last nine years, so something was muddying what should have been an open-and-shut investigation and arrest.

Evie reached over for a blank pad of

paper, divided the page into two columns, and numbered the lines one through twenty. On the left side she wrote *FACTS,* on the right side *THEORIES.*

Under FACTS, she listed:

1. Good grades
2. No history of problems with the law
3. No history of excessive drinking
4. Steady boyfriend
5. No roommate
6. Keys recovered in apartment
7. Phone ditto
8. Wallet ditto
9. Car in her parking space
10. No sign of struggle in apartment?

Evie put a question mark on that last one because she'd want to study the apartment photos with a magnifying glass before affirming it.

11. Last seen Friday night, 11 p.m., her block, walking to her apt building
12. Last text sent, Friday, 11:42 p.m., to her mom
13. Did not answer phone calls on Saturday
14. Did not attend church on Sunday
15. Did not appear in Monday classes

16. Credit cards not used after Friday night
17. Bank accounts not accessed after Friday night

What had Jenna been wearing that Friday night? If it was a unique outfit, and those clothes were in the apartment, Jenna had been home long enough to change before whatever this was had happened.

Evie scanned the reports. Friday's attire: blue jeans, a red college sweatshirt, tennis shoes, maybe gray. If Jenna hadn't had several close variations of that outfit in her closet, Evie would be surprised. Friends didn't remember her wearing jewelry. That wasn't helpful either.

She would find more details in the police reports and witness statements as she got deeper into those thick files, but for now this looked like the opening set of operative facts.

Under THEORIES, Evie started making another list. Her process was pretty simple: gather facts, speculate on possible theories, eliminate them with more facts, and eventually she'd find her answer.

1. Killed or still alive?
2. Missing by her own choice?

3. Stranger in apartment, lying in wait?
4. Robbery of apartment, she walked in on it?

Evie lightly crossed off number two — *Missing by her own choice,* though it remained readable. What she knew about this college girl indicated that was unlikely.

5. Boyfriend Steve Hamilton did something?
6. Former boyfriend Spence Spinner did it?
7. Abduction for ransom that went bad, with no ransom call made?
8. Anyone out there who would want to cause Jenna's family grief?

She needed a deeper look at the family. Brighton College was a private school and tuition would be expensive, suggesting either numerous scholarships and grants or the parents had money. Evie made a note to research that topic. Cops would have looked at the boyfriends closely, but she'd take another look there too.

9. If killed in her apartment, where did the body go? Hauled out when/how? Friday night? Saturday morn-

ing? Not a solitary sign of violent death?

10. Killed in another apt in the building?
11. Any other abductions, disappearances of women from this college?
12. Someone else sent that last text, not Jenna?

Evie stopped when she wrote down twelve, feeling an interesting tug. Maybe killed somewhere else and then someone takes her apartment keys, goes to the apartment, maybe to steal some cash (hard to know) or remove a connection that cops would otherwise find, photos on her phone or laptop, or to retrieve a gift given to Jenna. He (or she) sends text to her mother to misdirect when and where Jenna had been. *I'm back at the apartment,* sent at 11:42 p.m., only it's not Jenna sending it. Evie circled number twelve. She'd learned through experience to find areas not yet explored, or only glanced at, and spend more time there. She thought the cops had probably not pursued this particular idea.

13. Jenna was grabbed on the block before she reached her building, killed in some other building/

apartment on the block? (But her keys were there — she would have had them with her . . . killer returned them?)

Evie would need to know who had lived not only in Jenna's building, but in every apartment in the neighborhood — a whole lot of data to dig up and a lot of backgrounds to look into. Evie felt hope begin to rise that this case could be solved. Cops already would have looked at guys living in the area, but had they really *drilled down*? Systematically, building by building, across that block and others nearby? She could dig in with the benefit of hindsight. There could be a record of something off about the person she was looking to find. Kill one girl, odds were good you had committed other crimes in the last nine years. Evie put a star beside that idea.

What else? What other theories could fit the facts?

14. A good student. Was she writing papers for other students to make extra money? Helping someone cheat, now wanting to stop? Or she'd said no to someone who asked for her help to cheat?

15. She was a good student because she was the one cheating, buying papers and getting advance looks at tests from a TA?
16. She saw something she wasn't supposed to see and was killed to keep her from talking. A drug deal? A fight? What else happened that night in the area?

Okay, now she was finding herself in the weeds. Evie put down her pen and read back through her lists. She'd add more in the coming days, but enough was here that she might already have brushed up against the answer to this case.

Evie retrieved the photos cops had taken of the apartment and began to sort them out by area and room. She was interrupted by the front desk calling to say their lunch order had arrived. Evie walked down to get it, carried the sack to the conference room. "Mind if I join you?"

David turned from his whiteboard, smiled, and pointed to the clear end of the conference table. "I'd welcome the company. I'll be paused here in a minute."

It would be good to step away from Jenna for a bit. Evie divided the lunch order and pulled out a chair. Piles of folders filled the rest of the table, two laptops were open, and the PI's phones were neatly lined up. She watched David writing more notes on the long whiteboard, building his case overview. She started her lunch. "You're not linear," Evie remarked, intrigued by what he was doing. Client names, family members, neighbors, and friends all radiated out in various circle clusters.

David paused to unwrap his sandwich, gestured to the board. "It's people who interacted with him who can tell me his life story. And one of those people likely killed him. I'll deal with the timeline when I'm ready to break the alibi that's spun."

"You don't think he could just be missing, that he took himself off the grid and disappeared for some reason?"

David shook his head. "I find it easier to assume the worst. Then I ask the tougher questions."

"Interesting point."

He settled in a chair and opened a bag of chips. "You don't make assumptions to narrow down a case?"

"I run theories, play what-ifs, see how many different stories I can create out of the existing evidence. I try to simultaneously hold all of them as active possibilities as I explore for more facts."

"We have very different brains."

Evie laughed. "I'm often told I'm simply odd."

"Yours works. I'm just more . . . well, let's just say I shake the box of people connections and wait for the answer to fall out."

She wrapped up the second half of her sandwich for later and opened her own bag of chips. "I'm going to learn a lot just by watching you work."

David smiled. "With this case, I'm glad I prefer this approach. My PI disappeared sometime between Thursday morning and the following Tuesday morning. Throw a dart at a map of Chicago and its suburbs to sort out where it happened."

"Ouch."

"I chose a black hole for a case," David replied with good humor. "Saul didn't have someone he would check in with regularly. He used an answering service instead of a secretary. He was in contact with family, but not in a predictable pattern. There's no steady girlfriend in the picture that I have so far. By this time tomorrow I'm going to know just how deep a mystery I've got here. Even his car is missing."

"Your reputation will be well earned when you solve it."

"Or this will take a bite out of it. Solve

your case quickly, so you can come and help me out. I'll need it."

Evie laughed. "Ditto. Do you like hard cases?"

"Sure. It gives me something more to pray about."

Evie wasn't sure if David meant that literally, so she chose to let the comment pass for now. "I've seen enough paper with mine I'm ready to get out of here, go see the college and where my girl lived." She pushed back her chair and picked up the remainder of her lunch. "I'll be back by dark to join you for dinner. I want to hear the story of you and Maggie."

"By then I'll have opened all these folders and be ready for a break," David said. "Good hunting, Evie."

"You too, David."

THREE

Evie drove over to Brighton College, thinking about her case, trying to push what she did know toward possible answers.

At this point, it didn't feel like Jenna had chosen what happened. She didn't seem like the type of woman to take herself off the grid, walk away from her life, disappear of her own choosing. Not with a good relationship with her mother and the years she'd already invested toward getting her degree.

Jenna had no roommate, so scratch a personal collision of values — no college-style domestic violence, roommate doing away with roommate and successfully covering it up.

Jenna might have walked into her apartment to find unexpected trouble waiting for her. No indications of struggle could have been patience on the killer's part. Tucked in, lying in wait. Comes at Jenna when she's vulnerable, maybe after she turned in for the night, maybe after she went to sleep? Yeah. Maybe.

Someone hides for a couple of hours, though, they have to hide *somewhere.* Were there dead spaces in the apartment floor plan? Rarely used closets? She'd need to find out.

Evie reached into the console tray for another sweet-tart. Jenna Greenhill should, could and would be found. A real-life puzzle made this a good workday.

She drove onto the college campus shortly after two p.m., found a parking space near the quad. The open space of snowy ground was surrounded by buildings she assumed were devoted to various study disciplines — economics, chemistry, business, engineering, to guess a few. She picked up the backpack she preferred to a briefcase, locked the car. She could pass for an older student with the backpack, casual coat and boots, and that suited her for now. She'd look like a cop easily enough when that would better open doors.

From the groups of students crossing the quad, college hadn't changed much since she'd attended — clusters of young people heading to classes, trying to fit in a personal life around their studies. The couples stood out, for they were laughing, chatting with each other, and basically not paying attention to the rest of the world. What had changed were the smartphones and the messaging and scrolling through screens for information — looking at their cells, reading as they walked, tied into their slice of the world, defined by the music they liked, the style of news they preferred, and the people whose opinions they chose to follow.

The missing Jenna had walked this quad many times. She would have blended into this mass of humanity, not stood out. Some of her fellow students would have known her, most would not. Professors, teaching assistants, classmates in lecture halls, study groups, the social world of a dorm, then the apartment building, the hangout for pizza and the favorite mall — maybe three hundred people at the outside would have been in Jenna's circles? Forty or fifty people would know her well, another hundred would be casual acquaintances, another couple hundred would be able to place where they often saw her, the rest would be, "Oh yeah, the girl who disappeared, her photo looks familiar from the news."

Time had passed, but it wouldn't be that hard to roll back to when Jenna had been here. If someone around campus had caused her harm, that person likely had bothered someone else as well, possibly gotten kicked out of the college. Evie would check at the provost office for discipline problems, everything the campus security had worked on for the three years on either side of Jenna's disappearance. Cops would have pulled that information in the past, but it never hurt to get a fresh copy of the data.

Evie checked the campus map and headed toward the admin. building, hoping her badge would clear the way to some co-operation. First rule out the personal — boyfriend or ex-boyfriend at the time — then dive into the fellow-student pool of possible candidates and start eliminating names. That she would be walking the path other cops had taken before didn't bother her. She'd see facts in a different order, maybe make a connection they had missed.

Someone knew who had done this. Find him or her through Jenna or through other things he or she had done and connect back to Jenna. It was just a matter of working the angles to get the right one to come into the light.

It helped having the governor interested in what the task force was doing. It took only three referrals to get to the person who could make a decision about what she asked to see. She wouldn't get everything she hoped for, but she would get enough to be useful.

Satisfied with what she had put in motion, Evie strode across campus toward the apartment building where Jenna had lived. If she was lucky, the current resident didn't have afternoon classes and would be home.

"Jenna lived *here*? The student who disappeared years ago? This apartment?"

Evie tucked her badge back into her pocket and pulled in a sigh. The girl might be in college, but Evie's guess put her on the very young side of being a freshman. "The locks have been changed many times since then, security tightened with numerous cameras," Evie reassured her. "This block has had very little crime in the last several years based on data I've seen. I'd only like to step inside, look around, if you don't mind, get a sense of the floor plan of the apartment."

The girl named Heather bit her lip, but nodded. "Yeah, okay," and stepped back to let Evie enter.

It was a typical college student's small apartment, decorated by a young woman away from home for the first time, free to enjoy her own style and colors, but clinging to family and the familiar with photos and high school memorabilia on the walls.

"This is supposed to be one of the safe neighborhoods since the sorority houses, the sports stadium, and the bars are on the other side of campus. It's mostly premed majors and science types in this area."

"We're not even sure Jenna disappeared from here or if she had gone out again that night," Evie reassured. "She simply wasn't home when friends came looking for her."

The apartment was narrower than Evie had realized from the photos. A living room area to the left led out to a small balcony, to the right a small galley kitchen with a narrow counter, a table that doubled as a desk across from the counter at a window, then a short hall to a bedroom and bath. A guest stepping into the apartment would either have to step into the living room or into the kitchen-study area.

Evie noted where they were both standing. Heather had stepped into the kitchen entrance to let her enter the apartment. Jenna would have done the same if she asked someone to come in, automatically moving back into the kitchen between the counter and refrigerator to clear the doorway. It was a contained space, hard to escape from — you'd have to climb over the counter, and there wasn't much within reach to slow someone down — throw a toaster, a coffeepot?

"Is there a lot of street noise when you're sitting at the table studying?" Evie asked Heather, wanting to get her talking.

"If the balcony door is open, or the windows, it's steady noise, but you learn to ignore it after a while."

"What about the other apartments? Do you hear their music? Hear doors close as they come and go?"

"Sure. Late at night, you can tell in a general way that someone is still up — cabinets being closed, music on, voices in the hall when people come and go," Heather replied. "It's not a quiet building. It's got a routine that you start to recognize as normal. Who's most likely to come in late, the pattern of people's schedules. Sometimes when you're having people over, you can get a complaint to hold it down after ten p.m. We're pretty considerate of each other as we're going to be neighbors for at least a semester, and we've all got to study."

It was helpful information. It told Evie the witness statements from building residents when Jenna disappeared should be studied in detail for what they had heard and when. Evie scanned the apartment windows, checking angles from which others would be able to see inside. "The building manager, the super, any problems or delays getting stuff tended to that needs attention — a dripping faucet, broken latch, loose floor tile, that kind of thing?" Management of the building hadn't changed in the last decade, Evie had checked, so it was likely a few of the same staff were still working here.

"There's a maintenance number, and they are good about coming by. You have to leave a signed slip in their box downstairs with details on what is wrong, give permission for someone to come into the apartment if you want someone to handle the problem when you're not here."

There would be keys to the apartment somewhere in the manager's office, and Evie would want to check how easy it would be for someone to lift those keys, use them to enter the apartment, or make a duplicate for later. Procedures might have changed, some personnel, but certain things would be very much the same. "Laundry is in the building?" she asked Heather, trying to understand the dynamics of a shared building like this.

"On the first floor, past the mailboxes and the utility room. You can sign up for a specific laundry time for one machine or take your chances that the other is free."

"What's in the utility room?"

"They keep extra snow shovels, brooms, that kind of equipment available for tenants to use. It's left unlocked because there's not much there you would want to steal. Stuff has been spray-painted a bright lime green."

Evie smiled. "What do you do with your trash?"

"We're supposed to use the dumpster out back marked for this building, but if you've got a car and you're going out by the south parking lot, it's quicker to use the dumpster for the next building."

"Parking's constantly full? You have friends over, they're going to have to park where they can find a place and walk over to your building?"

"Mostly. It's always a challenge," Heather agreed. "You can get away with double-parking to bring up groceries, but you better be less than five minutes or someone is going to remember it was your car and make a fuss about it. We've got a parking space matching our apartment number, and mostly it's honored. But in winter it gets to be everybody for themselves when the pavement numbers get covered up. Most simply walk to where they are heading if it's anywhere nearby. It's just not worth moving your car and losing your parking space. And the bus is decent for going out to the mall — it passes through this block every hour."

That was useful to know. Evie pointed to the refrigerator. "Where do you get your groceries?"

"There's a decent grocery store two blocks east that most of us use. And every restaurant around here delivers in thirty minutes or less. This kitchen seems great when you look at apartment options. But having lived here a while, it would be better if they had made this area all office space and given us a half-sized refrigerator and a microwave rather than tie up all this floor space. No one has time or really wants to cook when it's just one person."

Evie remembered those days and mentioned lightly, "I kept my books where the plates were supposed to be."

Heather reached over and opened a cabinet. It was filled with art supplies. They shared a laugh.

The mood shifted to serious again as Heather asked, "Do you think something bad happened in this apartment?"

"If it did, I'll figure it out," Evie replied, keeping her tone matter-of-fact. "Think of it this way, Heather. You're in the one apartment the building manager worked the hardest to improve for security — new dead bolts, new window locks, a camera in the hall — not to mention it's been fully updated." Evie pointed out the living room, then the kitchen. "When Jenna lived here, that carpet was blue, the backsplash had a gold-checked pattern, and every wall was painted white. You've got basically a new place. Whatever occurred is history, and every apartment here has its own history, good and bad."

Evie looked back at the building from the front sidewalk. It showed its age, but it was well-maintained and matched others on the block, so likely it was built by the same developer. Odds were good the building stayed fully occupied, given it was cheaper housing than the campus dorms and was within walking distance to where classes were held. There would be people around, coming and going, at all hours.

Streetlights, wide sidewalks, with a patch of grass and a row of large trees in front of each building. The mature trees would leave dark pockets at night, blocking the moonlight and streetlights. The parking lot was visible from the street, but there were enough rows of cars to provide concealment if someone was careful.

Selecting this building, choosing apartment 19, risking going upstairs — Jenna hadn't been a random target, not if this happened inside. If it happened on the street or in the parking lot, that could be more random. Grab Jenna because she was the vulnerable one in a target-rich environment. Maybe the guy sat nearby, a van on the street, watching people come and go. Jenna walks across his line of sight and gets picked.

Right age, appearance — move when she's near your vehicle, snatch her fast, control her ability to cry out. Or maybe just walk up next to her with a question when she moved into a shadowed area and abruptly hit her hard, knock her out, and ease her into the van. Two minutes? Three? Try not to slam the van door or drive away too quickly. A public abduction was extremely dangerous, but that would increase the adrenaline and excitement levels of such a crime.

Evie felt a growing supposition that Jenna had walked into trouble that night. Either she was grabbed on the way home, and someone else sent that text to her mom, or she came back outside for some reason and was then grabbed. If an abduction on the street or in the parking lot, Jenna wouldn't be his first, would she . . . ?

Jenna had walked to dinner, the concert, then back to the apartment building, so the circuit of those places couldn't be far. Evie looked at her watch. With daylight left, she decided she had time to find the restaurant and the concert venue. She checked the restaurant name and location in the files she'd stuffed into the backpack, searched for it online, got directions. She headed north on foot.

She had the list of people who were in the group that night with Jenna, would track them down so she could interview them again, this time to ask about the details. Chinese food. Jenna's choice, or someone else in the group? The first time Jenna had been to this restaurant, or it was a place the waitstaff knew her by sight, remembered her usual order?

Evie found the restaurant in under ten minutes, studied it from across the street. An upscale place, probably an occasional destination rather than a frequent one, only when you wanted to splurge on a nice meal. They eat here, that takes maybe an hour of the evening, and then head as a group to the concert venue.

Evie looked up the Fifth Street Music Hall and was directed four blocks east. She walked that direction, finding herself mostly moving against pedestrian traffic flowing toward the college.

The Music Hall was a corner building occupying a good half of the block, tented canopies for entrances on both cross streets, a lighted marquee, the band *Five Young Guys* playing tonight, with the opening band, *The Chili Peppers,* warming up the crowd. *Smoke & Fire* was being promoted for Friday and Saturday nights. Evie had no idea who any of these groups were, but they must have a following sufficient to play here. Three expansive parking lots and a multistory parking garage were in sight of the building, suggesting weekends could be packed houses when a popular band was booked to appear.

Evie considered what it would have looked like that Friday night. Streets busy with cars, couples and groups streaming to the Music Hall for a concert, a lot of people milling around. The group around Jenna would have been one of many clusters merging together at the entrance. Someone could slip in behind her group, follow her inside — never be noticed, just one of the crowd. A popular concert would draw in music lovers from all over the area.

Had Jenna been a music groupie? One to hang around for an autograph? Or was she the type to enjoy the music because this was where the group wanted to go that night, then she was ready to call it an evening and get home?

Maybe she'd caught the attention of someone in the band or the crew that did the setup and teardown. "Why don't we meet up for a drink when I get free in an hour?" Or, "The band is gathering for drinks to end the evening, why don't you join us? Don't tell your friends, so they don't get jealous — it's a private invitation. I'll pick you up, or you can walk behind the Music Hall and meet me at the backstage door" — anything along that line would work if Jenna had stars in her eyes about a band member. Who was playing that night?

Evie tugged out the police reports, scanned them, but didn't see the names of any bands. Who in the group had made the dinner reservations, bought the concert tickets, put this evening together? She did track down that name. Tiffany Wallace. Evie shifted folders and got lucky. Tiffany's witness statement was in the set she had brought with her. She turned pages looking for the particulars. *After the concert we headed back to campus . . .* Tiffany's statement was filled with references to the evening's plans, the restaurant, the Music

Hall location, the concert was sold out, their group came and left together, lots of people were on the street as they headed back to campus — details, but not the names of the groups playing that night. Evie flipped through other witness statements, not finding the specifics she was after.

Her friends had seen Jenna alive after the concert, near her apartment, the cops hadn't been focused on the concert in the first hours of the search. Not unexpected. Evie was interested only because whatever had happened that night hadn't been solved, and this was a prime location for Jenna to have been spotted by someone who took an interest in her. The details she needed would be in the other documentation somewhere. She'd find it when she was back at the office.

She'd seen enough to tell her the core of it. Evie shoved the folders back into the backpack, dug out car keys, and reversed course. She'd come back with Ann for a more detailed excursion.

Jenna had been around a lot of people that night. Past midnight or one a.m., Evie doubted this was a quiet area on a Friday night. If Jenna had doubled back this direction after leaving her friends, someone would have seen her, noticed her, likely said

63

something when the area got papered with missing-person fliers and cops and friends were asking questions. Evie wanted to see the tip file, the called-in comments that cops might have looked at and not been able to do something with at the time.

She didn't know yet where the crime had happened. That felt like the critical missing fact and the most likely reason the case hadn't yet been solved.

Evie dumped her backpack on the desk and went to see what David was doing. The conference room whiteboard had been turned into a visual look at the PI's life. David was sitting on the opposite side of the table, studying the mosaic.

"Welcome back." David slid over an open bag of pretzels, and Evie pulled out a chair, took a handful. She hadn't worked with him long enough to recognize his mood at a glance, but she had the impression his thinking stints were probably as intense as hers, and interrupting was best timed for when he was ready for a break. She was rewarded for the silence with a smile and nod by him toward the board. "I've been looking through his files at the type of work he did. A PI doing his job is spying, sneaking around, collecting rumors and evidence to prove someone is a criminal or an adulterer or otherwise a bad person. *Really* bad people are the ones who tend to turn around and kill you."

Evie thought that was a fascinating observation, and considered the board. A missing PI defined "interesting" simply for the parallels with what law enforcement did plus the sheer number of directions it might go.

David scooped up another handful of pretzels. "I've glanced at his personal life. Saul Morris was forty-eight, never married, a clean record with local cops. He worked at a newspaper as a photographer before he got into PI work. Nothing showed up that set off alarms — no sex scandals, no revolving set of girlfriends, no gambling problem." He pointed with a pretzel at the photo of Saul's house. "Nothing was found in his place suggesting he was using or dealing drugs, trafficking in stolen goods, or doing some blackmailing alongside his investigating. Hobbies were sports and cars — several car magazines subscriptions, he'd paid to drive around a race track in a performance car — that kind of thing. He preferred to work alone, sole proprietor, no history of hiring any staff. His life was his PI business."

"An older guy with an interesting career," she commented, "maybe a few painful breakups with girlfriends in his twenties and thirties, so why settle down now?"

"Pretty much how I read it," David said with a nod. "He was actually pretty tame as PIs go. He was good with a camera, good at tailing people. He worked a number of infidelity cases. 'I think my spouse is cheating on me' kind of thing. He was getting referrals from satisfied clients, who told their friends about the PI who'd helped them out. It's sad when you think of it — the cottage industry that exists around infidelity. It looks to be about twenty percent of his business.

"He also did a lot of background checks. Prospective business hires, as well as people being considered for promotion to sensitive positions. Numerous traces locating people skipping out on debts and child-support payments. Some of his personal bills he paid by camera work — a newspaper needs a photographer on a breaking story, he'd stop what he was doing to take the job."

Evie was seeing a picture form as David spoke. "A realist about the work, a lot of jobs that would take five to fifteen hours, keep the client list full, the income diversified."

"I'd say that's how he was thinking," David concurred. He nodded at the board. "Notice what's not up there?" He gave her a minute to scan it. "There's no work for insurance companies, suspected fraud, thefts, the 'he said it was stolen and put in a claim, but he's actually still got it,' kinds of cheating attempts by people who aren't very good at it. There's also no work for lawyers, which is surprising. Most PIs are doing some trial-related work, probing the veracity of statements from defendants, trying to locate witnesses."

"A selective kind of PI," Evie said thoughtfully, intrigued. "So either business was good," she guessed, "or he lived thin as far as personal needs went, so he could be choosy about which clients to take on."

"From what I've seen so far, I'd say he was making ends meet, but it wasn't luxury," David replied. "He was living skinny in order to stay with the cases he wanted to work. I'm also not seeing what I would call work with the shadier sides of Chicago business — the business owner paying protection money to a crime family, a store dealing with a gang problem so as not to get their front windows smashed. Most PIs are doing some type of 'social counseling,' the 'back off' message delivery, the ex-husband

67

or boyfriend ignoring a restraining order. But my guy was avoiding that type of job."

As Evie listened, she realized David was revealing a rather extensive working knowledge of the PI business. She also noticed his handful of pretzels had become a neat stack as he idly flipped them into order in his hand while he talked. She was going to find the next weeks fascinating and had to force her attention back to the case itself, rather than profile the cop working it.

"My PI was the type who preferred to hang back," David continued, gesturing again with a pretzel toward the board. "He liked to observe, take photos, ferret out the secret. Based on the numerous photos on those laptops, this guy can blend in at hotels, at bars — social, comfortable in crowds. He's street-smart, can think on his feet. But that may have cost him his life, if he was too confident in his ability to handle himself in difficult situations."

David glanced over. "You look into the secrets people are keeping, you're going to find drugs, gambling, an affair, or a pretty elaborate fraud — the guy with two wives, a Ponzi scheme, embezzlement. I'm going to guess Saul followed someone, taking photos, got spotted himself, and paid for the error with his life — photograph a drug buy, get yourself shot. I'm inclined to think this case is going to come down to something that simple. He was doing a job that can be deadly. And for him, it was."

Evie studied the names on the board, not expecting to recognize anyone, just counting for a total. "Getting killed because of work, given the breadth of his clients, is going to make for an interesting exploration."

"The number of cases he was working at the time of his death is manageable. That's where I'll start digging first. If the answer isn't found in those, I'll then look at the closed cases. Maybe someone wanted payback."

"You sound pleased," Evie mentioned.

David smiled. "I am. I'm starting to understand this guy. I've now scanned enough files to know what he was doing in his job, and it's the job where he poured his time. That's a good chunk of work sorted out in just the first day." David reached for a bottle of water. "That's my case so far. How did your campus visit go?"

"Useful." Evie filled him in on her impressions of the college and the apartment building where Jenna had lived.

He nodded as she finished. "You're leaning toward a local crime, everything at the root of your case residing within blocks of each other."

"I am. Her world is contained. I think he entered it and chose her. Whether he was choosing a type — a pretty college student who was vulnerable, reachable — or choosing the person Jenna, I'm not sure yet."

"You'll find him."

Evie appreciated his certainty. "I will. Though I'm not yet sure it's a him. I'm thinking *her,* as that possibility is probably not something well-explored yet. It's there somewhere, the thread I need to find and tug." She pushed back her chair. "Italian, you said? I've got a few things I want to gather up to take back to the hotel, but then I'm ready for dinner. Don't forget, I'd like to hear the story of you and Maggie."

He laughed. "Okay, give me twenty minutes and I'll be ready to head out. We'll find some good food and then I'll tell you an interesting story."

FOUR

David suggested an Italian restaurant near the office complex, and Evie followed his SUV in her car. The crowded parking lot suggested the locals approved of the food and the prices. David requested a table to the side of the room so they would have some privacy, near enough to the kitchen they weren't going to get a close neighbor until the restaurant was full. Evie settled into the booth with a grateful smile, and the two scanned the menus.

David lifted his water glass. "To what will become a very long day."

She touched her water glass to his. "How much work did you bring along with you for later?"

"Enough to have me reading until well past midnight — I brought one of his laptops too. You?"

"I packed all Jenna's journals."

David laughed. "Yeah. The faster we know

what's there, the easier our lives become. So we'll work twenty-four seven the first few days."

"Not sure about your number, but ambition suits us both."

"It's the foundation of an interesting career," David agreed. He closed the menu. "Lasagna and a house salad, to help me decide how I like their sauce and seasonings, along with the appetizer special and hot bread, because lunch was a long time ago and any leftovers suit the hours of work still ahead."

She thought that sounded perfect. "A double on the lasagna and salad."

The waiter returned with their soft drinks, took the order, and brought a shared salad bowl and hot-bread basket.

Evie let David serve the salads while she split the bread loaf. "So start somewhere, David, and tell me about Margaret May McDonald."

He smiled at the way she said the full name.

Evie added, "I have to admit, you really threw me with Maggie's photo — it kind of scrambled my brain. Jenna Greenhill needs my attention, and I found myself instead wondering about the two of you at odd points throughout this afternoon."

David passed her salad over. "You'll like Maggie. She's got a thing about famous people too, sort of stammers when she meets other singers for the first time. It's really rather cute. She's still very much a fan despite the fact it's also her profession."

"She sells a lot of records."

"Vinyl, CDs, streaming audio, radio time — her music is everywhere, which makes for a nice icebreaker when I'm looking to find common ground with someone twenty years younger than me."

"How did you two meet?"

"We've known each other since high school."

He paused as the waiter brought the appetizer platter of colorful grilled skewers stacked with mushrooms, peppers, tomatoes, onions, and pineapple chunks. David nudged the ranch dressing and honey dipping sauce toward Evie, the marinara toward himself. "Are you a Christian, Evie?"

She deftly slid one skewer of vegetables off the stick and onto a shared plate. "Why do you ask?"

He sampled one of the mushrooms, nodded his approval. "There are two ways to tell this story, one of which is going to make less sense than the other depending on your answer."

"I am."

"A Christmas and Easter kind of Christian, or your Bible came packed in your luggage for this trip?"

She couldn't help but chuckle at his description. "It's currently sharing space on the bedside table with a J. D. Robb mystery and a Derek Prince book on biblical prophecy and the Middle East."

"Then I'll give you some of the nuances as I tell this." David accepted one of the slices of hot bread. "I was twenty-six, had just made detective, was settling into my career, when Maggie and I got engaged."

"Oh. Well, that's . . . unexpected." She found herself totally unsure of what to say.

He smiled. "I'll get to that in a bit." He buttered the bread and took a bite, settled into the narrative. "But first we'll back up.

"I'm older than Maggie by a few years. We actually went to different high schools. Our parents are good friends. Maggie had a talent for singing, wanted to see where it would take her, and the kind of events and places a new singer gets invited to perform can make for late nights. The band hadn't formed yet, she didn't want to make it obvious her parents were keeping an eye on her from the crowd, so I made it a point to be her guy, keep the social headaches away

74

from her, be a safe ride home. It began as a good friendship on both sides. But it's hard not to love Maggie, and I fell for her hard. We were going steady by her senior year in high school."

The relationship and romance began with the blessing of both families. Evie could see it. She ate some of the grilled peppers and pineapple as she listened, finding herself glad he was willing to talk about this. She would have been stumbling around otherwise, trying to figure out his history with Maggie and how it had developed.

"She has talent, wanted a band, and other performers met her and signed on, became her core group. Triple M officially formed after Maggie graduated from high school."

David reached for his drink. "She didn't hit it big right away. It was a steady climb through the ranks, playing everywhere they were invited, starting to travel as an opening band for others, then booking out weekends and beginning to get a following among the college crowd. They were working on their first songs for a recording when she turned twenty-three. That was the turning point. Her own music, some of them lyrics I'd heard her working on since high school — genuine emotion with a powerful voice. Triple M gradually became a featured band after that."

"You went to the academy, became a cop," Evie guessed, "while she's climbing her way up the music ladder."

David nodded. "Maggie would joke that I was her fallback if her career didn't catch fire. She'd marry me, be a stay-at-home wife, and I could bring home the bacon. We were talking marriage all the way back to the early days when I was in the academy and she was getting her first invitations to perform. But we wanted to wait until she knew how her career was going to go, until I had settled in with my job. We were going to be married when she was twenty-five, have kids by thirty — that kind of plan.

"So we got engaged. I'd be at her concerts most weekends. We were going to get married, have a long honeymoon during the three-month winter break when Maggie's concert schedule was clear. We were planning the wedding. Well, she was."

They both smiled, and he paused as their entrées arrived. Evie cautiously nudged the steaming lasagna bowl to the center of the plate, the cheese on top lightly browned. Her first bite confirmed her hunch — great lasagna.

"I was settled in as a cop by that point, while her career was beginning to take off,"

David said, picking up the story. "I was so proud of her, how she was handling it all. It was new to the rest of them too, the fame, the growing crowds." David passed his phone over to share more photos. "Their last concert in New York, backstage. Some of those guys have been around since the first days when it was college venues for the most part."

Evie scrolled through the pictures. Maggie looked happy. The ones of Maggie and David — casual shots snapped by someone using his phone — showed a couple very much in love. You couldn't duplicate that look in Maggie's eyes, that expression, without a deep contented love resting behind it. Evie quietly returned David's phone. What he'd been describing so far was right out of a fairy tale, friends in high school who stayed together as fame and fortune unfolded.

Evie looked across the table at him, knew the story was going to turn painful. "You and Maggie didn't get married as planned," she said quietly.

David met her gaze, sadly smiled. "No. We haven't. Yet. A car crash on the way home from a concert late one night shattered my leg, meant hours of surgery, months of rehab. That wreck changed the course of our lives."

He turned his lasagna bowl to more easily cut through the noodle layers. "I had dropped Maggie off at her home after that concert," he continued, his voice reflective, "and headed back to my place. We were both still living in Chicago then. Traffic was heavy, there was a semi in the lane beside me, a car trying to merge in, roads were wet. Police reconstructing what happened concluded the merging car misjudged speeds, came into the lane of the semi, the semi braked hard to avoid smashing into the car, the trailer fishtailed, caught the back passenger-side bumper of my car — I would still probably have been okay at that point — but the van behind the truck came into my lane trying to get more room to slow down and crashed into me at speed. The car and I ended up partially under the truck trailer. It took over an hour for fire and rescue to get me out. I was conscious for most of it, able to actually call Maggie so she'd know I was okay and not to panic when she came to the hospital. I was heading to surgery for my leg but otherwise had my full faculties.

"Both our lives changed that day," he said, looking over at Evie. "My daily job was no longer law enforcement, it was rehab. I fell more deeply in love with Maggie than ever, seeing how she handled those months. She pretty much set her career aside to be with me through the process."

David spooned himself another helping of salad, then seemed to turn his account in a new direction. "I met a guy named Bryce Bishop while I was in rehab. He had a friend from the military learning to walk again, and Bryce was his rehab buddy, someone to encourage and fill in rest intervals with sports and life outside the world of physical therapy. I'd see them most days, and we three got to be friends. As the months wore on, I didn't want Maggie putting her career totally on hold for me, so Bryce helped me bridge that gap — be the honest broker about how I was doing when Maggie called from some concert location. We both came to trust him as a good friend.

"Bryce is a strong Christian. He was comfortable talking about dying and what's after that, that if God existed it was worth asking the questions and coming to a con-clusion about it. I had a lot of time on my hands, I had come awfully close to death, and it's always in the back of a cop's mind. I started talking with Bryce about God, reading books he provided, thinking. We weren't a religious family, and I'd never been to church. Maggie didn't come from a church background either. So I'd watch videos of sermons with Bryce, talk over the questions they raised. It was a strangely captivating new world, this idea of God and angels and heaven and hell, a life beyond the touch-and-feel reality around me." He paused a moment, took another bite.

"I got to know Jesus," he finally said quietly. "He seemed like such a complex person, joyful one moment, gentle the next, warrior-like when needed, speaking with authority on every important matter in life. Jesus said that to see Him was to see what His Father was like."

Evie nodded but didn't interrupt the moment with a question.

"When you're a guy looking at his life," David went on, picking the narrative up again, "there's something about Jesus that resonates deep inside. He came to get a job done, to save the world, and He completed that mission even though it meant a painful death on a cross. He valued people without playing favorites, noticed those society overlooked. The ones getting life wrong, He challenged to start doing it right. He treated women with caring respect and was loving to kids. He was authentic. He showed what a man doing life well looks like. The fact He was the Son of God, had never sinned, you could see it in how He lived." David glanced at Evie, smiled. "I was baptized in the therapy pool five months into my rehab."

"Good for you," she said softly.

"Best day of my life in many ways," David agreed. "No one thought about the implications at the time. Things for me evolved, and getting baptized was where I was in that journey. I accepted Jesus was the Son of God, He'd died for me, had risen from the dead, and I wanted to follow Him, go all-in with the God who loved me like that. So I got baptized and publicly declared my faith."

He hesitated, then said, "It was assumed because I came to believe rather easily, that Maggie would have the same experience and find faith a step she could take as well, would join me in believing in God. She was with me through those months, listening to the conversations, asking good questions. It wasn't that this step was something I took without Maggie. We talked about it along with how the rehab was going and our lives and the wedding plans we were moving back because of rehab. It was just part of our lives, my thinking about God and coming to believe in Jesus."

He rubbed a hand over his face. "I can

still remember the day it struck me, when I realized I couldn't marry someone who wasn't a Christian. It was there in the Scriptures, when Paul tells us we should marry only in the faith, to another believer. To my thinking at the time, it was like 'Okay, that's another milestone I need to add to the sequence of things. Maggie will come to believe like I have, I'll get done with rehab so I can walk again, stand comfortably for the duration of the wedding, and when her concert schedule frees up, we'll get married, take that long honeymoon.' Only things didn't unfold that way."

Evie, understanding now where this was going, felt a growing sadness.

David put down his fork. "Had the car accident happened six months later, we would already have been married — God would have no problem with me believing and my wife would still be considering that step for herself. We would have our good life together. But we were simply engaged. And with that came a roadblock. We're in limbo. I can't give her a wedding date."

"I'm so sorry, David."

"Yeah. You can read the passage in Second Corinthians to mean something different, but that's stretching it to fit what you want.

I'd never felt such an intense battle in my spirit as during those next months. I was stuck between obedience to what God said and the word I'd already given to Maggie. I loved her. I had asked her to marry me. She'd said yes. I was the one who had changed, not Maggie. And it didn't seem like God was asking me to break the engagement. He was simply saying 'Wait, wait until she also believes, then have the wedding.' I finally found peace with the situation as it was. I wasn't going back on my word to God or my word to Maggie." He shrugged. "God is going to have to fix this for us."

"I hope He will."

David nodded. "Maggie's handled this so much better than me, with such grace. As time passed, I've offered to step back, to let her go on with her life. She deserves a good and happy life, the family she wants. She's wrestled with the question of faith with a sincere heart and hasn't been able as yet to accept it as hers. And she's equally wrestled with the question of moving on — at her request we've taken several long breaks in the relationship to give her some space — but she isn't willing to say it's over unless I too believe it is."

"She loves you."

"She does," David said. "Deeply. As I still

love her. For me to say it's over would be to say she'll never believe in God, and I can't accept that. Our marriage aside, I can't imagine eternity without Maggie in heaven too. So we're still on this journey. Initially, Maggie removed her engagement ring when the innocently asked, 'When's the wedding?' questions began to shred her spirit. She left it off to test what she felt about going on with life without me, and she moved to New York when her career exploded up another level in fame. I thought it best to give her space, stay in Chicago, but Maggie talked me out of that. She asked me to go with her, to be a person she could trust as her inner circle broadened with new faces. We would try life as friends. Being a New York cop would be a good career move for me, so I made the transition too. I enjoyed the work. And I could be there for Maggie, helping behind the scenes with her security, ground her by being a connection to her roots. I took this task-force job because she wants to move back to Chicago. She misses home.

"Two years ago she put her engagement ring back on. We're still a couple. Maggie wants that outcome. We may end up having the longest engagement in history if this impasse continues, but we're committed to each other, to the process. She will have all the time she needs to think about matters, ask questions, and reach the decision that she can believe also."

"That sounds like a wise place to be."

"It's what we have. She's never stopped trying to take that step of faith. She's never questioned my convictions or the sincerity of my beliefs. She's said many times I'm a nicer guy now that I'm a Christian than I ever was before. She likes who I'm becoming. But so far she struggles, hasn't been able to make the step for herself. She can't get her arms around the fact a man rose from the dead. That's so easy for me to believe now — *Jesus rose from the dead.* But for Maggie to accept it . . . she doesn't yet have the faith to see it as true."

"The Resurrection is the pivot point of history for a reason," Evie said quietly, understanding why Maggie's struggle would be there.

David finished his drink, nodded his thanks as a waiter stopped by and offered a refill.

"When Bryce got married to Charlotte, it helped," David said, "as Maggie and Charlotte hit it off and became good friends themselves. Charlotte believes, but also has some uncertainties. She struggles with why

85

God lets things happen. That's helped Maggie, to know it's a continuum, that doubt is something even a believer can wrestle with from the other side of the belief that Christianity is true.

"I rest upon this assurance in Scripture, that 'If you seek me, you will find me.' Maggie's searching with an honest heart. She doesn't believe yet, but she longs to do so. She'll connect with God one day. And we'll have our wedding, our good future together."

"It's a wonderful hope, David."

"It is." He smiled at a memory, and his voice lifted as he said, "In the meantime, life goes on. Maggie certainly treats me as her fiancé. She wants our dates, and the flowers, and the movies watched together. She calls when the sink backs up and asks my opinion on her new song lyrics, gives her thumbs up or down on the latest shirt I've bought, and still gets flustered when I'm taking her over to dinner with my parents, knowing they are going to drop hints about grandchildren one day." He grinned. "Anyway, thanks for listening, Evie. It makes it easier when people I work with know that background, especially when Maggie is going to be around often."

"I'm looking forward to meeting her,"

Evie assured him. She considered what else she wanted to say, for the trust he'd offered in sharing was significant. She wasn't ready to tell him her own past with as much candor, but she respected what he'd done. "You love her, David. You asked Maggie to marry you, and she said yes. If you broke your word to her, you'd be shredding something in your own heart and hers. You two are paused." Evie nodded, because that felt like the right word. "God may have known this was the only way to one day win Maggie's heart. Faith was relatively easy for you. But there are a lot of people in the world, like Maggie, for whom coming to accept the truth is not such an easy step."

"I've learned to understand that," David agreed.

Evie thought a good place to end this conversation was a request. "I'd like an invitation to the wedding, whenever that day comes."

David smiled and said, "I'm keeping a list current. I'll be glad to add you, Evie."

They said their good-nights in the restaurant parking lot twenty minutes later. Evie set the carryout carton on the passenger seat and backed out. At just after seven, she decided it was too early to return to the hotel. Jenna's journals could wait a bit. She headed back to the office suite. Working sane hours just meant living out of a hotel room longer, and that trade-off didn't take much thought.

FIVE

"I wasn't expecting to see you again to-night." Evie set aside her interview write-up and stretched her arms. It was just after ten p.m.

David set a laptop travel case on an empty desk. "It turns out one of my PI's active cases is an open murder. Saul was working for a husband whose wife was killed."

"That goes some interesting places."

"Go searching for a murderer, that's a nice way to get yourself killed." David shook off his coat. "I wanted to see the full file on it, and morning was a few hours too many away."

Evie smiled, completely understanding that sentiment.

David studied the aerial maps clipped on the second whiteboard she had rolled in. "They brought by your two map tubes?"

"A patrol officer delivered them," Evie confirmed. "Someone did a lot of my work

89

for me."

She turned her chair to scan the maps. The first tube had contained aerial images of the area around the college, taken in the late fall or early winter, so there were no leaves obscuring the ground. When the images were placed side by side, she had about a square mile of visual info — fences and storage buildings, alleys and bike paths, the semi-hidden features in a neighborhood that a local would know about and might use. Detectives had marked various buildings with numbered dots. An accompanying sheet listed forty-two locations, places she was finding referenced in interview files.

"I talked with a couple of Jenna's friends by phone tonight," she told David. "Her neighbor across the hall, plus a chemistry study partner. They both thought Jenna might have gone out for a walk that night and gotten shoved into a car or something of the sort, not been at the apartment when this happened. Jenna was known to take late-night strolls around the neighborhood, occasionally back to the campus. The student-union building and its coffee shop were open twenty-four hours a day back then — now it's just six a.m. to midnight weekdays."

"That takes this away from her apartment."

"The search area keeps expanding." Evie nodded toward a desk holding the contents of the second tube. She'd weighted down the corners of the oversize sheets to stop the curl.

"The second tube was equally intriguing. Photographs of buildings around the neighborhood, laid out in order on hand-drawn street maps. Some detail-obsessed detective wrote down the building address, the apartment numbers, and listed names of the residents. Both sides of Jenna's block are completely filled in. Blocks around Jenna's are partially complete with building photos and names intermixed with empty squares for ones that hadn't yet been researched. I'd kiss the guy who did that work if I could find him."

David laughed. "You're having a good night."

"I am. I'm mostly reading interviews so I have in mind what people told cops nine years ago and can compare it to what I hear from them now."

"A smart plan."

It was late, he'd come back to chase a good lead on his own case, and she didn't want to keep him from that. "I'm getting ready to head back to the hotel to start on Jenna's journals. I hope your active murder goes somewhere productive. You can tell me about it over breakfast."

"If I solve mine tonight, I'm calling whatever time it is."

Evie laughed. "I'd do the same."

David turned to the conference room. Evie brought up the music playlist for Triple M to give him some background music.

"Thanks."

"My pleasure." Evie gathered her things together, paused by the desk with the hand-drawn street map and building photos. Some residents' names had a checkmark beside them, others a circled C. According to the legend, the checkmark indicated an interview was on file, the circled C that the individual had a criminal record. The research work required to pursue various theories from her list had dropped by more than half.

The nice thing about a visual like this was being able to trail interviews back across geography. If Bob said he had a steady girlfriend, the guy across the hall should recognize the woman's photo as someone often around — this visual made it possible to determine who should have noticed something or who would be the person most likely to know something.

Evie scanned the names. There were more women living in the buildings around Jenna than she would have guessed. Guys seemed to favor a few — if she had to guess why, probably better gym facilities.

She traced a route Jenna might have walked that night, looking at names along the way she would want to re-interview. She needed someone who worked the late shift at a restaurant or local bar, someone coming home at midnight. If Jenna went for a walk that night, she would have been seen. *She runs into trouble on her walk or . . .* Evie traced her finger back to Jenna's apartment building *. . . or all this was superfluous because the crime was right here, and only here, in Jenna's building.*

A question to pursue further tomorrow. Evie got out her car keys and headed out.

Early Thursday morning, her phone showed one unread message. Expecting Rob, Evie pulled it up. David. *Heading to the office.* He'd sent it at 5:10 a.m. Ouch. She dropped the phone onto the second pillow. She was a morning person, but that was early even for her. She yawned and staggered into the bathroom, hoping a shower would wake up her brain, help her engage for the day.

A good man, David Marshal, she thought, even more sure of it after hearing his story last night. He would give Maggie as much time as needed to make that decision of faith, showing himself faithful both to his God and to his word to Maggie. Evie thought he was handling it beautifully, given how the situation had developed. And it had to be unbelievably difficult for him.

She was glad it was not her dilemma with Rob. He had been a Christian since high school. How he expressed his faith was different than she did, yet it was real for them both. David and Maggie deeply desired to be married but were caught in an impasse. Evie was in a limbo of a different sort. Rob loved her, had made it clear over Christmas that he'd like a life with her. There was a marriage proposal waiting if she wanted to say yes. And she wasn't there yet.

She owed Rob a call to get dinner on their schedule. They were, for once, within an hour's drive of each other. He wasn't in the habit of sending texts, and she wasn't the kind to send short messages either. She wanted eyes on him when they were talking, expressions, flow of conversation, not thirty seconds of information. They talked frequently enough that she knew the news going on in his family and heard anything unexpected that happened in his life. She gave him the highlights about her activities, but the rest could wait until they were together. So far it was a pace of a relationship that worked for them.

She made a mental note to call him, then wondered what it said about her that she was okay making that call at the end of day rather than reaching for the phone now. Rob was a good man, important to her, but she hadn't wrapped her world around his yet, wasn't sure she was ready to take that last step. She wanted more time and couldn't precisely say why, simply knew she needed it.

Last night's weather update announced another cold winter day — as if she needed a reminder in Chicago's January. She pulled out the warmest dress pants she had with her and an expensive suit jacket to slip over a black knit sweater. *Professional and approachable for interviews.* As she quickly blow-dried her hair, she planned her morning.

Jenna's best friend would be a good place to start. The woman had been studying fashion. Odds were decent she might still be in the Chicago area.

She would need to talk with Jenna's family today, but pushing a formal interview with them off for a few days would be wise; she would have better questions when she did sit down with them. This didn't seem like a family crime, but that possibility was pulsing to its own beat. Evie had seen too many fathers murder daughters not to leave it an open theory. Maybe a sibling collision — family member shows up at an unexpected hour, knocks on the door, Jenna leaves the apartment with them, trouble happens . . . it fit the facts as they so far existed, and she doubted cops had seriously explored the possibility.

Interviewing Jenna's boyfriend was also a priority. An older student than most, he'd been working at the campus newspaper, reporting on sports, been at an away game for the basketball team on the weekend Jenna went missing. Maybe he killed her, but the forethought to create an alibi good enough to hold up to scrutiny suggested a premeditation that didn't fit the current appearance of the crime. *Probably not the boyfriend.* The case would have been solved by now if that was it. The cops would have gone back to take another look at Steve Hamilton every time they revisited the case. But he'd still be a good interview for her as he'd have a unique perspective on Jenna.

Evie paused drying her hair to add another

theory to her growing list.

26. Was it an accident and a cover-up?

Late night, Jenna's out for a walk. "I was drunk, it was dark, I didn't see her, I hit her with my car. I took her body away and dumped it." A college guy, wanting to save his own skin, hid the accidental killing. If you grew up in this area, knew where to dump a body where it was unlikely to be found, it could fit the facts. Evie made a note to look at the aerial maps for rivers and lakes nearby.

College kids got drunk and drove vehicles — that was policing 101 around college campuses. She might be able to find a vehicle damaged that night by an erratic driver, maybe a vehicle repair or an insurance claim — those got filed and lingered around in databases. Or maybe come at it from the other direction: which college student had abruptly entered rehab in the days after Jenna's disappearance — killing someone would put a load of guilt on a guy. He could either become a raging alcoholic or get scared into going sober. There would be signs somewhere.

A drunk driver kills Jenna, manages to hide the body where it can't easily be discovered, or talks a friend into helping him hide the body. The combination of bad luck, accident, cover-up fit why this crime hadn't been solved.

The phone in her pocket rang, and Evie read the caller ID, said an absent-minded, "Hello, Ann."

"You're working, I recognize that distracted tone."

"Thinking mostly. I'm glad you called. I chose a missing Brighton College girl as my case. Want to help out?"

"It's actually why I called. Today and tomorrow are looking free."

"I'd love your help canvassing the college area. Want to meet me at noon?"

"Sounds like fun. You're buying lunch."

"I like those kind of deals. I'll text you a location. Thanks, Ann." Evie pocketed the phone, pleased to have that arranged.

She finished getting ready, then gathered up Jenna's journals and her notes, car keys. This was the sweet spot of a case as facts and theories began to bubble up in rapid succession. She had information to piece together, ideas to pursue. It felt like a good beginning to the second day.

Evie paused in the conference room doorway. David was reading what looked like one of Saul's case files. "You like working early mornings."

David glanced around, smiled. "Habit. I'm awake, I might as well go to work."

"Had breakfast?"

"Very early."

"I brought extra. Come join me."

"Glad to." He pushed back his chair and got to his feet, reached for his coffee mug. "I'll get a refill for this. Want coffee this morning?"

"Sure." She had chosen a desk not piled with her own case materials for a breakfast table. The carryout container she slid his direction held toast, bacon, and scrambled eggs.

"Nice."

"I was hungry." She opened a matching one for herself and shook her orange juice before opening it. "I read through Jenna's journals last night. A normal life. She didn't see it coming, whatever happened. She wasn't worried about anyone, in a stressful relationship with someone, coming off a bad breakup, nothing about troubles at home. Life was good, in a routine of classes, study-ing, time with her boyfriend. Free time was music and concerts and hanging out with girlfriends. A normal college life."

"Anyone else besides the boyfriend interested in her?"

"Nobody is standing out — not that she picked up on, anyway. I want the friend's take on that. Who wanted to be noticed that Jenna was passing over?" Evie shifted the subject. "I'm dying to know — where did the murder case take you?"

David spread jelly on his toast. "It may be my answer to this. The client is Nathan Lewis, a businessman in the city, wealthy, happily married for seven years. His wife, Caroline, was murdered in a grocery-store parking lot, middle of the day." David grimaced just saying it. "She's loading groceries in her car, she's stabbed once, she bleeds to death. Devastates the husband. Her purse was left at the scene, along with her wedding ring, expensive necklace and bracelet. So maybe a failed robbery and a panicked suspect, but it reads to me like robbery wasn't the original intent.

"Freemont's a middle-class neighborhood, a bit out of her normal geography, but she volunteered at a charity nearby and would often stop at the store to talk to an old family friend who worked for the in-store bakery.

"The cops looked at a lot of theories. Random crazy guy, random murder. Someone fleeing another crime tries to take her

100

car, knifes her, then runs when it goes bad. Maybe a kidnapping attempt gone sour. Or it was even more personal, someone hates the husband, kills his wife, or hires someone to kill the wife? She's a stay-at-home wife, charity work, law-abiding. She wasn't one you'd think of as a target. The husband falling apart may have been the goal.

"Saul had been working the case about a month when he disappeared. He was looking for rumors in the neighborhood. Did someone see something, hear something, but not want to come forward to talk to the cops? Maybe my PI found the guy who murdered the wife and got himself killed in the process."

"Going to talk to the husband?"

"He's on my short list to interview today," David confirmed. "His wife's case is still open. But I want to do some research first, see if the cops have a person of interest before I talk to him. It's been six and a half years, but I bet he still flinches when I say I have some questions about Caroline's death. I'd rather not do that to a guy without first doing my homework."

Evie could appreciate that. "Those open wounds don't heal. I'd like to tag along when you do go see him."

"Sure. I'll find you."

"Anything else looking hopeful?" she wondered.

"The closed files are giving me a lot of possibilities, people with a motive for payback who might like to see him dead. I've got twenty-two names so far, and the list is growing. People who went to jail for a few years or who had to pay a hefty amount in a divorce settlement because of an affair my PI proved was going on.

"He has some suspended files — the client decided to stop the work due to costs, or the PI and client were waiting for a new lead to show up before they started on it again. Saul could have been working a few of them on his own time, but those seem less likely as the source of this disappearance.

"The other active cases are all interesting in different ways." David consulted notes on his phone. "He was following a husband, a recovering gambling addict the wife thought might have relapsed. Saul's notebook — 'My take — the wife would be more relieved to hear he is having an affair than get the news he's gone back to gambling.' "

"She sounds stressed."

"If her husband turned up dead, I'd be looking at the wife," David agreed. "Saul was doing background checks for a vice-president job opening at a biomedical firm. Saul's notebook — 'One has a wife with a cocaine problem, one is keeping a mistress and a wife, one is sleeping with the CFO of a rival company, and one is getting ahead by routinely claiming his research assistant's work product is his own. Good luck with this hiring choice.' "

Evie chuckled, liking this PI's take on things, and David smiled in agreement.

"He was working for Nathan Lewis, the case I just mentioned. Saul's notebook — 'Stabbed once and walk away? This was never intended to be a murder. That's how it looks to me. Not sure how that helps the husband, given how he's grieving. Look for area robbery attempts; do it quietly, maybe find an answer there.' "

"A reasonable guess, given stabbed once does seem like an unusual murder MO," Evie noted.

"I agree. Which at the margins lowers the odds Saul found, and was killed, by a guy who didn't intend to commit murder in the first place."

"True. Case number four?"

"Saul was looking to find a Neil Wallinski, age sixty-eight, the estranged brother of a Carl Wallinski. The brothers had a falling-out over the settlement of their father's estate. Saul's notebook — 'Neil has lived in VA, KS, CO, WY, FL, NY . . . no wonder every PI who agreed to look gave up. Maybe staying ahead of ex-wives wanting to garnish wages? I think he's back in IL and just ignoring his brother.' "

"That one sounds promising just because it's such unusual behavior. He had a diverse set of active cases."

"Saul got around." David finished his eggs and opened the orange juice. "I want to talk with Saul's sister today, also with Nathan Lewis, start working down the list of people with motive to want him dead, see if I can jar something loose."

"I'm going to meet up with Ann," Evie told him, "canvass the college and surrounding area, interview Jenna's best friend and her boyfriend. I'm going to avoid doing a formal interview with her family until I know which direction to take my questions."

"Think something might be there?"

Evie shrugged. "No reason to think so, but I like having an unexpected theory tucked in my back pocket. Family interviews are inevitably so emotional, it helps occasionally to view them as possible suspects, otherwise I end up just wanting to cry along with them."

David considered that, and her, for a long

moment. "I'm intrigued to know you, Evie. No wonder Sharon mentioned you were able to hold the unexpected in mind when working a case. I kind of like that approach, as goodness knows family can be capable of any crime under the sun, even when they appear to have a perfect exterior." He gathered up his breakfast debris. "Thanks for the break. I needed this."

"It's a nice way to begin a workday — we should make this part of the schedule."

"I'm all for that. I'll pick it up tomorrow." David headed back to the conference room, mug in hand. Evie turned toward the nearest computer to check her email, see what of interest might have happened overnight. Her state job would intrude soon, but maybe she'd get another full day on her cold case before something pulled her away. The college had emailed her several of the requested reports. Evie sent the material to the printer. Nothing else required urgent attention.

She started making calls to set up interviews. She was able to schedule one with Jenna's best friend in person, secured one by video with the boyfriend when he got off work this evening, and was feeling confident enough about matters that she took a deep breath and dialed Jenna's parents.

"Mrs. Greenhill, this is Lieutenant Evie Blackwell, with the Missing Persons Task Force. Detective Newcrest said he spoke with you yesterday. I'm so sorry your daughter's case remains open. Would now be a good time to have a short conversation?"

Evie settled deeper in the chair and prepared to mostly listen.

Six

David returned while Evie finished up a call with Jenna's academic advisor. When he shook off his coat but didn't go to the conference room, she nudged her bowl of sweet-tarts toward him, got a smile of thanks as he took one and sat down.

"Thanks, Mrs. Cline," she said into her phone. "Yes, I'll call if I have more questions. I appreciate your time." Evie clicked off with relief. The woman loved to talk.

It wasn't hard to read David's expression. "That bad?"

"Yeah. I should have taken you along for the interview with Saul's sister. You would have melted. Cynthia Morris, forty-two, single mom with a teenage son. She made a point to let me know right off that she and Saul were stepsiblings — his dad married her mother. Then she gave me an hour on how good a brother Saul was. He stayed in her life even after the two parents divorced, his dad married yet again, and there was yet another set of steps for Saul to deal with."

"Loyal, caring."

David nodded. "He'd stay at her place if he was working on that side of town, be the uncle to her son, play some ball, be a good influence. He was there the week he went missing, came by that Sunday night, stayed until Wednesday morning."

David opened his notebook and read aloud, " 'He was in a mellow mood, not particularly busy with work, said he'd just finished a couple of long involved matters. For him, he was flush with cash, insisted on getting some repairs done while he was around, had the plumber out, got my car battery replaced. Being a nice brother.' "

"Oh, man," Evie said softly.

"Yeah. He mentioned to Cynthia he had a meeting with a client in South Harbor that Wednesday afternoon and thought he might hit a concert in Arlington Heights if he had time that evening. I've confirmed he had a ticket purchased for the concert on his credit-card statement. It's not clear he attended the concert, but a receipt on Thursday morning puts him at a gas station well north, in Gurnee. Cops at the time confirmed with security-camera footage it was in fact Saul using that credit card and that he was alone — their assumption is that he'd traveled north for work. After that the trail is stone cold. It's going to be his job that is the source of this. But family, particularly Cynthia, takes the brunt of his absence without a trace."

"That's the toughest kind of interview."

David put away the notebook. "It wasn't as emotional as you would expect, but very sad. She knows he's dead. She just wants answers, to be able to give Saul a fitting funeral."

Evie thought it would help David to talk about the rest of it. "What else did she say? I need to get my head away from Jenna occasionally, think about something else."

David smiled. "Now you're just being kind. You've really got a few minutes for this?"

"I do."

"Cynthia was worth the time." He took his notebook out again and read a few more notes. "He was into his cars, sports, liked baseball, would often go to a club to listen to live music, loved jazz, would attend a concert every few months just to enjoy the crowds. He was the guy every lady should marry, but no one ever did.

"Saul loved his work. He loved the puzzle of it, the search for how to answer the question were it an affair, stealing from their boss, or lying on their résumé. He considered it to be a good service to society, keeping people honest. The PI work came naturally to him. He liked people, could walk into any environment and be comfortable there.

"His motto was 'Follow the people, find the crime.' He'd be out on stakeouts, following people all hours of the day and night. He knew this city and its suburbs like the back of his hand. He'd hire taxi drivers to help him out, and sometimes borrow business vehicles from friends — a landscape truck, flower-delivery van, or a plumber's truck.

"Saul wasn't a particularly physical man, out to win every fistfight he might get into, but he could disarm tense situations and avoid altercations. If he couldn't disarm, couldn't simply leave, he'd throw the dirty punch and knock the guy out, or smash him with a bottle — he would fight to end it fast, wasn't going to be polite about it."

"That's useful to know," Evie observed.

"It is. She understood his personality and that's what's most valuable to me. She painted a picture so I can see him." David scanned the rest of his notes. "A couple more personal ones . . . she told me Saul was never going to be a wealthy man, he had too many people he'd slip a hundred dollars to when they were down on their luck, too many friends who needed help. He was generous of spirit, assumed you would get yourself on your feet again, believed you could.

"He was looking for a new apartment, a place where he could have a dog. He could live anywhere and it was time for a change, he told her.

" 'He'd brought this puzzle box over,' she said, 'one of those thousand-piece marathons — a Norman Rockwell painting of baseball players in a locker room. He'd set up a card table by the living room window and be hard at it when I got home from work. He wasn't the type to simply walk out of his life, leave things behind, leave his dreams. He wasn't a wealthy man, didn't have all the breaks go his way in life, but he was a good brother. A very good brother. He didn't just disappear on me.' "

David closed his notebook. "She loved Saul. And if he made that kind of lasting impression on her, chances are good his friends are going to have the same perspectives. This wasn't a family dispute that went wrong, probably not even a personal one."

"The rest of his family? She mentioned

more stepsibs."

"Scattered across the nation now; Cynthia is the only one within a hundred miles he saw regularly."

"The jigsaw puzzle is interesting," Evie remarked. "He was doing some thinking."

David nodded. "I thought the same, hence the written quote. A nice diversion, a puzzle, something to have in his hands while Saul lets his mind mull over another matter. I'd love to know what he was thinking about. I haven't come across a client being billed during that last week."

"Maybe one of the suspended cases, working it on his own time. Or a personal matter, something he wants to solve for a friend. A good-deed kind of case?" Evie proposed.

"That would fit him," David said, thoughtful. "He was working a puzzle, figuratively and literally, thinking through how to approach a problem. The question is, did it get him killed or did something more prosaic happen?" He raised a shoulder. "Something as random as looking for someone that put him in the wrong place at the wrong time?"

"The fact his car also disappeared seems as relevant a clue as anything else you have. It could have been a murder, and then an ordinary street thief takes the car that's been sitting for a day or two in a tempting part of town. But when no car gets found, no body, that tends to say they were disposed of by the same person. You'll find a lead somewhere, David, and figure this out."

David smiled. "Optimism is appreciated. I'm certainly going to try." He pushed to his feet. "Thanks for listening."

"You chose the right case, David. You've got the patience to talk with a lot of people — which is a good thing, given your whiteboard is about ready to fall off the wall it's so crowded with names."

David laughed as she had hoped. "I'll be doing some talking to people," he agreed. "I came back to pull the files of those who most likely would want him dead and then I'll be heading out again."

Evie set her phone alarm for her next interview, then turned her attention back to the four boxes of case material. Personal items first, she decided, and opened box two.

The nice thing about people's habits is that they leave trails, she thought — notes, lists, receipts, phone numbers. She picked up Jenna's purse, spread its contents on the desk, then opened Jenna's wallet. Library card, student ID, health-insurance card, a dentist's business card, an insurance agent with a renter policy number written on it. The checkbook showed occasional checks to a church, her landlord, the student-union bookstore.

Evie pulled out the less-organized bits and pieces in the front of the wallet. A reminder note to call Susan about volleyball, a Post-it note with a phone number and the name Chad, the time and place for a study group meeting, a diner's receipt for a chef's salad and Diet Coke. And then Evie stopped sorting items. She was holding a ticket stub with a swirling stack of cursive M's, a creative logo she immediately recognized. "David."

Her voice had enough urgency that he immediately appeared in the doorway. "What is it, Evie?"

She held it up. "My missing college student was at a Triple M concert the night she disappeared. I'm holding the ticket stub."

A long silence as he looked at the pink rectangle and then the whiteboard. "Tell me the date again."

She looked at the stub. "October 17, 2007."

"I was there," he said. "I'll never forget that date. I was onstage with Maggie for a few minutes at the end of that concert. It was the night of the car crash."

Evie didn't know how to respond. Maggie was a Chicago native, had come to stardom because the local college crowds loved her — this was one of the coincidences that came up in cases, histories overlapping. But it hit hard.

David dropped into a chair. "I can probably tell you a bit more about that night. It's not a concert I'm ever going to forget." He shook his head. "I'm sorry, Evie. The date on your case should have triggered the connection. I should have realized it had to have been a Triple M concert."

"I didn't think about that possibility either."

She handed him the ticket stub, its date still readable. He turned it over in his hand, a man lost in thought. He finally looked over at her, returned the ticket. "Maggie played concerts in college towns across the Midwest during those years. Does this help solve what happened to your Jenna?"

"I dislike coincidences. But they are usually just that. The fact we're looking into this case years later, and you happen to be dating Maggie? That's a random coincidence. Similarly, the fact it was the night of the accident with enormous impact on both of you. Lives do intersect, even in high-

115

population cities like Chicago." Evie paused. "But what are the odds if Jenna was at that concert, her killer was also?"

"College crowd, college-student victim, college-age killer?" he suggested with a nod. "That seems like a reasonable direction."

"Someone selected her at the concert, followed her home, did her harm," Evie stated. "The venue is just blocks from where she lived, an easy walking distance on a comfortable night. A mostly college-age crowd, a lot of others heading back toward campus would have walked those same blocks, it's not so obvious she's being followed."

"If it was a college student, you'd figure the cops would have solved it by now," David said. "It's hard to leave no evidence behind, but from what you've said already, there isn't much to work with along this line."

"Agreed." Evie hesitated to bring up a theory, but it seemed appropriate now. "Or go a different direction," she offered. "Someone from the band she might have been interested in? They met up later that night after the concert is over?"

He didn't immediately shake his head. "I knew Maggie's band members, her sound guys. The stage crew not as well, as they would shift around depending on the venue.

The band was beginning to pay its own way. They were making enough to draw a salary, small, but it was a paycheck. Eight men and women were the core of it back then — band, sound, a manager. I can get you a list of names. With the star-struck attention from fans, I'm sure there were more than a few phone numbers exchanged between fans and crew. Most of that core group were single then."

"You said band members have changed over the years? Sound guys?"

"Five of the original group were still with Maggie. Lives go different directions, and the travel, the concert life, are only glamorous from the outside. It takes a toll on marriages and on kids. And the crowds have decided there's one star on the stage, the rest are simply the support cast. It can hit your ego when the spotlight doesn't shine on you, but on the one you're making look good."

"I'm beginning to see why you went to New York to be Maggie's main security guy."

David smiled. "There are always dynamics going on between members working together. Maggie has been lucky over the years to mostly work with people who can wisely handle what they've signed on to. The money differential is also prominent — they all do well, but she's the famous voice." He leaned back, thinking, finally shook his head. "Evie, I may have liked some of those around her more than others, but I can't say any one of them ever stood out as a concern. These are guys Maggie worked with, and I spent a lot of time around them, with a cop's instincts for when something was off. They might have connected up with fans, but murder? That's a mind-set that doesn't play with what I know about them."

He considered it further and shook his head again. "Her security crew, they're mostly former cops, retired military. Even in the early days, security at a concert venue was tight. As the fame grew, security traveling with them became part of her life. These are guys who don't look the other way when a band member or sound person crosses the line. I might hear about it before Maggie would, but I would know what's going on around her, around her band members. We don't take chances with her or her reputation. If there was something off with a long-term member of her group, I have to think I would have seen it."

Evie thought that rang true. David would have seen it — a guy loving Maggie the way he did wasn't one to be careless about details. She took the conversation another direction. "Any chance there are photos of the crowd that night, anything left around from that evening?"

"Maggie was working with a publicist by then, so there would be photos for marketing purposes that might still be in the archives. And Maggie keeps a scrapbook for herself, adds to it from every concert. She likely has a few images."

"I think the concert was the opportunity," Evie suggested. "Jenna was away from her place until late, she was out and about, in a good mood, not cocooned in studying. She made herself accessible that night. Any concert would have been the trigger. It just happened to be Triple M playing that night."

David gave a small nod, accepted her attempt to lighten the connection, but then blew out a long breath. "I don't take prayer lightly, Evie, and I said more than one before I made my decision to join this task force. It's probably not chance that this is the county I selected or the case you picked. I'll think back on that time, see if I can come up with anything that might be useful. But let's not tell Maggie about it when you meet her. I'd rather not give her this kind of news to think about — not yet."

"Agreed." His perspective about God's influence intrigued her. Evie thought God was often involved in the details of her work, but David had an assumption that seemed much more certain. She hoped he was right, for it implied her case could be solved after all.

Her phone alarm dinged and she silenced it. "My interview with Jenna's biology class TA is in ten minutes."

"I'll let you get your questions organized," David said, standing. "That ticket stub, Evie, it's significant in at least one other way. It tells me your Jenna liked good music."

"Very true," Evie said, appreciating the lighthearted point. David walked back to the conference room. She picked up her notepad and added another fact to her list.

18. Jenna attended a Triple M concert
    the night she disappeared

"Evie, when's your next interview?" David asked later, stepping out of the conference room and sliding a stack of folders into a carry-on bag.

"I'm meeting Jenna's best friend in" — she checked the time — "thirty-six minutes."

"Mind if I tag along? I need a brief break from Saul before I start in on these conversations. I'll be switching from family who loved him to some people who at least have a motive to wish him dead."

Evie understood that whiplash. "I'd welcome a second opinion on what Robin has to say." She packed files in her backpack, not sure what she might actually need. "Why don't you drive? I'm meeting Ann at noon. You can drop me off with her and then go talk with your favorite person of interest."

"That would be Everett Gibson," David told her as they exited the office space. "He did six years for aggravated assault after beating a neighbor into a near coma. Cops strongly suspected Everett at the time, as he and the victim had past history, but they just couldn't break the man's alibi. Everett said he was settling a minor traffic fender bender with a judge's wife — for cash, untraceable, wouldn't you know — on the other side of town when the neighbor was attacked. An easy alibi to dismiss except the judge's wife backed him up. The case stalled. Saul got hired to look at that alibi. He managed to prove the judge's wife bought prescription painkillers off Everett on occasion, but that she hadn't seen him on the day in question. Once Everett's alibi was proven false, the case came together quickly.

121

The man took a plea deal for the six years."

"When did he get released from jail?"

"Two months before Saul disappeared. He continues to have a spotty record with the law. Everett's now in the county lockup for trying to steal a truck off a used-car lot."

"At least you know where to find him."

David smiled. "There is that. Getting him to confess to Saul's murder will be a challenge, given I don't know that he did it and there's zero evidence to suggest he did. For now, I just want to see how he reacts to Saul's name. The guy has a temper. That can be useful."

Evie nodded. "It should be a revealing couple of hours for both of us."

Evie met Jenna's best friend, Robin Landis, at a coffee shop across from the fashion design firm where she worked. David perched on a stool off to the left of their table, in comfortable hearing distance, but not in Robin's line of sight. Robin was willing to help, yet she was so emotional about her missing friend that Evie wondered how many details were being lost because of her eagerness to be useful. Evie found herself deliberately slowing the pace to try to settle the woman. She circled the interview back through less overt topics, taking notes in longhand rather than shorthand just to slow down the process further.

Eventually she asked, "Was Jenna having any problems with another student studying the same curriculum? A lab-assistant position a fellow student didn't get, an internship with only one slot — anything that might have put her in competition with others in her degree track?"

"That happens a lot when you get into the PhD programs, and Jenna was headed that route. She wanted to be a researcher at a biotech firm — it was a serious 'major goal in life' focus. She didn't want to go the medical-degree route but wanted as much as she could learn about diseases, genetics, and research methods as she could cram into her schedule. She was insane to carry the course load she did, but she was impatient to get the knowledge."

"Any reason for that?" Evie asked, curious. "Someone in her family was sick? She lost someone to a genetic disease?"

"Not that she ever said, and she would have. We were tight that way. It was more like, 'I can be the Einstein of my generation in genetics, the Alan Turing of biology' — she would talk that way. She liked to discover things, understand things."

Evie remembered an Alan Turing biography on a side table in a photo of Jenna's living room — something she'd been reading before she disappeared. "Was she a music lover? Was a concert something she would put into her schedule, even overloaded with studies as it was?"

"Live music was a big deal for her," Robin confirmed. "It was the only thing that would get her out of her serious study mode. She loved to sing, had a wonderful voice. I don't know what happened to her music collection, but she had hundreds of songs in her playlists and knew all the lyrics to them. An interesting band, a musical — that was her entertainment, her reward for all the work she was putting in toward her degree. She didn't have a lot of money, but her parents were good to her, slipping in a few extra dollars with her school fees for those kinds of evenings out."

"Triple M, the band in concert that night — was that Jenna's choice or simply the band playing that Friday?"

"The band playing that night. I don't think she had a special interest in them, though Jenna loved the song 'A Waiting Love.' She sang along with it, gave us a solo on the walk home as she sang it again. Tiffany had gotten a block of tickets so we could go as a group, and when people heard it was Triple M, they cleared schedules to be able to go.

"Jenna was delighted with the concert that night. The fact she had a boyfriend, it was a serious thing, and Triple M's music was focused on songs like that — the music was right up her alley. Jenna figured another year and Steve would ask her to marry him. She was anticipating it, dreaming big and loving life. Not just having a great personal life, it was also doing something great for the world at large, and that's why the studies mattered so much to her. She wanted to make a big difference in the world. Me" — Robin shrugged — "I just wanted to dream up fashionable clothes that didn't go out of style within one season. Sometimes it's weird, realizing we were such good friends. And now she's the one gone. . . ."

"She had a lot of photos of you in her albums," Evie mentioned.

Robin brightened. "That's nice. We were close — a college camaraderie of doing life together for a time. Jenna sat through all my failed boyfriend sagas, handed over the tissues and shared the ice cream. She made life fun, you know? She made it possible to sparkle. She was wickedly smart to have selected those courses, but she wasn't making a big deal about it. She just buckled down and did the work and could figure out hard things. She was kind of quiet, really calm, when the rest of us in the group had big highs and lows. I think that's why she was a good fit with Steve. He had that steadiness about him too."

"How were things with her boyfriend? Was there a former boyfriend still in the picture who might cause her to rethink matters?"

Robin shook her head. "It was Jenna and Steve all the way. He was working one of the sign-up tables on the quad when she was a newbie freshman going through orientation, and they struck up a conversation about the school paper and what he did. She didn't sign up to join the newspaper, but she started hanging around there some to see what he was doing.

"They clicked the first time they met, and it was Steve and Jenna pretty much thereafter — at least once he decided she wasn't too young for him. That first year he was playing it very safe, just a friend, but you could tell he liked her, and he was wise enough to come back around and ask her out on that first date just before the year concluded. It was" — Robin crossed her fingers — "like that between them after that."

Evie appreciated the image Robin was

sketching.

"By the second year, it's 'we're dating.' " Robin put it in air quotes. "Steve had made a point to meet her parents, and you could tell when around them, this is a couple that's going to be exchanging rings. I think he was the one making sure she got her degree without distraction before things progressed. She would have already been engaged if she could have made the decision.

"He wasn't Mr. College trying out his wings, figuring out who he was and what he wanted. He was Steve Hamilton, solid guy, career figured out, plan in mind, and Jenna was part of the plan. They were cute together, happy, content." Robin grinned. "That was so *not* a common thing on a college campus. Her friends were envious, me included, in a good way. She had a good thing and knew it. She wasn't risking that by making a mistake, getting her head turned by looking at another attractive guy."

"They were a solid couple," Evie reiterated. She tried to word the next question carefully. "Was anyone else interested in Jenna? A guy wishing Steve wasn't around?"

Robin thought about it. "Sure, there were guys who were interested in her. She was smart, but you could have a conversation with her. She was nice, and people noticed that. She had a relatively narrow course subject — maybe sixty people at most taking the same classes. There were guys she would have lunch with who formed a study group of sorts. Jenna mentioned a lot of them, but they were mostly tied to some class or another. She would occasionally connect two friends for a date. But if anyone was looking at Jenna with more than mild interest, she never mentioned it, and I never picked up on it."

Evie thought there was a line there worth pursuing further. "Was Jenna interceding in a friend's life? Someone got pregnant and was deciding what to do, a bad boyfriend breakup, someone not going to make the grades to keep scholarship money, that kind of drama coming into Jenna's life via someone else?"

Robin smiled. "I would be most of that, with the exception of the pregnancy. My boyfriend and I were all over the map — together, then not, back together again. Or my roommates changed again and some worked out well, while others did not. College is about highs and lows when you're twenty, emotions tended to run intense, and I wind up easily under stress. Add in finals week, the papers you had to write — there were pills floating around to keep you awake, others to wind you down. Jenna didn't go there, but friends of hers would, creating its own unfolding mini-crisis. If you needed to chill out about your life, you ended up visiting Jenna and dumping your troubles on her."

Robin paused, thought about it, then said, "I can give you the names of those who would've been in that circle of friends, but honestly it was typical college stuff. Tragedies at the time, but looking back, nothing out of the ordinary. Nobody was dealing with a violent ex-boyfriend or a suicidal depression or a body-image illness like bulimia. It was having to tell your parents you got a C or D on a test, seeing your ex-boyfriend now dating one of your used-to-be-girlfriends, that kind of tragedy. Not big-sized crises. No one getting arrested, or even getting particularly drunk and stupid. Jenna stayed above that churn, but she was there as a friend when you needed her."

Evie was getting a good picture of her missing girl. "Jenna was a loyal friend."

"Exactly. To me, with Steve, with others around her, Jenna stuck with you. She wasn't a fair-weather friend."

"Thanks, Robin. This was helpful."

"Truly?"

"Yes." Evie placed a card with her contact information on the table. "If you think of anything else that might shed light on what Jenna was like, or remember a particular friend she was helping around the time she disappeared, send me an email. Or just turn on a camera and chat about her, like you've done today, and send the video to me."

Robin fingered the card. "You'll let me know how your investigation turns out?"

"I will," Evie assured her.

Evie added a few impressions of Robin to her notes as David drove them to Brighton College, where she would meet up with Ann.

"Jenna was a good kid," David summed up. "Not the party girl or the leader, but a linchpin among her friends."

"A good description." Evie considered a conclusion, tried it out in words. "I think Jenna would have opened her door that night, even at midnight, even if it was a guy, if it was someone she recognized."

"She's thinking like a friend."

Evie nodded. "A boyfriend of a friend of hers — 'We broke up again tonight, you've got to talk some sense into her, Jenna,' that kind of pitch." Evie rolled the idea around in her thoughts, but it didn't want to settle anywhere. She knew names of Jenna's friends, only they weren't individuals with personalities yet, just names. She needed to talk with more of them to better fit her conclusion.

"Whoever did this likely shared her passion for music."

Evie glanced over at David.

"She's got the boyfriend in Steve," David explained. "She's not looking beyond him. Interested guy number two, how's he going to get some of Jenna's time? I bet he's around when Steve's out of town, sharing her interest in music. A guitar player, someone good on keyboards. Someone who could get Jenna's free time by having the one thing she's willing to let draw her out of her studies."

Evie realized where David was taking this. "Jealousy."

David nodded. "A tried-and-true motive for when a guy accidentally kills a girl. She didn't attract a killer because she likes to study the human genome. It's not just the Triple M concert. Music was the one avenue Jenna allowed in her life by her own choice. Music is how this guy found her. He knew her for years and wanted what Steve had — or he met her recently, but it's the same drawing card. Music."

Evie saw the leap he had made. "I'm not looking at music because it was Jenna's passion. I'm looking at music because it's *his.*"

"I think you're looking for a music major, a music student."

"Someone who would hear her voice and think *That's lovely,* share her passion, and think *That's my soul mate.*"

David nodded. "There's your thread. If he's on the campus with her, you're going to find him through his music."

Evie lifted her backpack from the backseat to look for the provost's office number, found the card, and made a call. While she got bounced around getting to the person who could find her the student rosters from that time, she glanced over at David. "You probably just set me on the track that's going to solve my case."

He simply smiled. "If so, you can buy me dinner, then help me find my missing PI."

SEVEN

Evie met up with Ann near Jenna's apartment building, arranged to ride with her, and waved David on to his interview.

"For efficiency, let's split up and start by following Jenna's credit-card purchases, get a look at where she liked to shop around the campus area," Evie suggested. They could show Jenna's picture around, hopefully jog owners' and longtime employees' memories.

Ann stamped her feet to clear snow off her boots and gamely nodded. With only a little irony, she said, "It's a beautiful January day for strolling around." Fortunately, it was a bit warmer than yesterday. Ann handed back Evie's page of facts and theories. "I like the music-student theory."

"David's suggestion on the drive over here. Music is this person's passion, I'm guessing, and why he chose Jenna. Or she — I'm not convinced yet we're looking for a guy. Jenna would have opened her door late at night to a woman without a second thought."

"I saw that," Ann returned, "and the 'literally moved her body'? You're good at seeing the scope of something, Evie, but that's just macabre. Possibly true, but beyond macabre. Although hauling a body away in a sleeper sofa carried out to a moving van does open one's eyes to what might not have been explored yet."

Evie shrugged. "College students move all the time. It's easy enough to use that to your advantage. 'The girl upstairs disappeared. I don't care what the penalty fee is, I'm breaking my lease and getting out of here.' Remove Jenna's body in a wardrobe box or that sleeper sofa, wipe your place with so much bleach it stinks because you have to at least get your security deposit back. It's a simple enough story to sell, which covers up a murder scene and gets rid of the evidence. I'll look at dates people moved out, see if something interesting shows up for residents in her building or buildings along that block."

"You think relevant paperwork is still around?"

"Between lease agreements, truck rentals, post-office address changes, student records, and DMV records, I'm sure I can find what I need. If this was a typical case, cops would have solved it already. The best way to use my time is to look wider than they did."

"You are doing that, Evie. A drunk driver hitting her caught me off guard too," Ann said. "I could see him dumping her body, but the blood on the street would be difficult to wash away."

Having already thought about that problem, Evie simply said, "A couple of drunks, hosing off the street where a friend threw up, it could be sold that way. It's late at night and you wouldn't see blood as red until the sun is up. The search didn't begin until Monday, and if Jenna had walked a distance, was a few blocks away when she was hit, the cops don't see that location right away. There were heavy rains Monday night. It would probably take two people or more in the car who hit her to cover up that kind of involved crime scene, or very good friends of a drunk driver willing to help him cover up such an accident. Still, it can fit the facts."

Ann considered that. "Sometimes life favors the killer and hides what happened. Yeah, we've both seen it."

They walked for a bit in silence.

"How's it working with David?" Ann asked.

Evie glanced over at her friend. "You could have clued me to the fact he's dating Margaret May McDonald."

Ann smiled. "It was a good surprise. The fact you didn't already know rather baffled me."

"I haven't stayed up with the music scene. I've had a busy life and all."

"David and Maggie will give you a crash course."

"I expect they will. We have had one unexpected overlap. My missing college student was at a Triple M concert the night she disappeared. David was there and briefly onstage with Maggie."

"I saw it in your notes. We've both seen those odd intersections in cases before."

"The Triple M concert could be a hunting ground. Maybe more than one of her concerts was a place to cruise for a girl."

"You think this guy did more than one murder?"

"There's just a nagging worry in the back of my mind that this case goes really bad. After last fall's Carin County, I'm wired to see the dark coming at me."

"That was about as bad as it gets," Ann agreed. "Okay. Assume the worst. Say he did do more than one murder. Maybe you can use that. The fact you're looking for the guy will likely get his attention. You have to figure he's keeping an eye on his past crimes, looking for activity, newspaper articles, public requests for information, that kind of thing."

Evie considered that and nodded. "So we draw him out. Sharon gets a reporter to write about the task force, our first cases, put out an appeal for the public's help. Maybe he decides to call the tip line himself, give some misleading information, inject himself into the case. I could use that."

"Ego has been the downfall of a lot of killers," Ann replied thoughtfully.

Evie liked the idea enough to stop their walk to make a note. "Anything that has me *doing* something is better than just hoping the case doesn't break that way."

"David will deal with it if that's where this goes."

"It's Maggie I worry about. You know their story?"

"Bryce Bishop is a good friend. I've known David and Maggie for years."

Evie wasn't surprised Ann hadn't said anything before. Unless her friends were in the same room with each other, Ann wouldn't think to make the introduction.

Ann kept secrets, and friends deserved their privacy. It was one of the first things Evie had learned about her. "I'm hoping the Triple M connection was simply the fact the college scene was Maggie's fan base, and any band playing that night would have been the connection."

"Odds do favor that, Evie."

They went their separate ways, and Evie stopped at a music store, then a restaurant, a card shop, a flower shop, another music store, showing Jenna's picture, searching for people who had worked and lived in the area for the last decade.

Ann handed over her notebook as they met again at a diner. "My faith in humanity is rising. Nearly everyone who was around when Jenna disappeared remembers her, the search, the speculation about what happened." The two found a table and ordered coffee.

"I'm hearing the same," Evie said, skimming through Ann's interview notes while Ann read through hers. "One thing I hadn't considered: Jenna's disappearance raised the fear level of an entire college campus. Girls didn't walk alone, boyfriends saw them safely inside and looked around their apartments, volunteer patrols were out with flashlights and phones to challenge any guy who was loitering. Whoever did this, if he was part of campus life, he was getting turned on by the fear. 'Look what I did. I'm responsible for all this. Everyone is talking about what I did.' "

"Creating fear in others can be a powerful fix, like a drug addict's high," Ann agreed, taking her first sip of the coffee. "It's an emotion that needs to be fed. Give it a year, the fear around campus subsides, he has to do something else to get it back."

"I've got a lot of data coming in on what happened in the years after Jenna's disappearance," Evie said. "If he was here, he probably tried to relight that fear, to experience it again. Something should turn up about this guy acting out again."

"How deep are your lists of names?"

"By end of the day, with the inquiries made, I'll have a large pool to fish in. The first target will be names appearing on multiple lists — a music major with a rape allegation would certainly get my attention. I'd like to give the researchers the top few dozen names by the end of the day so they can generate deeper histories over the weekend."

"I can give you some help on that data analysis."

"I was hoping you'd offer. It's gladly accepted."

As Evie drank her coffee and reviewed Ann's notes, she glanced over to her friend reviewing her own notes to ask, "Are you beginning to see a pattern here? The rumor mill has settled on about half a dozen theories, and we're getting the same rumors with variations on a theme, depending on which supposition the individual considers the most likely."

Ann held up Evie's notebook. "It's crowd-sourcing crime solving, the collective wisdom of a community on what happened to Jenna Greenhill. You have to admit, they're pretty good. They've nailed down the most likely theories on your master list."

"I find it interesting that the possibility she's alive still runs this hot."

"The need for hope," Ann replied. "To not allow for her to be alive moves the case from being depressing to being just black."

Ann closed the notebook and drank her coffee. "She's dead, Evie. This isn't another Shannon Bliss with someone taking her for a reason. To be alive after nine years, you need a reason. Jenna wasn't the prettiest, the youngest, the most outgoing. She was vulnerable, she got grabbed, but I doubt this kidnapping lasted more than a few hours at most."

It helped hearing another cop confirm what she also had concluded. This was a murder investigation without a body. Evie swapped back notebooks with Ann. "I hope her body isn't found in this neighborhood. I don't want to end the mystery by creating another memorial location residents have to pass every day."

"I sincerely hope it doesn't unfold that way either."

They paid for the coffee and stepped back outside. Ann pointed to the Music Hall. "Let's split up again. You take management, work your way down through security, sound and lighting staff. I'll track down janitorial employees and work my way through food and beverages, ticket takers, and dressing room attendants."

Evie pocketed her notebook and took out Jenna's photo again. "Sounds like a plan."

Two hours later they met up at the Music Hall entrance. Ann said, "I've got what you would expect — guys hitting on girls, drunk-and-disorderlies, three confirmed rapes linked back to these parking lots, several bands that are blacklisted because of drug use in the dressing rooms."

"I can add security footage of drug deals," Evie said, skimming through her notes.

"Pickpockets galore, a dozen fights, a fire-alarm prank to cause panic, an actual fire, three bands that managed to injure their own members, and five instances of fans with injuries after swarming the stage." She closed the notebook. "Given the number of concerts and the size of the crowds flowing through this place every week, that seems like normal crime to me over a decade. I've got names, promises for more names, but nothing that feels like a pattern, no other incidents that suggest someone works this location trolling for victims."

"Jenna seems isolated in that respect," Ann concurred.

Evie was glad to have this particular set of interviews completed. She checked the time. "Let's walk back to the campus. I'd like your impressions on the building where Jenna lived."

"Suits me." Ann fell in step beside her. "How's David doing with his missing PI?"

"He's having a hard time getting any traction. There's a wide time window between when Saul disappeared and when anybody noticed, and no clear geography for where something happened. There's nothing obvious in his personal life that suggests a reason as to what might have happened to cause him to go missing. So David has been going through the cases Saul was working on, looking for ones that might have a reason to want him dead. There are a number of names in the closed cases to work. And there's one active case that is promising.

"Saul was working for a husband on an open murder case. The wife was stabbed in a grocery store parking lot and bled to death. Maybe he found him . . . it's a theory at least. David is planning to interview the husband, Nathan Lewis, today to see if there had been a conversation, something not in Saul's notes, that might help identify what Saul had been doing the week he disappeared."

"Evie . . ." Ann slowed to a stop. "Actually, that might not be a good idea."

Evie stopped too, surprised. "What is it, Ann?"

"I've got someone undercover in Nathan Lewis's office right now, looking into who killed Caroline. I think the murder was done, or at least arranged, by someone close to Nathan."

Evie was stunned. "Wow. I didn't see that coming."

"Nathan's a friend. He isn't going to go on with his life until his wife's murder is solved; he won't date and put someone else in the crosshairs. So it's personal with me that the case get solved. If it turns out to be someone in Nathan's world, odds are he would have tried to tamper with the business, cause Nathan grief in other ways, before it escalated to targeting Nathan's wife. I asked someone to figure out if there was a pattern of trouble, to see if the murder of Nathan's wife was just the exclamation point in a sequence of things that had happened in Nathan's life."

"Who do you have working in his office?" Evie asked.

Ann shook her head. "Nathan doesn't know about the person's real reason for being there, so I can't give you a name. I don't want Nathan to know I'm looking at even those he considers good friends. The man has borne enough grief. But this seems to be the most effective way to get an answer."

"You want us to step back?"

Ann hesitated. "Has an appointment already been made?"

"I'll find out."

Evie called David. "Have you made an appointment to go see Nathan Lewis yet? Ann's got some info that might be useful to hear first." She nodded to Ann. "Thanks, David. Ann's coming over with me now."

She pocketed her phone. "He'll hold off

making the appointment. He's finishing up a conversation and then heading back to the office for a video interview. Let's go talk to David — I'm freezing out here anyway."

Ann laughed. "I wondered when the cold would finally win. You can drive, and I'll make a call on the way."

Evie entered the office suite with Ann, heard the music, and realized David had arrived back before them. "David, I brought company." She dumped her coat onto an empty chair and stepped out of her boots, determined to get her feet warm again.

David came from the conference room. "Welcome back. Hello, Ann."

"David. It's a pleasure." Ann gave the man a hug. "It's good to have you back in Chicago."

"I've missed being here. Please tell me you've got some really useful information for me, because I'm looking for something solid to build on."

"Of a sort." Ann draped her coat more neatly over another chair. "Evie mentioned your PI once worked for Nathan Lewis, and a whole array of intersecting matters clicked into place."

"Let me get you two some coffee to warm

you up, and then I'd like to hear all about it."

"I'd appreciate that." Ann gestured to the conference room, where he had been working. "Mind if I take a look while you're getting that coffee?"

David waved her in. "Help yourself."

Ann stepped into the conference room. Evie went with David to help get the coffee. "How was your conversation with Everett?"

"I like him for the murder. He was still steamed that Saul was the one who busted his alibi, put him in jail, and shattered a stable connection to the painkillers he also depended on himself. He had to come off his own addiction the hard way while in custody. That he could have killed Saul is clear. But to prove it, I need to fill in what he was doing during a three-month period after he was released. I have a couple of names to track down, people who might be able to help me with that question."

"You hope he said something incriminating to someone who no longer considers him a friend?"

"Basically. I'll be working names and having conversations around that very question. Any luck on your canvass?"

Evie thought about the notes they had taken. "A lot of useful conversation, but nothing that shifted the direction of things." She filled him in on the highlights while she got out cream and sugar, deciding she could avoid drinking her coffee black for once.

"It's good that you were able to get word out around the campus that cops are looking at the case again; it might stir up memories."

"I hope it helps. We passed out a lot of business cards."

They walked back to the conference room together.

"David, you've been busy." Ann accepted the coffee David handed her.

Evie studied the numbered list of names with interest; it was a new development.

"My list of thirty-eight people with substantial reasons to want Saul Morris dead," David explained, "from Charles Bell to Walter York. Most did jail time or suffered a serious setback in their professional lives because of Saul's investigative work. That's my target list for interviews."

Ann tapped number eight — *unnamed person who killed Caroline Lewis.* "I think the person who killed Caroline is someone close to Nathan. I've got someone undercover in his office right now looking into that possibility."

"Well, *that's* interesting news."

Ann pulled out a chair at David's gesture. "Nathan's a friend, the case needs to get solved, and someone working on it from the inside can more easily run down possibilities. I made a call on the way over here and had dates pulled. The last contact Nathan had with Saul was on August twenty-second — it's in the file as a phone update. Saul was canvassing the area, people were being talked with, queries were out, but he had nothing new to report."

"That date fits what is in Saul's own paperwork," David confirmed. "Saul disappeared in the days after September eighth."

"If Saul had found out something about Caroline's murder, that knowledge didn't have time to reach Nathan. There's nothing in Nathan's records to indicate they spoke that week."

"That closes down one hope I had," David said with regret.

"Nathan has had three private investigators work alongside the police over the years. The other investigators looked into Saul's disappearance based on the same assumption you had. I asked to get copies of whatever notes they made regarding Saul for you. Hopefully their notes might narrow down where Saul was last seen."

"Thanks. You've got a better chance of finding anything useful working from the inside of Nathan's office than I do hoping to re-create Saul's work for him. So for now, I'll move on to other possibilities."

"If you have specific questions, I can try to get you answers without having to go to Nathan directly." Ann pushed back her chair and stood. "I'm going to spend a few hours helping Evie data-crunch on her names. If you have something specific come to mind, I'll be around."

David smiled. "We both appreciate that help, because after Evie solves her case, she's doubling up to help me solve this one."

"I'll take getting these two cases solved however it comes about," Evie said with a laugh. "I'm ordering in food, as I still owe Ann lunch. I'm thinking steak sandwiches. Want in?"

"Sure."

Evie ordered them a late lunch while Ann made a brief call to her husband, Paul. It was nice, having a friend helping out who understood this kind of work.

Evie wrote the question *Who Killed Jenna Greenhill?* on her whiteboard and then numbered one through twenty-four down the side. "We fill up the list with the highest-probability names so that researchers have something to work on, then I'll send you home."

"Paul is taking me out to an arcade late tonight — we're working a small matter for a friend on our own time — so I'm yours until then." Ann settled in at an empty desk. "Give me the apartment lists, the names of those who lived in buildings on Jenna's block. I'll start cross-referencing names with moving records, arrest records, school records, disciplinary actions, and look for signs of trouble in their lives after Jenna disappeared."

Evie found more answers to inquires in her inbox, all with attached lists of names. She passed printouts to Ann, then dumped the accumulating reports onto a flash drive for her use. "You'll want to reference those big sheets of paper on the far desk for the resident lists by building."

"Thanks." Ann plugged in the flash drive and brought up the reports. "You've been busy."

"I learned by watching you. The more data, the better the odds of finding an answer. If I've tossed a big enough net out in the last thirty-six hours, I've now got his name."

"Given your wide array of theories, I'd say you're covering the bases."

"That's my hope." Evie turned her attention to the music majors, began cross-referencing for the same indications of trouble.

Papers turned, keyboards clicked as they scanned the screens. Evie wrote the name Harold Jefferies at position twelve. A music guy suspected of using a date-rape drug, he had played guitar in a band Evie remembered being mentioned in Jenna's journals.

"You'll want to list Philip Walsh," Ann said. "Put him at five. He's been questioned twice regarding home break-ins with sexual assaults. He lived on Jenna's block, moved two weeks after she went missing, never graduated. He's been arrested four times for theft — he likes lifting handbags from the back of a chair and walking away."

"That's promising." Evie wrote in the name. She added Candy Trefford on the list at number ten. According to her interviews, the ex-girlfriend of Steve Hamilton had a temper, a strong jealous streak, and was in the original police investigation as someone cops repeatedly returned to speak with.

Evie added the name Mark Reynolds at number nine. "This one catches a lot of maybes. He's a music major. He lived in the building next to hers. My interview notes have him dating one of Jenna's friends, and that relationship breaking up in high-drama acrimony the month before Jenna disappears. He's got a history of alcohol infractions, drunk-and-disorderly arrests, two DUIs, and I've got him in rehab twice after Jenna's disappearance, according to prior police conversations."

"He's worth a conversation," Ann agreed. "Let me give you what may need to be number three on that list. Aggravated assault, rape charges stuck, tossed out of school, lived on her block, and did more jail time recently for sexual assault of a girl who looks a lot like Jenna. Adam Wythe."

Evie wrote in the name. "It's not going to be a comfortable list when we're done."

"It never is," Ann said.

Evie squeezed in another name at the bottom of the board, taking the list to twenty-seven. The number of guys with a history of trouble regarding women who lived in the area around Jenna's apartment was disturbing, given this was supposedly the quiet side of campus.

"We have our first volley of names. Thanks, Ann. It's a good place to be for day two."

"A useful beginning," Ann replied. She marked her lists with Post-it notes and handed them on to Evie. "There are a lot of names still to go through."

Not a surprise, as Evie was barely halfway through the music-majors list. "Tomorrow's problem. We'll see what the researchers come back with on these. I figure cops have looked at most of these names in the past, but they caught our attention for a reason. Looking at someone with the benefit of additional history sometimes reveals more."

"Finding a name on that list who's now in jail for an abduction-type event or killing would narrow the search very quickly." Ann gathered up her coat, stepped to the conference room door, said good-night to David.

Evie walked her out. "I appreciate the help today."

"It's a pleasure, Evie. I miss this work on occasion. Stack up whatever you most want to tackle tomorrow and I'll help you move that mountain."

"I'll do just that," Evie promised.

Returning to the office, Evie remembered she still needed to call Rob. She considered the time, made the call, and wasn't surprised when his private number rolled over to his voicemail. "Hey, Rob. I was thinking about you and wanted to say hi. I'm about an hour away. Let's meet up for dinner, whatever night works for you. I'll come your way.

Hope your day is going well. Mine is."

She pocketed her phone. He'd call her back, or text, depending on what was happening.

Back at her desk, Evie sent an email with the twenty-seven names to her researcher at the State Police. He'd disperse them to others and funnel back the results of criminal and general background checks as they came in.

David joined her to study the assembled names. "Think he's up there?"

Evie scanned the list once more. "I'd give it maybe a thirty percent chance," she guessed, trying to be optimistic. "How's yours coming?"

"I've finished reviewing Saul's closed cases. I'm at forty-two names with motives to want him dead. I'll see which ones lie to me in interviews and hopefully narrow it down to a top ten. I have a feeling there are a lot of Everett types in that data with minor and major infractions.

"I've been able to pretty much eliminate the other active cases," he added. "According to people I've spoken with, Neil Wallinski was eventually located in Alaska. The VP position was filled four months later by a name not on the candidate list Saul was checking out. And the gambling husband died in an early-morning car crash a year after Saul's disappearance; he'd been playing poker most of the night. No one seems to have benefited from Saul's disappearance in those situations."

"It's good to have at least those checked off," Evie commented.

David smiled. "It's a start. There are a lot more I need to close with this one." He gathered up the used coffee mugs. "You ready to call it a day?"

It was after six p.m. Evie weighed her options. "It's been a long day, but it's still relatively early. I'll put in another hour here with things I need to read. I've got an interview with Jenna's boyfriend after he gets off work, and I'll probably do that later from the hotel. And I still want to try to get through Jenna's laptop tonight. What about you?"

"I'm meeting up with one of Saul's neighbors and a longtime friend, Dell Langford. I've got calls out related to Everett that hopefully turn into conversations. I've got others on my list who work nights — delivery package sorting, bartender, bouncer — so I may try for some late-night conversations. I'd like to end today with the same kind of movement you're getting with yours."

"I've benefited from help. You are making progress, David."

"It's that this case seems stuck. The way through that is to get out talking with people."

"How many people have you spoken with today?"

David paused a moment, then said, "Ten. His sister, along with the woman who worked the answering service and handled his business calls, his two landlords for the business location and rented home, a friend of Saul's from his newspaper days, his regular auto mechanic to see if there was anything about his car that might help me find parts if it had been stripped, a taxi driver Saul paid occasionally to help him out, Everett, Everett's cousin, the other three active-case clients. Make that twelve. The rest of the calls were trying to track people down." David smiled at the look she gave him. "Busy is not productive. You know there's a difference."

"You never know where the right answer is until you locate that lead going somewhere. Don't work too late is my advice, but I'll likely be going until midnight so it would just sound foolish. We're both sprinting when we should be doing a more settled jog."

"Any idea how Sharon, Theo, and Taylor are faring?"

"I was going to ask you that. I really don't want to be the last unsolved case in the county."

David laughed. "We're sprinting for a reason. It's called 'fear of looking bad.' Or ambition. Or just plain stubbornness. These cases have remained unsolved for too long, and justice needs to be done. Take your pick."

"Probably all of them. On that, I'm going back to work," Evie decided, turning back to her laptop.

"I think we're well-suited for these cases." He turned to take the coffee mugs back to the break room. "I'm fixing another pot of coffee."

EIGHT

Working at night was mentally more laid back, and Evie didn't mind putting in the extra hours. She pulled out police reports from the first box and started reading again, looking for additional facts for her board. She liked the style of the cop who had written most of these reports — clear without being verbose. He had been putting in the extra effort to find out what happened. It showed in the depth of the questions he'd asked, the number of interviews conducted.

She turned the page, saw the next report had been misfiled with a date earlier in the search. *Jenna's driver's license is missing from the wallet.* Evie read that, stopped, shook her head at her own oversight — she'd walked right past this when inspecting the wallet's contents herself.

She picked up her pad, added it to her Facts list and circled it twice.

20. Jenna's driver's license is missing

Evie leaned back in her chair and let the information play through her mind. First, could it be a fact unrelated to the disappearance? There were reasons Jenna might have taken her license out. She could have slid it into her pocket as proof of age, was dashing out for a quick trip and didn't want to take her purse. But her car keys were still in her apartment, so she wasn't driving somewhere, and she wasn't a drinker according to the interviews.

How often did someone actually need to get out their driver's license? Evie ticked off five possible reasons: after being stopped for speeding, ID when writing a check, at bank tendering a check for cash, entry to a club with an age restriction, proving age for buying alcohol. Maybe a number six with TSA ID requirements at the airport. Jenna likely hadn't used her driver's license in months, probably wouldn't even have noticed it gone. This could be a months-earlier crime. How many other drivers' licenses were reported missing among college students that year? If it were an identity-theft ring, it wouldn't be just hers getting lifted. Evie flipped the page and wrote a note to look into this further.

The security chief at the Fifth Street Music Hall had shown her video of pickpockets working the concert crowds, security's own variation of a top-ten tape since it was such a routine problem for them. Jenna's license could easily have been lifted the night she went missing, or at any concert she attended before.

If whoever took Jenna's license did so to find out where she lived, that would answer a major question regarding *who* and would eliminate anyone who already knew the address — the boyfriend, the ex-boyfriend, most of her study group, her girlfriends and *their* boyfriends.

If you were a stranger, but had the license, there was no need to follow her home. You could get there ahead of her, study the neighborhood, decide where you would park, how you would get away after the crime.

It fits the case. She tapped the pencil against her notepad as she thought it through.

If there were a lot of missing licenses around that time, it pointed to a crime ring involved in identity theft. But a smattering of licenses lifted, someone was hunting information for a type of girl, would only pursue it if where she lived looked like a reasonable place to wait for the victim's return.

Evie started making phone calls, glad some officers were still at their desks. She asked for missing licenses in the years around Jenna's disappearance — those reported stolen, those replaced as lost. Cops would have pursued this back then, and the records they pulled at the time should be in the electronic archives. Yet it never hurt to request records a second time.

David came in, carrying coat and gloves. He paused by her desk as she hung up the phone. "You've got something. I can hear it in your voice."

"Her driver's license was missing from her wallet."

He considered that statement, grinned. "Another one of those key facts leading to an answer has just landed. You don't have the name yet, but it's there. It's sitting just out of sight."

"I think you're right. He trolls concerts for girls he likes, or knows ones from campus who share his love of music, lifts their drivers' licenses to scope out where they live, and acts when he thinks he can get away with the crime. Music is his thing, his passion, and that's going to give him up."

"When's your next interview, or are you done for the night?"

She glanced at her list. "Ten minutes. Then another in an hour and a half."

"Come take a walk after this next interview, divert for half an hour so your brain can let it simmer there for a bit."

She smiled at his suggestion. "Sure, I could use a break. But I'm bundling up like an Eskimo for this walk and hanging on to you. These are dress boots, not for hiking. And from the looks of you, snow is coming down again."

David smiled. "Maggie's not the jealous type. We'll find hot chocolate or something. You owe me the story of your guy, since I've told you mine and Maggie's."

"Rob Turney. My guy." She saved them some time and punched in the website for the firm where he worked, brought up his bio. "Read. I'll never get the job details right," she said, motioning toward the screen.

David came around the desk, started reading. "You're hanging out with ambition of its own kind," David mentioned as he finished.

"He's kind of like Ann. He keeps introducing me to famous people in business and finance, but I don't have a clue who they are, what they do, why I should know them."

David laughed.

"He's a dealmaker. That's what I think best describes him. And he's trying to close the deal on marrying me."

"I wondered," David said with a smile.

"Yeah. It's kind of nice and also kind of awkward — his parents don't think I'm good enough for him. He does. And I've stumbled into realizing I care more about their view of me than I probably should."

"Finish this next interview, then we'll walk, find hot chocolate. You need to shift over from figuring out a case to figuring out your life. And I just need a break. They were good interviews, but it all needs to meld for a while."

"If only solving my life was that simple."

He tapped the pad of paper on her desk. "Where's the sheet with the two columns outlining your personal decision?"

"I'd have a lousy time living with myself if I reduced it to yes-or-no columns."

"It's how you think, Evie. Sometimes putting it on paper is what digs up the truth so you can look at it squarely."

He had a point. The alarm on her phone sounded. Her next interview with the boss of Jenna's boyfriend at the newspaper shouldn't take long. "Give me a few and then let's go for that walk."

Evie finished her notes as David reappeared in the doorway. "Learn anything useful?" he asked, putting on his coat.

"Jenna did some work for the newspaper — student opinion pieces, that kind of thing — published under 'Anonymous.' They sourced out various subjects to different students. I'll be able to read more of her own words now that I know which articles she authored."

She bundled up, scarf over her lower face, and they headed out. The street was well lit. David pointed to a coffee shop on the next corner. "So tell me more about Rob."

"I have no idea where to start."

"Do you love him?"

Evie glanced over at David, wondering how to put her situation into words that would make sense to a guy who was head over heels in love with his girl. "I like him. A lot. I think at times I love him. But I have a history with canceled weddings that tends to make me jittery when the subject comes up."

"Define jittery."

"Three engagements that didn't make it

to *I do.*"

David winced. "Ouch."

"Yeah. All were ages ago. As I described recently to a friend, they were good guys, and any one of them would have made a fine husband. But I didn't fight very hard to keep a wedding in view once the relationship began to go south. I was looking for something I thought a guy could give me . . . to fill the void I was feeling, make me complete. I grew up, and grew out of that stage in my life.

"Rob is different. He's more . . . what? Aware of us, of me? I'm different too. I run stretches where I'm certain it's not him, then it rolls back toward he really is the guy. We're at the point there's a marriage proposal on the table if I want him to ask, want to say yes. It's already bedrock certain on his side. He wants a future together."

"You're uncertain what you want."

"Uncertain more about the idea of marriage than about Rob, I guess." She struggled to find the right words. "I want something in my life that is a contrast to my work, something that isn't what crime scene I walked into recently. Cold cases are actually easy compared to my day job. My phone is going to ring tonight, tomorrow, and it's going to be some police officer in a small town dealing with a double murder, asking for state help to sort out the scene. Or it's going to be an arson fire that leaves people dead, matching a string of them across the state. Those weighty phone calls will always keep coming, and I'm good at solving those critical cases. But to be able to shut that door for a while, have another life — it's something I need. And maybe it's why I actually do love Rob. There's not a single crime-scene detail that's going to be part of our dinner conversation. He's 'normal life,' if someone of his standing in the financial world has a normal life. I'm making a decision about marriage, about Rob, but it's also what he represents. A life outside of being a cop. And I don't want to choose Rob merely out of a desire to balance out my life. That just wouldn't be fair to him."

"You sound like you don't expect others to understand that heartfelt desire for a life different from being a cop," David said.

"I get it, Evie. I certainly understand. But for a cop to have a life outside of the job, it's you who has to be able to 'turn it off' when you leave work, as much as the other person needs to be a safe place. What you want to find is as much about you as it is Rob."

Evie thought about the last couple of days, nodded. "I read Jenna's journals late into the night — rather than watch some movie or read a book. I spend evenings adding new ideas to my master list of theories. And I know — just for a moment in time — I would resent the phone ringing, interrupting that work, even if it was Rob on the other end. Work is this chase, this ongoing puzzle that grips at my time and thinking until it's resolved and I can put it back in its box. After that, until I open a new box, I can be as lazy about work as anyone would like, totally leave it behind. But when a case is open and the details are soaking into my head, it's 'How can I get this solved? And please don't distract me.' "

"Which do you want to tame?" David asked. "The desire to do the job or the impulse to be annoyed with the interruptions?"

Evie smiled at the question. "Ann and I have had the conversation whether God just wires some people to be cops. I can't help it, really, this habit of wanting to run real-life puzzles to the ground. It's not that I want to be this single-track person, but it actually does matter to me to figure things out. And when it's a real-life crime, doing it fast matters to people. I don't have an easy way to tone down that intensity — it seems to spring up of its own volition."

"To use your analogy, God wired Maggie to be all about music," David told her. "You take a break in a conversation, and she's jotting a song lyric or two in the margin of the newspaper she's reading. She can't help herself. Her mind thinks up music all the time. Create a pause point, create stillness, and her mind comes alive with rich refrains. It's like a tide of music flows in any time there's an opening. Who's to say that the producing of ideas, the what-ifs that so suit your job, aren't also wired into how your mind works? You may never shut it off, Evie. When there's a puzzle to chew on, your mind keeps turning it over and generating solutions until it's resolved."

"You don't do that."

David shrugged. "I work cases differently. I'm looking someone in the eye, listening to what is said, watching for the lie. I'm intense but in a different way. I give the work my focus and a lot of hours, but it's not doing what you describe as your process. To each his own. We both get the job done."

"How to have a life when that's how I work, that's the mystery," Evie said. "When you're having a meal together with Maggie, she's humming a few bars and asking what you think, 'Do you like this song fragment?' With me, I'm likely thinking, 'I bet he gutted the guy with a fishing knife, and he's probably still got the knife in his tackle box' — not exactly the kind of remark you can share across the table. And when my mind is there — on a murder or something worse — it's hard to shift back to pleasantries about the blueberry muffins being extra good this morning."

David smiled. "Point taken." He pulled open the door to the coffee shop. "Job collisions and how your mind works aside, do you *want* to get married?"

"That seems to depend on when you ask, which is part of this problem — I honestly don't know."

He ordered two hot chocolates with extra whipped cream. They started the walk back, Evie's hands wrapped snugly around the warm cup.

"You really do need to make one of your two-column lists," David advised. Evie simply nodded, not sure what she'd even put on one.

They walked a minute in silence.

"An observation, Evie? If you wanted to get married, you'd be saying yes to Rob. You haven't told me one concern yet about him — his character, his job, his history —

just that his parents don't see you as the right one for him. It's a good sign when a guy makes his own choice rather than simply echoing his parents. Given he loves you, he's probably the right guy."

Evie nodded. "The question really is, do I love him?"

"I'd say that's *the* question," David agreed.

"I'm probably overthinking it."

"I'll make a guess you tend to do that," David replied lightly.

Evie smiled. "How did you know you were in love with Maggie?"

"Everything in me said I loved her — emotions, heart, dreams. She was it."

"You're not going to be much help."

David laughed. "Can you see yourself spending a lifetime together?"

"Yes."

"Do you miss not seeing him?"

"It's more like . . . like I would deeply feel the void if he were not around to be with. But we're not everyday close, like some dating couples are. You probably talk to Maggie more than I do Rob."

"Make your lists, Evie," he said around a chuckle. "There's a reason probably unrelated to Rob that has you shying away from marriage. 'Single' isn't the answer unless it's actually what you want for yourself. And you really don't strike me as one who wants to spend her life on her own. Your voice softens when you talk about him."

"Ann has some reservations about him being the right guy for me."

"She knows you both well?"

"She knows me as well as anyone. Rob she's met a few times."

"Then listen to her concerns, weigh them on your list. And quit grimacing over the idea of a list — it's just a tool, forcing you to think clearly on paper, a way to dig down to the root of a matter that has you so uncertain."

"It's the very fact I need to make one that has me grimacing. You didn't have this kind of stress when you thought of a future with Maggie."

"Sometimes love comes easily, and sometimes it's the most challenging decision a person ever makes. That reality doesn't make one way right and the other wrong, it just is. The love underlying marriage is more than an emotion, more than a set of facts adding up to a decision. It's the choice that this is the person I'm going to stay with for the rest of my life. It's something you have to make with your head and your heart, Evie. It's a decision with consequences.

171

More time can be good and helpful, adding new information. But when it's time to make the decision, you need to make it. Avoiding that step doesn't get you anywhere productive."

"You make it sound so . . . well, so easy, David."

He opened the door to their temporary offices. "Not easy. Just necessary. Life is mostly captured in the decisions we make, the choices, the pivots. You're at one of those points. Accept it, Evie. When it's time to decide, you pray, you think, you listen to your mind and heart, and then you make the decision."

Evie found herself reviewing once more the known facts of her case as she drove back to the hotel. Like an oyster forming a pearl, it had become an irritant she couldn't ignore. She wasn't chasing a ghost. Someone had made Jenna disappear. She wished she could see him more clearly — the outline of a person would make it easier to fit a name to the shape.

"I don't think it's my guy's first time," she whispered to herself. She needed to dig into similar events tomorrow — the last remaining line of inquiry she hadn't actively pursued yet, beyond asking the FBI to generate data.

The missing driver's license might be a trophy that could cross between cases. Choosing someone at a concert, that might be a pattern. The clean abduction without witnesses might point to method. The better she understood Jenna's situation, the easier it would be to spot related cases.

The car's radio shifted to a Triple M song, and Maggie's clear, strong voice caught her attention. She focused on listening to enjoy the song. Knowing Maggie's history with David, Evie understood now the deep well of emotion Maggie drew from to put into her songs. She had a lot to offer people who were also waiting for love in their lives.

"God, if Maggie can accept that Jesus loves her, she's going to find herself in an ocean of love, not only married to David, but enjoying a love relationship with Jesus forever," Evie whispered.

She wished she knew how to solve truly hard problems like Maggie's questions about God. How did you explain that when God raised Jesus from the dead, it was *the* sign Jesus was in fact His son and savior of the world? It was the proof Jesus was who He said He was, that He had the authority on earth to forgive men's sins as He claimed and could give eternal life to everyone who called on Him. The call of Jesus was so simple — "Follow me" — and yet it took a step of faith to say yes and trust that He would be there to meet you. If Maggie could take that step, she'd find that Jesus was indeed there. But no one could do it for her. Evie could only imagine how deep the ache was in David's heart as he yearned and prayed for Maggie to believe.

"God, would you help Maggie find you this year? Please help *somebody* describe you so clearly that she can see your outline in their words, realize you are really there, and accept you. Please plant that seed of faith in her heart. I know how richly you love her. This is something you are eager to accomplish. Let it all come together this year, however it needs to unfold. That would be such a relief to David, and a blessing to Maggie. Thanks, Dad."

She was so relieved God understood people better than she did. Maggie's questions came from a lifetime of experiences, and somewhere in that history was the obstacle that needed to be cleared away. There was a way to reach faith in God. Evie wished for both David and Maggie's sake that their journey moved forward in the next months.

As she turned toward the hotel, her

thoughts drifted back to the questions she wanted to ask Jenna's boyfriend during their conversation. She would be speaking with him in about thirty-five minutes.

At two a.m., Evie draped her arms around a pillow and considered getting up to watch an old movie. If her brain didn't shut off soon, she was going to have to do something. She'd finished both books she had brought with her, a nice break, but then reality had returned. This case had theories churning around like a storm-tossed sea.

The interview with Jenna's boyfriend had been a spectacular bust. She'd thought Robin had been hard to shepherd through an interview. Steve . . . he was willing, even eager, to talk about Jenna, but Evie had vastly underestimated the crosscurrents and undertow within him.

Over the last nine years Steve had pushed hard to solve what had happened to Jenna. He was now such a walking conglomerate of mashed-together interviews he'd had with others, that whatever he had known at the time was layered over and intermingled with hundreds of conversations he'd had with Jenna's friends and neighbors after her disappearance. Whatever original facts he had for investigators were only going to be found in the notes from his initial conversations with cops.

That realization had buried her hopes that their conversation would be useful, but it had taught her something she'd need to better grasp as she worked numerous cold cases, and so the time spent had been helpful in that respect.

She'd seen three major facets to Steve tonight. He was a guy still grieving the loss of someone he'd loved. He was still a reporter — sports at the time — but Jenna's disappearance had moved him into news reporting where he still remained, and he asked probing questions of his own. Finally, he was still very much the wary, careful, non-named suspect, the boyfriend cops had repeatedly talked to in informal and formal interviews, trying to break his alibi or show him as somehow complicit in Jenna's disappearance. This case was history, but for Steve it was very much part of his personal history, his life story, with pain for his loss, and pain at the question marks still hanging over him.

She felt sincerely sorry for the man. Like Jenna's parents, Steve needed an answer to be able to move on with his life. The only thing the interview had really done was confirm to her that Steve hadn't been involved in whatever crime this was. Jenna's disappearance had haunted him and torn up his life in ways it wouldn't have done had he been responsible for the crime. If he were guilty, he'd simply have been relieved to have gotten away with it and have distanced himself from the event.

What happened to you, Jenna?

Her brain seemed stuck in an aimlessly spinning solve-it gear. She had facts, theories, but nothing had jelled into substance. That had to shift. She'd start looking at specific names tomorrow, Evie decided, dig out someone to focus on and see what she could find. It had to be better than these endless middle-of-the-night cogitations.

Evie pushed back the covers. She'd brought Jenna's laptop with her to the hotel but hadn't yet gotten to it. She would see what Jenna had been working on before she disappeared, who she'd been talking with via email, what websites she'd been visiting.

Evie turned on the table lamp, set up the laptop, powered it on. "God, at this time of night, what's on my mind isn't elaborate — where did this crime happen? Who was involved? What thread will lead to something useful? All those useful five W's and an H are just hanging out there. Help me make progress on this. Thanks." It wasn't an elaborate prayer, but it was better than sitting here working alone in the middle of the night. God was up. She might as well talk with Him.

She yawned as she brought up Jenna's email account. The inbox had 816 messages. Evie laughed softly. "Why don't you read these for me, God, and tell me which handful I should care about?"

She started scanning subject lines. An hour of this should either put her to sleep or give her something useful. Right now she'd take either outcome as progress.

NINE

David had texted that he'd pick up breakfast, so Evie didn't stop on the way into the
office Friday morning.

He was taking off his coat as she entered
the office suite, so she must have been following him in traffic. "Not as cold out there
today," he commented.

She laughed. The digital sign at the bank
she'd passed had said twelve degrees. "I'm
glad my car's battery is hearty or I'd have
been stranded many times over by now. We
need March and that first thaw." She
dumped her coat and gloves onto her office
chair. "Thanks for breakfast."

"My pleasure."

She found plates and napkins as he un-
packed the sack. "How did your conversations go last night?" she asked.

"Surprisingly successful. The fourth name
on my list is Grant Quince. Saul proved the
man stole money from a business partner-

ship to support a drug habit, and he ended up doing four years. He's a bad liar, and the month before Saul disappeared, Grant got two parking tickets on the same street where Saul's office was located. There's also three assault charges on his record."

Evie nodded as she bit into her breakfast sandwich. "That sounds very promising."

"He says he doesn't remember where he was when Saul went missing, but I could practically smell the fear on him. It could be the drugs — he's clearly using again by the look of him — but it could be what he knows."

David shared his hash browns with her. Evie appreciated the salt and the crunch and tried to remember they weren't good for her even as they tasted wonderful.

"Number six on my list — Bradley Vine — was caught in an affair, lost his marriage, his reputation, and with it most of his business clients. I found out through his ex-wife that he'd hired a PI to investigate Saul, hoping to get him arrested for trespassing, picking a lock, something that would get his license pulled, cause him some grief in return."

"Not as promising, but more creatively interesting."

"The guy he hired is more thug than

investigator, has a history of using his fists to get information."

"Now I'm liking that lead more."

"I'm still looking to find the guy he hired — Vincent Lane — so I can have a conversation about what he might have done. I could see a confrontation going too far, and whoops, Saul's dead.

"Thomas Ford at number twelve was suspected of selling backroom inventory from the electronics store where he worked. Saul was hired to figure out what was going on. When Thomas realized he was being tailed, he backed up and smashed into Saul's car with his, tried to pull Saul and his camera out of the car during the altercation that followed, ended up doing three years for possession of stolen goods found in his apartment. He got out of jail, beat up the owner who had hired Saul to follow him, did another year in jail for that. Next time he gets out of jail, Saul's car goes up in flames one night. No arrest on that car arson, but the timeline clicks."

"Why isn't he your lead suspect?" Evie wondered.

"Tom didn't lie when I interviewed him. Admitted what he did, drew the line at what he didn't. Cops interviewed him after Saul disappeared. His alibi at the time was a short-term job hauling furniture with a friend in Wisconsin. It's got major holes, as it's only a couple hours' drive back here, but cops confirmed he was in Wisconsin. Tom stays on my list, but I tend to believe him when he said payback was payback, and he's not one to murder a guy."

"You did have a good night," she said after a sip of orange juice.

"It felt like progress, something I sorely need." David finished his first egg sandwich and wadded up the wrapper. "My plan for today is to track down more names on that list, have more conversations, see what other rocks I can turn over." He motioned with his second breakfast sandwich. "How's your day shaping up?"

"Ann and I are going to spend most of it doing interviews of people on my whiteboard list. The background reports I'm getting confirm we have the right names to consider."

David nodded. "A productive day is ahead for both of us." He gestured once more with his sandwich. "If you happen to see a for-sale sign on a decent house, jot down the address. I'm officially house hunting."

"Sure. Looking for anything in particular?"

"Ranch-style, two-car garage, a little grass,

not on a major street. I can fix it up. So long as the neighborhood is low crime, I'm good. Maggie will be living in Barrington. I figure if I split the distance between the airport and the tollway, I'll have the shortest commute I can arrange between my personal and work lives."

"I'll keep my eyes open," Evie assured him. She'd never actually owned a house, always rented, so it would be interesting to watch David settle in someplace.

After breakfast, David headed to the conference room while Evie turned her attention to Jenna's files. Cops had considered some similar cases. She found those reports, went online to see their current status. Three of the five were still open. She looked deeper at the two solved ones, the arrests made. The individuals involved didn't seem like possibles for Jenna's disappearance. Evie cleared a section of the whiteboard and put up photos from the three still-open cases.

She didn't know what pieces truly mattered — attending a concert, the missing driver's license, no sign of struggle in the apartment, the body not found, Jenna's appearance and personality, or something else entirely. The FBI report on missing women was in her inbox. She opened it and found it ran sixty-two pages. A lot of college girls had gone missing over the twelve years Evie had asked for.

She had about thirty minutes before Ann would join her. She began to read the five-line abstracts for each entry. She found a case in Indiana that sounded like a match, pulled up the file to read the summary, added another photo to the board. Missing college girls . . . Jenna Greenhill was one of a larger subset of crimes.

The interviews went about as Evie had expected. "Ann, do you get the feeling the last person these people want to remember is Jenna Greenhill?" she asked, walking away from an automotive garage where Benjamin Reece worked.

"It's certainly less cooperation than we get from her friends."

"At least it confirms we've got the right names." Evie marked off number five. They weren't going to get a confession out of someone, but she would settle for hearing a lie and seeing acute nerves kick in. She was mostly hearing stress and anger that cops were out asking questions again.

"Who's next?" Ann asked.

Evie had lined them up in order of geography to limit drive time. "The ex-girlfriend of Steve Hamilton, Candy Trefford. Has a temper and a jealous streak, and in the last nine years has had three restraining orders filed against her."

"I like the idea of it being a woman," Ann remarked, opening the car door. "Gender bias aside, Jenna doesn't see it coming if it's a woman, and when cops did interviews, asking if people saw anything out of place that night, those questioned are going to be thinking male, not female."

Evie, behind the wheel, entered the address for directions. "Exactly. I'm thinking Candy viewed her first name as something to live down, let herself get a temper, had a 'you'd better take me seriously' attitude toward guys."

"Makes sense. We've both seen it. Live against type, be aggressive with the world."

Evie nodded. "Steve was a nice guy. Candy didn't like him moving on. And Jenna is the target of that anger. It's plausible, if I could figure out how it played out. The easiest was to get Jenna in Candy's car, hit her, dump the body somewhere. The text message to Jenna's mom throws the timing off, but it's possible Candy sent the text, then returned Jenna's keys, phone and purse to her apartment, walked out."

"It's possible, yes."

"I've had that text anchoring me to the apartment because the phone was there. But Jenna's phone could have been anywhere when that text message was sent. No one looked at Jenna's apartment until Monday. That gives a lot of time to return those items without being seen. Wait till it's absolutely clear, deliver them to the apartment. That's pretty easy to do if you've got forty-eight hours to figure out when to walk up those stairs."

"We've been looking too closely at her apartment as the location for this," Ann confirmed.

Evie nodded. "I think Jenna went for a walk that night, and then trouble happened. The things put back in her apartment, the text to her a mom, are probably simple cover-your-tracks steps to throw off the original investigation — and now me. I'd be better off looking at the person with the strongest motive to kill Jenna, then just back into how they accomplish the crime to fit the facts I have."

Ann smiled. "You've got your hands around this case now."

"Hopefully I do. Saturating myself with the facts seems to have put it all into better order in my head. I need to ask Steve if Candy ever tried to make up with him after

Jenna disappeared. He didn't offer that information in our first conversation, but jog his memory a little and maybe it's there — he'd brushed off Candy's overture as not going to happen so had forgotten it."

Evie scanned house numbers as they entered the right subdivision. "According to my researcher, Candy's working as a hostess at a restaurant three nights a week, does sales work at a car dealership on weekends. She drives a red Toyota. There." She spotted the car and house and slid into a place at the curb.

They walked up the sidewalk, and Evie knocked. The door opened within a minute.

Candy Trefford was a beautiful woman, significantly more stunning than her driver's license photo suggested, and thin as a rail. Evie had her badge out and showed it as she spoke. "Ms. Trefford, I'm Lieutenant Evie Blackwell. I have a few questions for you regarding Jenna Greenhill." The blank look lasted a few seconds before the name clicked. Disgust was the emotion that passed across Candy's face first, Evie noted, surprised.

"She's finally been found, that boyfriend-stealing cheater?"

"I gather you weren't friends," Evie dryly responded.

187

"She shows up freshman year, hangs over my guy like a piece of gum on your shoe, and manages to poach him when I'm out of town seeing my folks. She wasn't *anybody's* friend if they happened to have something she wanted."

"You mind if we have this conversation inside?" Evie asked. The woman was a talker, and to Evie's view of things, that could make her a gold mine of an interview.

Candy pushed the door wider and stepped back. "You didn't answer my question. Did she finally show up? And who's this with you?"

"Ann Falcon is working with the task force looking at the case. Jenna's not been found, Ms. Trefford. We're talking with those who knew her."

"I knew her. Didn't like her. And those who saw under the surface mostly steered clear too."

The house was a basic floor plan, maybe twelve hundred square feet, but it had been carefully decorated, modern in style, furnished more for looks than comfort, Evie thought. They weren't asked to sit, thankfully, as they stepped into the living room. "Besides your boyfriend, what else did Jenna acquire?"

"Grades, for one. She was tight with the

TAs. You'd see her back in the professors' offices, the labs where grad students worked. She was getting inside help to make those grades. Steve was so enamored with how smart she was, but truth be told, she was mostly a cheat."

"Any particular TA she hung out with more than others?"

"Jacob something. A grad student who ran the lab area. I know she was two-timing Steve with Jacob — I saw them kissing."

Evie's attention sharpened at the remark. Candy stalking Jenna was like a camera clicking nine years ago. She might be the murderer, but if not, she had made herself the reporter on the scene. "Jenna have any other guys hanging around?"

"The drummer Kyle Lee with the school performance band would be around her place, and the guy who manages the music shop, Tyler something, she'd be out with him for coffee."

"Were you around the campus that week-end Jenna went missing?"

"Steve was reporting on an away game. I went to the game, which is what a girl should do when her guy is there."

"Did you speak with Steve?"

"He was hanging with the guys, avoiding me in public so he wouldn't have a scene with Jenna when he got back. She was friends with the stats guy, would ask who Steve had been with on road trips, checking up on him. The guys were laughing about the leash she had him on. We talked some at his room Friday night, but I didn't stay over with him if that's what you want to ask next."

"When did you get back to campus?"

"Sunday afternoon? I like to shop. I heard all the hubbub Monday night when I was leaving class — one of those tuition-money theft requirements you have to take to graduate, *postmodern interpretation of the English classics* or some such stupidity. Still burns me the name was the most interesting thing about the class."

"What do you think happened to Jenna?"

"How should I know? She probably charmed some other guy, and he got tired of being played. With Steve out of town, Jenna was doing whatever she wanted to do that weekend, probably ran herself into trouble."

"You ever see her at a bar drinking? Doing drugs?"

"That I can't say she ever did. She was straitlaced, that one, made a face at people having a good time. Nagged Steve off even a beer, poor man."

Evie closed her notebook. "I appreciate your time."

"That's all you want to ask?"

"Did you cause her harm or know who did?"

Candy made a face. "Wasn't me. And I'd thank whoever did rather than tell you their name."

"I can see why cops on the original case liked to talk with you, Candy. Why don't you give me the names of your friends from back then, someone who might remember you were at that away game, shopping that weekend?"

"I hung out with Nancy and Iris, sometimes with Lisa." She dug a phone out of her pocket and read off full names and numbers. Ann jotted them down. "They'll tell you the same as I did."

"I expect so," Evie agreed. "Thanks again for your time."

Evie scanned the photos on the walls as they walked out, finding Candy in casual shots with a range of different guys. Candy had the looks that would have made guys come calling, but none appeared to have stuck. Losing a boyfriend to someone else had become a sharp sting that didn't get forgotten. A sad fact for Candy, and a useful one for Evie. It had kept those memories alive.

"That was enlightening," Ann remarked as they got back into the car. "So which picture is more accurate, the one drawn by those who liked Jenna or by someone who didn't?"

Evie thought Ann's question was right on point. "Candy was watching Jenna in a way no one else was. Didn't like her, but paid super close attention to her. Others who didn't like her mostly ignored her. The guys we've interviewed mostly look at her picture, shrug and say, 'Yeah, I saw her around. I saw a lot of girls around. Nothing particularly special about Jenna. Until you said her name, I wouldn't have remembered it.' Doesn't mean one of them wasn't the one who did Jenna harm, but across the board she wasn't a fixation. They weren't eyes-locked-onto-the-photo when I showed it, remembering an obsession with her. They mostly didn't know her. Candy Trefford — she *knew* Jenna, in her own warped-interpretation way."

"So what do you do with it?"

Evie was wondering the same thing. "For starters, how about we look for more people like Candy who didn't like Jenna? To begin with, others with the same major. Let's find

192

out what was going on with the TAs — if there was some inside favoritism. Or this is simply a bright student with a shared focus on an obscure subject, already making friends among the grad students she hoped to work alongside one day."

They called the interviews done at four p.m. Ann had a standing Friday-night date with husband Paul. Evie turned in and parked beside Ann's car. "Thanks for the help, friend."

"It made for an interesting Friday. Paul will enjoy the highlights," Ann said with a smile and handed over the notebook filled with her own observations. "I remember now why I often went home with a head-ache . . . interviews with people who have something to hide or who are being hostile just for the sake of giving cops a bad day."

"We caught our fair share of both today," Evie agreed. "I did think Joe Mueller was going to run when he saw the badge. For an instant I hoped we'd caught a lucky break and stumbled onto the right guy."

Ann smiled. "I saw that too. He was the only one who looked relieved when he heard we were there to ask about Jenna Green-hill."

"Yeah," Evie said with a chuckle. "I'd care

193

about what he's got going that makes him nervous around cops, but that would take more energy than I have left. Did we learn anything today that felt substantive to you?"

"We met a few interesting people like Candy, several bad guys, but not, I think, anybody who directly caused Jenna problems."

"Regretfully, same conclusion," Evie said.

"But your list of twenty-seven is slimming down. Same time tomorrow?"

Evie gave a nod. "I'm not going to turn down that offer."

"I figure if you're going to be working on your weekend, I'll at least keep you company."

"I'm getting more coffee," Evie announced, stopping at the conference room door. "And whatever I can find to toss in the microwave. I saw popcorn packages in the vending machine. Want your own bag?"

David turned from his laptop. "Sure."

She nodded and left. *He's had a good day,* she thought. He'd been humming before he realized she was at the door.

Back with bags of popcorn for both of them and a full mug of coffee of her own, she decided the warmth was worth the slightly stale taste indicating too long in the pot.

"My timeline narrowed," David said casually, only underscoring his relief. He saved the page and closed the document. "I've confirmed Saul's movements for part of Saturday. Around four p.m. he was talking with a Neil Wallinsky, spelled with a *y,* who lived over in River Glen, a good two hours west. The age was right, but it wasn't the Neil he wanted. From there I have him back in Chicago just after eight p.m., talking to a guy in Arlington Heights about the location of a card game maybe happening in Englewood."

Evie glanced over the whiteboard's list of Saul's active cases, spotted the one she remembered. "The husband thought to have returned to his gambling problem."

David nodded. "Sounds like it. The guy died in a car accident about a year after Saul disappeared, so I can't ask him if he was playing a game in Englewood that night. But it fits why Saul would be asking about a game."

"Tell me about the guy who remembers this nugget."

"Okay. That's Brad Olmer," David replied, satisfaction in his voice. "The guy was in Saul's book as an occasional source — he worked security at clubs, after-hours parties, *and* the occasional off-the-books card game. Saul paid him fifty bucks for solid answers to his information needs. Brad heard there was a game going on, but didn't know where, didn't have any solid info for Saul. He remembers the date from when he told Saul it was his sister's birthday. Saul peeled off a hundred, said to make it a nice birthday gift, and Brad was feeling guilty about that."

"Not his sister's birthday."

"Not by a couple months. It was the last time they spoke."

"According to Saul's sister," Evie remembered, "Saul was flush with cash, had been getting some things repaired for her, and the spontaneous gesture fits him."

"Feels that way," David agreed. "Let's say Saul persists in trying to track down the card game, drives around Englewood, spots his gambler's car, maybe stakes out the game to get a photo of the guy leaving. That puts him in the area until two a.m. or later Sunday morning."

"Could Saul get himself in trouble simply watching till the game breaks up?" Evie asked. "Guys leaving a location . . . it's hard to jam someone up over that kind of photo. The husband is in trouble only because the wife already suspects what's going on."

"Security on a card game maybe is going to rough him up if they think he's there to bother the game. But kill him? Not for sitting in a car watching a parking lot."

"Crimes in the area at that time? He saw something else and took a photo of it, or someone thought he had?"

David nodded. "That's where I'll look next. Saul's neighbors didn't see him coming or going that weekend, didn't see lights on at his place. He missed watching the Sunday football game with the usuals at the neighborhood pub. That suggests he didn't make it home from Englewood Saturday night."

"He works odd hours, maybe neighbors simply missed it."

"True. In which case he got home early Sunday morning, maybe went out later with his marked newspaper looking for a new place to rent, and walked into trouble. Unfortunately, the newspaper that would tell me that is probably in the front seat of his car, wherever that is."

Evie laughed at his dry tone. "Been there. Solve the crime first, and you can have all the evidence you need for what and how. Any more sources like Brad Olmer in Saul's notebooks?"

"Thirty or so," David replied. "Cops talked to them, but I'm making the full rounds again. Time gets people more willing to talk about facts safely in the past." He gestured to the numbered list on the whiteboard. "Another five names also got crossed off the possible list. They're glad Saul disappeared, but I didn't get vibes that any of them had been involved." David took a handful of popcorn. "Anyway, that was pretty much my day. Yours go anywhere interesting?"

"Candy was fascinating." Evie gave him a thumbnail sketch of the interview.

David smiled. "Jealousy with an extremely good memory."

"It's the contrast of how she views Jenna and the descriptions from other friends that has me curious. I need to find a few more Candys, those in Jenna's world who didn't like her. It could be a long step toward solving this mystery."

"Use whatever works. About ready to call it a night?"

"I need an hour to enter notes, but then I'm out of here."

"I was going to order in a pizza and do some more database work. I'll make it a large if you want."

"Anything without onions. Thanks."

Phone tag with Rob about dinner arrangements hadn't connected yet, and it wasn't going to come together tonight. It was a rare week they didn't share a meal, but he was working on something that had left his message sounding particularly upbeat, and she no doubt had sounded similar.

Evie settled at her desk with her notebook and Ann's, focused on getting the notes of their interviews organized into the laptop.

It felt as if the case had moved forward today, though it wasn't quite clear yet what precisely she was reacting to — maybe the broadened perspective about the victim. Candy had gone from a person of interest to someone shining a light from a different angle on Jenna. The seeming clarity of the original interviews had gone out of focus. That was the interesting shift. Rather than be bothered by it, Evie thought it might be the key that took her toward her answer. Get the whole truth about Jenna to bring her back into focus again, and the task of finding who would want to cause Jenna trouble would likely solve itself.

She liked days that had movement. This indeed had been a good day.

"More possibles?" David asked. Evie glanced over as David joined her, pulling on his coat. He nodded to the whiteboard. "You've put up a couple more pictures."

She turned to consider the photos and names. "Missing college women. Nothing exact to Jenna, but in the ballpark. I've been avoiding this direction, but it feels necessary."

"It's been nine years. If he's not been caught, what else has he been doing? It's logical, Evie."

"Thanks." She studied the board once more. "I do think there is at least one before Jenna simply because of how clean her disappearance is, but I don't know what I'm looking for — another missing person, a sexual assault, maybe a failed abduction?"

"It could be anything," David said.

"What I'm hoping is that if Jenna was close to his first, she was also close to where he lives. I think the first ones occur on very familiar ground, where he'd have some comfort with how to get away, hide, a plan if things went wrong, alibis in place, friends who would cover for him. He would have started to branch out only after he got more success, been confident enough to take action in a place he'd never been."

"Reasonable assumptions."

"It's a big field to wander into — the FBI report has a lot of names."

"You understand Jenna pretty well now. She's your template. Cases that are a match are going to feel like hers, either in the victim type or case details."

"Jenna does feel like it's personal — concert, apartment on the second floor — he chose her, whether it was actually Jenna or a certain type. Seems specific enough that he took risks to get to her. I don't think you make that kind of connection on a twenty-minute 'she'll do' pick in a random crowd of students. Someone took time with his decision. Anyway, I'm going to be working this approach when I'm not doing more interviews."

She glanced at his coat. "You're obviously heading out again."

David gave a rueful smile. "More interviews, here I come. I plan to pick up the pizza on the way back as my reward."

Evie laughed. "Thanks again."

"I'm praying for Saul's remains to turn up. It would save me a lot of time."

She blinked, realizing David was serious. "Truly?"

"You're not praying that same kind of thing?"

"I hadn't even considered it." And she was rather shocked that she hadn't. God certainly knew where Jenna was buried.

"Try it. That prayer can't hurt. 'Jesus, what am I missing?' is also a favorite of mine. He knows the answer to that question too."

Evie smiled. "Thanks. I needed the reminder."

David tugged out his gloves. "God appreciates justice even more than we do, so it makes sense that He'd be interested in helping us find it. I like to lean hard against that when I feel like I'm banging my head against a stone wall."

Evie's phone rang, and she felt a flash of relief at the caller's name. "Hi, Rob."

David stepped away to give her some privacy.

"I'm in town and wrapping up for the night," she confirmed.

"Go ahead, meet your guy," David mouthed.

She nodded agreement. "I'll see you in a little over an hour."

"I'm bailing on you to have dinner at Rob's," she reported to David as she hung up, saved her work, and logged off.

He smiled. "Watch me do the same when my girl gets into town next week. Enjoy your evening, Evie."

"I will. See you tomorrow, David." Evie felt a renewed shot of energy at simply having Rob in her plans for the night. She pulled on her coat and gloves and headed out with David.

TEN

Evie curled her feet up under her on the couch, watching Rob over an oversized mug of hot chocolate she'd chosen over a glass of chardonnay, enjoying listening to details of his week as he put away the remains of their meal.

"We're doing a deal with The Lewis Group on a television station," he told her, "buying it from Nathan and merging ownership with one from Atlanta and another two located in Virginia."

She could hear the satisfaction in Rob's voice — certainly the deals, but also the people he was working with. He liked running with "the big dogs," as he joked on occasion. The deals were large, had more on the line, got noticed by the press, and written up in the business sections of major newspapers. Rob was good at what he did, was respected by the decision-makers. She liked that about him.

She didn't try to follow the intricate specifics of what he described, but she liked listening. The money and business transactions that had him fascinated were just things, not life and death, though they caused similar stress. Her perception was different. She would never appreciate them with the same satisfaction he did and couldn't easily pretend that she did. But she knew he loved the work.

"Boring you?" Rob asked with a grin as he walked into the living room with his glass.

She smiled. "No. Just drifting a bit as I listen. It's been a long workweek." She shifted the hot chocolate to the coffee table and curled into him after he joined her on the couch, gave him a hug and simply leaned against his chest. "I missed you."

"Very much mutual, my Evie." He put a hand under her chin, lifted it for a gentle kiss.

He took good care of her — the meal, the quiet evening. He also liked to show her off, take her to events, out to dinner, to parties where friends and business acquaintances could meet her. But there were also nights like this one where he simply wanted a shared meal with her at his place.

"Fifteen days since we last spent an

evening together — far too long a stretch," he mentioned. "You might start forgetting me."

She smiled at the teasing tone. "As if . . ." She gave a contented sigh as she sat up to reach for her mug, idly wondering if that was one of the ties she had given him. He'd relaxed, nixed the suit jacket but still wore the loosened tie. It suited him, her banker boyfriend, a semiformal look even when choosing comfort.

She wondered what he'd say to Ann having someone undercover at The Lewis Group to figure out who murdered Nathan's wife. Their worlds did intersect, if not collide, at times. She smiled to herself. Not her secret to tell. Knowing Rob, he'd take in the news and rather quickly deduce who it was. He made it a point to know his clients and their associates. Someone new in the circle around Nathan would have been noticed.

"My parents were wondering if we might like to join them for dinner at the mayor's charity benefit next Friday night."

And their lives overlapped yet again. She nearly told him that David knew the special guest who would be performing that evening, but thought better of it. She didn't think Rob would have more than a glancing knowledge of Triple M even if she did mention the name. "I'd like that. I can't promise, but I can try to be there."

"I'll arrange tickets then. And tell Mom and Dad to go easy on expressing their concerns."

She had wondered how Rob was taking their remarks. "They mean well," she offered, willing to give them the benefit of the doubt.

"I'll be charitable and say they're just not used to making small talk with a cop."

She smiled at his dry comment. She thought Rob was handling it about as well as he could, given his parents had someone very different in mind for their future daughter-in-law. Evie turned to lean against him once more, and Rob rested his arm around her. She felt content to share the couch and just enjoy being held. "Whether or not I understand it all, it sounds like you had a productive week."

"I did. Like to tell me any more about yours?"

Evie thought about the missing girl, then back to the arson fire with fatalities she'd worked before the task force began. Neither added anything useful to the evening except to bring the weight with her. "No. Thanks, but no."

"Okay." Rob gave her shoulder a squeeze and let the silence linger, giving her room to suggest a topic. They often spent evenings just talking, time together they both enjoyed. When she'd finally realized she could truly relax with him, it had moved their relationship a long way forward. She didn't feel she was "onstage" with him, like she needed to put her best foot forward, fill silences with confident, sparkling words. He gave her room to be herself, and she loved that about him. Some nights they'd end up reminiscing about high school or sharing jokes they'd heard; other times they would talk about what was happening in the lives of mutual friends or make plans for things they would enjoy doing together. Simply *life shared,* and she loved the freedom that gave her with him.

Now he asked lightly, "Have you thought any further about my question?"

Marriage. The *big* question. "Yes, I've thought about it." She considered following his lead to that conversation, but decided against it. Some subjects weren't addressed well when one was tired. So she bent the conversation slightly in another direction. "Actually, I've been thinking a lot about us. What do you like best about me?"

"Are you asking for a list?"

She would have stirred, but he ran a comforting hand down her arm. "I've actually got a long list, so it's a good question," he responded, and she heard the smile in his words. "I'll mention the first handful. I like the fact you're not dazzled by 'stuff' — by my world, that you have your own world you get lost in, one that's meaningful to you and to others. You're never going to be a wife who's pressing her husband for the next gift of jewelry, the next big house, or chasing another rung up the ladder. You'll let me build a home I'd like, and you'll appreciate it without craving more. You have the ability to appreciate my world, genuinely enjoy it, and yet be content. I like that about you, Evie. You have what you need, and that's enough for you.

"I'm a man of ambition in my own way, with a vision of what I want for a home and family. Wealth is part of that, a legacy I can pass on to my children and grandchildren, as well as quietly distribute to causes and individuals crossing my path. You give me room for all of that. I like the fact there's not competition between us."

Evie wasn't sure how to respond, so she didn't try to find words. She did feel out of step with his wealth, but it was beautiful, his home and the flow of his life. Rob was gifted at knowing how to put together a life that worked for him. There was comfort in that she didn't feel pressured to fit herself into his world — simply invited to join her own with his, finding parallels and intersections along the way.

"Want a few more?"

"Sure." She laughed. "So far we're good."

"I like your smile," he said simply, "the way your face lights up when you see me. I like that you enjoy the simple things, like fussing around in the kitchen, running with your dogs, and curling up to watch a movie, even one you've seen before. You know how to enjoy yourself.

"I like how you're kind to my parents, even though they haven't been all that welcoming to you." He turned to face her as he continued. "And I admire you for being a cop. You have a sense of right and wrong in you that runs deep and doesn't waiver. You're a good compass for me. When you don't like something, I think about it twice, because there's a reason it's rubbing you the wrong way. You keep me far away from trouble." He paused. "I told you it was a long list."

She smiled her thanks. "You're being particularly kind to me, Rob," she whispered.

"You're drained emotionally right now, giving the truth a particular impact," he replied gently. "Let me mention another big one. I like that you have a passion for God. It's different from mine and expresses itself differently around people. I'm more about the certainty of God, the fact He cares about our decisions, how we've lived. You seem more relaxed about that, confident in God's grace. You easily interact with people who come from criminal backgrounds, accept them as simply as you do victims who have lost faith because of what occurred. You seem able to reach both extremes, to live in a place where God is bigger than the particulars of how life happens to unfold. Those are all good things, Evie."

"It helps me that you see things from a different perspective," she replied. "Our sharing a love for God gives me a solid place to stand even when I'm not sure about the rest of . . . well, you and me. I'm confident about what you think about God and how your life revolves around your faith. It's . . . reassuring," she decided, looking for the right word.

"It is. We're good for each other, Evie." He let the silence return.

Evie wasn't sure if or where to take the conversation further. This relationship had begun to dig deep into both their lives, and it was obvious in what they were willing to risk in discussions. She wanted to match Rob in candor, but she didn't have things clear enough in her own mind yet to know how she wanted to reply.

"Shall I mention that I see where you struggle too?" Rob finally asked gently. "You're not confident in yourself, Evie, and I don't understand it, but it's a constant in you and doesn't seem to go away. It's not so much a weakness as it is a vulnerable place. I can see its effects. It's what creates that internal pressure to be worth the trust someone has placed in you. The task force, doing a good job — it's not just to impress the governor, your boss, those working with you, but to reassure yourself you're good enough to be on that task force. That sense of not being good enough is something I'd love to see fade away one day."

Evie knew he had nailed that one. "You do see me pretty clearly." She shifted away and fully turned toward him on the couch, grateful the conversation was honest but not putting her in tears. She loved that his smile was kind as he looked at her.

"I see a good life for us together if you want that, Evie. I'd like to marry you and build a home with you, a family. You can be a cop and have a life with me — goodness knows they need a good detective around here. I don't mind the interruptions your job brings. My job interrupts life too. So long as we both can step away from work to be a couple, a family, it can be a good life." He reached over and feathered his fingers through her hair and, after a moment of silence, said quietly, his smile a bit sad, "And still you hesitate to know how to answer."

She understood that sadness and gave him back as much honesty as she could. "Rob, you see the threads of you and I twined together and making it work, and I just . . . maybe it's that lack of confidence showing itself in another way. I feel the peace when I'm with you. I love how you laugh at my jokes, tolerate my distracted mind when work is still capturing my attention, and that you enjoy life with me. The fact I'm not in a cop's world with you, and you're not going to bring up a crime or lay something similarly heavy on me — that is *life* to me.

"I'm never going to understand the deals, the money, with the significance you feel. I care for you more than any man I've ever met. But I look at us together and figure I'm not pulling my weight. I'm not being the one you need. You'd do better with a wife who can relate to your world, can socialize with your partners, charm your potential clients, be an asset to your life. I can try, but people are going to sense that I don't fit in. Your world is a game of skill, moving money and people and things around, and I appreciate that you're gifted to do it well. Yet it really just seems like a game to me, not life and death, and no one is going to bleed when the day is done. And that reaction in me . . . well, it doesn't feel right. You deserve better than that."

He was starting to smile, so she hurried to add, "You need a wife who wants the 'stuff,' at least enough to appreciate what it is. I'm more puzzled and lost when it comes to material things. I enjoy a couch that's comfortable, a home that's spacious, and the security that's reliable. I love being part of your comfortable life, but I wouldn't put in the effort it takes to build that for myself. I'd rather go solve something that mattered to me. And that's what bothers me. What you do *does* matter. But then I come into your world with its true pressures and headaches, and I'm thinking, It's just stuff. What's the big deal? That's the last thing you need a wife to be thinking about when you've poured everything you've got into creating a comfortable life."

His smile broadened and turned into a chuckle. "If only you realized what you're saying, Evie. Do you really think I didn't understand that about you the first day we met? You're always going to think, 'What's the big deal? So you lost some money, go earn some more. So you lost the deal, there will be more.' It's actually one of the core things I *love* about you. You honestly don't care about the outcome because there's a world out there where if my deals work out or not, if I earn a bonus or not, the world spins on regardless. It really doesn't matter. It's a kind of vanity and striving after the wind. I like that you're always going to ground me to the truth that my world is just not that big a deal in the larger picture of life and death, sorrows and problems I can't even imagine.

"I do it because it's fun. I'm good at numbers, love to negotiate, bring people together, overcome obstacles. When good deals are struck, people prosper, lives improve. It helps people when a good man makes good deals. That's a role I was designed to play. And maybe *play* is the operative word here. But it's not the end of the world. I need a wife who knows that and reflects that truth to me. It gives me balance." He smiled as he ran a hand down her arm. "You give me balance.

"All too often people in the role I fill are warped into thinking the money, the power, and the prestige are the important things, and that's all they can see. You, on the other hand, are incapable of getting blinded by the success, the wealth. You'll call it foolishness when it goes to excess, and laugh at the false pressure of it. You'll help me find ways to use it to invest in others. I want someone like you in my life, Evie. I want *you* in my life. You're the balance to this world I live in. I'm wise enough to deeply desire that. Just like in some other ways I think I'm the balance you need for the often dark world you live in. You need me too. It's okay to build a marriage there."

She understood why he was so far ahead of her, was comfortable with the desire to be married. He'd figured out what he wanted, needed, and he loved her. She just wished she was at the same place he was. "Rob, what if I'm just not ready to step into marriage? What then?"

"Why the doubts?"

She tried to find the words. "Maybe I'm too young. I know, I'm thirty-six, it isn't a rational feeling. But as much as I wonder if it should be you and I, it's that sensation that I'm not ready, that I need a few more

216

years to grow up. 'Banker's wife' is a title, a role that doesn't sound . . . well, *possible* to me.

"I can step down from the State Police, take a local job, be a detective in a local precinct. I can figure out how to coordinate life between your job and mine. I can even envision kids one day. What I can't see is *how* to step from what I have now over to that." She shook her head. "But the truth is I really don't know why I'm hesitating. If my feelings for you need more time to develop or I just need to let go of the fact I'm single and let the word *couple* now define who I am. I don't know. Maybe I'm just scared." She leaned her head against the back of the couch, wishing she knew her own heart better.

Rob didn't immediately answer, taking time to absorb the words and finally nodding. "I think part of it is you don't see yourself flourishing in that new picture, Evie. You're in it, making it work, but it's not somewhere you develop and bloom in fresh ways. That's what I hear in your words. It's not adding 'more and better' to you, just taking away some of what you are right now."

She hated to think that maybe he was right. "You'd make a wonderful husband,

Rob. I know my life would be blessed being with you. I also know I'm damaging things between us by not being able to say yes. I deeply regret that. I just can't put into words why I'm hesitating. A great guy wants to propose and I'm not saying yes, *yes*!? It just doesn't make sense. I don't know what else to say except I need more time to figure out what is going on in me."

"Evie, you trust me — easier than you can say the words *I love you*. Do you wonder why that is? Maybe I haven't sparked something in you you're hoping to find. Or maybe what you're hoping for doesn't exist. If it does, it's possible I'm never going to be the guy who can click with that. I can answer the question why I want you in my life. I love you, Evie. I would treasure having you with me for the next fifty years. I'd enjoy building a home and family with you. But you need to be able to answer why you want me in *your* life," he continued. "I'm a safe place in the storm, a refuge away from the life-and-death reality of your work. I'm a good guy, a good provider and someone to relax with. I'm good company who likes you being around. All that is a solid foundation. What's the rest of it, Evie? That's been enough for an exclusive relationship. But the rest of it? Am I the guy you can't live without?"

"Right now you are," she whispered. "I lose you, Rob, I lose the safest person I've ever known."

He held out his hand, waited for her to grasp it. "You *are* safe with me, Evie. And if what you really need is to acknowledge that your heart isn't yet ready for marriage, you should feel safe enough to say that to me. We'll take a break. A year, two years, let time help sort this out. If you can take this step, I want to marry you. If it's not going to happen — at least not now, is my earnest hope — then let's step back. I don't want to damage something I value more than I can say by pressuring you, but we can't simply stay where we are. Let's either go forward together or step back together."

He was right, and his reasoned, careful, logical summation was one of the reasons she felt so safe with him. "How long are you going to let me think about this?"

"Why don't we talk about it again on, say, Valentine's Day?"

He was giving her enough time to let her heart settle. "Yeah. Okay." Her smile was full of regret. "I'm being a lot of trouble."

He chuckled. "You're worth it, Evie."

She had to blink away tears. "Something inside me must be broken," she whispered, "for this to be so difficult for me. My parents are happily married. It's like this alien thing crept in and confused me somewhere along the line."

He laughed at the image. "We'll get through it."

"I'm truly sorry for this place we're in. I never have wanted to cause this kind of turmoil."

"You *are* a bit of a distraction on occasion," he conceded, "as my attention isn't always focused on the meeting I'm attending. *Does she, or does she not?* It's all right. Like I said, I saw the vulnerable part of you from the beginning. That it shows itself when you're considering a change to the very center of your life doesn't surprise me. Saying yes to marriage, reorienting your life, *should* be a very big deal. You are a cautious turtle in many ways — you don't move very fast, and you hide very quickly."

She wrinkled her nose at the image but knew he was correct. "I'm scared of getting hurt," she whispered.

"I know."

"Are we okay?"

"Yes." He crossed his heart like a little boy. "Promise. We'll settle this by Valentine's Day. You work better with a deadline."

She laughed, but it also made its own kind

of ache that he knew her so well. "I didn't want to talk about this tonight. I guess I'm glad we did."

"It was time." He leaned forward and kissed her, drew a smile. "Yes, we're good," he promised. He picked up the remote. "Find us a half-hour comedy. We need something to laugh at together."

She was grateful. "Thanks." She took the remote and began searching.

It helped, having said the words that she was okay with for now. Evie relaxed with Rob, enjoying the comfort he offered far more than the sitcom. She felt him idly twisting a lock of her hair around his finger even as he laughed with her. He was a good man — different in his priorities, his style of living, from her. But she could trust him with her heart, and that mattered most of all. If she wanted it, theirs would be a safe marriage for her. There was enormous appeal in that.

When their evening came to an end, he drew her into a hug at the door before walking her out to the car. "I love you, Evie. You know that."

"Yes, I do." She met his gaze, and the smile came easily. "I know that," she repeated. "God blessed me with something truly extraordinary when you asked me out on that first date. I don't doubt that."

"Good." They walked together to her car, where he took her keys to open the door, then kissed her good-night. "Text me when you arrive. When you're halfway down the state, I don't worry so much about you as when you're driving across town. I know the drivers here, their bad habits."

She laughed. "I will. Valentine's Day is a definite, even if I have to haul myself back from the other end of the state."

"Before that we'll fit in a couple of dinners, lunches, walks — whatever is doable when we're this close. I don't apologize for wanting to make it as easy as possible for you to say yes."

She tugged his head down and kissed him. "This matters too. I'll see you."

He helped her into the car, closed the door. Her return smile was a little shaky, but as she backed out, she was feeling lighter than she had been on the drive here, knowing a decision was coming . . . and when. This relationship would be settled in a matter of weeks, either moving toward a wedding or the mutual decision to move apart. Things wouldn't be staying the same.

Finding a missing college student suddenly seemed like the much easier task.

■ ■ ■ ■

"I didn't expect you this early after your evening with Rob," David said, entering the room with his mug of coffee plus one for her.

Evie glanced at the clock, saw it was just after eight. "I realized I wasn't going to sleep in today, so I thought I might as well come in and sort some more names. Thanks for the coffee," she added.

"I'm working through Saul's suspended cases," he said, "looking for one he might have shifted over to on his own time. Maybe he went from the card game in Englewood Saturday night to check out a lead on one of the suspended cases." David gestured with his mug, not joining her at the desk as he sometimes did but not heading back to work either. "Your evening go okay?"

Evie heard in the question the "we're partners" tone — interested without prying. She smiled at its camaraderie feel. "It was fine."

"Hmm," he said, looking at her more closely. "You've been crying."

She had some, on the drive from her hotel, thinking about the frightening possibility she would make the wrong decision.

223

"No, it's okay. He'd like me to decide what I want by Valentine's Day."

"Ahh." David leaned against the wall, shifted his weight to get comfortable. "An interesting choice of day on his part. He really wants a yes."

"I know."

"Think about it, pray about it, decide," he said, turning serious.

"If I'm distracted some the next couple of weeks, that will be why."

"You'd like to push it aside for now, focus on work?"

"Pretty much."

"Then from experience I suggest you find the thickest report that needs the most concentration and start reading there. While you do that, I'll take a break and go get a box of Dilly Bars from the Dairy Queen so you can retreat to ice cream and chocolate whenever your mood needs a lift."

Evie felt a small smile start near her heart. "That sounds wonderful."

"Cold feet about marriage doesn't mean it's not the right decision," he said, pushing away from the wall.

"I wish that was all this is. You've wanted to be married for years, and can't. It must be odd, watching me struggle to make this step you're eager to take when the door finally opens."

He shook his head. "Maggie struggles to take the step to faith that I made so easily. You struggle over the step to get married. Different struggles, but from considering the two of you ladies, not so different at the core. Are you loved, can you love back, is it safe to commit to this forever relationship? You're both surprisingly cautious, given each of your chosen careers."

"When does Maggie get into town?"

"Thursday midmorning. She has the charity event Friday night, then it's back to New York on Monday. She officially moves to Chicago at the end of the month, but movers will begin bringing furniture and belongings to the Barrington home in a few days."

"Any ideas for a housewarming gift?" Evie asked.

"What she loves are flowers. Find something in a pot that reminds her of spring coming and you'll hit the sweet spot. Anything else you need while I'm out?"

"I'm good."

David lifted a hand and headed out.

Any one of the task-force members would have been good company, but David was particularly great, both for the work angle and her personal life. He liked people, liked her, and asked good questions. Evie took his advice. She sorted out the work on the desk and picked up the thickest document, the FBI report, and started reading.

ELEVEN

The morning's sunlight was giving her a headache, and last evening's discussion with Rob weighed on her concentration. Evie rubbed aching eyes as she studied the case board. She was probably overthinking this. It wasn't hard to find cases that were similar to Jenna's. She'd chosen fourteen from the FBI report from the last dozen years, plus she still had the three cases the original cops had thought sounded similar. The problem was narrowing it down further.

She was sure she had something here, yet there were too many cases to all be her guy. Two, maybe three, might be his. Assuming — and that was still a big reach — that Jenna hadn't been a one-time-only crime.

Evie shook her head to try to jar her concentration back into focus. It was now nine o'clock on Saturday morning. She was certainly a touch sleep-deprived, not a good way to proceed to make significant decisions. She picked up her empty coffee mug to get a refill. The only positive thing at present was that none of the photos on the board showed much similarity to Jenna. She hoped that by going through the full files, she'd be able to eliminate at least half of the possibles, which would then leave her with much less to ponder.

"Evie."

The urgency in David's voice drew her into the conference room. "Got something?"

"Something," he replied, paging through a thick folder. "Take a look at this."

He slid the folder toward her and began thumbing through a stack of thinner folders. "You're holding the research for one of Saul's suspended cases," he explained.

She opened it, found newspaper clippings, scanned through them, and halfway into them realized what David had. "Well, this is indeed interesting." She was looking at newspaper accounts of Jenna's disappearance.

"My PI was looking into your missing college girl."

"Which case connected to it?"

David pulled out a smaller folder. "Tammy Preston. Give me a minute to read the details. I looked at these suspended cases earlier, but the red flag only went up when I saw that research folder."

"Take your time — you've certainly got a captive audience. Are you going to finish that coffee?"

"Just poured, it's yours," David replied with a smile after a glance at her.

She nodded gratefully, drank most of it, and then began sorting through the other items in the folder. Articles on a Wisconsin high school football team and its star running back. Several Jane Doe remains discovered. A variety of announcements for musicals, theater performances, and concerts in Chicago during a two-week period eight years ago. Then the news on Jenna's disappearance.

"This isn't good."

Evie looked up at the tone in David's voice. She'd heard a lot of cops say those words over the years, and with that tone the words were underselling how bad it actually was.

"A Wisconsin family hired Saul to look for their missing daughter, thinking she might have traveled from Wisconsin to Chicago," he murmured, studying a sheet in his hand. "She had a history of taking off, was of age, revolving boyfriends, living with a girlfriend rather than renting on her own. But she had always called, stayed in touch with the mom. Then it just went quiet. A pretty girl, but not striking. Five-foot-four, auburn hair, one hundred forty pounds. Twenty-one when she went missing." He slid the photo to her. "Something about her led Saul to look up the newspaper articles on your Illinois college student. You've been looking at cases possibly related to Jenna. Is this girl one of those? Tammy Preston?"

"No, I don't recognize the name or photo. But I can check the full FBI report and see if I passed over the name. Time-wise, do both our cases overlap? My girl went to a Triple M concert the night she disappeared. And now your PI looked into my missing girl?"

"Think God is trying to tell us something?"

Evie wondered, shook her head. "I don't know anymore."

"Tammy was last seen on a Sunday night. She had attended a concert two nights before." David handed her the slimmer file. "Look at the band, page three."

She turned pages. " 'A Triple M concert,' " Evie read, a sense of dread coming over her. She looked over at David. This bit hard.

"Yeah." He sighed. "My PI suspended his

investigation because the family had asked him to spend no more than five thousand dollars for his time, but he was on the scent of something telling him these cases were similar. He might have tagged onto the concert link. The parents were thinking their daughter had left on her own, had hooked up with a new boyfriend they would find questionable, but Saul was wondering if it wasn't something else."

Evie went back to the beginning of the folder, reading the paperwork in Saul's neat handwriting. " 'Tammy wasn't in college. That's why she's not on my board, why she didn't get picked up in the search for similar cases years ago. But she's the right age and lived near a college campus.' "

"The date she went missing puts her a year after Jenna."

"That could fit."

"After two years with no contact from her, the police elevated Tammy to a suspicious missing. Her body has never turned up."

Evie took a deep breath, let it out. She was holding a case file that was likely also her guy. "Someone likes Maggie's music, likes those who like Maggie's music? Is he traveling around to her concerts, or is it any concert that attracts a college crowd?" she wondered. "Jenna Greenhill. Tammy Preston. Two missing college-age women, living within a hundred miles of each other, both attend a Triple M concert the weekends they go missing. The raw numbers say it could be random, but it doesn't feel random."

"Find a third, it's not random."

She pushed back her chair. "I've got an Indiana case on the board that had a missing driver's license, my best prospective match for Jenna. They had recovered a body days later. Let me go pull the full file."

Evie sat at her laptop, found the FBI report and case number, figured out how to get from her Illinois police account over to the Indiana police database, then sent the full case report to her printer. She grabbed up the first ten pages, leaving the rest to print, and was reading as she walked back to the conference room. "Case highlights: Virginia Fawn, a student at Indiana University, went missing on a Saturday night. Body was found on Thursday three miles outside of town. Probably smothered. Her purse was near her body, cash and credit cards in her wallet, but no driver's license." Evie scanned the summary for more details. "Boyfriend repeatedly questioned. Where was she before she disappeared?" Evie searched the pages. "The day of her disappearance, a credit-card charge at Famous Eddie's Burger Palace, 4:42 p.m., followed by a credit-card charge at State Fairgrounds, 6:12 p.m., for eighty-four dollars and change."

"Stadium seating, forty bucks a seat plus tax," David guessed.

"It sounds like a concert," Evie agreed. "Let me get the rest of the report off the printer. Maybe the interviews will tell me what band was playing."

"No need. I've already got it." David had turned to his laptop and was searching the band website history page. "Triple M played at the Indiana State Fair, April 28, 2010."

"A date match." They stared at each other.

"Three cases," David said, fury in his voice. "He's been using Maggie's concerts as his hunting grounds."

"I'm so sorry, David."

"Jenna, Tammy, Virginia. And Maggie, the connecting point. You've now got more than casual crossovers on your case, Evie. I'll try not to step on your toes, but we will *find* this guy."

"Partners all the way until it's solved," Evie promised. She didn't want to touch the emotions coiling in him — she had no idea how to defuse them. Instead, she would put her attention where she could help, and that was on the case details. They both knew there might be other young women once they dug deeper.

"An obsessed fan?" she wondered aloud. "Or a vendor maybe? T-shirts? Food? They would travel the circuit just like the bands."

"That's a good idea."

"He's picking off college students, has to look young himself to blend in, not get remembered when cops start asking questions. So, someone close to their ages. Jenna was twenty-one, Tammy the same —" she paused, checked papers — "Virginia, twenty-three."

"He's in his early thirties now," David guessed. "I need you to dig into the other similar cases on your board, tell me if there are more Triple M overlaps or more missing driver's licenses. I'll send the band-history page to the printer so you have concert dates and locations. We need to look for missing women around all those concerts. Virginia Fawn went missing six years ago. What's he been doing since then?"

"I'll do that next," Evie agreed. "Ann is already on her way in. She can make sure we don't miss a name. I'll call and get us time with the Indiana detectives. Virginia's body was found — there's got to be something useful to work from with the physical evidence."

"I'll push on Tammy's case in Wisconsin. Work with Saul's notes, get the missing-persons file from their local PD, talk with Tammy's parents, find out if they hired someone else after Saul. I hate to rip open their grief, then tell them we're working a similar disappearance in Chicago, but it's what has to be done."

"Go see them in person? Make a road trip and link up with the local PD?"

"I'll feel it out. If not today, Monday."

"I'd vote for today. It's only . . . what, a three-hour drive? Seeing the area after having viewed Jenna's in detail, it's going to click that these are similar cases or toss them apart as being separate."

"Going today does make sense if we can pull it together." He looked at the time. "Let's make that call in two hours."

Evie suspected as soon as they let it be known the three cases could be linked, getting others to join them in the search was going to be the easier part. The real challenge would be in coordinating things so that the various PDs didn't step on each other.

Evie knew of one decision that could be made right away. "Don't say anything to Maggie, David. This guy likely moved on to another hunting ground as he grew older, has probably been caught related to another crime by now. We figure it out, we make sure he's in jail, but Maggie doesn't hear a word of the overlaps we discovered. She had nothing to do with this, didn't inspire it — it's just bad luck he likes her music."

"I agree about Maggie, and I sincerely hope you're right about his already being in jail. It will make it easier to charge him with three murders once we crack the case."

"Does this help in any way figure out Saul's disappearance?" Evie asked, hoping to move him onto another track.

He considered that, shook his head. "Saul had a lot of suspended cases he could have picked up and worked on his own time, but there's no obvious indication he had been looking at this one when he disappeared. Nothing noted in the file suggests he had a new lead."

"Didn't Saul's sister mention he was considering a concert that Wednesday evening? I know you've got Saul's movements now traced through Saturday night, so I'm not implying a concert is related to Saul's disappearance too, but what concert was he talking about? Did you ever figure that out?"

"It was in Arlington Heights, a band called the Fly'rs, lead singer Evelyn. It's a soft-rock group. There's nothing in Saul's notes to suggest he was going to that concert for work reasons. But maybe . . ." David got up to add another note to his whiteboard. "Maybe Saul did choose that concert for a reason.

"Tammy had been at a concert in Wisconsin," he went on, "and Saul had been looking at news articles about Jenna's disappearance after she went to a concert. Maybe he was checking out this one in Arlington Heights because someone working there had also been part of the crew at those other two — someone doing stage setup, a food vendor, possibly someone as extra security. Multiple concert venues mostly use the same union workers. Crews shift locations depending on the crowd size. That's the most likely reason I can come up with for Saul being at the Fly'rs concert. But if that's the case, my PI — who took extensive notes on everything — either didn't write that lead down, or he had a notebook on him when he disappeared, with a name of interest he was pursuing."

"Union workers at the various concert venues," Evie mused, "that's another useful list for us to review." Something significant could be there, she thought. "Saul was at a concert, David. It wasn't a Triple M concert, but it was a concert where he might have been working a lead. It would be a nice tribute if somehow Saul is the link to solving this."

David nodded. "I'll start making calls to get info on those who worked the different concert venues. Then I'll find out what concerts Saul attended after he took on the Tammy Preston case — he usually charged his ticket purchases. If he was onto something, we'll find an increase in his ticket purchases. And while that keeps me occupied, get me the bad news on how many missing young women overlap with Triple M concerts."

"We've got possibly three," Evie replied. "I'm willing to predict it's not more than a handful in total," she offered, knowing it would sting, but anything less than one a year would be a blessing in such a case.

"Let's hope." David glanced up. "Jesus, help Evie find them all. We need to know what we're dealing with."

"Amen," Evie said. "Set your alarm for two hours. We'll make a call regarding Wisconsin then."

"Agreed." David reached for his phone and set an alarm. "Go wide in your search, Evie. Missing one now is worse than doing work on a case we later eliminate."

Evie was already planning the method for the search. "I'll use the concert dates and locations and look at every case within a certain window of time regardless of age, gender, or college affiliation. I'll first make sure your Tammy Preston shows up in the list, then let Ann verify the ones I think overlap." At David's nod she added, "Do you want to call Sharon? You've got the most insight on how we handle this with Maggie."

David hesitated, shook his head. "Your case, your call."

"Then for now, I'll just say we might have an overlap out of state and we'll know more once we see the files. We're putting out the requests for those now."

David smiled his appreciation.

"We solve this and move on," Evie suggested lightly, "because I hate cases that turn personal. It takes all the fun out of the job." She actually got a brief chuckle out of him, considered it a good sign that he would be able to temper the anger this overlap to Maggie had caused.

Evie left David to make his calls and turned her attention to matching cases against Triple M concert dates. She sent full case reports to the printer for the photos she had on the whiteboard. If they didn't crack the case by the end of January, she would be very surprised. She just didn't envision much sleep in her near future.

Evie made her own calls, to Ann to alert her to what she would be walking into today, to her researcher at the State Police, and then to their task-force boss, Sharon Noble.

"Do you want help, Evie? Theo can shift off his case, Taylor off his," Sharon offered.

"I don't know how big this is yet or if we're actually dealing with false-positives simply because of the law of large numbers. Thousands attend these concerts, pickpockets work the crowds, a high percentage of concertgoers are college-age women, and every year a few of them go missing. What we've got now may be only smoke and mirrors. David is motivated, and I'm dug in until this is set to rest. Ann can give us some time. For now, we're tagging other states for data because we're being thorough, not because we want FBI and other cops thinking *multistate murderer* and stepping in."

"I can keep that at bay for a while."

"I appreciate it, Sharon. David and I both do."

"I'm hoping it's just smoke, Evie. Some of these cold cases are going to lead to guys who have committed multiple crimes, we know that. But if that's our first county, it just gives us more press interest than I would like at this point. We need some light and good news to go along with dark and heavy arrests."

"Which way is yours looking?"

"The missing wife and two daughters left an abusive situation and are likely still alive somewhere. The woman's sister is so nervous with my questions, I'm beginning to think they could actually be living in her neighborhood. Theo suspects his missing teenage boy was killed by a high school classmate and has it narrowed down to a couple of names. Taylor knows who killed his businessman; he's just got to find the body or come up with new evidence so the DA will file charges without one."

"So you're all basically flying through your cases," Evie remarked.

"Pretty much," Sharon agreed. "But we didn't step into quicksand, which it sounds like you and David did. Tag us, however and whenever you want help."

"Thanks, boss."

Evie clicked off, genuinely pleased the rest of the team was making good progress. Jenna's case was breaking open and that was a good thing. Add the still-fragile intersect with one of Saul Morris's clients and it wasn't bad for the first week of the task force's time. And it wasn't so much them. Evie was beginning to see what David already thought — God's hand was in motion, helping them find justice. "Thanks, Dad," Evie whispered.

TWELVE

Evie heard David's phone alarm and laid down the report she was reading, shook her head at Ann's inquiring look. She'd let David decide what he wanted to do, but she thought they needed a break.

He joined them, and Evie thought he looked as stressed as she felt. He'd been making calls. She didn't ask — he'd volunteer what was useful.

"I talked to Sharon, we're good there," she told him, unwrapping a roll of sweet-tarts to share. "We've got Indiana detectives on a conference call for Virginia Fawn at three o'clock. I figure we can take it from either here or on the drive to Wisconsin. The full case file sounds a lot like Jenna — missing license, Triple M concert, no sign of struggle at her apartment. Additional facts, her body was discovered, the autopsy says smothered. I've got copies of the full report for both of us, and I've sent Indiana

PD everything we have on Jenna."

She nodded to the board. "I've whittled my seventeen possibly related cases down to twelve, but am still working through them. There are no other matches on Triple M concerts yet, but it's too early for that to indicate much. To make sure we don't miss a related disappearance, Ann and I are starting with the first concert date in the band history and working our way forward in time. It's going to be a few hours of database work to have a solid answer on that question."

David seemed to relax a bit and nodded his thanks when she was done. "Okay. Good." He turned to greet Ann. "When the governor asked if you wanted to help the task force get up and running, I don't imagine you thought you were volunteering for actual case work like this again."

"I'm glad to help out, David," Ann replied with a smile. "It's amazing how seductive a good puzzle can be. You've got yourself a mystery, but one that's going to get solved now that it's got some links," she reassured.

David nodded toward additional photos now on the board. "Jenna, Tammy, Virginia. Let's hope it stays at that . . . or only a couple more."

"Under five would be good news. The

database work is time-consuming," Ann added, "but the core of it is straightforward. I can keep the search flowing if you two want to head to Wisconsin. Paul's got some good researchers who can help me out, I'm sure."

David looked to Evie. "What do you think? I tracked down the detective who has the Tammy Preston case. He's off today, but he'll come in if we want to meet with him. I've got copies of Tammy's file printing now. No surprise, it's rather thin. If we want to do interviews, he'll make introductions to the family."

"We wait, we risk January weather issues. The drive will give us time to talk through what we do have. I vote we go."

"Then we go. I'll let him know we're coming."

Evie handed him a Post-it note from her monitor. "There's one other data set to put into motion before we leave. I'm sure Maggie has obsessed fans — that goes with the territory, right?"

"Disturbing emails, letters," David agreed, "people we profile as budding stalkers. Security keeps photos on those we know are the most dangerous to her."

"If he's a devoted fan, he's likely written Maggie."

David considered that. "The most disturbing mail is kept for a lot of years on the assumption the person is either already a problem or will be one in the future. We've been updating the threat file for the ones living in Chicago, particularly given her planned return to live here. So I can get a current list of security worries. But if he's killing women and being careful about leaving a trail, he's not going to be sending creepy mail — 'I want to kill for you, Maggie' and the like. We already would have been on it. Names going at least nine years back, I know them."

"The admiration ones — softer tone, 'I love your music, I'd follow you anywhere,' " Evie suggested.

"Okay, I'm catching what you mean. She gets a lot of that kind," David confirmed. "Those notes don't get saved unless an obsessed tone comes through. But maybe we can source names. A thank-you letter goes out to people who write her, and those envelope addresses must be generating from a database. We can run the correspondence names against all three of these case files — Jenna, Tammy, and Virginia — and maybe a name turns out to be common in each."

"Another solid place to start looking. He follows Maggie's concerts, he likes Maggie's music, he's ninety percent likely to be in her fan database too."

"It's a massive list, but I'll get you those names."

Evie tried to get a better picture of how the guy might show up. "I think he would reach out to Maggie, share his admiration of her music. He doesn't want to draw attention to himself, wouldn't come across as a threat but as a devoted admirer. 'I've been to all your concerts, I love the way you sing, I play your music all the time.' Like that. But he isn't choosing women who look like her, he isn't going for her physical type, so this may not be an actual Maggie obsession. He's probably not going to have a room turned into a shrine for her, her pictures all over the walls. It's the style of music, the lyrics, the event, the concert gathering — it's the combination of her music and fans that sparks his interest."

"Which narrows it down to every male attending her many concerts, but I see where you're going here," he said. "I think you're right that he's not Maggie-obsessed — she's just the forum, the draw. The crowd that shares his enjoyment of her music is his hunting ground. I'll see if we can source names and addresses for those who ordered concert tickets from the band's website.

That data probably goes back at least a decade, since her accounting firm is fanatical about keeping income-and-expense records in pristine shape. The music world is mostly a cash business, one that gets audited frequently. Most orders are for two to ten tickets. If we look for single-ticket purchasers, for these specific dates in history, maybe we get lucky."

Evie heard some much-needed hope in his voice. "Make some calls to her accounting firm, maybe we get *very* lucky," she suggested. "I've heard that band groupies try to be at every concert. But someone nine years ago, when the band was just getting its footing, and him being at these three specific concerts in Chicago, Wisconsin, and Indiana? That's not going to be a long list."

"Let's hope he ordered tickets off the band's website for at least a couple of them," David said. "I'll make the calls, then tell Wisconsin PD we're on our way. Thanks, Evie. A good idea."

She waved toward Ann. "Joint idea. Ann's been educating me on the music business, what a concert is actually like."

David smiled. "I promise to take you both to enjoy one of Maggie's, show you the real deal from the backstage preconcert prep to switching off the lights when it's all over. A great experience. Maybe not so great the next couple of dozen times you try to go from beginning to end."

They all laughed, and David and Evie gathered up items for their trip north.

Milwaukee was colder than Chicago, people were friendlier, and the case that had brought them here was even more incomprehensible than Jenna's disappearance. But Evie now had enough details from Tammy Preston's life to reach some possible conclusions.

As they returned to David's SUV beside the candy store where Tammy occasionally had worked, she tucked her notebook back into her pocket and put some of those thoughts into words.

"This doesn't feel like Jenna to me. Tammy lives one street back from small retail shops — the town's version of a downtown square — sharing a ground-floor apartment with a girlfriend. The college is nearby on a map, but it's really not when you see the area in person. Two different worlds, Jenna's and Tammy's. Locals live on these blocks, mostly single-story smaller homes, the student apartment building itself another outlier. You'd want to go east to blend in with the college crowd living off campus."

"Tammy had a different life than a college student," David said. "But this area still might have suited our guy. No good lighting around the apartment building, mature trees, tall shrubs, just eight parking spaces squeezed in behind it. Someone waiting on Tammy to arrive home wouldn't be noticed by people out walking their dogs. He could wait unseen, watch her arrive."

"That itself is another shift. Jenna walked back to her apartment after the concert. Tammy would have driven. And Tammy doesn't live alone, not a setup for someone lying in wait. Then there's the time gap. Tammy went to a concert on Friday night, but she didn't disappear until Sunday evening. Why stick around? The building location and roommate presence can be explained away, but the time delay? Why stay from Friday night to Sunday if he came to town just for the concert?"

"It doesn't make sense that he would," David agreed, "unless this is where he lives, and Chicago — Jenna — was his road trip. He wants to target Tammy but has to work around the shared apartment, and it's a hard crime to pull off. Maybe Tammy was always the real target and he used Jenna a hundred miles away as a practice run. Jenna was easier — lived alone, walked home. Then he came back and went after Tammy, his intention all along."

Evie considered it and felt the case slide onto a new footing. "That would solve a lot. Jenna is a clean crime, so even if hers was a practice run, it's still probably not his first. Let's look through crime reports from this area for his first crime. Maybe the move to a college girl developed as a way to blend in when out of town. Your suggestion about music as his world still seems the likely way we tap him. We begin with Tammy and Jenna both at Triple M concerts. He's choosing them because they're overlapping into his chosen world of music. Maybe he's a music major — not at Jenna's college, but here in Milwaukee."

David started the vehicle and kicked on the heater, let the engine idle while they talked. "I like the feel of it being a college-age guy. If someone sees Tammy with him, they just think 'new boyfriend,' not registering that this is someone to be worried about."

"I lean toward young too," Evie replied. "The more I think about Jenna Greenhill and why she went missing . . . it's not her — the fact she liked strawberries and read philosophy and studied biology and wanted her postgrad work to focus on the genome — none of that is relevant. He wanted the outline of her. He wanted the female college student who liked Triple M music, who had a nice smile. I believe he chose her that night at the concert. He followed her home. And he took her. Tammy *sort of* fits that profile, but her disappearance . . . it feels different.

"Why Tammy?" she asked, continuing her deliberations. "What did he see that made him choose her? You're talking serious premeditation to practice with a crime just to commit another crime. We need to understand a whole lot better who Tammy is." And even as Evie said it, she found herself looking over at David and shaking her head. "No. It's not this. Feel how complex the motive just got when I made that proposition. A college guy wanting Tammy picks her off coming out of work one evening; he doesn't do a trial-run homicide to practice *how* to grab her. If Tammy was his target, he would have gone for her first."

"Yeah, it gets complex with our proposed age of the offender," David said. "It's linear — Jenna then Tammy then Virginia, with a common motive threading through. Maybe a growing addiction to abduction and killing?"

"Which brings us back to the core question. Was Tammy one of his, or is this simply a girl who took off once again, looking for a different life but ran into trouble? She liked music, had even sung a bit to earn pocket money, yet the rest doesn't fit Jenna."

"Consider this possibility," David offered as he checked traffic and pulled out of the parking lot. "Assume Jenna is his. He's attending a Triple M concert the next state over, away from home, enjoying his night as a young man surrounded by college girls, and something clicks. He wants an even more exciting end to this special night. So he lifts Jenna's driver's license, stakes out her place, abducts and murders her, hides her body, and he gets away with it. It goes so well for him that the parts of that night form one cohesive whole. A year later when he goes hunting again, wanting the same thrill, he starts with the same band Triple M, same choice of a girl attending the concert, so he can experience it all again."

"That connection works for me, David — the first murder setting the parameters he's going to consider important."

David nodded. "Part of the whole, the memory he's trying to re-create. And it's the outlier components that might make Tammy one of his. Assume for now this is his hometown. To act here is more risky, a place where he's known. But Triple M is literally coming right to his doorstep. He wants that thrill again. So he goes to the concert, planning to re-create his success. He sees Tammy there that Friday night, lifts her license, wants to do something, but once he sees the building and the roommate situation, he loses the nerve. He walks away from the evening he had built up in his mind, totally frustrated. He thinks about it for forty-eight hours — stews about it. She's right there in his hometown, drives by her place several times, getting more frustrated, and then he's got up his nerve again. He's able to snatch Tammy when she's on her own, out of the sight of witnesses, does the crime in his hometown, gets away with it.

"He's had two successes now. He's enjoying this. But he's learning. He goes farther afield for the next one, to Indiana. He keeps the constants he likes: Triple M concert, the driver's license to see where she lives, get there ahead of her. But he's out of the area quicker. He doesn't take time to hide the body now. He's deciding what is necessary to protect his identity and what he doesn't need to care about. He's has a third success with Virginia." David's voice turned hard. "But he doesn't go quiet. Not for six years.

Not if Jenna and Tammy and Virginia are all his kills."

Evie was nodding even before David finished. "That fits, David. I really think you just nailed it. Illinois with a Triple M concert and Jenna. So target another Triple M concert in his hometown, select Tammy, persist even when it doesn't go as planned, succeed again. Move on to Indiana and Virginia Fawn with what he's learned. This time leave the body rather than take time to dispose of it."

"He persisted with Tammy because he could. We shift our focus, as he likely lives around here," David said. "So the question on the table now is how do we want to start that search?"

"Someone who lives here, has traveled to Illinois, to Indiana — let's start with speeding tickets in Wisconsin heading south around the dates of interest. He's got a long journey ahead, I bet he ignores the speed limit leaving town, wanting to get the road trip behind him. And music majors at the local college are still a good fit. Anyone in Maggie's fan base who lives in Wisconsin? I think it's the same set of questions we're asking about Jenna, just changing venue. And we'll want to add anyone who went to Brighton College who previously lived in

Wisconsin, whether they graduated or not."
Evie had her notepad out. "Anything else
come to mind?"

"Local crimes here. You don't start at
murder. It's a small enough town the police
probably knew the names of the teen boys
they wanted to keep an eye on."

"Saul had research material on a Wisconsin high school running back," Evie said.
"We need to look at why."

"He's here, Evie. Somewhere around
here."

"It feels good to have the sense we're on
the trail now."

David glanced over, offered a wry smile.
"Or we've just talked ourselves into a
detour. Keep that in mind. All of this could
be a rabbit trail."

"I always keep that in mind. The most
brilliant ideas can turn out to be errors. You
just don't know it until it plays out if you're
setting up to whiff the ball or hit a home
run. A batting average of one in three is still
really good, so I've learned to love brilliant
ideas — eventually that's where you succeed."

"I've got a baseball fan riding with me?"
David chuckled. "Nice. Where to next?"

She checked her watch. "Let's head over
to the police station and the conference call

with Indiana. Then let's talk to Tammy's parents, hopefully get some more names of friends to talk with while we're here. After that, back south. It's time to start generating more lists. I'm going to shoot these ideas on to Ann, let her add more queries to the database work she's doing for us."

"Don't tell me how many cases she's found overlapping Triple M concerts. I want to see the details when I hear that bad news."

Evie glanced over at him. "The last time I asked that question, Ann said, 'Ask me later, and keep your focus on Tammy.' She's keeping us in the dark. But whatever the answer, we're going to find the guy and end this. It could be soon with the thread we've got to pull."

"I sincerely hope so. I don't want to even consider the implications for Maggie if we haven't resolved the case by her next concert. She's got one at the McCormick Center on March seventh."

Six weeks. Evie prayed it didn't take them that long. "There's time," she said.

Just after seven p.m. they rejoined Ann at the Ellis office complex. "I'll carry my backpack and your briefcase," Evie offered, "if you can manage that box Tammy's parents gave us."

"Thanks." David slid over his briefcase. "Don't wait for me — it's cold out here. The box is heavy, but I'll be able to open the doors."

Evie didn't need further encouragement. She headed toward the building as he retrieved the banker box from the trunk. Everything Tammy Preston's parents had pursued to find their daughter was highlighted in the materials. They pleaded with them to read through it — they hadn't given up the hope she'd simply run off and might be out there, still alive.

The first thing Evie spotted as she pushed open the office doors was a large fruit tray on the first desk, then a tall bouquet of flowers and glass bottles of Carin County Root Beer chilling in a chest of ice. The flowers she could easily guess were from Rob, who loved sending arrangements to brighten her temporary offices. The fruit and cold drinks — *Paul,* she thought, *a gift for Ann,* with likely their mutual friend Gabriel Thane's involvement. The local brand of root beer was one of the best exports Carin County offered. She scanned the rest of the room, and her sense of order settled.

The head of the Chicago FBI office, Paul Falcon, was sitting at her desk, munching from a big bag of M&M's. The other desks were equally occupied.

"Welcome home. We migrated," said Sharon.

"So I see, boss. Hello to all of you." She nodded at Theo and Taylor, put down the briefcase and backpack, shed her coat, and stepped out of her boots. It felt . . . nice, walking in and finding friends at the end of a taxing day.

David came in and stopped, equally surprised.

"There's room for that box over here," Theo said, pointing.

Evie waved at Paul to stay seated and simply perched on the edge of her desk. "Where's Ann?"

"Food run. I type faster than she does, and more people scurry around when I ask a question." He smiled as he said it and reached over to pull up a nearby chair. "Sit, kiddo. We're up to speed on Tammy Preston — Ann's filled us in on your notes. We thought it would be useful to push the rest of this question into place tonight so that you and David can catch your breath."

"It's bad, isn't it?" David stated, interpreting why everyone was here. "The number of Triple M matches?"

"Not so bad," Sharon said firmly. "Sit.

Drink. Eat. We'll drag out the whiteboard with details after you've gotten some food in you."

Evie was ready to hand the weight of the day off to the others. She settled into the chair Paul had offered. "Pass me a root beer, David, and someone tell me what Ann is bringing in."

"Sautéed chicken, baked potatoes, coleslaw," Theo replied. "Ann's putting it on Paul's credit card since the FBI is being nice to us tonight."

"So you've solved your missing high school student?" Evie asked Theo.

He smiled. "No shoptalk for thirty minutes. But yes. I'm in a race with Taylor for who gets a closed file first."

"I'm in the race for last," Evie figured. "I want one-sentence updates before I eat. Taylor?"

"I'm ninety percent solved, but he's dead."

"Sharon?"

"Eighty, but only because I don't want to show too much optimism. Mine are alive."

"Three closed out of five, with people alive in one," Evie summed up. "Not for public notice, but that's a great outcome."

"I certainly can live with it," Sharon agreed. "We'll get Jenna and Saul figured out and make it five for five." She came over to offer a chocolate chip cookie from a bakery bag. "The flowers have your name on them, Evie. I've been dying to ask. Your guy?"

"I'll look at the card later, but I would assume so. Rob likes sending beautiful arrangements."

"Nice." Sharon pulled over a chair, and Evie asked her about any new wedding plans, more than willing to stay with the no-work rule for a while longer.

The group migrated to the conference room for their meal, moving folders aside to make space. The chicken was delicious, and talking slowed as they enjoyed it. Evie was well satisfied as she finished her coleslaw and final dinner roll. She let the conversation drift around her, about sports and politics and family.

She already found the task force easy to be with. David was now involved in a detailed conversation with Paul and was more animated and relaxed than he'd been in days. Paul was drawing the rules of an aerial golf competition on the back of napkins. Drones would soon be changing sports, creating brand-new ones, if the people Paul talked with were to be believed. *Drone golf, coming to the sky near you.* Evie had to smile — *such a guy thing.* She'd impress Rob with her bit of insider sports information when they had their next dinner.

Ann caught her attention and nodded toward the outer office. Evie picked up her root beer, joined her friend. "You put together a really nice evening — feel free to do this anytime you like," Evie mentioned.

"It sort of evolved when Paul decided he could spare a few hours of his Saturday to help out on the database work. Then Sharon called."

With just the two of them in the room, Evie crossed to the flowers, pulled out the envelope, checked her name on the front, and drew out the card. She hadn't done so earlier because occasionally Rob wrote delightfully personal messages she wouldn't want to share with the others. She smiled, and because Ann was someone who would understand, offered her the card.

It was a sketched drawing of an archer with a bull's-eye, an arrow in flight.

"You know I have my reservations about him, Evie, but this" — Ann held up the card — "*Evie's on target.* Without needing to say the words, Rob is encouraging. I'm glad to see it."

"He gets me, Ann, in some ways better

than I do myself. I don't have to wonder if he asked me to marry him with a misguided sense of who I'd be as his wife. We're very much mismatched in other ways, yet he sees that as a good thing. He likes the counterbalance."

"Well, the flowers are lovely, the message even more so. I see what you mean about his liking to brighten your life."

Evie studied the floral arrangement. "I feel uncomfortable about the price tag, but I also have a sweet spot for beauty. I think these are tiger lilies," she said, lightly touching a petal. "And whatever the purple ones are, they always make me smile."

"I admit, I elbowed Paul. 'Look what Evie's guy sends her!'"

Evie laughed. "Yeah. It feels good to be romanced."

The group came trailing in, and David leaned back against one of the desks. "I'm grateful to you all for the help, the hours of work on a weekend, and the meal. It's appreciated. But it's time. Let's get the bad news over with."

Sharon nodded. "Theo."

Theo rolled a whiteboard out from the storage closet — Ann's handwriting — neat, precise, accompanied by photos.

Not as bad as Evie was braced for. She

glanced at David, saw fleeting relief on his face. Not nearly as bad as he, too, had been prepared to see.

"Five cases," Ann said into the now-quiet room. "We're pretty sure it's only five, David. We've searched every concert date and location Triple M has played in the past. We've been debating case details for a few hours, eliminating those we conclude didn't align.

"In date order, Chicago, Wisconsin, Indiana, Ohio, and back again to Indiana. Jenna Greenhill, Tammy Preston, Virginia Fawn, plus now Emily Close and Laura Ship.

"The Triple M concert connection held for the five, though there were differences on other case details. Three bodies have been found, all smothered. Two still missing — Jenna and Tammy.

"He's traveling. Even the crimes have a travel component to them," Ann continued. "The bodies were on back roads outside of town. Lived here, found here. Lived here, found here," she indicated on printed maps. "The yellow dots are the concert venues. Not all these victims walked home from the concerts — some lived miles away.

"He's choosing reasonably big cities," Ann suggested, "good-sized concert turnouts, college towns. He grabs and goes. That's what it looks like on first review. Someone able to blend with the college crowd, maybe drives a van, likely a van. He's waiting at her place, comes at her when her guard is down. Then hauls the body away in the middle of the night. There are no signs of a break-in at these apartments. But the overall essence of the crimes suggests he might be picking their locks and getting inside, lying in wait. Theo suggested we should be looking for a teen with a B&E conviction — where he got his confidence — or even a locksmith now in training. He isn't worried about how to get access without witnesses."

"What you two have theorized about Wisconsin and Tammy," Sharon said, picking up the summary, "makes a lot of sense for the trigger. He was successful with Jenna, that set a pattern in his mind, and he's been re-creating that evening. The concert, the lifted driver's license, being at the apartment ahead of them. He wants to experience it again. The cause of death for the last three makes it very likely Jenna was smothered too."

"I think it's worth noting that the two cases without bodies are the earliest two," Evie said.

"He got tired of the whole process. Just dump the bodies somewhere they won't immediately be found, move on," David guessed. "We talked with Indiana PD at length about Virginia Fawn. They worked that case hard as an active homicide after finding the body. I assume the other two already discovered will have been worked in a similar fashion."

"Yes," Taylor replied, "I talked with Ohio on Emily Close, and Theo's looked at Laura Ship. Forensics haven't given further answers, so I don't think we're going to get a break there. The best hope right now is that when the lists from all five cases get crunched, there's an overlap that will focus like a laser on someone, open a new line of inquiry."

David nodded. "Jenna and Tammy are the cases among the five that haven't been worked as hard. The theory that this guy lives in the Milwaukee area needs pushed hard."

"We're in agreement on that," Sharon said.

"What are the odds we're wrong on this grouping?" Evie wondered, studying the grid of case detail overlaps and differences. "Tammy's the only one not attending college. We may have her on the board, and it's not one of his — though he simply might not have known she wasn't in college. But maybe Jenna and Tammy are his, and the other three with remains located are someone else's crime. What do you think? Fifty-fifty we've just created a group that is a distraction, unrelated to what happened to Jenna?"

"I lean toward Jenna and someone before Jenna being linked," Ann finally said into the silence. "I agree she doesn't feel like a first crime. The three recovered bodies could easily be someone else's doing. Tammy is an outlier. She disappeared two days after the concert, wasn't in college, had a history of leaving without word. While your centering this guy in Milwaukee is a high probability, it's also possible Tammy simply got into trouble after leaving home. You're as likely to be looking at three separate groupings as you are at one person behind all five."

Paul leaned forward in his chair. "There's a Triple M concert connection that wasn't seen before, and that needs investigation, whether it solves Jenna or not," he put in. "I'm adding FBI manpower and resources for the three who were smothered, mostly to keep Indiana and Ohio cooperating with each other. Anything you need from my team, just ask. They'll be your eyes and ears in other states."

"Good. Thanks, Paul," Sharon said.

"I'm inclined toward your not telling Maggie about this," Paul said to David. "Keep it out of the press for as long as possible. If every famous person felt responsible for the crazies that come around, we'd have little good music or art."

David smiled his agreement. "I do think music is the link, and it's the link to him. The victims' paths cross with him because of their mutual interest."

"Let's dig there on all five of our possible cases," Evie proposed. "But we keep coming back to Jenna. She's going to be the pivot point. She attended a Triple M concert and is missing her driver's license, so if there is a grouping, she's in it. Solve hers, we just might sort out which of these other cases are his."

Sharon nodded. "Good. Evie, you keep your attention on Jenna. If we're wrong about this connection in some way, we need you to find the right answer for her. David, push on the Triple M connection, as you've got the access to the info from Maggie's world. Paul's guys can take another look at the forensics from Indiana and Ohio, see if the recovered remains can offer any further clues. I'm guessing I'm within a week to ten days of wrapping up my case," she added.

"Theo and Taylor are even closer with theirs. We'll join you to provide extra help as we get freed up, on this or on Saul's disappearance."

"Thanks. It's a workable plan," David said, the group's nods mirroring his around the room.

Theo and Taylor headed out while Sharon, David, Ann, and Paul set themselves up around Evie's desk, still kicking around ideas on how to proceed. Evie was getting ready to call it a day, but she found the discussion too fascinating to leave just yet.

"Can we get credit- and gas-card data going back nine years?" Sharon wondered. "If so, I think we can spot this guy by the fact we have five data points. He had to fill up with gas, the distance tells us that. And I doubt he'd make these trips entirely on cash. I also doubt he's gone to the trouble of getting new cards. We know which highways he likely traveled to get to each concert, the gas stations where he might have stopped, and have basically a seven-day window on either side of these concert dates. It's a gigantic data set that's not likely to yield many false-positives — not if we can show a card name was used in Wisconsin eight years ago during a particular week and that name was used in Indiana six years ago during another specific week."

"I'll take on that inquiry," Paul offered, "put a researcher on data we can still get access to and run the correlation." He made himself a note and shifted his attention to David. "Do we want to do anything further about Maggie's fan mail? FBI can take a look at the most troubling ones."

"I'll take you up on that," David said. "I can source you the flagged emails quickly, make arrangements for the physical mail of concern to be sent back here from New York."

Evie offered an observation that had been simmering during the last few hours. "The three bodies discovered were all smothered, no other signs of trauma or particular physical injuries beyond a bruise or two. Just suffocated and the body dumped somewhere not that far away. Does that seem odd to anyone else?"

"It does seem unusual," David agreed. "Not violent, not sexual. It's just . . . *Shut up. Be quiet. I want you dead.*"

Evie nodded. "It's both personal and rather abrupt, and . . . it feels somehow female to me. I know men smother women, husbands do it to wives, boyfriends to girlfriends. And we've got three victims recovered who died that way, which indicates it's the killer's preferred method. But was Jenna's like that, personal and abrupt? I haven't been thinking that way for a motive with her, and yet it fits. And now I'm back to this not being a stranger crime, but someone who knew Jenna."

"Candy's more the type to take a swing at a rival than smother her," Ann suggested. "But maybe it was someone of that general type, the don't-like-Jenna crowd." A pause, then, "Maybe what drew interest to Jenna was the opposite of what we've been assuming — it was dislike, rather than like."

Evie pondered that idea and slowly nodded. "I'll come back to that later, as it's a really interesting idea. Jenna was chosen because someone *didn't like* her. But for now, I'm wondering the opposite. Consider the other extreme. I wonder if Jenna opened the door to a friend that night, a girl who had a fight with a roommate, who says, 'Can I sleep on your couch tonight?' And in the middle of the night, upset girl walks into Jenna's room and smothers her to death."

"Ouch."

"A bit of crazy going on, 'Jenna the girl with a perfect life, and I can't stand the fact my life is the opposite,' so kill the perfect one."

"It would have to be a rather strong girl to carry Jenna down a flight of stairs, to a vehicle, and get rid of her body," David pointed out. "And you would most likely be looking at Jenna as a single crime, because I don't see a crazy female driving to different states smothering other women — not doing it in a way that doesn't get her caught."

"True. Still," Evie said, "I'm going to let that idea roll around in my mind for a while."

David closed the case report he'd been reading. "We need tomorrow off, all of us, to get some actual rest." Sharon was already nodding. "Come Monday we hit this fresh, correlating lists from the five cases, focusing on Milwaukee and the possibility he lives around there. We're going to find the guy who did these crimes when we start to push in multiple places. He's been smart, but the pattern is his weakness."

"For Maggie's sake alone, we have to nail this down," Evie agreed. She pushed to her feet. "And on that note, I'm heading out. Thanks again, Ann." She smiled at Paul. "Nice to have your help today too. David, text me if you think of anything urgent. I'll plan to bring breakfast Monday morning."

"Thanks. Night, Evie."

She took two of the flowers from the vase

and headed back to her hotel.

Four and a half hours of sleep was not enough. The phone was ringing into the darkness. With a groan, Evie reached for it, read the caller ID, clicked it on. "Lieutenant Blackwell." She listened to the state dispatcher, rubbing aching eyes. "Tell him three hours. I'm on my way."

She punched David's speed-dial number.

"This can't be good," he answered.

She envied his ability to sound fully alert at such an hour. "An arson case with fatalities in Petersburg. I'm now multitasking."

"Get someone to drive you."

"Yeah." She covered a large yawn. "Someone's been hitting homes this way across the state for the last year. Anything other than this level, I'd be seeing if I could pass it on."

"We're going to be doing mostly data analysis for the next few days. I'll keep you in the loop."

"I'm fine with someone else solving Jenna's disappearance while I'm on something else. You get a lead, run with it. Catch this guy, David."

"Done." She heard the smile in his voice. "Good luck catching your arsonist."

"He equally needs catching. I'll be back

273

as soon as practical."

Evie called highway patrol to catch a lift with another cop heading south, looked around at her things once she was dressed, decided she would be near enough to her own place that she could make a run there to get clothes and a bed, and left her hotel room intact. Her car would be in Ellis while she was in Petersburg, but it couldn't be helped.

Twenty minutes later, she walked out, turning her attention back to the Illinois State Police Bureau of Investigations position she'd spent a career working to earn.

THIRTEEN

Evie walked into State Police headquarters after seven hours at the crime scene, talking by cell to the arson investigator still there. "The fact the victims were shot and killed before the fire was set tells me this is a different unsub. Does the fire itself say the same, Cole?" She headed up the stairs to BOI and her office. She wished she could stay downwind of herself — her coat, clothes, and hair reeked of smoke, and her eyes stung from all the ash floating in the air. She needed a shower and eye drops, and as soon as she had the prior case files on their way to the detective heading up this case, she was going home.

"The last five fires were all multiple origin points inside the home," Cole told her, "done with an accelerant of gasoline and whatever liquor was handy to pour. The fire path was designed to trap residents on the second floor without egress. This one, someone tampered with the water heater's gas line to fill the basement with natural gas, then dumped what I suspect will be black gunpowder on the staircase carpet and across the kitchen to the back doorway, and lit a match.

"This guy had probably never set a house fire before. He thought about what he wanted to do — overthought it, actually. Brought the gunpowder along, but wasn't sure how wide to trail it, probably used an ice pick on the gas line. He wanted the fire to destroy evidence of the murders before the firefighters could arrive. He was trying for a fast, explosive fire, but didn't know how to do that. He mostly scattered debris when the house blew up rather than burning the evidence. He had to have come close to blowing himself up along with the house."

"Premeditated and targeted — he was after this specific family. That's what the murders and the fire tell me. He came with a plan."

"Yeah, a different guy, Evie."

"Thanks, Cole."

"You sound relieved."

She was too tired to pretend she wasn't. "It at least makes it a local problem rather than mine. You need anything from me as this proceeds, I'll come back or get on a conference call."

"I'll do that, Evie. I'm good for now."

She turned on lights in her office and dumped her coat on one of the two visitor chairs, slid the phone into her pocket, ignored the contents of the inbox already stacked high. She logged on to the database, found the files she'd promised to send, took thirty minutes to write a summary of the five cases she'd been working, so the detective could quickly get up to speed without having to wade through the thick reports. She was sure her arsonist was different from this guy, but if the situations were reversed, she'd want to make that determination for herself. She gave him everything he might need, pressed the send button.

Logging off the system, she laid her head down on folded arms. She could catnap right here for a couple of hours, then catch a ride home with somebody. It was tempting if she didn't so desperately need a shower. Her gym bag was in the trunk of her car back in Ellis. Using the gym here meant rummaging through whatever abandoned clothing was in the lost-and-found. She couldn't fathom putting her current attire back on after finally ridding herself of the smoky smell.

A light tap on the door, a familiar voice.

"Welcome back."

She didn't bother to lift her head. "Go away."

A reporter was prowling the building. Commander Frank Foster, the man who led the Illinois State Police, had three sons. Two had become cops, one a reporter. She trusted Michael. He was off-the-record when he visited the building, unless he asked to go on-record. She even liked him, had dated him a time or two. But that didn't mean she wanted to see him right now. She had to look as bad as she smelled at the moment, and she still had a little vanity left.

"You haven't been around the office in a while."

She turned her head on her folded arms toward the man leaning against the doorjamb. She figured it had been two months since she'd last spent five consecutive days in this office. She was constantly surprised to find she hadn't been relegated to a desk in the bullpen during one of her extended absences. "I haven't. You looking for someone in particular?"

"Dad's tied up on a call. This arson isn't one of yours."

She should have realized, given the fatalities, he would have been on the scene of the house fire. He'd probably already talked with Cole and the lead investigator. Mike cultivated good sources and used them to write solid news pieces. "No. It doesn't look like the same guy."

"I was heading to the cafeteria. There's a stack of silver dollar pancakes calling your name."

She gave a faint smile. "Thanks, but I need to get home."

"In that case, I'll give you a lift."

She merely lifted an eyebrow.

"You arrived on scene via the state patrol, and I imagine your car is still in Ellis. Jenna Greenhill is coming along?"

She didn't bother to be surprised that he'd taken the time to dig out which case she had elected. "It's been a busy first week for the task force."

"I can imagine. C'mon." He reached in his pocket and swung his car keys in the air. "You'll sleep much better in your own bed."

He had the habit of mothering her at times when a case went sidewise on her. She'd found it irritating when they'd dated, but now it was more on the endearing side. He was a man who liked to take care of her, not unlike Rob. As much as she'd gone a different direction with their relationship, some core refrains remained.

She went with him. And when she fought

sleep within minutes of settling in the passenger seat, she simply closed her eyes and let herself drift off. He knew where she lived, knew where to find the spare key, and her dogs liked him. With Michael she could turn off the world when it was necessary to do so. He knew too much about her job and the cases she was working for her to have continued dating him. But the friendship they still had was authentic and safe. And she was tired in a way that went down to her bones. A safe guy suited her just fine right now.

Evie thought about Michael as she drove a rental north Tuesday morning after cleaning up some urgent items on her desk. Last night he had awakened her in the passenger seat of his car, nudged her through her own front door, shared an enthusiastic hello with her dogs, and left her with a casual but well-meaning good-night. *A good man.* One she could regret losing, even though she'd been the one to bring the relationship to an end. She'd never figured out how to integrate dating a reporter and being a cop. Their work lives had overlapped in ways she hadn't been able to deal with — almost worse than if he'd been another cop. She admired him even more for accepting that decision and neither walking out of her life for good, nor trying to bring her back. He'd chosen to remain a friend.

Dating him had taught her something about herself. Michael ran on short deadlines to deliver hard news, his life was always going to be about the case details, and hers was equally driven by the need to solve the real-life puzzle of it and bring justice. They fit together well and yet the very thing that fit them together was the reason it hadn't worked as a relationship for the long term. She needed a distance from the job. They had tried limiting how much the case conversations were in their personal lives, and for a season that approach had worked. But to not talk about their days left them having voids in what they discussed, and to talk about the days spiraled naturally into trying to help each other out. . . . The reality of that pendulum dynamic swinging from not enough to too much had never found a way to settle in the middle. She'd made a difficult choice, and as a result, a great guy was now a friend rather than her husband. She didn't regret the decision, but she ached every time she saw Michael, missing those good moments of her dating life with him.

A lot of good men had been in her life

over the years, she mused, and Gabriel Thane was another one of those, but one with a different balance — or unbalance — to it. As sheriff of Carin County, Gabriel was mostly a cop doing "protect and serve," very different from her life as a detective. Gabriel lived in the community, would likely serve it for decades, knew the families, and long after the crime was solved, a victim helped, the offender tried, Gabriel would be using what had happened to try to improve safety in the community. He was a solid guy, a good guy. But she hadn't opened the door to the relationship that could have been there. She wasn't a reporter's wife, and she wasn't a sheriff's wife.

Am I a banker's wife? That question was now back center stage. She'd been answering that question with, *No, I'm not a banker's wife either,* even before Rob had asked her to consider marriage. But she wasn't sure of that response anymore. Rob Turney was as different from a Michael Foster or Gabriel Thane as she was going to find. If her cautions were encompassed by work overlap, she'd solved it and found a great guy. She would have no work overlaps with Rob, be free of the weight that had led her to back away from Michael, to not consider Gabriel in a serious way. She just needed to say yes to the idea of getting married to Rob, then make the necessary compromises that would come with choosing him.

But in a way she didn't understand, she found herself torn just thinking about saying yes. She felt herself shift toward a prayer that had been forming for a while, and she finally risked putting it into words. "God, I'm not interested in a long conversation right now, I'm still too tired for that. But I'm aware the days are going by and I'm not getting my head — or my heart — around Rob's proposal.

"I really don't see how I can be married and have the career I do now. That seems like part of this. But there's more. And I guess I'm asking if you'd like to dig it up for me and show me what's going on inside. Because I truly don't understand it. Rob wants to marry me, and I'm dragging my feet. I need help. And you're my 'go-to guy' for perfect help. You're always honest with me, and always say things in a kind way. I need that inner mirror right now. I just want a day, more sleep, some space before you and I have that in-depth conversation, but I do need it, and I realize it needs to be soon. Okay?"

Evie felt some of the stress come off her chest just having the prayer out there. She quietly listened to see if God wanted to say anything in reply. The thought that came to mind within a moment was a Scripture, the beginning and end of a longer passage she knew well. *"Come to me . . . and I will give you rest."* The peace accompanying the gentle words settled her emotions. "Thanks, God."

She knew she was loved, that God cared about sorting it out with her. She didn't know how it would get resolved, but it wouldn't be her floundering around, trying to find the way forward. God would help her out. She was pretty sure she was destined to be married. She didn't want to be sixty and single. But the who and the when, the right choice — she often felt as though she was walking through a thick fog. It was hard to be confident about her personal life when she was so afraid of messing it up. God would be her help like no one else could, for He knew her and loved her. She'd trust what He had to say.

Evie checked the time on the latest message from David and decided to stop at the hotel first. She parked her rental, arranged for its pickup, and headed up to her room for her backpack. Ten minutes later, she settled into her own car and turned toward the office suite.

David was just walking into the building, saw her arrive, and waited as she parked. "Welcome back. So, not your arson guy."

She shook her head as she retrieved the backpack. "Different accelerant, and the three fatalities had been shot. Local cops are looking for a brother of one of the victims." She didn't bother to describe how grim the scene had been. David would have worked more than one arson fire in the past. "I've been keeping up on your notes," she told him.

"Lists are being crossed with lists, producing baby lists."

Evie laughed at his analogy.

"There are a few possible candidates with Wisconsin speeding tickets, and the union folks who worked various concert venues yielded two names of interest." David held the door for her. "As soon as the background reports come in, I'm going out on interviews."

"Your note this morning said there was good news regarding the credit-card data?"

"The historical credit- and gas-card info we would like to search was sold to marketing companies for analysis, the data stripped of names, but it still shows card numbers and full purchase histories. Since what they label historical data is anything over three years old, we've got the data set we wanted without even having to argue for a warrant. With the names gone, we cannot correlate them across various cards he might have used. But if he used the same gas card or the same credit card on at least two of the five dates of interest, there's going to be a hit. With that, we can get a warrant for a name on that card number, then turn *that* name into other card numbers, and *presto,* we can search to find his travels in all five cases."

Evie grinned. "I love that news, David. We need the data, and companies still have it since they're turning it into a profit of pennies per card."

"More like fractions of pennies per card. But it's free income, simply selling information about what somebody's already bought. Marketing companies love the data. The FBI does too, from the sound of it. The only drawback is the size of the data sets, how long it takes to crunch for an answer. We may be looking at a week unless there are early matches."

"Whatever it takes. It puts someone in a specific place and time years after the fact — that's good info to have."

David unlocked the office suite. Evie stepped inside, saw Rob's flowers had been transferred to her desk, two new whiteboards had been added, and a dozen new boxes were stacked by the east wall.

"That's Maggie's physical mail that's considered suspicious. The box with the red lid has the top concerns. They try to sort out incoming mail and match it with other letters sent by the same individual if possible, but a lot of it isn't signed, so they go by writing style."

"The emails she receives?"

"The most troubling ones went over to the FBI this morning. Ones from the Midwest are getting special attention, as are those where the sender tried to mask the email's origin."

"Good." Evie lifted out her master notepad filled with facts, theories, and ideas to help pull her mind back into Jenna's disappearance. "We think this is someone keyed into Maggie's music, so the probability that he's written her is likely — what, in the ninety-percent range?"

"I'm willing to lean that direction. But he's not going to want to stand out. The odds that he's in these boxes is low."

"I'll take any odds. Want me on her physical fan mail?"

"Sure. Just brace yourself if you haven't worked with fan mail before. I'm finishing the box Tammy's parents sent back with us, using it to generate yet another list of names we can use in the comparisons." David moved over to where those materials were now spread.

Intrigued by his caution, Evie crossed over to the fan mail, opened the one with the red lid. She soon realized why David had said it held the most disturbing correspondence — letters that ran ten pages, single-spaced, laying out the hidden messages in her lyrics she had especially coded for the sender, those who wanted Maggie to marry them, some who gushed with delight over having received a signed photograph, sending travel arrangements to be picked up at the airport on arrival.

"This mail is just . . . strange," Evie said, rather shocked.

David paused to glance over. "Welcome to the world of the general public writ large. About one percent of the people who like Maggie's music are at the ends of the bell curve for normal. The vast majority are, as you say, strange, but mostly harmless. A few, though, can tip toward violence when they feel affronted by Maggie's lack of reply or encouragement. You can't fix them — you

288

simply stay aware of who is out there so a problem doesn't become more than a problem."

"How many people are on the 'concerns list' for Chicago?"

"Her security has photos of about two hundred people they make sure don't get near Maggie. Another four hundred would be considered a concern."

Evie pulled out the thickest of the folders — indicating individuals who had sent the most mail — as she was looking for a person who'd been writing Maggie for close to a decade, back to when Jenna disappeared.

"Not all this mail is creepy." She held up a piece of light pink paper from a handful of similar pink pages in one of the folders. "Song lyric suggestions." She read a few of the pages. "Some of these are pretty good. Why is this folder in the problem box?"

"It's a possible source of lawsuits. Song lyrics are a really touchy area. You write a hit song, fans have sent similar ideas, maybe somebody claims the idea was plagiarized — how do you protect yourself from the honest fans who think a song was partially their idea too? So it's policy that song lyrics never get to Maggie. Those who do send her material get a rather personal letter, explaining why Maggie can't read their lyrics, then they're provided places where they can submit song lyrics and receive compensation if an artist wants to use their idea. Writing hit songs is a business all its own. Maggie's an exception since she chooses to write her own material. Most singers are not songwriters — different skill sets."

"I had no idea."

"One doesn't see the realities of a career unless you're within that sphere. The same with us. It's not glamorous being a cop, in spite of the TV shows. It's mostly talking to people, paperwork, and trying to figure out who to talk with next."

"Glamour it is not," Evie agreed. She flipped through the letters on pink stationery. "This woman has been writing to Maggie a couple times a month for the last . . . wow, eleven years."

"Holly Case?"

"It's signed Holly, yes."

"We've actually met her. She's a waitress, has a good voice, loves to sing. But she's shy, never got up the courage to solo at church, coffee shops, weddings — that early stage where a singer builds confidence, and maybe a career down the road. We put her in touch with some people. She now sings backup occasionally for a recording company here in Chicago. She keeps sending lyrics to Maggie, a safe outlet for her because she knows Maggie will never see the material and so can't reject her as not being good enough. It's sad, but until she's ready to send her material where it might be used, there's not much that can be done. She needs people in her life who have faith in her. She's got potential, just lacks self-confidence. Maggie can't save everyone, and *Holly* is often a code word between us when we encounter similar dilemmas."

Evie read a random dozen pages of the lyrics, closed the folder. Holly was using Maggie as a security blanket for her song lyrics rather than taking a risk and possibly failing at something she loved. Evie wasn't going to judge. She was sitting on a marriage proposal because she couldn't find the courage to take the risk.

But that did raise an interesting question. "Assume for a moment the five women were abducted by the same individual. It would suggest the killer has confidence in his ability to commit a crime and get away with it. Do you suppose it's frustrated rage driving him? 'I wanted to be a success, and the doors never opened for me'?"

"Killing young women with bright futures ahead of them so they can't fulfill their dreams?" David asked.

"Something like that," Evie said. "To smother someone isn't rage. It's ending something — a person's potential, voice, life. It's that 'Shut up, I want you dead.' Smothering is a different kind of personal."

"Not quite the same as strangling someone, but still, it's face-to-face murder, and that's personal."

"There's something in that thought that fits this. I just can't see what it is yet."

"Keep thinking — you'll have that light-bulb moment."

She was back to the idea it was a woman. *Smothering the victim feels female . . .* Evie opened the next folder and found cutout letters pasted on a page with death threats, a lot of them. Her adrenaline shot up. "You've got here a writer calling her foul names and wanting to kill her, done in letters and words from magazines. The folder reads 'Kevin Ought.'"

"He's sending them from a psychiatric jail facility. They haven't figured out yet how he gets them smuggled out, but she gets one about every other month."

"Ouch."

"I don't worry that much about the obvious mentally disturbed. Maggie isn't the first person they have fixated on, and someone in their neighborhood or family is going to be addressing their problems with the help of mental-health authorities long before they could show up on Maggie's doorstep. It's the one who's just crossing over that line, from devoted fan to fixated fan that is the worry. They're unpredictable, and they don't detach from their fixation easily. Typically someone else has to become the focus for them to let go of Maggie, and that just transfers the problem to another. So we are careful about Maggie's personal whereabouts. She'll post social media comments after she's been somewhere, loved it, and left — not in anticipation of being there. The common-sense precautions that make her difficult to locate in advance."

"Looking at these letters, I'm glad she takes them."

Evie lifted more folders out, then paused as a thought hit. "What are the odds the guy we're after will be at the charity event Friday night?"

David looked up from what he was doing. "Her first appearance in Chicago in years? High. He won't be inside, not at five thousand a plate with their running background checks on all the guests. But odds are high he'll be among the rope-line fans. I already talked to security working the event, and there will be cameras on the crowds, so we can review footage with that in mind."

"Good. Thanks."

"I'm not taking chances with Maggie. We can also assume he'll have a ticket for her scheduled performance at the McCormick Center on March seventh. We've got until then to find him. I don't want a conversation with Maggie on whether to cancel the concert to avoid another missing-person photo going up on that board. So we find this guy before then."

"We've got time to get it done," Evie replied. She paused as she realized what she was holding. "David, look at this one." Evie walked over to him with it.

I love the way you look when you sing "A Waiting Love." You're looking right at me.

"There are more in that same vein. A lot more." The thick folder held letters all on a blue paper, computer-printed in a fancy script, unsigned, but the similar messages laid out the same way on each.

"Yeah. Maggie's got an obsessed fan. She has them, Evie. I've added some of those letters to that folder over the years. The blue paper reads male, the choice of a fancy script and the text itself reads female, but we've drawn a blank trying to track down the sender. Can you tell if security has had any better luck with recent letters from this individual?"

She reviewed the document in the front of the folder, was pleasantly surprised at the depth of the investigation to identify this sender. "No fingerprints on the letters, and the envelopes carry prints of postal employees only. That's what has me wondering about this sender." She sifted through the folder. "These letters go back ten years. A fan who takes that kind of care to conceal identity, to not leave prints? And has done so for years?"

"Some people are paranoid about fingerprints."

"He doesn't sound paranoid. If he's already a criminal, wants to conceal his identity, but is drawn to Maggie, so he hides his fingerprints — doesn't that sound a lot like the person who did Jenna harm?"

David weighed the question. "Okay. For the sake of argument, say they are from the same person. How do we use the letters to help us find him?"

"They're all postmarked in Indiana. Two of our five possible matches are women killed in Indiana. Would Indiana be a false clue, in line with no fingerprints?"

"The postmarks are probably an attempt to mislead."

"So someone who does not live in Indiana." Evie spread out numerous letters from the folder across the desk. "What do you notice? What I see — mentions of specific songs, specific lyrics, all admiring in tone. He's into the title and words of the songs more than just the music, suggesting maybe he writes lyrics too. Some of these letters are from this last year. He — or she — is still following her."

"Agreed," David said, considering the letters. "The blue paper is the same shade, so the same brand, possibly all from the same ream of paper used exclusively for writing to her. But as promising as this is, Evie, there are dozens of similar people in her world. The lack of fingerprints is on the odd side, given the notes themselves seem pretty rational. I'd like a photo of this guy for Maggie's security to carry with them — she doesn't need to meet him — but ten years of writing letters without the letters escalating much in content still suggests someone reasonably harmless to her."

"So I should be looking for someone who wants to meet Maggie," Evie said, "who talks about seeing her at a restaurant or visiting her home, something other than a history of questionable fan mail."

"Not necessarily. I think the *tone* here is the right fit for who you want. Your guy uses Triple M concerts as his trolling ground to select victims. He's into Maggie and the Triple M band enough to be a fan who'd write to her. He's paranoid about revealing his identity, so he leaves no prints. He stays with less traceable paper and envelopes rather than email or comment posts on her website.

"All that sounds like the guy you want, Evie. But I would have expected over ten years to see less mail than this, being more selective about when he writes her, and something in the mix would change, would say or imply he did something. 'There are those who sing your songs and don't know all the words. They fill in whatever words they decide fits. I won't let them botch your song lyrics anymore, Maggie. Your lyrics are perfect.' Something like that."

"He would have shifted into the occasional creepy letter."

"This guy isn't static if he's killed Jenna and a few others. How he sees Maggie will have migrated over the years too. That's assuming the cases on the board are all his. We may be looking at clusters of two or three different individuals' crimes."

"I'm inclined to think the three smothered victims are linked, but maybe not to Jenna."

"Exactly." David scanned the blue sheets, then stacked and placed them back in the folder. "The unsub we're after will have changed over the years as the crimes happen, and his behavior, any letters he sends, will reveal that." He handed the folder back.

"A good point." Evie returned the folder to its box and went on to the next one. Sorting through all that was here was going to take hours. She glanced at the conference room, aware they had shifted attention away from the other case while David helped her solve this one.

"Your PI, David. You were going to check out crimes that happened around the Englewood area, where Saul may have disappeared that Saturday night. Later today I'll spend an hour looking at that for you. I don't want to leave his case entirely cold while we pursue this one."

"I'm sure Saul would understand," David replied, "but thanks, Evie. We'll get both cases resolved if they can be. It just makes sense to push first where there's movement, and Jenna's case feels that way, and may still be flowing into current crimes. Saul's looks to be ended."

FOURTEEN

Evie studied the latest database matches. Ticket purchases made at the Triple M website yielded sixty-two names in common with at least three of the five concert locations and dates. There were twelve matches for all five concerts. A strikingly high number of matches, she thought, given the dates went back nine years, with locations crossing four states.

She started at the top of the list and went hunting for what she could learn. Kyle Kendrick, 18 Hillcrest Road, Pawnee, IL. That put him south, in the middle of the state. He'd bought tickets to all five concerts of interest. Was he still living there? She pulled up the DMV database and found that he still lived at the same address. He was forty-three now, placing him at the high end of the likely age range. She searched the marriage and divorce records but came across nothing under his name. She moved to business records and found his name and address under business ownership. She tracked the business number in the *Doing Business As* database and came up with Shirts for You. She found a matching website with a shop address in Pawnee, IL. Kyle was a T-shirt vender who, going by the website content, followed a lot of popular bands.

Probably not Kyle, she concluded, but she doubted he was the one going out to the concerts and actually selling the shirts now that the business looked to have prospered. He'd hire a college kid, provide a ticket to the concert as part of the deal. She'd probably find Kendrick or his shop name in the vender list at the various concert venues. She could ask who he had paid to work the five concerts; maybe she'd get the same name for all five. She picked up the phone and made the call, found Kyle a rather puzzled but cooperative man willing to dig out that answer for her. She thanked him for his help and moved on to the second name.

Lucille Johnson, 79 Marigold Lane, Evanston, IL. DMV showed her to be sixty-nine. A bit more digging came up with the surprising bit of info — she was a music-magazine staffer. Evie made another call and this time got a recording, left a message that she would be interested in talking with Lucille about concert venues in the Midwest.

She was going to have to wade through a cottage industry that had latched on to the Triple M band as a lucrative group for business reasons to get to the fans buying tickets because they loved the music. But the only way to separate the groups was to identify each individual. Evie could feel the clock running as she followed names and generated information. Some she found in the business-license database, sometimes there was an arrest on file, while for others there was a permit issued — T-shirt vender, ticket broker, food vender. They all were efficiently buying tickets to every one of the concerts, taking the discount by ordering directly from the website. But these kinds of leads would be buying tickets for a lot of bands, and for now she wanted only Triple M fans.

She found her first probable fan — Garry, with two r's, Nichols, 552 Rowlings Road, Gurnee, IL. That put him close to the Illinois-Wisconsin border. DMV showed a Garry Nichols now resided in Chicago. He would be the right age, thirty-one now. She searched for a criminal record, found a long one. Multiple drunk-and-disorderly arrests, short jail times, a B&E — that caught her attention — two restraining orders issued four and five years ago, cited as at fault in a traffic accident causing injuries two years ago. "Garry, you and I need to get better acquainted." Evie sent the information to the printer.

She heard the door open, glanced around to see David. She looked at the time, realized it was later than she had thought. "How were the interviews?"

"Productive, but negative. I can eliminate both union guys."

"Well, I've got more names — those who bought multiple tickets through the band's website."

David smiled. "More names is always a good thing." He pulled free a yellow sheet of paper taped to the conference room glass door. "You've found there was trouble in Englewood around the time of Saul's disappearance."

She'd taped the page there to make sure she didn't forget to tell him. "A bookie was murdered that weekend. And a domestic disturbance ended with a husband shooting his wife. There were three B&Es, two car thefts. Someone was eventually charged in every case. It might make sense to ask at least the B&E and car theft guys, 'Did you see anything that night?' They're out of jail now and look to be living reformed lives. Who knows, but one of the car thieves might have taken Saul's car. We're looking for information only, and if we're willing to pay to get it, maybe something helpful comes our way."

"That's a very good idea."

"Great. I need to rebuild my hoard of good ideas. It's been thin the last few days."

David laughed. "I'm going to write up these notes, then I'll help you work those ticket names."

"Thanks."

Later, he worked from the bottom of the list up while she went down from the top. They'd come up with eighteen names of interest when they brought the workday to a close just after eight p.m. "There are some strong candidates here," he said. "We'll spend tomorrow doing interviews, hopefully catch our man off-balance when we show up at his door."

Evie nodded. "The fact it's Maggie's guy knocking on his door? There will be a re-action if he knows who you are."

"It's not going to be the guilty reaction you're hoping for," David cautioned. "Most, if not all, of the names on this list are going to know me on sight. I'm Maggie's guy, and these are the ones buying multiple tickets because they like her music. They'll not only recognize me, they can probably tell you all kinds of gossip about me."

"Then we'll look for someone who recognizes you and is also sweating because you're a cop."

David smiled. "I'll take 'fear of a cop' as a good clue."

Evie walked out with him to the parking lot, unlocked her car, and tossed her backpack on the passenger seat. "You interested in a movie? The new *Fast and Furious* sequel is playing." It would do them good to stop thinking about work for a few hours.

"I'd normally take you up on that after a day like this, but I want to stop by Maggie's house tonight, check security, make sure the furniture delivery and arrival of some of her things went smoothly. She's due in Thursday midmorning."

"You want company?" Evie asked, hopeful.

"Sure. Let me follow you back to the hotel, you can leave your car, and we'll ride out to Maggie's together."

"Anything else surprising or interesting happen while I was gone?" Evie asked as they drove to Maggie's place.

"I went to several open houses Sunday," David replied.

"I'm glad. Tell me about them."

He clicked his phone on and passed it over. "Check the photos I sent Maggie. There are a couple there that would work at the right price."

"You'd like owning your own place."

"I like the tinkering it lets me do. The tree I plant, the shrub I cut out, the projects like putting in new windows or building book-cases. A home of my own means hands-on — and there's always something to do."

"I can see how that can appeal if you're into DIY projects." Evie showed him a photo. "Tell me about this one."

She got him talking about the different homes, the pros and cons of the properties, keeping him on a subject unrelated to work. She peppered him with questions, because he was likely to ask her a personal question in return, about Springfield or about Rob, and she'd rather avoid that tonight.

"You're chatty this evening," David mentioned.

"Yeah. I'm distracting us both with your home search."

David laughed and slowed as he entered a rather pricey neighborhood in Barrington. "It's not a gated community, but they have a neighborhood association, and a private security presence patrols these blocks. It's staffed by a mix of retired cops and military guys. Response times average two minutes."

"I hope she never needs them, but it's good they're here if she does."

"They're decent guys, solid skills, and they were all thoroughly vetted once Maggie decided on this place."

Even in the darkness, Evie could appreciate the surroundings. The landscape had some roll to it, curves in the road. Mature oaks provided continuity and, even without their leaves, a sense of canopy above the roadways.

This was a community with some historic homes walled off and gated, other more recent ones with expansive snow-covered grounds sloping up to the house. Spacious, but not McMansions, many set within sight of one another. It was a neighborhood, if a wealthy one.

David slowed for a curved driveway, the property surrounded by a tall stone wall. He punched in the security code at the entrance, and tall, black iron gates swung open. He pulled in and parked on the left side of the drive.

The house was fairly close to the road, the side yard filled with trees. Built of stone, it blended beautifully with the landscape, designed to follow the slope of the land. The smaller front yard had been laid out in crisscrossing walkways and tiered flower beds for what must make an inviting array of color in the spring.

"She has a beautiful home. I can't wait to see it in daylight."

"Maggie took voice lessons here, from a retired singer who had a famous career in the eighties. This has been her dream home ever since. When it came on the market a year ago, Maggie considered it a worthy reason to return to Chicago."

David sorted out keys as they walked up to the front door. Evie studied the house, the recessed entry, the lighting, began to pick up signs of the security that had been added. David unlocked the door, entered a passcode on the security panel, paused, tapping his finger on the wall to count time passing, then entered a second code.

"I like the fail-safe system," Evie noted.

"It's useful. Do things in the wrong order, the patrol is on scene to check it out. Miss one of the steps, it's the equivalent of calling 911. We're set at maximum security right now since the house is empty."

David turned on lights for the main floor. The entryway welcomed them, a long closet for coats, a comfortable bench on which to sit and put on boots, two tall tables for flower vases. The marble floor curved into a spacious cream-carpeted great room, a couch still wrapped in shipping plastic set in front of a fireplace. Two blue-and-silver-striped wing-back chairs flanked the couch. A grand piano commanded attention. Beyond it was another seating area with love seats and a square ottoman facing a large television.

The floor-to-ceiling windows showed a large backyard bathed in muted ground lighting, a pool now covered for the winter, a spacious patio with bench seating and tables and chairs set near a stone outdoor grill. Farther out, Evie could see the high wall circling the back of the property. "Maggie is going to be very comfortable here. And safe."

"I think so. She wants this — the yard, the flowers, the property — to call home for the next thirty years. When she lived on the sixtieth floor of a high-rise and her apartment number in the building was a protected fact, security was an easier matter. But it didn't have the setting of a normal life that she wants."

Evie smiled. "I can imagine."

David slipped off his shoes. "Yours are fine

— it's habit for me. I want to glance at what furniture came today, snap a few photos for Maggie, then check the last security upgrades that went in this month. Feel free to wander around. This'll take me about thirty minutes."

"Sure."

Evie took her time, disappearing down a hallway, getting a feel for the place. The layout was nice: two powder rooms on the main level, separate pantry, mudroom, the spacious living room, a formal dining room, and a well-laid-out kitchen. Entertaining twenty or thirty people wouldn't feel tight here.

She opened a kitchen cabinet, found dishes and glassware, opened random drawers and found towels and utensils in place. Pictures, awards, coasters, and candle holders rested on the dining room table, waiting for Maggie's decision on where they should be placed. Framed artwork leaned against the walls in many of the rooms. Evie walked over to study some of the watercolors in the living room. Maggie liked ones with a light touch and soft colors.

David came back, phone to his ear. He waved toward the fireplace before pocketing the cell.

"There are cameras throughout the

house?" she asked, curious.

"Yes. I know it's creepy at first, but you learn to let it go. They're on when Maggie requests it, when she has guests over she doesn't know well or when she's throwing a party and sensor security for the grounds are turned off. They're a security blanket of sorts, for Maggie and for me."

"Aren't you worried someone could hack the system, turn on the cameras to watch her?"

He shook his head. "One of the benefits of having the finances for really good security, it's all encrypted transmissions from here to the Chapel Security offices, and it flows over our own equipment, not carried by any public network. Someone can't casually stroll into those offices, press a button to turn on cameras here. But to bulletproof it further, there are fail-safes. She can't be watched without her knowledge. I can tell the cameras are on right now."

"I suppose it's the price of fame, having to prepare for trouble. But it's sad that it's necessary."

David shrugged. "You've got a system at your own home because you're a cop and someone might show up who doesn't like you," he pointed out.

"Yeah, two retired military dogs, both of

them vigilant about uninvited guests," Evie agreed with a little chuckle.

"It's the same basic rule of thumb for Maggie. Try to keep her home life private, and use common sense for the rest." He glanced out the window. "I want to look around upstairs, then walk the backyard. Come on up if you like." Evie followed him.

David paused at the first bedroom, still empty. "There are five bedrooms, one of which Maggie will use as a studio. She likes writing her lyrics at home — probably here as it gets good morning light."

He moved on to the master bedroom. Furniture in place, the bed made up, lamps on bedside tables, two upholstered chairs and a round table by the window. The suite didn't have much character without Maggie's personal things yet, but the bedroom looked comfortable and feminine.

David turned on lights in the walk-in closet. "There are safe rooms in the house on each floor. They were put in when the house was originally built." He found the mechanism, and the back closet wall slid nearly silently to the left. "If an alarm sounds for an intruder coming in a window or door, Maggie has agreed to move to a safe room while security resolves the problem. That was our compromise for her not living in a fully gated community."

The small room beyond the sliding wall could handle three or four people, Evie gathered. A shelf held stacks of pillows, blankets, board games, water bottles, and what looked like a box of chocolate bars. Beside a small refrigerator was a discreetly placed commode. Evie decided she wouldn't want to be in that room for more than an hour — basically like an elevator in size. "I've never seen one before."

"Nothing elaborate, but once the door closes and seals, she's safe. No one can get in, and she can't come out — not until security or the police open it. It's twelve hours before you can open the door from the inside. It's heat-resistant and has its own air supply. You'll be bored but okay, even with a tornado ripping through the area."

"That entryway wall with the bench — behind it is another safe room?" Evie asked.

David smiled. "Yes. You've got a good eye for spaces. It's entered through the mudroom off the hallway, with the same design as this one. The police and her security are notified when one of the safe room doors seals."

"Let's hope these rooms are never needed."

"I doubt they ever will be. But I sleep better knowing the house has them. We call them the bad-weather plan for tornado sirens. Any other reasons remain unspoken."

David finished his walk through the second floor, and then they headed downstairs.

"Maggie lives a very public life as a performer," Evie mentioned. "Keeping her personal life private . . . all this matters. She is blessed to have you arranging things for her, David."

"Thanks for noticing." He sat down on the bench to put on his shoes. "Maggie jokes about the security, but she counts on it working."

"It's only going to get more intense, the more her fame grows."

He nodded. "There's room for security on-site, but hopefully that's still a few years away." David took out keys to lock up the house. "I appreciate you coming with me, Evie."

"She's found a beautiful place to call home. I hope she's happy here for years to come and that one day it's a family home, with your wedding photos on that fireplace mantel and your shoes permanently under the entryway bench."

David's chuckle held a bit of sadness, yet he said, "I do like the image of that. Give me about ten minutes to walk the backyard and I'll be ready to go."

Evie finally gave up looking for a television show to watch. *I should have stopped and bought a book.* She would have called Rob, linked up with him for dinner, but he was in New Jersey for a wedding his parents had talked him into attending. The plane trip there and back was one she was glad to have missed.

She picked up her collection of facts and theories on Jenna, read through them again, but found nothing to spark another line of inquiry. They now had several hundred names across the five missing women, even before they considered fans related directly to Maggie. Odds were good they had the name of Jenna's killer. Time and patience and a steady push would identify him.

In some ways the case had turned boring — it was simply elimination work now, going name by name, the inevitable middle-of-the-case syndrome. Hours would be spent on it, but the answer would appear out of that effort. Evie had faith in the process, even if she couldn't predict how long it would take. She sighed and set aside the notepad.

She wrapped her arms around one of the pillows she'd tossed onto the couch. *Quit ducking it, Evie,* she told herself. *Now's the time to at least get started on David's assignment.*

She reached for a new pad, turned halfway into it to provide privacy from casual glances at the top page. She divided the blank page into two columns, numbered the lines one through twenty, being optimistic on the number of entries. On the left side, she wrote *Stay Friends,* and on the right, *Get Married.* And then she let herself think about Rob Turney.

She began with the right column, Get Married:

1. He loves me
2. He's a good guy
3. I trust him
4. He wants to marry me — his decision is made
5. Options to explore for a job change that would eliminate most of my travel — move to the local PD, work with a private security firm, or _____?
6. I like his home, his lifestyle — more upscale than mine, but not impossible to bridge for my personal comfort
7. I'm at ease with his core group of

friends, even though we don't have much in common
8. If I want children, it's time I marry

She didn't write *I love him.* Though it felt true, to say "I love you, but I won't marry you" felt incredibly harsh. So for now she didn't add it to the list.

Under the left column, Stay Friends, she began with the obvious:

1. His mother wants someone else for him — she's in good health, I'll likely see her weekly for the next thirty years — mother-in-law tension is a real issue — do I want to live under that cloud of being a disappointment?
2. My indecision tells me I do not deeply want to be married or I'm not ready to be married
3. I've already had three failed engagements — do I want Rob to possibly be a fourth?
4. If we stay friends — a big "if" — I could remain a state detective with its required travel and no job change
5. I could become head of BOI one day if I stay with the state — a dream of mine

6. My dogs are going to hate Chicago
7. Rob will always be a finance guy, and I'll always see that world through a lens that says it's not life-or-death — that's not a very supportive-wife attitude
8. Sam

Evie stopped. If she and Rob stayed just friends, she wouldn't have to tell him any further details about her brother Sam's death. She felt relief wash over her just at the mere thought of not having to have that conversation.

Eight *Get Married* items, eight *Stay Friends*. At least it was an equal-opportunity uncertainty, she concluded, reading over the lists again. "Jesus, what else should be on these lists?" She thought about it carefully.

After a while, she added five more to *Get Married:*

9. I would enjoy being a wife
10. We could have fifty years building our shared history — the sooner the wedding, the deeper, more satisfying that history will be
11. We're already solid friends, know each other well
12. Rob enjoys spending time with me

13. I'd like to share my life with someone, and I could see doing that with
Rob

Under *Stay Friends,* she wrote:

9. Ann has concerns about him, and I
value her perspective as a trusted
friend
10. A lot of good guys have been in my
life, and I've always moved on —
something in me is deeply vulnerable in a way I don't understand
when I never let myself settle into
"forever" with one of them
11. I want Jesus to be the center of my
life, but I'm already giving him less
attention than I'd like. In my head I
want more time with him, and yet I
avoid making it happen. I'm not
afraid of what he'll say, as he's
always kind and wanting to help
me. I think I'm afraid I can't be
fixed. . . .
12. I marry Rob and he dies on me

She felt God open her eyes even as she
wrote it down, and she literally hurled the
pad across the room. *Of course that's the
problem. Jesus is safe because He's already
come back from the dead and isn't going to*

die on me like Sam. The last thing she wanted was to wear a ring from someone who would die on her and leave her like Sam had.

She got up from the couch, feeling like she wanted to kick something. She left the pad where it had fallen, scooped up her coat and keys. She was significantly behind on her gym and shooting-range time. She'd use the county sheriff's facilities, burn through a couple of hours with some intense exercise.

Her brother was dead — she'd already said goodbye to one family member. There was no way she was going to live with the fear of losing another person she loved. She'd rather stay single than survive that pain again.

FIFTEEN

Evie brushed her hair the next morning, a Wednesday, ignoring the tired face and eyes in need of makeup looking back at her in the mirror. She was relieved when her phone rang, interrupting her thoughts. "Yes, David," she said absently, setting the brush aside.

"Evie, I just got a fascinating call from Sharon. There's a body in Englewood, or more accurately, a skeleton."

It took a moment to reorganize her thinking away from her own problems and Jenna's disappearance. *The missing PI.* "Bones?"

"In a wall. A classic wall-up-the-problem crime scene. Want to come?"

Her mood brightened at the question and the total change of focus. "Sure. I can meet you in the lobby in ten minutes."

"I'll have the heater on max."

"Thanks."

Evie added another layer of socks before pulling on her boots. "God," she whispered, "if you arranged this just for David, it's so cool. I appreciate the distraction too." She needed the break. She could put both Rob and Jenna on the shelf for a while.

She made sure a pair of gloves were in her coat pockets, picked up a new notebook, ignored the pad now resting upside down on the table, and headed out.

The directions Dispatch provided led to an older section of Englewood and a long, brick three-story building surrounded by a high chain-link fence. The multiple dumpsters, debris chutes, and scaffolding anchored to the roof on the north side all indicated the place was undergoing a much-needed renovation. A gathering of marked and unmarked cars at the south end of the building told them this was their target.

David pulled in beside the coroner's vehicle, and Evie got out with him, turned up the collar of her coat. The press was already on-site, for she recognized the vans with logos and call letters. The officer holding the logbook for the scene wrote down their names and badge numbers at the door. "You'll find the excitement on the second floor, south end," he said, waving them toward a stairway.

Upstairs, it was easy to locate the crowd at the end of the hall, clustered around a small restroom, one marked with a *W*. The toilets in the four stalls and the wall with sinks remained, but construction workers had cut out a side wall and taken down the stall doors — with haste over neatness from the looks of it. They had more carefully cut out a six-by-six-foot section of the concealing drywall for better visibility. That piece, along with what looked like a hammered-out hole in it, was being examined by crime-scene technicians with bright handheld lights.

"Those are definitely skeletal remains," David said dryly beside her, and Evie couldn't help but smile.

The skeleton leaned to the right, held up by the collar of a leather jacket that seemed to be caught on a nail. The rest of the clothing had disintegrated for the most part, with some short strands of hair remaining around the skull. The bones were still mostly in place and visible because gravity had been stopped by something that appeared to be chunky gray clay.

"Is that cat litter?" David asked as they got closer and could see the detail of what had solidified into honeycombed chunks around the skeleton.

The technician worked something out from the wall at about the height of the skeleton's pelvis, turned at the question, held out a handful of the gray matter. "About twenty bags of it is the working theory." Other technicians were carefully removing more of it from either side of the remains, placing softball-sized lumps of the material in rows on a clean piece of canvas laid out on the floor.

Evie glanced around. The scene had been a busy one for at least a couple of hours, she thought. Cops were now mostly waiting for assignments, the newness of the discovery worn off, but still interested in watching the work while doing other business by phone or text. The detective in charge stood off to one side, supervising the process.

David walked over to make introductions, Evie following more slowly since it wasn't her case.

"Captain Whistler," David said, reading the man's nametag, "I'm David Marshal with the Missing Persons Task Force. My partner, Evie Blackwell. You're the one who called our boss, Sharon Noble?"

Whistler nodded. "They found a wallet with an expired driver's license about where his back pocket would have been. It made

sense you'd want to see the body in context"
— the captain passed over an evidence bag
— "seeing as how you've been trying to find
this guy."

David checked the license. "That would
be my Saul Morris." Obviously relieved, he
offered the evidence bag to Evie, then
looked again at the skeleton. "I'm going to
guess he was dead before he went inside
that wall."

"I'd say shot in the chest, then the drywall
went up," Whistler said. "A lot of stuff was
shoved in there with him." He indicated a
makeshift table sitting under a window.
"That's where we've put what's been lifted
out so far."

"Thanks," said David.

Evie moved to the table with David. Items
were being cleaned off by hand, using a
small, soft brush to remove the cat-litter
gunk. Another technician was taking photos
and writing up an inventory. Evie was elated
to spot a litter-caked camera, one of the
older professional types with a motor drive.
"One of Saul's cameras was with the remains? That's going to be a rich find if any
photos can be recovered."

The technician paused to point with his
brush. "The lab might be able to restore
some images either from the film or the

memory card, depending on which he was using. It's a dual-type camera. The battery compartment looks like battery acid ate through it, but the vacuum seal of the body has held together."

"Care to give odds?"

"Better than seventy if he was using film. An exposed negative is going to be good until it decays. Forty percent might be high if he was using the memory card, but images on those older cards are actually more retrievable since they used thicker memory cells."

"I'll take those odds."

They saw the wallet's leather had mostly survived, including its contents of ruined cash and business cards, plus two stained credit cards. David used his pen to gently shift a photo still intact under the plastic sleeve. "Cynthia and her son. Saul's sister," he noted when the technician glanced over. "This wire spiral" — David pointed with the pen to an encrusted ball of gunk — "is it the edge of a notebook? The guy was known to carry one."

"Could be," the technician answered. "There are some remains of his shirt in there. You can see the collar, the front line of the pocket. We'll peel apart the layers at the lab. Maybe you've got a readable notebook inside."

"And this?" Evie asked, studying a larger piece.

"That looks like what came out of a car's glove box. You can faintly make out a vehicle registration card on top, and on the side, part of an insurance card — see the logo? I think the thick mass at the back is a car manual."

"So," David said, "they tossed everything he had with him into the wall, cleaned out his car and threw those items in as well. Both efficient and fast."

"What else might be here with him?" the technician asked.

"A phone is likely, and maybe some folders of case materials," David guessed. "He wasn't one to regularly carry a handgun, but he was licensed for concealed carry."

"We'll keep you informed on what gets found."

Evie walked with David back over to watch the work being done at the wall. Technicians were carefully recovering items around the bones. If they removed a piece too soon, the lattice of cat litter would cascade down in a heap, and with it the bones. The lead technician eventually took hold of the skull and with great care eased it out of the vertical tomb. Evie turned away, not needing to see this part.

Captain Whistler came to join them. "How far along was your investigation?"

David slid hands into his back pockets but kept watching. "I'd filled in the timeline on Saul's disappearance to Saturday, eight p.m., when he was looking for a card game here in Englewood. A client's wife thought her reformed gambler of a husband had relapsed but didn't want to confront him without being certain. I'd guess from what we see here that Saul was working that case when he ran into trouble."

"A useful lead," the captain responded. "It's going to take the day to get the remains out of there, factor in lab time on the recovered items, medical examiner's report, putting together the history on this building to figure out who might have thought it harmless to entomb him here. We're looking at several days just putting our arms around this scene and what it can tell us. Consider this a shared investigation for now. I'll want your take on the items found with him, whatever else you have for leads. So talk to anyone you like, read any reports you want to see. In a few days we'll have more information to guide how everything proceeds." He paused, smiled. "I'm guessing we take the bones and homicide off your hands once you've done all the work and can tell us what this all means. Your boss is on her way to sort that out."

David simply smiled. "You'll find me in agreement with that plan, Captain. I'd like to stay with the case long enough to see the details, button down some open questions I have, but you'll find me eager to hand it off to your homicide detectives. I'm one guy, and this is going to get very involved. We're in the middle of a hot chase on another missing person that equally needs my attention."

"Good enough." The captain nodded to the group off to their left. "Detective Jenkins will coordinate getting you anything you need. He'll be running point for both of us."

"Thanks, Captain." David stepped over and swapped business cards with Jenkins.

The detective said, "I'll stay on the body and scene recovery. Once we wrap up here, I'll find you so you can fill me in on the case details."

David nodded. "That works. Who was first on scene?"

"That would be me." An officer stepped away from the watching group of cops to offer a hand. "Frank Taft, my partner Owen Nevins. We took the dispatch call."

"Who found the body?"

The officer pointed down an intersecting corridor. A woman was sitting at a makeshift plywood table set up near the other end of the building. "Lori Nesbitt. The man pacing around is her boss, Nathan Lewis. He owns the building. Lori says she found the body, called 911, called building security, then her boss. Time on her call to us was 5:38 a.m. She was standing with a security guard at the first-floor doorway when we pulled up. Her boss arrived about twenty minutes behind us. We found that wall mostly intact. She'd punched a large hole in it with a hammer, and the skull was visible if you looked in with a flashlight. It was still a functioning bathroom then; construction workers didn't start to dismantle it until crime-scene guys directed what they wanted done."

"Okay, thanks," David said.

Evie's attention had spiked at the mention of Nathan Lewis, and she saw David's had as well. Saul had been working for Nathan Lewis, looking into his wife's murder. And Ann had said someone was working inside The Lewis Group right now and pursuing the same question.

Evie followed David as he headed down the corridor toward the two. Rob had done business with Nathan on occasion, admired him, while Evie had never had an opportunity to meet him.

It was quieter at this end of the building, the echo of voices subdued. "Ms. Nesbitt, Mr. Lewis, I'm Detective David Marshal. This is my partner, Lieutenant Evie Blackwell. It's been an interesting morning for you, I take it."

The woman gave a ghost of a smile. "That's one way to describe it."

Evie caught Nathan's surprised look in her direction, gave him a brief smile but didn't extend the introduction by mentioning either Rob or Ann as common friends.

David turned to Nathan as he got out his notebook. "How long have you owned the building?"

"Maybe thirty-seven days? Around there. I doubt the contract lets me void the deal for including a crime scene."

"We'll be looking into all prior owners," David assured him.

"Between 2008 and 2012, it would have been RB Electric," the woman interjected. David gave her an attentive look. "The officer gave me the date on the recovered driver's license. I was rather insistent they tell me something. Had I uncovered a man or woman, dead a year or a decade?"

She offered without being asked, "I know the data on the building because I helped

research the property before it was purchased. RB Electric went bankrupt in 2013.
A lighting company based out of the Neth-
erlands bought the building from the bankruptcy court to use as warehouse space for
their US division. They added the fencing,
updated the security, but then their needs
changed and the building has sat unused.
The Lewis Group bought the building from
them in late December."

"You found the remains, Ms. Nesbitt?"
David asked.

"Yes. And please, call me Lori."

He nodded. "No one else was in the building?"

"Security was downstairs. They'd let me
in around five this morning. I had a meeting with the site foreman scheduled for six
to prioritize today's work — multiple crews
would have started at seven."

David perched on the edge of a tall stool.
"Okay. Lori, what were you doing with a
hammer slamming into drywall at five this
morning?"

She gave him a faint smile. "Curiosity is a
stubborn trait." She glanced at Nathan, than
back to David. "I'm new on this job — I've
worked for The Lewis Group since mid-
November. It's my first community rehab,
and a lot of buildings in these four blocks

are now ours . . . I mean, his. It's rather interesting work, and Nathan, for some reason he didn't explain, has put me in charge of this building, made me the arbiter between the architect and the foreman. I was here early, putting in some of my own time working on the details.

"It's been bugging me, that lady's washroom, every time I used it. It felt awfully cramped, certainly not wheelchair-accessible. I'd seen the schematics of the building, and there were no heating or cooling ducts running through that area to explain why the dimensions were so tight. I figured the building had been remodeled so many times that there might be an old staircase or something back there. It paced off about that amount of offset. If that was the case, we needed crews focused there today since it would be significantly more demo work than we'd originally anticipated.

"The wall was going to come out soon anyway, so I figured I would take a look. I punched a hole in the drywall, and there was his face looking back at me, the jaw and teeth still kind of smiling. Freaked me out, let me tell you. I screamed so loud I probably sent every mouse and rat in the building fleeing."

Nathan lightly laid a hand on her shoulder. "I'm sure they were already far away just from your hammering."

She chuckled. "I don't mind the things that run, Nathan. It's the spiders the size of quarters that give me the shudders."

Evie smiled at the humorous way the woman worded it. The sight of a skull would have freaked anyone out, and a woman mostly alone in a building under construction — she'd been fully within her rights to yell. "If you could share copies of that building research with us, it would help us out considerably," Evie put in.

Lori looked toward Nathan and got a nod, looked back at Evie. "Sure. If you don't mind copies of copies, there's a folder of building research materials in the office downstairs — everything from when this building was built, its various owners, to blueprint changes and the permits issued for electrical and mechanical work. You can take it all with you. I've got a duplicate folder at The Lewis Group building."

"Perfect," Evie said.

Lori turned her attention to David, considered him for a long moment before observing, "You know who he is — the man in the wall. They called you in because you know. They wouldn't tell me his name."

"Saul Morris was a private investigator

who's been missing for six years."

Knowing what was coming, Evie kept an eye on Nathan. David had timed things well. Nathan went pale, and then anger surged into his face. He stepped away from Lori, swung toward the windows. "Well, that burns it."

"Who's Saul Morris?" Lori asked, bewildered.

"A private investigator looking into my wife's death," Nathan replied abruptly. He squeezed the bridge of his nose, shook his head. "This can't be related, Detective. Nothing he was working on for me would have had Saul this far south. Caroline was killed up in Freemont." Evie watched his anger, fascinated by the quickness of it, along with the rapid way he'd reined it in, dealing with such an astonishing fact.

"We have a sense of what he was working on, what likely brought him here, and it wasn't your wife's murder," David said.

Nathan seemed marginally relieved at that news. "Still, it's not only beyond sad to realize he's been dead, hidden here all these years, but you know better than I do that it incriminates me. I could have bought the building, hoping to permanently cover up the scene when I heard about the new missing-persons initiative. And now my newest employee rather steps in it, finds the body, and calls the cops before calling me."

Lori laughed. It sputtered out of her so that she slapped a hand over her mouth as she shook her head. "Sorry," she gasped, but still laughed around it. She caught her breath. "If you could hear and weigh what you just said. You sound rather foolish, Nathan. My boss or not, you've got an inflated way of viewing your importance. Some of the time at least, like now."

Nathan started to smile. "It's nice to know you have a healthy respect for the guy who signs your paycheck."

The tension in him had broken. Evie studied Lori, more interested now than ever in this woman who'd discovered the missing PI. When Lori glanced over, Evie offered a brief smile. *Oh, yeah. Ann's chosen well,* she thought.

David said into the pause, "Nathan, would it help to simply clear the question? Did you have anything at all to do with Saul's death?"

"No."

"Then we'll figure this out. I've seen more odd coincidences than this in a case, though you now being the owner of this building is certainly unexpected. Give me some facts. When did you start looking at doing work in Englewood?"

"Jordan Lake with Helping Hands, Inc., started mulling around the idea of a community rehab here about a year ago. I'm basically his banker on projects like this. The concept didn't gain traction for this calendar year until Governor Bliss won the election. He's hoping Helping Hands can double the number of its employees over his four-year term, and a project of this scale is one way to rapidly ramp up hiring.

"I gave the project to Lori to pull together. If building owners see me on the other side of the table, they know I've got deep pockets and can make the decision to meet their price. They see Lori across the table, she tells them she might like to agree to that higher price for the building but can't, they tend to stay more reasonable in the negotiations. I watched her acquire seventeen buildings with cash left under the cap she was working with, where I would have struggled to acquire fourteen for the same dollars. She did an incredible job."

"Thanks," Lori said softly. Then, "So I'm not fired?"

Nathan gave her an amused look. "You do too good of work to fire you, though the price of a crime scene is going to need some reconsideration. I'm still not sure how you got Tyson Fenny to sell. The property at the end of the block," he explained for their benefit. "Adult entertainment and liquor. It was critical to acquire if we were going to change the atmosphere of the neighborhood."

"What are you going to do with it?" Evie asked, curious.

Nathan shared a look with Lori. "Probably a roller rink, give kids a place to work out some aggression in a well-padded way. But a church wants a footprint in the neighborhood, and that place has got the sizable parking lot required. What goes in where — that's the next issue on Lori's plate. It's time I moved her off demolitions."

They all chuckled at the comment.

"It sounds like quite an opening project with your new job, Lori," David remarked. "You said you started working for The Lewis Group in November. Were you working for a real-estate firm prior?"

"No. The accent tends to give me away. I worked for Estate Services, Ltd., out of their Houston office for the last decade. If beneficiaries live in several different states, or you've got a complex family situation — exes and steps — you'd hire the firm as executor of your will. I'd arrange appraisals, liquidate assets, handle transfers of ownership, according to what the client had outlined. I spent a significant amount of time traveling and I was ready to settle in one place. That happened to be Chicago."

"Something I've come to appreciate more with every passing week," Nathan added.

David tucked his notebook away. "I appreciate you both staying around for this."

"We've been shifting people to work at other sites, moving deliveries of materials to later dates," Lori replied, nodding to paperwork in front of her. "I need to talk with Scott downstairs, the security guard who was with me. We've been told this will be a crime scene for at least forty-eight hours, that someone is likely to remain on-site even after we resume work."

David glanced around. "I imagine the odds are good if a body is on the second floor, there's going to be one on the first floor."

Nathan grimaced.

"Sorry about that," David said.

"Well," said Lori, "at least it will solve one question we're debating between the architect and foreman. We're definitely gutting this entire place."

Evie caught David's attention and held up her phone. "Sharon is here. Lori, if you can get the building history info from the office downstairs, I'll start on the next piece of this puzzle. You have Detective Jenkins's number?" Evie handed over business cards for herself and David.

"Yes." Lori gathered together an elegant-looking portfolio and slim leather briefcase. "I'd rather avoid that end of the building if you don't mind, so let's use the north stairs." Nathan headed that way with her.

"Let's regroup downstairs after you speak with Sharon," Evie suggested to David. "If you want to head to the lab or stay on-site while they do a preliminary search of the building, Sharon can give me a lift back to the office."

David nodded. "Give me twenty minutes. I'll get a sense of the politics unfolding and then we'll see what makes the most sense."

The press corps was settled in for the long term, most of them walking around with insulated coffee mugs, talking on cells. An enterprising assistant had rounded up some portable heaters and arranged for the brewing of gallons of fresh coffee, enough to fill several large thermoses. The anticipation of someone on the second floor discreetly capturing a photo of the skeleton in the wall would have any self-respecting reporter hanging around with a roll of hundred-dollar bills in hopes of scoring such a scoop.

Evie unwrapped a sweet-tarts roll as she scoped out the neighborhood. Plywood covering broken windows and faded *For Rent* signs told an all-too-familiar story. Manufacturing businesses disappearing, gone either to bankruptcy or relocation, had collapsed local incomes, with that impact then rippling through the restaurants, clothing shops, hair salons, drugstores, and on and on.

Six years ago, Evie mused as she looked around, *this would have been an odd place to hold a card game, with Englewood already on a downward slide.* But it likely had an organized-crime connection already entrenched, preying upon the community's desperation — payday loans, get-rich-quick schemes, liquor sales, petty crimes. In such an environment, "RB Electric" would have been a good front for what really went on here.

A good-sized building, she thought. A night of gambling, with booze and music and women, could have been hosted here when Saul came around with his camera. Saul could easily have gotten himself killed for interrupting a moneymaking enterprise. No panic, just kill him, cover it up, and go on with business.

"Standing out here in the cold?" David asked as he joined her.

"Watching interesting dynamics," Evie replied in verbal shorthand. She nodded to where Nathan was holding a passenger door open for Lori. "You missed most of it. When Nathan Lewis stepped outside with Lori, between the press hollering for a statement and his own people wanting to be recognized as the most helpful employee, there was a near stampede."

David smiled. "Sorry I missed it."

"He's not letting her drive herself back to the office. So she finally passed the keys to her car to the site foreman and suggested Nathan should buy her breakfast then, but she has to be at the office for a scheduled ten o'clock call with someone whose name I didn't catch. I think Lori protested mostly so he could have a polite fight with someone."

David laughed. "I'm going to lay odds you just told me all that just so I'd have a reason to be distracted too."

With a smile, Evie said, "We all need a little levity after such a grim morning. I know it's hard on you finding Saul this way, knowing he got zero dignity in death."

"It is."

"Let's go figure out who murdered him.

341

We can give this case the day, get the details sorted out for homicide, who'll be taking it over." Evie considered him. "But breakfast first. I'm thinking silver-dollar pancakes."

"Enough maple syrup, I'll eat twenty dollars' worth."

"How about that local version of the Pancake House over by the hotel?"

"Works for me."

She waited until they were in the car and David had maneuvered back onto the open street before she said, "Ann has someone working at The Lewis Group. I'm thinking we just met her."

David nodded. "Lori Nesbitt. I've been wondering the same thing. Did you read 'cop' in her demeanor?"

"Something more interesting. She knew where the body was."

David drove in silence for a block. "I didn't want to go there. She's a forty-something woman in an expensive suit, working for the last decade in Houston. How does she know where a private investigator gets buried six years ago in Chicago?"

"I've got a few thoughts on that." Evie figured her idea would go down better over food, when David was occupied and had to hear her out. "But we need coffee first."

David glanced her way, amused. "All

right. Then we'll shift the subject for a minute. What happened last night? If you slept, it wasn't much."

"Let's not go there either." She turned on the radio. "We'll find the local news or something."

"You're just stacking up questions for me to come back to later."

"Women like to be mysteries."

He laughed. "Point taken. We'll eat first."

"So what's your theory on Lori Nesbitt and Saul's remains?" David asked as he cut into a stack of pancakes.

Evie set down her second cup of coffee, considered how to word her speculation. "Lori buys seventeen buildings, including this one? She's the one who finds the body? She knew there was a body there. Either someone told her the body was there, or she heard a secondhand rumor that he was. She opened up that wall intentionally. It's easy enough to realistically scream, it would still have been a startling sight."

"I'll concede her reason for taking a hammer to the wall at five a.m. was unusual, but it's the odd kind of truth that often is exactly what really happened."

"David . . . work with me here. She found a body. *Whack whack* with a hammer and

343

there's a skull looking at her. Come on. You're not wondering?"

He considered the problem. "She said she worked at Estate Services in Houston, and I'm fairly sure she wasn't lying about that. Easy enough to check it out. Maybe a client says, 'Hey, want to know a secret? I'm dying, so it doesn't matter if I tell it. I buried a guy in a wall in Englewood, Illinois, six years ago.' Or maybe, 'I heard about a corpse that's hidden in a wall in Englewood.' "

"If her job connects her up with information like that, she picks up the phone and calls the cops to check it out," Evie replied.

David thought about it, nodded. "What are the odds she was in fact an attorney at that firm, not simply a staff executor of somebody's will? She handled seventeen building purchases without breaking a sweat — sounds like a full-blown attorney to me. You know Ann and the friends she tends to collect. Stands to reason Lori is more than she appears. She knows something but she can't legally tell anyone, so instead she uses the information and gives cops the body."

"She's got the demeanor and self-assurance to be a lawyer, I'll give you that," Evie agreed. "But if she's a lawyer, why underplay what she did for Estate Services with Nathan? Why not tell him she's a lawyer? There are ways around attorney-client confidentiality; she's not required to cover up a crime."

"So, you've got a dying client who tells you about a hidden body. Maybe Lori doesn't know precisely which building — the client didn't give her an address, just described the place and said it was in Englewood. She mentions the problem to Ann, and Ann says, 'Hey, I know someone who'll be working in that neighborhood and I need a favor to solve what happened to his wife. Come to Chicago and help me out. You can look at solving your mystery while you're here.' Lori goes along, seeing Ann's request as a valid reason to come to Chicago. As to Nathan, Lori didn't tell Nathan she's an attorney because he would stick her in legal affairs and Ann wanted her in a job closer to him — searching to find someone who had caused him problems and ultimately killed his wife."

"That fits. I rather like it, in fact." Evie reached for more maple syrup for her pancakes. "Now, who went from Chicago to Houston who would have information about a body concealed in a wall?" she asked idly.

David narrowed his eyes at the question.

Evie smiled. "Come on, go there too."

David picked up on her subtle point and immediately protested it. "No way was I looking at someone with knowledge of the Witness Protection Program."

"C'mon, the building fits — an old warehouse, a rough neighborhood? Card game. Gambling. Body in a wall. I'm thinking *gangsters,* organized crime. You said yourself it was likely a client who told her about the body. Somebody in Chicago who knew about that body went into WITSEC in the last six years, and got relocated to Houston. And that somebody in WITSEC told Lori about it. She used that knowledge and went *whack whack* with her hammer, gave cops the body."

David laughed at the visual whacks Evie gave the air. "Maybe. It's an interesting ball of twine you just rolled out."

She nodded and stabbed another piece of pancake. "We need to ask Lori if a client told her about the body. It stands to reason that whoever told her was either the person who killed Saul or was involved in some other way. We'll get a confession of the crime, even if secondhand."

A server came by and refilled their coffee mugs. David nodded his thanks. After the woman had moved on, he offered, "You would think if all this shakes out as you've described it, Lori would simply tell us the story. 'I heard this rumor in Houston from a client, decided to check it out since the building sort of fit the location he described. Wow. Body found. The client's name was Joe Killer. I'm sorry, but the client is dead now.' But Lori doesn't say a word, just gives us the body."

Evie grinned. "Exactly. It's a WITSEC situation. That's how she knows the truth. And why she can't tell everything she knows. Maybe the guy who told her isn't dead yet."

"I agree it's a theory worth a conversation," David replied. "Do we talk to Ann first or Lori to figure out how much of this theory might be true and how much is us whiffing at a good pitch?"

"My experience with Ann is that she tells you what she wants to say and no more, so I vote we start with Lori."

David nodded. "Lori it is. But first we do basic cop due diligence, see if Saul answers who murdered him with a photo on that camera, or a name in that notebook. We also need to check out what she told us about where she worked, when she moved here."

"You're spoiling my fun by wanting evidence."

David was still chuckling as he signaled

their server for the check. "Thanks for the mental detour, Evie — the brain-twisting what-if you just spun out, no doubt so I wouldn't brood on the fact that my poor guy was buried in a wall." He put breakfast on his credit card, handed it to the server.

"You're welcome. But I wasn't entirely filling time. I think it's a reasonably good theory. Lori knew there was a body in that wall. It's the only thing that really works."

"We shall ask her just that, and soon. For now, let's head back and see what the lab geeks might have for us. We need to dig into RB Electric. If we find out it was mob-owned, your theory gets even more interesting."

Sixteen

"There are photos on Saul's camera!" Evie slapped David on the shoulder hard enough to jar the coffee he held.

"So I just told you," David replied with a laugh. "You need some more sleep, Evie."

"It's just awfully exciting. What floor?" She stepped ahead of him onto the elevator at the crime lab.

"Adam said fourth, room 419. He'll meet us there."

Detective Ben Jenkins was coming down the hall from the other direction as they exited the elevator. They waited for him to join them and then entered the door marked *Imaging.* Evie was expecting white counters and lab equipment, beakers and sinks. Instead, it turned out to be a conference room with several wall screens and an old-style overhead projector.

The wall clock said 4:18 p.m. She was so ready to have something tangible to tackle.

She'd spent the day learning about the building where Saul's remains were discovered and the businesses that had last occupied it. Her brain was spinning with tax filings and bankruptcy court accounting documents.

RB Electric had the smell of an organized crime family business front. The owner was the uncle of a man who'd been arrested on racketeering charges, who also had done jail time for money laundering. But RB Electric itself looked legit, paid its taxes, had twenty employees, had gone bankrupt only when clients stopped buying the equipment it manufactured. That filing had been in order. If they had been using the company as a front, they were taking advantage of the truck fleet, not laundering money through the business accounts themselves. Five trucks were sold during the bankruptcy, all with lift gates and more than a hundred thousand miles on each of them. It would have been easy enough to load contraband and make an extra stop on the way to a customer, use RB Electric for the resources and building it offered, but otherwise leave it a legal business.

Evie paced the room while David and Ben compared notes on the rest of the crime-scene recovery. The skull indicated Saul had taken a hit on the back of the head, probably with a baseball bat. The ribs showed a gunshot to the chest. Breaking up all the cat-litter chunks to see if the bullet had settled somewhere in the wall tomb would take another day. It was solid, steady progress. They knew *how* and *where.* She wanted something to point to *who* and *why.* The noon newscasts had led with the recovered remains, so anyone involved now knew their handiwork had been discovered. Another real unknown was how many other bodies might be found in the building.

David had decided they would talk with Saul's sister in the morning, once the remains had been transported to the medical examiner's office. They would tell Cynthia it likely was her brother while the medical examiner worked to make it official. It would be good to have that hard conversation behind them.

The door pushed open, and an older man carrying a thin box joined them. Evie was relieved to see the lab coat — she liked science guys when it was evidence she was looking for.

"Thanks for coming so quickly, detectives," the man said. "I'm Adam Billings. I've been coordinating work on your retrieved evidence. I have good news and bad.

The bad first. The notebook in the shirt pocket is a mass of pages bonded together. I doubt we'll be able to separate them. The good news, the camera had been shooting film, and there was nearly a full roll of exposed frames in the protected well of the motor drive. What I have to show you now are the negatives we've since printed to ten-by-twelve."

He opened the box he'd set on the table and took out an inch-thick stack of photo paper. "As these are time-stamped, I'm just going to lay them on the table so you can see the chronology. The last photo is Saturday, 10:16 p.m. The first ones begin on Wednesday." Adam began to place the photos along the length of the table.

"Oh, wow. They survived really well," Evie noted, surprised. She was looking at a crowd of young people, some with arms in the air, some dancing, mostly facing the same direction. Good compositions. She could tell Saul had been a photographer for a newspaper before changing careers. Many shots came from a slightly higher vantage point than the crowd. *Probably stood on a chair,* she thought, *or maybe a bench.*

"The concert Saul attended Wednesday night," David said.

Evie nodded. "That makes sense. He must

have started with a new roll of film after he left his sister."

The concert photos went on for nearly forty shots — crowds, then a recurring face in the crowd, and finally ones that cropped in just the young man. He looked to be early twenties, had a neat haircut and wore a black T-shirt sporting some band's logo. David picked up a photo to study it closer.

"Does he look familiar to you?" Evie wondered.

"Vaguely. These are six years old. I have a feeling I've seen a more recent photo of him. Maybe a union worker at one of the concert locations? I was searching the entire list of names in the DMV records."

"We know Saul was looking into concert connections for Tammy and for Jenna. That he'd found a reason to focus on somebody at another concert makes sense."

"Tammy — *that's* where I've seen him. This guy reminds me of a boyfriend of hers from her high school days." David pulled his notebook out, started flipping pages, then stopped. "Lucas Pitch," he read with satisfaction. "Saul was tracking down Tammy's former boyfriends. I can see him doing that on his own time, case suspended or not. He would've liked to find Tammy. If this is Lucas, he was at an Arlington Heights concert six years ago. Maybe he's still in the area. I ran the name through Illinois DMV," he added, "and didn't get a current match, but we'll dig deeper."

"A good lead."

David tapped the next photos. They changed to several of an overgrown lot within a block of homes, taken from different vantage points. "This must have been what he was doing up north in Gurnee Thursday morning. The time stamp is close to when he stopped for gas. But I haven't run across anything like a land dispute."

"Maybe a favor for a friend? Or he was looking to buy the lot and build himself a home?" Evie asked.

"Could be. Yet another mystery, if it turns out to be relevant."

"Can you make out the street signs?" Evie lifted one of the photos to check. "Maybe it's Gradley with a cross street beginning with *Tri.*" She passed the photo to Ben.

"I'm thinking that's Gridley — the name of a former mayor in Gurnee," Ben said. "It shouldn't be too hard to find this lot. The house number here . . . it looks like a forty-six."

Evie focused on the mailbox number. "Forty-six," she agreed.

David had moved on to the next group of

images. "These are from Saturday afternoon — I can tell even without the time stamp. This guy is Neil Wallinsky, who lives over in River Glen." There were ten shots in all, six of a neighborhood and a particular home, four of the man, one taken without his knowledge as he walked toward a mailbox, the other three casuals with him looking into the camera.

"You have to admire Saul. He put in the hours for his clients," Evie commented.

"He enjoyed the job," David said. "Cynthia underscored that."

The next five were taken over a twenty-minute period, all of a gorgeous sunset. "Very sad," Evie said, thinking about Saul's last views alive.

"Cynthia might be relieved to have these. Her brother had seen some beauty the last night of his life," David replied, "had paused long enough to capture it."

Evie looked over at Adam. "Can you make duplicates of these five for his sister?"

"I don't see why not. They're confirmation that he was alive past this particular time of day, but otherwise, not evidentiary."

Evie nodded her thanks.

"The next time I know Saul's location," David said, "it's eight p.m. and he's talking to a source in Arlington Heights, looking for a card game he's heard is going on somewhere in Englewood. I hope you can tell me a sunset isn't the last photo I'm going to get."

"It's not." Adam spread out the final thirty photos. "My hunch, these are what you're looking to see."

It was night, the first obvious difference from the previous ones. These were taken with a long lens, meaning a cropped effect on the subjects. Lighting was dim. Evie doubted her own camera would have been able to get even a faint shadow in such conditions. Saul's skill was clearly evident — he'd manually held the exposure open on some of these images.

The photos were mostly of men exiting vehicles, the figures caught in headlights, or some on a sidewalk with a streetlight providing angle lighting. Five photos showed groups entering the RB Electric building through a side door, with light from inside shining out and showing features clearly.

"We're working on the negatives to enhance the contrast. My guess, you'll get another twenty percent clarity. And since some are of the same individuals, frames can be digitally combined to heighten more details."

"We'll need that photo enhancement and

more," David replied calmly, but Evie heard something in his tone that made her glance over sharply. David pushed one photo up from the spread. "Recognize him, Ben?"

Detective Jenkins looked closely and smiled. "I do. And isn't this interesting?"

"Who is it?" Evie asked. David had worked in Chicago for years before moving to New York. That he would recognize a major criminal player didn't surprise her.

"The organized-crime boss for the greater Chicago area, Henry Grayson, has two sons. This is the middle one, Blake. And this" — Ben tapped another photo — "is Blake's one-time bodyguard, Tony Churchill."

"So who killed Saul?" Evie wondered aloud. "The middle son? His bodyguard? One of the security people watching for problems that night?"

"We may never know," David cautioned, "but we can pop news of a recovered body, the fact photographs exist, and do some squeezing on who might know something, beginning with the bodyguard. Whatever happened that night, you can bet it had Blake's approval, before or after the fact.

"Given the number of people Saul managed to get on film during forty minutes, this wasn't a table game," David proposed. "This was a multi-table, bring-a-guest affair. Probably blackjack, roulette, and poker, hosted at an out-of-the-way business controlled by the Grayson family. RB Electric is going to tie back to the Grayson family."

"Very likely," Ben agreed.

David tapped the last three photos. "Here's the gambling husband Saul was looking for — fitting in a way. Saul was doing good work right up until the end of his life. The last pictures Saul took were of the husband, who had taken up gambling again. If this guy hadn't died in a car accident a year later, he would be the perfect interview about that night."

"Serious gamblers at this level tend to keep on gambling and eventually come to our attention," Ben put in. "We'll see about identifying the other players in these photos. Maybe someone will talk to us. There were a lot of people there that night who might be willing to speak with us.

"The fact your missing person was buried in that wall," Ben went on, "with these being the last photos he took, either he decided he could safely get closer to get a better picture of what was going on — maybe went up a back stairwell at one a.m. and got himself hit with a bat, then shot in the chest — or more likely someone spotted him, hauled him out of his car and upstairs to see what Blake wanted to do, with the same outcome."

"That fits with what we're seeing here," David agreed. He motioned to the thirty pictures. "It's good his death didn't happen in an obscure back alley. People were around, security, Blake's inner circle, others coming to gamble, waiters, setup and teardown personnel. Add employees that actually worked at RB Electric come Monday morning. You can leverage a few names you know to tell you *who else* was there and build a pretty sizable list of people to interview."

"I'm guessing we'll be officially taking this case off your hands tonight," Ben said. "News is already out about the skeleton, and there may be more than one body in that building. We need to move with some speed to find these witnesses."

"I'm fine handing over what we have," David agreed. "I can get you and a couple others briefed tonight. Let's hope a slug turns up so that ballistics can tell us about the gun involved. How do you think the Graysons handle this?"

"We put out the word we want to talk to Blake, he's likely to walk into the station with his lawyer two hours later," Ben replied. "He's smooth that way, answers your questions but never admits or says anything specific. He's also ambitious, impetuous, and not as careful as his old man. He's got a temper. He likes to get even in person for perceived slights. He likes the connections and the power his family wealth and business give him. He's been questioned in at least two other murders, but nothing has stuck thus far.

"Blake's been trying to prove to the old man he would be as good as his older brother at running the business. But rumor has it the old man isn't buying. Sounds like when Henry decides to step down, he's appointing his cousin to take over rather than pass it to Blake."

"You said two sons. What happened to the elder one?" Evie asked.

"There were actually three sons, but the youngest died in a boating accident as a kid," Ben replied. "The eldest son, Caleb, left the family about ten years back, has built quite an empire of his own, and done so within the law from what repeated investigations and audits have determined. You want to retire from organized crime, get out of the life? You go to work for Caleb. At least that's the word on the street. And if you do, you don't talk about what you know from the past — that's the implicit deal."

"So no one needs to shoot you to shut you up," David said.

Ben nodded. "It's an interesting dynamic. Caleb's a lawyer, a good one from what I hear, representing all those who work for him, who pretty much enforces that no-comment policy when cops come around. He lets us do our jobs, doesn't interfere, but doesn't particularly help either. Sort of a mediated peace — no one shoots his people, and his people don't talk about anything from their past . . . or anybody else's. He'll bend that occasionally by handing us physical evidence — a janitor just found a gun hidden in a heating duct of a building Caleb bought — that kind of help. He's big into real estate, mostly low-income neighborhoods, single-family homes, apartment buildings."

"Real estate. That's interesting."

Ben smiled. "Either someone like Caleb keeps the buildings together and in good repair or they end up needing to be rehabbed like what's happening in Englewood right now. I wouldn't be surprised if the size of Caleb's world isn't larger than his father's by now," the detective added. "The two are careful to keep the peace, staying out of each other's geography. They're still on good terms, but the brothers — to say there's tension between Caleb and Blake would be a major understatement. The eldest brother left and still gets dad's approval, while the middle son is too wild to ever get his dad's admiration, and knows it. Chicago crime's problem is liable to get even more dicey when Henry retires or dies."

David smiled. "I should have stayed in New York a few more years, as we just got done with a similar shakeout there."

"We're not looking forward to the inevitable transition," Ben said. "The hope is that the control passes on to the cousin, who can hold things together until Blake here gets himself arrested and jailed, removed from the equation. But so far we haven't put together a case that can hold up in court."

"You'll eventually build your case. Maybe this one with Saul is it — if these photos let you pry up some people to testify about what happened that night."

"We'll push hard," Ben said.

Evie found the story of the Grayson brothers fascinating. "That's rare, that someone leaves a crime family and is still alive."

"The eldest son has talent and a good business sense. He's the sort of man who, were he born into a different family, you'd think would make a good federal judge or an honest governor. There's got to be some deep-rooted ethics in him to have walked away from the money and power of his family in order to build something legal and free of that influence." Ben looked across the images spread out on the table. "David, the photos from the concert and the guy Saul was focused on, why don't you take those and see what you can find out? It might help you with that other disappearance — Tammy Preston, was it? I'll start working IDs for the people gambling that Saturday night. We'll meet up at the office where you're working in, say, three hours? I'll bring my team with me, and you can bring us up to date on the Saul Morris case."

"Sounds like a plan," David agreed, gathering up the concert photos of Lucas.

"So do we tell local cops our suspicions about Lori?" Evie asked David as they rode down in the elevator. "Someone tied to *the* organized crime family in Chicago is involved in Saul's murder? If Lori knew a body was in that wall, it's no longer a casual matter . . . or how she came to know it. And if one of her Houston clients told her about the remains, it's likely she might be able to identify that person as someone in those photos."

"We ask her ourselves first," David replied after considering the question. "If she was acting on information someone told her who's now dead, that's different from if he were still alive. We don't want to lose sight of what she's potentially doing for Ann — solving who killed Nathan's wife. The cops start looking at why she's in Chicago, how she had info about the body, then suspicions overshadow what she's doing at The Lewis Group, and whatever she has found to date there grinds to a halt."

Evie went quiet as they walked out of the building, waited until they were in the car. "We've got time to swing by The Lewis Group offices. Why don't I give Ann a call now, ask her to have Lori come down and meet us? That way we have it settled before you talk to the Englewood detectives. If we want Lori to speak with them directly, we can make arrangements for her to come talk with them tonight, maybe keep Nathan in the dark about Lori's real reason for working for him."

"All of this presupposes that Lori Nesbitt is in fact working for Ann and did know a body was there. We may be totally off, Evie."

"I don't mind looking like I stepped in

scrambled eggs."

David laughed at the image. "Call Ann. We've got time to make a stop." He put the address for The Lewis Group in the GPS and pulled out into traffic.

Evie made the call, closed her phone with satisfaction three minutes later. "Ann didn't seem surprised at the request. I'm going to take that as confirmation Lori and Ann have talked since the body was found this morning. Go around to the staff entrance on the south side of the building. Ann will have Lori meet us there."

"We don't tell Lori about the photos," David clarified.

"No. Just ask about how she knew about the body. And take it from there, depending on the answer we get."

Twenty minutes later, David pulled up to the building, and Lori appeared, opened the back door and slipped into the seat. "I'd say someone here knows Ann well. You've got questions?"

David and Evie had both turned toward Lori, and Evie began, "Thanks for coming down. You're helping out Ann in Nathan's office?" she asked.

"Yes."

"Making any progress?"

"I think so, and Ann's right. Someone has

been making trouble for Nathan from inside the firm going back at least eight years. That it escalated to killing his wife? I have some theories but not enough facts yet to put a name out there."

"I'm glad you're digging into it," Evie said.

"Who told you where to find the body?" David asked.

Lori blinked, considered him, then smiled faintly. "A guy named Philip Granger, who was a client of Estate Services, Ltd. I learned after he died that he was in WIT-SEC. His landlord called me since I was listed as his emergency contact. I was at his apartment before the US Marshals got there. Granger had left a letter alongside his will with a few details. He didn't say who the dead man was, just that he'd walled up a body in Englewood, Illinois. There wasn't an address for where, only a description of the scene.

"I gave the US Marshals the letter, waited for something to happen, even subscribed to a Chicago newspaper and watched for anything about a body discovered in Engle-wood. For whatever reason, either the US Marshals didn't pass on that letter or it was deemed too unspecific to act on by local authorities.

"Anyway, when Ann asked me to do a

favor for her regarding Nathan, and I realized I could possibly solve my curiosity about this mystery at the same time, I said yes. I figured I could narrow it down to five or six buildings in Englewood, then get cops to do a radar scan of the walls or something. When I saw this property and the permits, the building changes, I realized Philip had to be referring to a building in its prior condition. He was describing RB Electric, because the fence, the last building modification, hadn't been made yet. It fit, so I took a hammer to a wall and wow, a body, just like the letter said. I'd thought I was on a wild goose chase up until then."

"Why didn't you tell us this when we first met?"

"With Nathan hovering? He doesn't know why I'm here. The man I knew as Philip Granger is dead — I doubt that was his real name — and all I had to give you was a body. You've literally got everything I know. I figured silence worked in my favor."

"It had to be a surprise, finding out Philip was in WITSEC," David said.

"Caught me off guard," Lori said immediately. "It was a rather vanilla will, stated he had no living relatives, left his estate to the preservation of wildlife. The US Marshals went through the remainder of his things, then handed the apartment and its contents to me to process according to the will. They seemed a bit irked a letter had been included with his will with such information in it, but otherwise it wasn't such a big deal."

"How did he die?"

"The ME said natural causes — he was a steady drinker, and his body finally said enough."

"We'd like you to identify a photo of him for us, so we know the Philip Granger you were talking with, hopefully to get a real name," David requested.

"You can call the Houston medical examiner and ask for the file. His photo has to be part of it. Or check DMV records in Texas since he had a valid driver's license in that name when his will was notarized four years ago. If those draw a blank, I can look at photos or try to work with a sketch artist, but just to warn you — I'm not too good at descriptions."

"You're a lawyer, Lori?" Evie asked casually.

"No."

Evie studied her. "Why the lie to that question? The rest has been reasonably truthful, the facts, although the sequence . . . maybe not so much."

Lori faintly smiled. "I used to be a better liar. I'm not a lawyer anymore." She didn't offer anything else.

Evie blinked as it clicked who she must be talking with. "Oh . . . I thought you were mostly a legend."

Lori's smile broadened. "I'm very much real, but thanks for the compliment. I've really got nothing else useful to offer on this case. The body was it. I wish you luck with solving it from here."

"Thanks, Lori," Evie replied. "Let me know if you need any help with digging out what happened to Nathan's wife."

"I'll do that." Lori slipped out of the car and headed back inside.

David had watched in silence as the last part played out. "Clue me in, Evie."

"She'll never say it, but I think she's the WITSEC death attorney. Or was. She must have retired."

David turned to look at Lori reentering the building. "You think . . . ?" He tapped his fingers on the wheel, then nodded and carefully pulled back into the heavy traffic. "Explain what you mean so I don't say something in reply that tells you more than I want to say."

Evie smiled. "She truly is an estate at- torney, but she's also a US Marshal. Her clients were all in witness protection. She's the one who figures out how to settle their estates without compromising the program. The people in their lives from before WIT-SEC don't know where they went, their new name, and those who meet them after WIT-SEC have no idea of their former life. The wills get complicated when you're distributing money and belongings from someone who has to remain a ghost to those receiving an inheritance. I've heard rumors the position existed. But to meet someone who's held that role, that's a pretty big deal."

"Lori Nesbitt."

"It fits. Just shift what she said from being, 'Oh my, my client was in WITSEC and left me a letter, what shall I do?' to that being a normal part of her job description. It makes better sense."

David thought about it, smiled. "Theoretically, yeah, it would flow better. I've seen one of those WITSEC on-death letters," he mentioned. "About four years ago. A man died, and the letter arrived through channels to the NYPD. It was ten pages long, detailing crimes he knew about firsthand or had heard about. He'd been in WITSEC for twelve years, and it was clear he wanted to have the last say in life, was writing mostly to get even with old adversaries rather than to clear his conscience. We were able to make fifteen arrests based on the details in that one letter, even with the rather dated information."

"I've seen one in my career too. A shorter letter, about six years ago. It had information about a series of vandalisms to farms, a guy causing damage to grain silos, destroying airflow so that the feed inside them would rot. The damages ran into the millions of dollars, and there wasn't a single lead. The one who wrote the letter entered witness protection after testifying in a murder case. He wanted to get even with his cousin, who was doing the vandalisms, but had promised his mother not to rat on a relative, so he waited until he died to get even.

"I asked Ann about the letter when it arrived, and she said she'd dealt with a handful of them during her career. Apparently, to encourage those in WITSEC to be detailed in their on-death letters, there's a deal made. If the material is ever used while they're alive, they get immunity for everything in the letter. If I'm right about Lori, she would have been the one getting her clients to write those letters."

Evie looked over at David while he steered

through the lanes of traffic. "Say in this case Philip Granger was one of her clients. She wrote his will. She also talked him into writing an on-death letter. She would have read that letter in order to decide if it was worth giving him immunity to use the information while he was still alive. So his letter describes a past crime with a buried body. Maybe the body gets found by other means, and cops make a case against Philip as the murderer. Oops, we gave him immunity. So the decision in his case is to let the letter sit there alongside the will and hope the body gets found by other means.

"A few years pass. This Philip now dies in Houston. Lori hears the news. She happens to be in Chicago working for Nathan. So Lori knocks a hole in the wall and gives cops the body. She must know scores of secrets like that one. If I'm right, the on-death letter Philip Granger wrote — or whatever his real name is — will arrive in due course through whatever official path those things take. Lori simply saved us some time and used what she knew to give us the body sooner rather than let some random construction worker get the scare of his life and possibly damage the evidence."

David thought about that sequence of events. "I'll accept that Lori somehow came to know where the body was and 'found him' in order to give the skeleton to the cops in a neater fashion than some construction person might have done. The rest of it is . . . well, conjecture and speculation."

Evie shrugged. "No one would ever confirm I'm right, even if I was. The WITSEC death attorney knows an enormous number of interesting secrets. The identity of that person, even after they retired, would have to be carefully protected. It does make me wonder, though, if Lori Nesbitt is even her real name."

"Evie . . ."

She grinned. "I know. Letting it rest. I just like spinning stories of WITSEC and spies and skullduggery. It lightens an otherwise miserable day."

David laughed. "I'll concede that."

"Do we need to tell Englewood detectives anything more than what they already have in Lori's statement?"

"We'll pull a photo of Philip Granger and see if he's in one of the photos Saul took that night," David proposed. "See if we can learn his real name. Why was he in WITSEC? He must have told cops something useful in another case to get moved to Houston. The fact he's dead is going to complicate things, but maybe he had a relative who would also know something about the night Saul died. We make sure those names show up on the Englewood gamblers list. If necessary, we say a source gave us the names, but we don't have to bring Lori into it."

"That works for me," Evie said.

It was midnight when Evie walked the Englewood detectives to the door after their briefing in the Ellis offices. They would be back with a van in the morning to pick up all the boxes from the Saul Morris case.

She pushed open the suite doors and realized David had once more turned on the Triple M playlist. She found him sorting folders into a box. "That went well. They liked your whiteboard wall."

He glanced over his shoulder, smiled. "Saul's life, recorded in the names of those who knew him. I only wish something here pointed more specifically to who killed him. We know why, where, and when, mostly how. We still don't have *who.*"

"Blake Grayson. Go to the top of the list for who pulled the trigger and actually killed him, and maybe evidence one day confirms it."

David fit a lid to the box. "Given who Blake is today, they'll have their hands full trying to find someone willing to talk. But it's their problem now. In one day my case goes from being a stuck mystery to mostly resolved. It rarely happens this elegantly."

"You want me to come with you tomorrow when you talk with Cynthia?"

"I would, but grief is a complicated reality. It's probably best she not have to deal with a new face when she hears the news. I'll make sure she has a friend or neighbor to be with her before I leave. So" — he set another box on the table — "tomorrow it's back to Jenna Greenhill."

Evie could barely remember the last detail she'd been working. Multiple concert ticket purchases by loyal fans? "You could pursue Tammy Preston's high school boyfriend, Lucas. Maybe she ran off with him and got in trouble. If we can take Tammy off the list of similar crimes, this gets simpler, even if it means we lose the theory that the guy lives around Milwaukee."

"I'll take another look for Lucas," David agreed. "You look staggeringly tired, Evie."

"How come you're not? We got called out to the scene at like seven a.m. — and I'd had a short night."

"Adrenaline hasn't faded yet, I guess. It's nice having an answer to prayer be so obvious, even though it's a grim scene. And you still owe me an answer on that short night of yours."

"We'll pass on my story. But given it's Chicago in January, I should have realized any answer from heaven would have to be indoors. If I'd been sharper on the mark, I could have guessed he'd be found in a floor or a wall, and looked smart when I turned out to be right."

David laughed. "A missed opportunity. Why don't you plan to sleep in tomorrow? I'll join you at the hotel after I've talked to Cynthia. Maggie gets in tomorrow, and I've promised her an introduction to you before the charity event. Maybe we'll do that as well."

Evie had lost track of the calendar. "The mayor's event is this Friday night, forty-eight hours from now? I need to go shopping."

"You'll find something wonderful, I'm certain."

"It's not the dress; it's the inevitable high heels to accompany it. You're comfortable with Maggie's security for this?"

"Given the number of VIPs attending, Maggie will be in one of the safest locations in the city Friday night. I'll confirm again tomorrow that there will be security video for the rope line for us to review. I think odds are good the guy we're interested in comes to see her arrive. It's one reason I'm so relieved to be able to pass along Saul's case, which needs devoted attention to reach a conclusion. I need to be focused on who is using Triple M concerts."

"Maybe we'll get lucky and spot a familiar face. We should be able to ID the diehard Maggie fans by looking for those who leave the minute she disappears inside."

"We'll start there." David finished the last box and added it to the flat cart. "Come on, Evie. Let's call it a night and head back to the hotel."

She gladly went to get her coat.

Seventeen

The hotel restaurant at 10:40 a.m. on a Thursday had just two other guests in a room that could seat forty.

"It went that bad with Cynthia?" Evie asked, pushing a Diet Coke across the table as David approached.

He pulled out a chair, sighed as he sat down. "Just sad. She'd seen the news, wondered if it could be Saul. I told her the medical examiner is going to need another week to confirm ID, but based on what I'd seen at the scene, it was her brother. It helped a lot having copies of those sunset photos for her."

Evie simply nodded, imagining the difficult meeting for both of them.

He picked up a mushroom from a basket of appetizers she had ordered, then pointed to her pad of paper. "Master list? Where are you at right now?"

"Just reviewing old theories on what happened to Jenna. This vast gulf between how Candy saw Jenna and how her friends describe her has my attention. Jenna was a lot more complex than she appears."

"I remember you mentioning it at the time." David nodded to the third plate. "Ann's going to join us?"

"She's across the street buying a gift for Paul. She asked me to order her a cheeseburger and fries."

"We'll make that two then — sounds good whether this is breakfast or lunch."

"Three."

David smiled, signaled the waiter, gave the order.

"So how do you resolve who was the real Jenna?" he asked.

"Find more people who didn't like her, if that's possible. I'm not particularly hopeful, though. Even if they didn't like her at the time, they feel bad about her disappearance, and it determines how they want to describe her today. So I've decided I mostly want to talk with her sister."

David lifted an eyebrow. "I think I'll sidestep that conversation. A guy asking her to dish on her missing sister could dampen the flow of information."

Evie smiled. "Hence my asking Ann to come along."

Ann appeared as she spoke, a bag from an upscale men's shop in her hand. "Hi, David, Evie." She sat down, settling her purchases in the empty seat. "I don't know why I assume shopping for Paul is as easy as walking into a store and making a decision. Men's clothes are worse than women's. All the fabrics and colors and patterns you have to hit just right — a shirt with a subtle stripe, or is it checked, does it need a solid tie or can it contrast in pattern? It's dizzying."

They all chuckled, and David said, "I'd suggest finding an employee at the store who does know how to do it, then say, 'I need pants, shirt, tie, jacket, keep it under five hundred,' and come back later to pick it all up."

"Sounds like a better plan. But at least I know Paul doesn't have this particular shirt or tie design anywhere in his closet. So score one for originality. David, I am very curious about your day yesterday."

"A fascinating day. Saul Morris's remains are located, official confirmation to come, and Englewood detectives have an interesting murder investigation ahead of them. We've now handed the case off to them — hit in the back of the head, shot in the chest, and entombed in a wall. Connections to

Blake Grayson are strong enough they'll be looking at him to have either done the murder or approved it. Finding enough for an arrest and taking it to trial is an entirely different matter."

"Sharon asked Paul last night for anything the FBI had on Blake Grayson, so I imagine it's going to get worked from a couple of angles now," Ann mentioned.

"Good to hear," David said around a drink from his soda. "Lori Nesbitt found the remains."

Conversation paused as the waiter brought three plates to the table and refilled soft drinks.

Evie picked up her sandwich. "So, Ann, why don't you tell us about Lori Nesbitt?"

"What do you want to know?"

"Is it her real name? Is she the WITSEC death attorney? Is it true she's retired now? Why didn't you tell me you had recruited a top-shelf cop to get close to Nathan?"

Ann picked up one of her French fries. "He needs a wife. She'd make him a good one."

"On that note . . ." David said, picking up his plate, "I am abandoning this conversation to you ladies, retreating to a side table where I can call Maggie and ask what she's doing right now. She should have landed in

Chicago about forty minutes ago."

The two laughed and waved him off.

It was a comfortable lunch, sorting out the lives of people Evie knew only in passing. Ann was good at matching people up, had a track record suggesting her instincts were solid for who would click together. Lori Nesbitt and Nathan Lewis were on Ann's list of people to connect.

Evie got Ann to confirm Lori was retired, but couldn't get confirmation on it being from law enforcement. She accepted the counsel to let it go. Ann kept secrets, and would be keeping Lori's for the duration. But it was fun to wonder about the woman's true story. Given Ann's particular circle of friends, Lori could be someone who had worked for WITSEC, or she could just as likely be similar to the Grayson brother, leaving an organized-crime family behind, now in witness protection herself, rebuilding a new life in Chicago. Whatever her story, Lori was an intriguing person, of that Evie was certain. Ann didn't put someone next to Nathan she didn't trust and deeply like.

Evie used her teeth to remove a stuck glove, slipped out of her coat, glad to be back in the office.

"How'd it go with Jenna's sister?" David asked from a desk where he'd set himself up near the office windows.

"Surprisingly, Marla confirmed Candy's take on Jenna." Evie raided a bowl of pretzels before walking over. "Candy's basic charge against Jenna," she continued, "is that she came in and stole her boyfriend. Jenna's sister, in more polite words, said that was exactly what Jenna would do if the right situation presented itself. Jenna liked guys and had the 'good girl' image to dangle out there. Without it being too obvious, she caught more than her fair share."

"A predator with a nice smile," David replied, intrigued.

"Well, an opportunist at least. I'm guessing someone besides Candy didn't like Jenna getting her hooks into her boyfriend and so went after Jenna."

"Steve was out of town that weekend," David recalled. "If Jenna had someone else she was involved with, odds are decent she talked with him that Friday. Maybe the girlfriend overheard the conversation, was there to confront Jenna when she got home from the concert."

Evie nodded. "That could be the scenario." She nodded to the box of photo albums and scrapbooks Jenna had put together. "I'm going to sort through the photos Jenna decided to keep, see if I can find some casual shots suggesting one or more 'other guy.' She didn't want to lose Steve, but she wasn't ready to quit with flirting — maybe another version of catch-and-release?"

David grinned at her humor. She looked curiously at his laptop screen. "Lucas Pitch?"

"Tammy's boyfriend is now a concert promoter in Ohio. I've got an interview with him by Skype in —" he glanced at his watch — "twenty-eight minutes."

"Nice."

"If Tammy was taking off on her own that Sunday night, it makes sense she might have been in touch with her high school boyfriend, or she might have looked him up as part of her travels. He was living here in Chicago at the time, working at a music shop off Kliborne Avenue."

Evie looked to the two whiteboards, where the five possible case details were laid out as a grid. "You remove Tammy, it puts them all going to college. You remove Jenna, it's even tighter."

"The missing driver's licenses say Jenna is linked to the three whose bodies were recovered," David said. "I think she'll match there rather than be a stand-alone."

"Maybe. We need the case before Jenna. It'll be something more subtle than a disappearance, but it's back there. An assault, a B&E — something."

"Search B&Es around your college and pursue pickpocket arrests. Go back in time on this guy. Start looking for what he was doing when he was fourteen through twenty."

"I'll put my time there next," Evie agreed.

"I told Maggie we'd come by this evening about seven," David mentioned.

Evie wished she had known that when she got dressed this morning. She looked okay, but just okay.

David must have read her expression and said, "You look fine — Maggie goes casual whenever she can."

"I need to get that housewarming gift."

"You can take a rain check on that. She'll be flying back to New York Monday morning. A plant would die on her before she's in town for good."

"I'll get her something nice later then." Evie went back to her desk. "We're going to find this guy, David," she said over her shoulder. "Before you have to tell Maggie someone has been targeting women at Triple M concerts."

"We will."

He sounded less stressed than he had some days ago, which was a good sign. She'd be extra careful when in conversation with Maggie tonight.

She moved her backpack from the chair and pulled over the box of photo albums. They would get a break in this case, though probably not as dramatic as with Saul's. But something would turn up, and the answers would fall open at the right page like a book. She was ready for that moment.

Evie brought up a playlist so that they could listen to Maggie during the drive to her home. "She's got talent," Evie said. "However Maggie's managed the dynamics of her career, she's done an excellent job of deploying that talent wisely. I love both her singing and her lyrics."

"It's a gift. One she's continually thrilled by," David replied. "She loves hearing a song she's written come together as a finished piece. It's like a painter completing a portrait or a pitcher throwing a no-hitter game. That *I did this* delight when something excellent gets crafted."

"Any advice before meeting her?"

David smiled. "Be yourself. She'll like you. She's got a soft spot for cops. Especially me." They both laughed.

They were soon driving through the exclusive neighborhood of Barrington. David entered the drive, punched in the security code, and the gates opened. A silver sedan was parked in front of the garage, and he pulled in beside it. "Would you relax, Evie? She's a nice woman."

"I'm sure she is. But this is her lovely home, and she sings before tens of thousands of people —"

"It's her day job."

Evie laughed at David's comeback, forcing herself to shake off the nerves. She saw lights through the windows on the main level, artwork visible on the walls as they approached the front door.

David used his key, and music from overhead met them, not so loud as to be overpowering, but at a volume to delight as a clear voice sang along. He reset security. "We're here, Maggie," he called.

The singing stopped, and they heard footsteps skipping down the stairs. "You're early! That's great."

She launched herself at David with a confidence she would be caught, and she was swung around in a hug and hello. "I'm loving the house, David. And it's so nice to be back here!"

"Glad to hear it, Maggie." David set her back on her feet, his arm around her shoulders. "Maggie, this is Evie Blackwell. Please be nice — she's a bit nervous about meeting you."

Maggie laughed and offered a hand. Not a beautiful woman, Maggie was more comfortably pretty, with a real smile rather than simply polite. "Welcome, Evie."

"It's a pleasure, Maggie." The woman was in jeans, the hole in one knee from wear, not fashion. The shirt was equally loved, a blue cotton with a fire-station logo, faded from many washings. Evie felt overdressed and let herself relax. "I've been listening to a great deal of your music lately. You have a lovely voice, and your lyrics capture my head and my heart."

Maggie beamed her appreciation. "Thank you, Evie. It was God's surprise to my family. The rest of them can't carry a tune." The three laughed together.

Maggie turned to David, grabbed his hand. "Have you eaten? Say you haven't even if you have because I'm hoping you'll cook. You just missed the hordes, which you probably don't mind all that much. Ashley has been helping me hang the artwork, and she just went to meet Greg at the airport. The makeup and hair crews just left —

they're bringing on new Chicago-based assistants," she explained, "and needed a practice session before tomorrow's event. We've settled on blue for my gown. It's been like the decision of the decade to hear them wrestle that one through. Rehearsal is at one p.m. for sound. The band's already at the hotel and swear they're settled in nicely. With all that going on, someone forgot to mention dinner, and it's dawned on me I'm starving. It's like ten p.m. in New York. I've got two hours of energy left, and then I'm going to wilt like a lily without water."

David smiled at the rundown. "So long as you're not fussy about the menu, I'll figure something out."

She patted his chest. "Thank you. And since I know better than to ask about your workday when it's only been over for like ten minutes, I'll leave it that you look very tired. You can tell me why after we eat."

Evie caught David's glance before he answered and read its meaning easily enough. *Don't disagree with what I'm about to say.* "I'll think about that, Maggie."

"Rough week, not just long day?" Maggie asked, concern furrowing her brow.

"It's had its moments," David said. He nudged off his shoes and set them aside, seemed to make up his mind as he turned back to Maggie. "My missing PI is mostly resolved, although we may never be able to get justice. Evie is making good progress, but it's probably tied to other crimes the guy might have committed. We're both in need of an evening without work."

Maggie held his face between her hands and kissed him. "Okay. Nice attempt at not telling me the full story, David. But work doesn't normally bother you this much, even sad cases like this one."

"We'll talk about it later."

"We will." Maggie waved them toward the comfortable seating arranged around the room, and Evie made a quick decision as they sat down.

"Maggie," she said, "my missing girl was at a Triple M concert the night she disappeared. David is trying to avoid telling you that. I'd like to request to look at your albums — any photos you might have from a concert on October 17, 2007."

"The night of the car accident," Maggie realized.

"Yes. David pretty much had to tell me the history of you two once we realized the overlap. I don't mean to be the one stirring up old pain, yet I could use anything you might have from that night. My girl might be in the photos, and I might be able to

390

identify friends of hers I haven't spoken to yet."

Maggie nodded. "You'll have it — or rather, you will when it arrives on Saturday. There's a box marked concert albums. You'll need to sort through it to figure out which one has that October date. Some cover multiple years."

"I appreciate that, Maggie. I'll be careful with them," Evie reassured. Maggie had just solved another problem without having to be asked, granting access to a range of concerts albums. They might find useful pictures from other Triple M concerts. "I know David was trying to avoid dragging you into our work, plus stirring up that particular set of memories."

"It was a night that changed our lives," she said, reaching over to slide her hand into David's, "and one I now realize also changed someone else's life. What was her name, your missing girl?"

"Jenna Greenhill. Twenty-one, a college student, and she loved your music. She left her apartment sometime after returning from the concert, about eleven-thirty that Friday night — probably about the time you were arriving at the hospital and David was going into surgery," Evie suggested, deliberately misstating the time estimates. David said he hadn't been freed from the wreckage for an hour after the crash, and the ER evaluation would have added more time to that.

"It was a very long night. David went into surgery just after two a.m. The surgeon came out to see me about six o'clock, said the surgery had gone well and I could see him," Maggie said quietly.

"And that expression is why I was trying to avoid dragging this question into our evening," David put in. "You can't fully enjoy your return to Chicago," he said with a little smile, "when we've been recalling car crashes. So let's shift to more interesting subjects like dinner, or how the music is coming for the album, or Evie's boyfriend."

"Hey," Evie protested good-naturedly. Yet she wouldn't mind talking about Rob if it would help David turn Maggie's attention away from the subject she had introduced.

"She's sitting on a marriage proposal, Maggie, and hasn't figured out if she wants to say yes or no," David commented, sealing her fate.

Maggie, her attention caught, turned to Evie. "That must be a story in itself, not unlike ours," she remarked with a smile. "So what do you want to do, Evie, tell David to button up or tell me the rest of the story?"

There was more than just kindness and good humor in the question; there was sympathy and a great deal of empathy giving life to the invitation.

"I don't mind sharing the story, as it never hurts to get a woman's opinion on such matters. His name is Rob Turney," she said, her tone turning playful, "and your David looks like a great catch only because you haven't met Rob and realized you settled on your guy too early."

Maggie laughed. "David, you'll have to fuss over dinner without help. We're going to go unpack while we talk." She turned to Evie. "Come on up. I'll probably ask for advice on where to put things — an occupational hazard. I like to hear alternate opinions."

Evie followed her. "I like helping people move in. It's the one time the house is still a place of possibilities."

"Oh, that's a perfect description! I might borrow that line in a lyric. We'll be upstairs, David."

"I'll call when it's ready," he said.

Evie followed Maggie up the staircase. The room next to the master bedroom had been transformed into a dressing room. A pair of closets were being filled with custom-made stage gowns. "I'm unpacking the professional apparel in here, as it would take over the master bedroom if I let it. I'm working my way through the wardrobe boxes. If you want to continue hanging those dresses, I'll match up the shoes. The trick is to locate the ribbons sewn into the shoulders, so when you put them on the hanger, it's the ribbons holding the weight rather than the shoulder material."

"I can do that." Evie understood clothes well enough to appreciate the skill that had gone into crafting these gowns. Boxed individually, they were layered in tissue paper and grouped together within larger traveling wardrobe boxes.

She encountered a lemon-yellow silk in the first box and nearly sighed with delight at its beauty. Stage lights hitting it would make the fabric shimmer like the early sun. *The perks of a performing career are clothes at this level of design,* she thought. She carefully lifted out the dress and hung it on one of the padded hangers, slipped the ribbons into place, added it to the others in the closet.

"David said you're singing tomorrow late in the program. Will you be able to join him for the meal?" Evie asked.

"I'll be missing dinner. If I want to get through a performance, I don't dare touch anything in the hours before I'm on. It's butterfly city."

"After all these years?"

Maggie laughed. "When I started this career, I didn't know what nerves were. A performance is nothing but things that can go wrong. What if I miss the pitch on a high note, or mistime a breath and can't hold the tone, or draw a blank on the words as I begin the second verse *of a song I wrote*? I love singing, I love the crowds and the enthusiasm and people enjoying the music with me, yet still I'm terrified at being the one leading the experience. Music is to be shared, but I find the recording studio *so much* easier than live performances. It's free do-overs whenever I need them."

"Will you ever quit performing live?"

"Probably not. I need the fear — it motivates me to do my best work. The songs would be a step less true if I wasn't driven to get every bit of the music and the words right. Not perfect — I don't have the skills for that — but right."

"I think I understand."

"Tomorrow night I'll change after I sing, come join David for the dessert course. I like to have him be part of the audience at events like this. Seeing him there is a huge boost, and he can give me the straight scoop on sound, lighting, balance with the band — those kinds of things."

Maggie found the pair of shoes that perfectly matched the yellow dress, slid them on the shelf above it, said over her shoulder, "Your Rob Turney sounds like a good guy."

"You'll meet him tomorrow night at the charity dinner. And his parents."

"Ahh. A wealthy family? Or a political one?"

She must know the ticket prices. "The parents have 'politically connected' wealth. Rob is more on the earned-wealth side of things, a dealmaker who likes working in the financial world."

"You really like him, Evie. I can hear it in your voice."

"I do. My travel schedule is a problem for us. I work for the State Police when I'm not doing this task-force job. It makes it hard to build a life in Chicago when I'm rarely here."

"Being a cop is how you think of yourself?"

"It is. I enjoy solving real-life puzzles."

"You could become a private investigator, do that work for yourself."

Evie paused as she unboxed a red dress. "I've never even considered that for myself. That's a pretty big oversight. Especially considering David's been living inside a PI's world and giving me an up-close look at it."

"If you can handle not having the authority a badge brings, I imagine it's got some interesting benefits for what you do — when, how."

"It's something to think about," Evie agreed. "I'm so sorry for how it's been with you and David. You've been very gracious with him, given the limbo his decision about faith has created."

"I've decided he's my guy, for better or worse," Maggie replied, placing more shoes on the shelf. "I've stepped away from him twice, thinking it was better to accept reality and move on, only to find myself coming back. Walking away sounds like a solution until you try it and find your heart stayed behind. I loved David before he found his new faith, and that love had time to sink deep roots. The car accident and his decision following it took us on an unexpected turn, but it didn't damage the love we feel for each other."

Evie wasn't sure what to say. That answer just made it clear how deep the impasse was affecting them both.

Maggie sighed as she sank down on a nearby ottoman. "I've thought deeply about this quandary I'm in. There isn't a better life waiting for me out there, married to someone else. There isn't a greater love for me to find. I could form a different life and be content, find a different love, be fairly happy, but I would always regret what I'd let go. I don't want to start over. I want what my heart has always wanted since high school — to be David Marshal's wife. I suppose I'm pretty stubborn on some matters. But the truth is, being in limbo with David is actually the lesser pain than the alternative."

"Wow." It was the only word that fit the emotion Evie felt. She wondered if David had any idea how much Maggie really loved him.

Maggie half smiled, paused, looked around the room. "I try very hard not to seem bitter when I talk about this, or angry at the religion David chose to believe, because I know his sincerity, that he never intended to hurt me. I'm honestly not hurt inside anymore. I'm just puzzled because I can't make sense of it. David accepts that this Jesus is alive. I don't see how it can possibly be. But I know you believe like he does — he mentioned that in one of our calls when you had first started working together. I'm glad he's got a friend he can talk with."

Evie set aside the next boxed gown and sat down on an upholstered chair facing Maggie. "It will feel pretty gentle, Maggie, that moment of 'Oh, I see it now, I understand now.' It's something God, the author of faith, does for you over a period of time. His Word settles in your heart. You can't will yourself to believe, but you can read the Bible with an open mind and listen to what it says. That's your part. God is very willing to take you to that moment when you understand and accept it as truth. His promise is that those who seek Him will find Him."

Maggie nodded. "David has shown me those statements from the Bible. That is what I hope for this year — actually, what I've hoped for every year as this has evolved, this faith you two talk about so easily. But it's not so easy, Evie, not for me."

"No, it's not. It's just wonderful."

Maggie laughed. "I watch David and realize it's all that to him. He's a better man now than he was before. I can see the changes, good ones. Finding Jesus has been a good step for him. If the same thing comes true for me, I'll be glad for it. I just . . .

well, I just don't understand it yet."

"Did you decide to come back to Chicago because this is where you two have the deepest roots to your relationship?" Evie wondered.

"Partly," Maggie replied. "Life starts running by too quickly when a career takes off. It's all constant opportunities. I wanted that in the early years, to have a singing career, then to reach for what was possible with this talent." She smiled at Evie. "But I've realized the career will become my life if I let it. It never slows down — always a need for new songs, another concert, the next album, an interview — it's mostly an exciting, fulfilling life that has no natural boundaries or checks on itself. I've decided I want to impose a few, to dictate the pace of my life, at least give it a try. That's easier to do when you live away from New York. Chicago is busy, but it's not that almost frenetic grasping for more. I want to spend some time with Charlotte and Bryce, asking more questions about faith, have hours with David less hectic than New York."

"I'm glad for you both."

Maggie's phone chimed, and she looked at the message. "David says dinner is served. Let's go see what miracle he's managed to work."

David had put together an easy meal of chicken and fried rice, alongside slices of fresh tomato sprinkled with parmesan and balsamic. Evie listened to the two of them sync their lives back together as she ate the tasty meal. They talked about the house, what of Maggie's was shifting from New York to Chicago and when, logistics for the next day's charity event, some things going on with mutual friends. Evie was enjoying this glimpse into their lives.

"I'm sorry, Evie," Maggie interrupted herself. "It's like listening to shared to-do lists. Not particularly interesting conversation for our guest."

Evie smiled, shrugged. "I'm enjoying the meal, I didn't realize David was such a good chef. Getting your world transitioned halfway across the country is a major undertaking. It's not only you, but the band, your staff, the business partnerships."

"Most, thankfully, aren't doing this move," Maggie responded. "Planes are constantly flying from here to New York, and the internet is even faster. We'll figure out how to make things happen here as well as there. It's just going to take a lot more planning." Maggie gestured with her fork. "I speak from experience, Evie — relationships can handle a significant amount of travel and still stay bound together. But it's meals like this, time spent actually together that the phone and texting can't replicate. I love the work I do, but if it costs me too many evenings with David, it's asking too much."

Evie understood where Maggie was coming from, thinking of the recent meal with Rob. "Then I wish you both many more evenings like this one, and I'm glad the two of you are returning to Chicago. I've really enjoyed working with David."

"He's like you, Evie, he loves solving real-life mysteries. He likes being a cop."

"A fact I'm grateful for. His input's been invaluable on my case."

"You two are getting awfully close to shoptalk," David cautioned, picking up his plate. "I found ice cream for dessert. Sundae or milk shake? What's it to be?"

He ended up fixing three milk shakes. "So what's the biggest, heaviest item I can deal with, Maggie?" he asked as they finished the shakes.

"Greg promised to put the music room equipment together, get it all connected and working properly. You want to tackle setting up the planters and lights for my herb garden? I'm thinking that south wall in the mudroom gets decent sunlight and would be a perfect place for it. It's also close to the kitchen."

"I can handle that," David said.

"The boxes are in the garage," Maggie told him. "Meanwhile, Evie and I are going to go finish unboxing and hanging the gowns."

Their evening wrapped up an hour later when David caught Maggie's yawn. "You're starting to fade," he teased, rubbing her back. He'd joined them upstairs when he finished his task and had started unpacking her books. "Those on East Coast time need to call it a day."

Maggie walked with them to the front door. "Thank you for coming with David, Evie," she said with a hug. "I'll see you tomorrow night."

"It was nice meeting you, Maggie." Evie stepped out to the car to give the two a few minutes for a private good-night. She envied them the ease and comfort they had with each other.

David slid into the driver's seat, started the car.

"You have a very nice girlfriend."

"Thanks," David said. "I'll get a chance to meet Rob tomorrow?"

"And his parents."

"Don't fret too much on that score, Evie. They'll eventually warm to you." He smiled.

"I find you're hard to resist."

"Let's hope that's not just optimism. Maggie, now — in spite of the commotion from her move — seems ready for tomorrow night."

"The songs she's been asked to sing are longtime favorites, so it's less stressful than working in new material. But she's very aware the mayor is hosting this, and the room will be filled with society types. She'll be glad when her part is over."

"Rob's going to want to introduce me to several of those people."

He grinned. "I imagine you'll survive the evening too, Evie."

He drove them back to the office park and pulled in beside her car. "If you're going inside to work, I'll come in with you."

Evie considered that, reached for a quarter in the change dish. It was just after nine p.m. so either would work for her. "You call it, we work another hour, otherwise it's the hotel."

He nodded. She flipped the quarter and he called "Heads" as it dropped to the floor. He turned on the overhead light so they could see it. "Heads."

Evie scooped up the quarter, put it back, and pushed open her door. "I don't mind working at night. I find my ideas are more . . . free form."

"And I'm willing to put in the hours, because it's the only way this thing gets finished. With a case like this one, you push until it's figured out."

"How very true, David."

He locked the car, and they headed inside.

EIGHTEEN

Evie had been looking through Jenna's albums and scrapbooks earlier, particularly at the photos of guys. The materials were still spread across the desk, and she turned her attention to the girls. She'd interviewed most of Jenna's girlfriends — all those from the group at the concert that night, several more from shared classes. But there were always one or two more who might know something, those on the periphery of her inner circle. Even interviewing the boyfriends of those in that outer circle might lead somewhere useful.

One photo struck her as particularly interesting — Jenna with two of her friends, singing together on a karaoke stage. A jacket matching best friend Robin's dress was draped over a chair on the left side of the photo. Two girls were sitting at the round table, one Evie recognized as the girl living in the apartment across the hall from Jenna.

The other girl wasn't happy, that was clear. In a room of smiling and laughing people, this girl obviously wasn't in a good mood.

Evie searched through the pages, found the girl in one other group photographed on another night of music. Guitars rested on stands on a low stage beyond the group's table. There were no names written on the back of either photo, but she knew someone who might know her.

Evie looked up the place where Candy Trefford worked as a hostess three nights a week. It was getting late — a good time to chase down the woman. "David, I'm running out to get an answer from someone I spoke with before. She works nights. Anything you want me to bring back?"

She looked around when she didn't get a reply, saw his concentration on a photo, holding up a hand to request a minute. "Sorry," he said eventually. "Yeah. I'm good. The FBI lab people taking another look at the three smothered girls think they have a partial print — a composite from three marginal partials lifted at the three scenes. It's this." He pointed to the photo on his screen. "I see what they're doing, the science behind it, but it's going to be a challenge to get a judge to accept it."

"Did they get a database match?" she

asked, coming around to look at the screen with him.

"They just started running it. This thin of a partial is just going to create another list of names."

Evie's chuckle turned into a laugh. "David, that should be stenciled on a wall around here," she said, shoulders shaking. "We're the master list creators — music majors, drunk drivers, pickpockets, guys with criminal records living within four blocks of Jenna, loyal fans of Triple M, friends and enemies of Jenna." She finally quit laughing, added, "And that's before we add all the details of the other four possibly related cases."

"I admit, I can't help but be amazed at our tenacity," David agreed, matching her humor. "We're going to pin this guy down somehow, someway. It's inevitable now."

"I am off to get a name to go with this photo," Evie said, holding it up, "and should be back within half an hour."

"Watch for idiot drivers on the ice out there — nighttime brings out the drunks."

"Such fond memories you bring back from when I worked patrol," Evie joked, then headed out.

At ten p.m., the Ocean Wave Restaurant's

incoming guests were down to a handful. Candy stood at the reservation desk talking with a server. She stiffened when she saw Evie. "I'm working tonight."

"You can spare five minutes." She nodded to the privacy of an empty area by the drink station. Candy's reluctance was evident in every step.

"I'm not here to ask about Jenna." Evie held out the photo and tapped the girl sitting at the table. "Tell me about this girl."

Candy glanced at the photo. "Wannabe Maggie?"

Evie felt the shock all the way to her toes. "Yes, that one. What's her real name? Then tell me everything else you know about her, please."

Candy cast a suspicious glance at Evie. "Am I getting her in trouble?"

"I don't even know her name, so probably not, unless she's done something seriously bad she shouldn't have. Help me out here, Candy."

"Lynne Benoit. Music major, good voice, wanted a career as a singer. Devoted Triple M fan. A little weird. Over-the-top ticked off when someone messed up a song and didn't sing the lyrics as originally written. I've seen that scowl on her face so often I don't even need to guess the problem. Jenna and her pals were improvising lyrics again."

"Lynne ever get that break as a singer?"

"Not that I've heard. She worked backstage at the Fifth Street Music Hall during her college years, for all I know still does, trying to snag a manager or connect with a band, another performer. It wasn't much of a job. She was the dressing room staffer — basically a gofer — bringing in food and drinks, finding misplaced curling irons and shoe boxes, whatever performers and their staff needed. But to listen to her, that job was the highlight of her life. She plastered autographs and photos of everyone who played at the Music Hall on her walls. Maggie was everything she wanted to be one day — great lyrics, the band, the singing career. She was trying to copy her style. Lynne was probably Maggie's most devoted fan."

"You said she was weird?"

"She wasn't good at reading social cues. Didn't get that Jenna saw her as the misfit, was simply playing fairy godmother by letting her be around the group who had it all together. Even I felt sorry for Lynne when I saw how they were using her just to show how nice they were. Jenna always had the do-gooder image going, but it was so she'd be noticed. It wasn't real."

"Jenna gossiped about Lynne, laughed at her behind her back?"

Candy shook her head. "More subtle than that. Lynne made Jenna look good — 'See how accepting I am of this out-of-place one?' But she didn't like Lynne, wasn't a true friend. She didn't want her to succeed and become someone. Just let her flounder and didn't clue her in, didn't help her." Candy looked away a moment, then back to say, "Put a good boyfriend with Lynne, some guy who's kind, someone who 'gets' her, he could have steered her to a successful career. Lynne had a strong voice and the desire to make it in the music business — if someone had bothered to help her, to coach her. But Jenna wasn't into helping anyone but herself. I wasn't into music, so Lynne's help couldn't come from me. I felt sorry for her, but she didn't realize what was going on and, far as I know, never did realize it."

"For somebody who comes off a bit snarky about life, Candy, you see and sum up people pretty well. What happened with Lynne after Jenna disappeared?"

"Don't know." She lifted her palms. "Jenna disappeared, Lynne wasn't around anymore. After a while, I mean, she just wasn't doing anything with Jenna's friends. She was part of the search, handing out flyers, was over-

411

the-top distraught that the police couldn't find Jenna. She got kind of spooky for a while. I remember Lynne wanted to do a memorial event with songs she'd written in Jenna's honor, and she got locked on what might have happened, where they should search next. She wasn't picking up on the fact that people didn't want to talk about Jenna anymore, but were moving on. After a while, Lynne just drifted away into her own world again."

Evie pocketed the photo. "Thanks."

"That's it?"

"Yes. I have no idea if Lynne was involved in what happened to Jenna or not. From your description, probably not. But I'll look hard enough to eliminate the possibility. You know that solving what happened to Jenna matters, and cops aren't going to leave the case alone until it's figured out. So if you have another name you want me to consider, Candy, I'll be glad to hear it." She waited a beat.

"Kayla Quim," Candy grudgingly offered. "Her boyfriend worked for a music company repairing and restoring guitars. Jenna was making a play for the guy. Kayla would have taken that very personally."

"Jenna sure was getting around for being known as Steve's girlfriend."

"She liked being the benevolent queen bee in the background pulling people's strings. I know you don't see her that way, but I'm right about this. While Steve was her latest catch, she was quickly looking elsewhere when he wasn't around. I think what happened to Jenna was the result of her stepping onto the turf of a jealous type, and paying for it. I'm the jealous type and I can see that happening. It wasn't me, my alibi always did hold, but there are more women like me out there, the kind cops like to suspect. And Jenna had a knack for making a person furious."

Evie felt something click with Candy's words.

"Thanks, Candy." Evie pocketed her notebook and offered a twenty. "For your time. I'd buy a meal and leave a tip, but then I'd have to spend hours at the gym working off the calories."

Candy chuckled. "Been there. It's been a slow night, so thanks."

Evie said goodbye, headed out, replaying the conversation in her head, feeling again that jolt when Candy mentioned, *"Wannabe Maggie?"* The only question at the moment was how hard they could push on this tonight versus waiting until morning.

Evie started the car, got the heater going,

and checked the time before making the call. "Ann, sorry about the late hour, but do you remember talking with a Lynne Benoit at the Fifth Street Music Hall?"

Her friend thought for a moment. "Check my notes. She's the one who fingered the groups who had been banned because they did drugs in the dressing room."

"Did she say anything specific about Jenna?"

"She remembered the search for a missing college girl but couldn't recall the name — that kind of comment."

"She knew Jenna. There are photos of them together."

"She did *not* tell me that," Ann replied, her voice lifting. "We need to have another talk with Lynne."

"I'm going to drive by the Music Hall, see if there's a concert playing tonight. If so, I hope to catch her at the end of a work shift. Want to join me?"

"Count me in."

"I'll call you back if it looks promising. If not tonight, we'll track down her home address for a conversation first thing in the morning."

Evie said goodbye and drove to the Music Hall. She called David as she drove, setting up her phone for a hands-free conversation.

"Hey, Evie."

"I've got a name for you. Lynne Benoit. Candy looked at the photo and said 'Wannabe Maggie?' when I asked if she knew the girl."

"Oh, boy."

"Yeah. She's still living in this area."

"I'm pulling up DMV now. The name doesn't click as one of Maggie's problem fans."

"Lynne works backstage at the Fifth Street Music Hall. Think back to the concert the night of your accident, being backstage with Maggie. Lynne would have been an overeager staffer, ready to get anything Maggie might need, was probably working the dressing room area."

"That describes a lot of people. But cross it with a devoted fan and that contact could have sparked an obsession," David said. "Hold on here . . . okay, DMV shows six matches for the name."

"She was in college with Jenna, so you're looking for late twenties."

"It's going to help to see that photo you have of her from nine years ago. None of these images are ringing a bell. Wait . . . okay, here — I think the one you're looking at is a Lynne T. Benoit. The age fits, and she's still in Ellis. She lives at 37 Garver Road."

Evie felt a surge of adrenaline. "I recognize the street. That's about midway between Brighton College and the Fifth Street Music Hall. Single-family homes are along that stretch. Ann and I walked the cross street to it."

"I'm checking property records now. I get a Nancy and Kevin Benoit, property purchased in 1982, probably her parents. Lynne would have grown up in that house. Goes to the nearby college, lives at home, works at the Music Hall. Let me guess, music major?"

"Another yes. That night was huge in Lynne's life. Getting to meet her idol, a photo with Maggie, an autograph, to speak with her in person, help her get ready to perform — Lynne would have been layers above cloud nine by the end of that evening. She leaves the Fifth Street Music Hall after that experience, she's not going to want to go home to her parents, be alone in her room. No, she's going to want to share every detail with friends. Who better with than a girlfriend who was at the concert?"

"Jenna."

Evie nodded as she drove. "I don't know much about Lynne yet, but put Jenna and

Lynne together, something gets said wrong about Maggie, or Jenna steps on Lynne's dream to make it as a singer one day — according to Candy, she had talent — maybe Lynne lashes out at Jenna and that ends this mystery."

"Where are you now?"

"On my way to the Music Hall to see if a concert's on tonight, catch Lynne at work. Ann said Lynne was vague on the search for a missing college girl, but I've got photographs of Lynne with Jenna and her friends. Lynne is conveniently erasing Jenna from her memory, something you might do if you had a hand in her death."

"Call me if there's a concert and I'll come meet you. Otherwise I'll start digging up more data."

"Will do. I'll know in about fifteen minutes."

Lynne Benoit . . . Maybe Jenna had disappeared because of a *her.*

The Fifth Street Music Hall was lit up, but there weren't the cars and crowds to indicate a concert. Evie debated finding the night manager, getting a read on Lynne, a copy of her employment records, but reined in the impatience. Odds were high Lynne would be working tomorrow night. The marquee announced the band *Priceless* was being promoted for Friday and Saturday nights, with *The Chili Peppers* once again warming up the crowd.

Evie called David, then Ann, letting them know a conversation with Lynne would happen in the morning. She then drove south to Garver Road and slowed enough to snap photos of house number 37 as she passed. A well-maintained, single-family two-story home, bushes lining a narrow driveway, a detached garage behind the house, probably three bedrooms, built in the 1950s. There was an older model blue Civic parked in the driveway with both a college bumper sticker and a Music Hall sticker. The plate read LYN 3356.

Evie relaxed. Tomorrow morning there would be a conversation with an actual person of interest. Lynne had downplayed the fact she had known Jenna. The rest was speculation. But it was David's approach of looking for who lied to you. Lynne had made herself a person of interest.

Returning to the office complex, Evie parked and took her time walking across the slippery parking lot so she didn't land flat on her back. She did, however, put on a burst of speed down the hallway, took two deep breaths, and swung open the door.

"Tell me she still looks good."

David laughed. "Catch your breath, Evie." He swung back to the screen. "Lynne Benoit looks incredibly interesting." He stood and gestured to the whiteboard and the new data he was building. "Her social media is a treasure trove of Maggie trivia. She actually acquired a photo of Maggie and me having dinner last month at Revere's Pizza in New York. I didn't even know it was out there, and I keep pretty good track of things like that. Lynne's in Maggie's fan database, no surprise there. She's flagged for having repeatedly sent song lyrics via email, so there's a file kept on her. But nothing in that correspondence has crossed the line to suggest a security concern, so no separate security flag.

"Up in the right-hand corner is a printout of her email dated the day after the concert in question where she met Maggie. Wow, did it ever register as *the* event in her life. Obsession, here it begins. There are 672 emails in her folder now, a big number but by no means a lot. There are some fans who email daily. Still, it's up there. Once it touches a thousand, someone would routinely run a background check, and I would have heard this name. Lynne has bought tickets from the band's website for Illinois and Wisconsin concerts — but not the one Tammy attended in Wisconsin — as well as bought every kind of band memorabilia: T-shirts, posters, coffee mugs, key chains. She's got a bunch of Triple M stuff."

David reached over to the printer now spitting out additional pages, scanned them quickly. "Moving on, she owns a Honda Civic, has since 2006, so was likely driving it during her college days. One ticket in the last year for speeding, doing thirty-four in a thirty-mile zone — some cop must have gotten up on the wrong side of the bed that day.

"Graduated from Brighton College," he said, reading from the papers. "Looks like it took her six years, suggesting some part-time enrollment since I have her on the dean's list for three semesters. She appears in the college alumni newsletters four times — twice for musicals she performed in, twice for stage performances where she sang, all local events. She's an only child, no birth records for siblings, no adoptions on file for her parents. No criminal history. She's apparently single, no marriage or divorce on file in this state."

He flipped further through the printer pages. "Employment is with the Fifth Street Music Hall for the last eleven years, with several breaks lasting a few months, and one with a stretch of eight months." He held up the pages. "I woke the Music Hall owner, didn't tell him who I need info on, just asked if he was going to make me get a warrant. He made a call, told their accountant downtown to send me whatever paycheck records I wanted to see." He thumbed through them again. "These are all the paychecks issued for her social security number. I don't have it down to days and hours worked, but we can see gaps when she wasn't getting paid."

"Nice. You've been busy," Evie said.

"Give me a name and there's all kinds of information available. I'm just getting started if you want to wake a few more people up tonight. The college strikes me as a good place to look further."

"Let's talk it through. I took a few photos of the house." Evie handed David her phone, walked over to the aerial map and attached a Post-it note with the address on it, studied the neighborhood around it. "If she's still living with her parents, she's probably got decent spending money. She could travel to enjoy the music she likes. We can see if the credit card she was using at the band website shows her traveling out of state."

"The FBI is busy chewing through historical credit-card numbers along the travel routes, and we can ask them to search out her card number in that data set," David agreed. "Nothing in Lynne's social media suggests she's traveled outside of, say, a hundred miles, even on vacation. No posted photos of the ocean, New York in the summer, 'Here's me skiing in Colorado' kind of shots.

"I don't think she's attended a recent Maggie concert, at least not since Maggie moved to New York," he noted. "And it surprisingly doesn't look like she was at the St. Louis concert last year. There's nothing in her email correspondence that raves about seeing Maggie in person and how great the concert was. A devoted fan is going to splash that in big, bold terms. This obsession isn't fading, but it's not getting Lynne on the road. She might be tied to here because of family — a parent in ill health or the like. But I don't think from what I've seen that we're looking at someone who ever did the concert loop into Indiana and Ohio and left behind three smothered victims. Her emails didn't change tone during those years, and they should have."

"Okay. That's useful to know." Evie studied the information on the board. "So this is the life of an infatuated fan."

"Pretty much," David confirmed, "but one we haven't considered to be of particular concern, and nowhere near our most-dangerous list. The next circle over from obsessed is groupies, those who do have the freedom, with time and money to travel to every show. They're not always as passion-ate between shows, but will know the music just as deeply. Lynne's not a groupie, even though she appears to be an *all*-things-Maggie trivia buff, or a stalker, not even an overly obsessed fan — those want to marry Maggie or ask if they can have her trash. The requests get a bit strange."

Evie smiled. "The things I'm learning about the music world astonish me. So Lynne's an obsessed fan, but a normal one."

"Basically."

"Does her social media show a current boyfriend? Links to other bands?"

"There's no boyfriend she's highlighting in current pictures or mentions spending time with. She steadily puts up posts about bands appearing at the Music Hall, but she's loyal to Triple M and Maggie. Other music is 'good' or 'I liked this' or 'this singer is promising.' But it's not the gushing you get about Maggie, what Lynne thinks of her newest songs."

"How early do you think we can talk with Lynne?" Evie asked.

David weighed the question. "She's accustomed to working nights, so I doubt she's an early riser. The Music Hall opens its doors at five p.m., staff probably start work around three p.m. for sound checks, four for concession prep. If she's working the dressing room, let's split the difference — she works an eight-hour shift, three-thirty to eleven-thirty p.m., with a half-hour dinner break. That matches up with the recent paychecks.

"We can sit on her house early, probably see her parents get the newspaper, leave for work, and wait for Lynne to appear. Or we can deliberately ring the doorbell to wake her up once we think she's alone, catch her off-balance. Low-key would be to stop by the house at noon, one p.m., figuring she's either up by then or getting up. 'We have a few more questions about the Music Hall. We would have called, but we were in the area and thought we'd see if you're home.' Or we can deliberately approach her at work, then it's routine. 'We're making sure we didn't miss anyone last time, and oh, did you say when you spoke to Ann that you were friends with Jenna?' "

Evie could see advantages to all three options. "At the house is the most promising, though I think it's better to have her parents out of the picture when we make the approach. Lynne sees you, she's going to enter orbit — Maggie's boyfriend is *here* at *my house* talking to *me.* We can use that if it makes sense to do so or keep you in reserve."

"Use it. She's going to get an adrenaline spike, and if I'm the one asking the questions, she's going to find it very difficult to lie or be that careful in choosing her words. With something to hide, the most revealing moment is when they're talking without a lot of time to think."

"I'd be feeling guilty with you taking the lead, knowing how she'll react, if I didn't need that utter honesty from her on every fact she has about the night Jenna went missing. But I'm rather relieved to know we'll get the truth in one conversation. We can figure out if we should be looking at Lynne or clear her of any involvement."

David studied the whiteboard. "Lynne's local, has lived in that neighborhood all her life. She would know where to hide a body so it doesn't get found. She's got a personality that can lock on to things and make them bigger than what they really are. She gets asked by a cop about the college student who disappeared and *doesn't re-member they were friends?*" He shook his head. "She over-anticipated how to handle the question because she has something to hide. She could have had a falling-out with Jenna that night, lashed out, and her friend is dead. You may have found your answer to Jenna, but unless we can confirm Lynne is making road trips that aren't obvious from this first look, it probably doesn't answer the three smothered victims. But let's go see Lynne."

Evie nodded. "Let's try for casual, noon or one p.m. at her house, before she goes to work. We were in the area, a question came up about the Music Hall, you work in the dressing room area, likely know the answer, can you help us out? If she hasn't already recognized you, then it's, 'Oh, by the way, this is Maggie's David. We heard you're a fan of the band Triple M —"

David lifted both hands, palms out, to stop her as he laughed. "I think I can do it a great deal smoother than that, but yeah, that's probably the best way to play it. We approach it low-key and then take the conversation in the direction we want. If I can get a look at her scrapbook, her Maggie wall — she'll have one or both — I'll do so and see if I can spot anything far enough back to be useful around these five concert dates. If she attended one of those other concerts, there's going to be a ticket stub, a photo at the concert, something. I've been to enough Maggie concerts that I can recognize stages, outfits, band members, and pretty much date a photo to a specific show."

"Great. It's good, the fact you think like a cop."

"I am one."

Evie blinked, realized what she'd said, and laughed. "Sorry. I occasionally get you stuck with your 'Maggie's boyfriend' hat on, and it covers up the one that says 'super cop.' "

"Nice save."

She grinned. "Yeah. It does mess me up at times, realizing who you are. By the way, what *do* Maggie's friends think about her being engaged to someone who's a long ways away from the music business?"

"They're puzzled — probably much the same as yours are since you're considering life with a finance guy of some acclaim."

"True enough." Evie forced herself back on topic. "Okay. You'll get Lynne going on her life story, showing you ticket stubs and photos of Maggie, I'll take copious notes to back up the recording on my phone. We don't walk out until we're convinced Lynne is either our person of interest for at least Jenna or she's ruled out."

David grinned at the way she said it. "Okay." He considered her. "You wearing down from your own adrenaline yet?"

"Sort of. At the margins. Sitting on my hands until noon tomorrow is going to have me climbing the walls."

"You need to crash the rest of the night. We both sleep in, then we go back to a few of Jenna's friends, ask a bunch of questions we don't care about, then casually bring up Lynne and see what they say. We'll pursue what her credit-card number tells us, look at Jenna's albums to see if there are any other girls like Lynne who might have been overlooked. Or else you can just hit the gym for a couple-hour workout before lunch."

"What I really want is to have the case solved before the charity event tomorrow night."

David visibly jolted. "A fact that just turned on a lightbulb. Lynne's not going to be at the theater tomorrow night, Evie. Maggie's in Chicago, Lynne's going to be there. She's probably already arranged time off so she can get a good position on the rope line. Or get inside." He slid around the desk, spun in his chair, shifted the keyboard over. "Okay, the guest list tomorrow night . . ."

Evie watched over his shoulder as he accessed the security list.

"Good," he said as he scrolled down. "Lynne doesn't have a ticket to the event — not a surprise given the steep price. Let me confirm she's not registered at the hotel, hoping to get a closer vantage point from inside the building." He picked up the phone, made a call, got hotel security on the line. He asked a series of questions and waited. He shook his head.

"So not a hotel guest either," Evie said.

David hung up. "No. Not under her name, or booked with any credit card that has her mailing address. So, a reasonably confident no. I'll make sure hotel security and Maggie's security have current photos of her, know she's likely to be present.

"I'll adjust Friday night based on whether Lynne is where I expect her to be. Visible at the rope line and screaming her excitement, waving like mad, that's fine, expected and good news. Lynne not being there to see Maggie — it's not that she decided not to come; it's that she's found a way to get in even closer. Lynne's been in dressing rooms for music groups for eleven years, would have collected names of hair and makeup people, publicity types, managers, not to mention musicians and singers. At least a few names in her world have gotten to where they could attend an event like this or open that possibility for Lynne."

"And now *your* tension level is up," Evie said, having seen the shift in David from casual planning to stopping potential trouble for Maggie.

He shook his head. "There are several hundred names on Maggie's security list that raise my tension level just like Lynne, some of whom I *know* are trying to figure out how to get as close as possible to Maggie tomorrow night. It's why we screen her limo's chauffeur, why we have photo ID badges for those backstage. I do feel it deeply when I'm working security for Maggie, which is one of the reasons I've chosen to remain in law enforcement, not do this full time for her. Other people I trust are feeling a similar tension and covering the bases for her. Not just the event tomorrow night, but security for her home, keeping watch on her parents."

"Tell you what," Evie said. "If it's anywhere near doable, why don't we aim to solve this tomorrow, or at least by Monday? Because if it's not Lynne, you've already convinced me that whoever is picking out women at Triple M concerts is going to be at that rope line to see Maggie at her first event back in Chicago. We'll be able to move this case tomorrow one way or another."

David nodded. "I put it at seventy percent that our answer shows up at the rope line. So at least we can go from lots of names to lots of photos."

"Ooh, how true, and that hurts. But it's our reality." She looked once more at the board, then reached for her coat. "Let's go back to the hotel, David. This is tomorrow's problem."

"By the way, did you find something to wear for tomorrow night?"

"I did. Still looking for shoes, though. I'll have to fit that in tomorrow morning."

"Maggie likes me in black tie. She says I look dashing." He pulled on his coat.

"I can imagine you do. Rob, he manages to do it without trying. Just picks a suit out of his closet and fits the part."

The crisp breeze outside felt refreshing. Evie turned her face up. "Nice — in very small doses."

David chuckled. "So we'll dive into it back here in the morning, Evie, but not so early we need a pot of coffee to wake up."

"No earlier than nine a.m. Deal?"

He nodded and turned toward his car.

It would be hard to sleep past seven a.m.,

but she'd do her best. "I'll update Ann tonight," she called over to David, "and pray the state doesn't call and step on me."

"If you do get called, I'm waiting on you for the Lynne interview. You made a good find."

"It does feel like that." Evie unlocked her car and lifted a hand. "Thanks, David. Good night."

"Night, Evie."

It really felt like she had a probable answer. Sometimes great pitches still fouled off or became less than the home run she was after. *But it will come. If not tomorrow, in the next few days,* she told herself as she drove to the hotel. *Lynne Benoit . . .* It was rare the first name that surfaced was the right one, but female, local, Jenna's friend of sorts — it was all clicking in the ways a murder often happened. Just add the discovery of a well-hid body, and Evie had the Jenna Greenhill case resolved.

She could let the FBI figure out the three other victims in Indiana and Ohio, give Milwaukee PD some new ideas on Tammy's disappearance. As the outcome for her first task-force assignment, she could live with that. Actually, it was her second assignment if she counted the practice run in Carin County. But solving the case was what mattered, getting answers for Jenna. She was tired but hopeful, and that was a good way to end the workday.

NINETEEN

Evie clicked her seat belt into place. "That filled up an interesting hour. Thanks." They had been running down leads on both Saul and Jenna, filling in the hours until they could go interview Lynne. Talking to one of the gamblers identified in Saul's last photos had been a useful interview.

"A fascinating man," David said, "one whose gambling addiction has been dominating his life for twenty years. The names he provided will be helpful." He glanced at the time, started the car. "Let's go find your shoes for tonight — by then it will be time to drive over and see our Lynne."

"That's very much a *yes,*" she replied.

David nodded, backed out into the street. Evie found the name of a nearby mall, keyed in directions, then went online for shoe stores closest to which entrance. "I assume you're coming in while I shop?"

"If they've got a bookstore, that's where

I'll be. Find me when you're done."

She smiled. "I can do that."

Evie had known David had done it on purpose — the break at the mall and something else to think about before Lynne's big interview. It had helped. She followed him up to the Benoit home, let him ring the doorbell just minutes after noon. She hoped what followed would go as well as their timing.

The woman who came to the door was Lynne's mother, and her DMV photo hadn't done her justice. She looked younger than her years. "May I help you?"

David already had his badge and credentials out, showed them casually as he smiled. "Mrs. Benoit — Nancy, if you don't mind — I'm David Marshal, and this is my partner, Evie Blackwell. We're working on an old case of a missing college student, Jenna Greenhill. We're in the area for interviews this afternoon, and we had a question come up regarding the Music Hall that Lynne might be able to quickly answer. Would she happen to be home?"

"Of course. Please, come in out of the cold. It's never going to thaw, the way the weather is this year." She turned to the stairs and called, "Lynne, would you come down

435

please? We have guests."

Nancy motioned them toward the front room where a fire cheerfully blazed. She had apparently been watching a *Jeopardy!* episode she'd recorded, as it was now on pause. She studied David with interest. "You're Maggie's boyfriend, aren't you? I'm not so behind on the times I didn't hear you were in town — that skeleton they found, your name in the news. Lynne will be overjoyed. You're helping out with Jenna now, are you? It's sad, what happened with her, just so very sad."

"Yes, it is, Mrs. Benoit. You remember the case?"

"No one talked of much else for several months. It was the lack of any clues that was so puzzling. When you live in a neighborhood for thirty years, crimes like that leave a large hole in your sense of safety. Thankfully, it's been the only crime of its nature in those thirty years. I'm not saying the college doesn't breed some trouble, and girls certainly have to show common sense at night, but most of the families around here are smart enough to know the college crowd comes and goes as a constant refrain. They don't bother us, for the most part, and we let them be."

"Who is it, Mom — ?" Lynne mostly swallowed the last words as she took the final two steps into the front room. "Oh my, oh my, oh my, oh my . . . !"

"Take a breath, child," Nancy said kindly but firmly, and Lynne swiveled her head quickly between David and her mom.

"Oh, hi. Wow!"

David smiled, and Lynne flushed scarlet.

"Hi back to you, Lynne. I hear you're a fan of Maggie's," David said.

"Only absolutely forever! I've got her first recording from Chester Hill, the one she did with Steve Ross at the Cup and Bell, and I just acquired a copy of Marissa's wedding program with the original lyrics Maggie wrote. Oh, my goodness, why are you here? I mean *here* here? Did I, like, win the ticket? The actual ticket to a table at the charity event tonight? I know just what I'll wear —"

"I haven't heard yet, Lynne," David interjected. "The mayor's office is the one doing the drawing."

"I've already got the night off to go into Chicago. Just being there is important. There's going to be so many celebrities coming to hear Maggie sing, but to be inside would be incredible."

David smiled. "Then I hope your name

gets drawn so you can have that experience."

Lynne looked from David to Evie, over to her mom, then back to David, her expression full of delight and also questions.

"They need some information about the Music Hall, Lynne. Related to Jenna," her mom filled in.

"Sure. I talked to someone last week asking questions about the Music Hall and Jenna. It was a Triple M concert the night she disappeared. Maggie was incredible, her singing that night. She brought the house down."

"Ann was doing interviews with me last week, and you spoke with her," Evie said, and Lynne's attention turned to her. "You were helpful, Lynne. Your job in the dressing room gives you insight on the bands no one else has, and the fact you've worked there for so many years is also invaluable."

"It's a great job. They pay me to do a job I'd do for free, given how many musicians and singers I get to meet." Her attention shifted back quickly to David. "Maggie was absolutely the best of all of them, ever. She gave me songwriting tips, autographed my program, and I've got a photo with her playing the guitar in the dressing room. She even asked my opinion on a song she was putting together. I wasn't bugging her," Lynne hurried to add. "I was just there if she needed something — it's my job. But there was a lull with the sound check, and she had twenty minutes to fill. She wanted to talk, asked about how the crowds were when the Music Hall was full and what I thought of the acoustics, did I have any tips about the stage or lighting. I was so nervous I would say something wrong, but I could tell she was nervous too — can you imagine it? *Margaret May McDonald* nervous about singing! I would have never thought it. She laughed and said I was the best for helping settle her nerves. She sang wonderful that night. I'd heard her several times before, and I knew she was going to be spectacular. She absolutely was. I thought it was the best concert ever."

"Maggie did sing wonderfully that night," David agreed. "She was trying out some new songs, which always makes her nerves particularly acute. I'd say she was right, if she said you were helping her calm down."

Lynne beamed. "I told you, Mom."

"Yes, you did, Lynne. But there are other things to talk about now." She looked to Evie, then David. "You came with a question about the Music Hall?"

"Your daughter has worked there for a

439

long time," David began. "And I was there that night when Maggie sang, with her onstage briefly at the end of the performance. It struck me that the Music Hall's pretty expansive the way it's laid out. I'm curious, Lynne, if there's been any remodeling done, like new exits added as the fire codes changed, more office space, or new configuration to handle updated electronics to enhance the concert experience — that kind of thing."

"Why ask Lynne rather than the building owner or manager?" Nancy interjected.

"Mom . . ." Lynne protested.

"We're not implying anything or suspecting anyone, Mrs. Benoit. It's simply easier to ask questions about the Music Hall when we're not actually standing in it. Working backstage like she does, Lynne would have seen the changes as they happened."

"There used to be a stage trapdoor — you mean things like that?" Lynne asked.

"Yes, just like that."

"They had to board it over for a few years because it opened to a ladder underneath the stage. Then they took that whole section of the stage out and put in a motorized lift. Now the entire section of floor can be raised or lowered by four feet. And they took out offices rather than add them, so the Hall could have an official standing-room-only section." Lynne gazed at the floor for a moment, thinking, then looked up in relief. "They put in more restrooms. And the place used to have pretty uncomfortable seats, but they've replaced them all, twice now since I've worked there. Not that anyone sits once a concert is under way, but you do notice before things start that it's more comfortable than before."

She glanced between them. "It's not a complex building — just the entrance halls with concessions for intermission and restrooms, the backstage area for performers, and offices upstairs for security and management. The sound and lighting guys have lots of storage rooms tucked around all over the building, and the janitors need big equipment to work on the floors and carpets to keep them clean. But they mostly rip out the carpet every couple years and repaint everything. Rather routine, you know, how stuff is done. Does that help?"

"It sure does," David replied.

Evie, busily taking notes, nodded her agreement. That hall was a labyrinth for people who knew it well. If Jenna had gone back to meet someone, there were ways around getting noticed. Something bad happened with the manager, just schedule the carpet to get ripped out since it was getting worn, put a repaint job on the schedule, and watch the crime scene disappear.

"You've noticed a lot of bands come and go, the equipment they bring in, how they like to configure things, practice," David commented.

"Sure. Sometimes I go in early so I can watch the stage configuration. Mike — he's the electrician there — sometimes he'll see me in the seats watching and send me for the cables he needs, or call out the connections he wants made, because I know where everything's stored. I keep the dressing rooms neat and everything arranged in its place, but it's nothing compared to Mike and his cables and cords. It's everything put back where it belongs, and everything checked to be there, before you leave wrap-up. Sometimes it's two a.m. before he'll release the crew. He's a good teacher. I can put the dressing room back in shape and have its inventory checked in under an hour now, when it used to take me almost two."

"You stay after the concerts to straighten up, put things in order — it's not a job for the next morning?"

She shrugged. "You wait until morning, then the next band comes in early, and they suffer in the chaos because you weren't ready for them. The Music Hall has a reputation for taking care of its performers, and it would be bad if I was the reason for something less. Every band deserves an excellent dressing-room experience."

"My daughter takes her job very seriously," Nancy said with a smile.

Lynne shot an embarrassed look across the room. "Mom wants me to be a bank teller or work for an insurance broker, because I'm careful with the details. But the Music Hall is better than any other job around. There are great perks besides just getting to meet great people and hear all the concerts. They constantly have new posters going up and others coming down. I've got dozens and dozens of band posters in my collection, and some are worth serious money as collectibles."

She looked toward the stairs and then back to David. "I've got one of the best Triple M concert posters ever printed, but it's framed on my wall. I'd love to show you. And maybe you could sign the playbill from the concert that night? Alongside Maggie's? Please?"

"I could do that for you, Lynne, sure."

"What a day to have not made my bed!" She turned toward the staircase. "Two minutes, then come up? I'm on the right at the end of the hall." Lynne ran up the stairs, two at a time.

Nancy looked between them, her worry showing. "You really came here to meet her, not to be asking questions about the Music Hall, didn't you? You wonder what Lynne was doing the night Jenna went missing."

Evie stepped in to take that bullet. "Do you have any reason to think Lynne was involved with Jenna's disappearance? You're her mom, you love her, you know her. Is there anything that has caused you concern in all these years?"

"No." The shake of her head was firm.

"Then relax, Mrs. Benoit, please. Yes, I wanted to meet your daughter. Jenna had photos of Lynne in her album. We're meeting and talking with all Jenna's friends. Lynne just happens to be one of them with a unique perspective because she was also at the Triple M concert that night."

"We're looking for someone who is a fan of Triple M," David said quietly. "Someone who travels, who may have been in Wisconsin, Indiana, Ohio, as well as Illinois."

Nancy's hand slowly lifted to her chest. "Oh no . . . there's more than just Jenna missing?"

"We don't know, Mrs. Benoit. We're trying to figure that out."

"Lynne hasn't traveled much. A concert in Milwaukee, a lot of downtown Chicago trips to see musicals, but that's about it," she answered shakily. "She's got talent and a passion for her music; she just hasn't had the break yet that gives her a chance. Maggie is both inspiration and role model, and she's also a star to adore, has been for a decade. Lynne's wall of fan memorabilia is . . . extensive."

David's smile was comforting. "I understand fans, Mrs. Benoit. My famous girlfriend still screams when her favorite performer walks backstage to say hello. Not to mention the time Maggie got Bono's autograph after a guest appearance at an awards ceremony. I thought I was never going to get her off the subject of Bono, his music, his band, his career, his lyrics."

Nancy gave a glimmer of a smile. "Yes. I can relate to all the trivia."

David tapped his watch. "I'll go up for a bit, Nancy, if you'd like to come with me. No more than a few minutes, though. We're on a schedule today."

"That's fine, go on up. It's kind of you to indulge her and sign Maggie's program."

David nodded and headed upstairs.

Evie wanted to go with him, but there was still too much ground to cover, and it was the mom who could best help her.

Nancy looked back at her, a bit uncertain. Evie very lightly moved back to their conversation. "I know it was stressful when Jenna disappeared. Did you know Jenna well? Lynne and Jenna were friends?"

"Yes, and it was a very hard time."

"How close were they?" She saw the instinctive hesitation and pressed as much as she could risk. "Please, I can only know Jenna through the insights of those who did know her. It's important to get a clear sense of how you saw things."

Nancy sighed. "Jenna was a music connection for Lynne, and I liked that about her. But she wasn't one of Lynne's close friends from the neighborhood, like the girls Lynne went to middle school and high school with, who came over for sleepovers and movie nights. Jenna was a lovely girl, polite, good manners, bright, someone who enjoyed the college experience and classes. She filled a gap when Lynne was in college, gave her someone to socialize with, as Lynne's friends mostly went to the state university rather than Brighton."

The woman looked away a moment. "It hit Lynne hard when Jenna disappeared. She searched the neighborhood and college with such intensity I seriously worried about her. But maybe I can say it this way: it was the placeholder Jenna provided in her life that Lynne missed more than the friendship. They didn't have a tight personal connection — I could tell that whenever I saw them together. After a few years, Jenna's absence was no longer a topic Lynne brought up. I was relieved. Lynne was able to move on, when so many times something like that would get her stuck, fixated, and she'd struggle to let it go."

"Thank you, Mrs. Benoit." Evie closed her notebook.

"Tell me honestly you're not looking at Lynne."

"You're Lynne's mother. Have you ever thought there was something to be concerned about?"

"No. Until today, it has never crossed my mind."

"If Jenna and Lynne had some kind of 'collision' that night, I doubt Lynne would have remained a Maggie fan, loving one thing that happened that night while desperately trying to block out another experience. That doesn't seem likely or even possible for Lynne — fixating on one, ignoring the other."

Nancy's smile held relief. "No. It doesn't sound like Lynne."

447

"Then simply help me rule her out. The night of Maggie's concert — do you remember what time Lynne got home?"

"Yes, because it wasn't till dawn. She was floating, that one. She first came home with her autographed souvenirs around eleven-thirty, then took off to write her music. She came home for breakfast at seven with this thick set of song lyrics, sang several as I scrambled the eggs. She was happy, bubbling really. Whatever Maggie described as her writing process, Lynne latched on to it like a duck to water.

"It's not unusual, that schedule," Nancy went on to explain. "Lynne doesn't want to head straight to bed after a concert, and I can't blame her. It's the end of a workday for her. She's been around a thousand people, and music is her thing. She needs a few hours before she can settle down to sleep.

"So she'll join others from the Music Hall for the midnight movie at the 4-Plex and then head to the restaurant next door and read until dawn. Or she'll go over to a girlfriend's, watch TV or DVDs, stretch out on their couch. She has a deal with me — she settles where she's going to be by midnight, and once we both carried phones, she'd text where she was. The college years, she'd join friends at the campus union and take the early morning hours to study. If she's out at night, she's always home for our breakfast at seven."

Evie opened her notebook and added some shorthand comments for David later.

Nancy smiled. "I know sometimes she would go join her boyfriend, Jim. He'd be closing the coffee shop at midnight, and they would hang out for a couple of hours playing music. He would walk her later to the destination of her choice. He was good to her. They shared similar circumstances — working evenings, each living at home, not wanting to go straight from the job to bed, but not wanting to disturb the folks. His dad owns the music store over on Tailor Street and the coffee shop beside it where they've got a small stage for live music. Lynne still sings there at least once a week, trying out her songs. She would haunt that music store as a child, learned what she knows about keyboards and guitars there, always ready to learn something more.

"I liked Jim the best of her boyfriends — Jim Ulin — he was good for Lynne during those college years. After him Lynne was seeing Brad Nevery, a nice boy, just a bit rough in his language. He works as a mechanic over at Bushnell Autos. She's between boyfriends now — by her choice, I think. Jim comes by occasionally to compliment a song she wrote, ask if she's sung it for me yet. He's got a good heart, that boy, didn't go the college route but made himself something without it.

"Lynne's father and I, we're lights out at midnight, and it's hard in this old house not to hear someone moving about, even when she'd be doing her best to be quiet. She deserves to have some space — her music, her friends. She'd get an apartment of her own, but stays because she knows her father needs the certainty of someone being here, and I still work morning hours. If Lynne is a bit quick to fixate, she comes by it from her father. He hears sounds and thinks someone's breaking in, can get himself in a panic. But when family is here, he's fine. We make it work. She deserves a life of her own, and I give her what space I can."

"I don't see someone stressed about her life and wanting out of it, Nancy," Evie commented. "She's happy. That's not a bad place to be when you're her age." Evie glanced at her notes. "Jim was her boyfriend throughout college?"

"More like friends from grade school on, really. I hoped it would turn serious one day. Jim's managing both the music store and the coffee shop now, and his dad's mostly retired."

Evie heard David and Lynne, knew they would be coming down momentarily. "You've got a good daughter, Nancy, one who strikes me as happy with her life. I'll figure out what happened to Jenna. It may shock a few people at first, whatever the truth is I eventually find. But it's probably going to be a case where, on second thought, it's not difficult to see. If there's someone in the neighborhood who's a person you have wondered about, would you call me?" Evie offered her card. "I promise, I eliminate quickly ninety-nine percent of the names that go on my list, yet every one of them takes me another step toward the truth."

"I'll call you. If only because the truth removes all the questions once Jenna is found."

David rejoined them, and Evie knew him well enough to see he was thoughtful but not stressed. "Mrs. Benoit," he said, "Lynne has a rare and classic Triple M poster in mint condition, one I also have on my wall. If she ever decides to part with it, I would be pleased to buy it for Maggie." He smiled at Lynne as she stopped on the bottom step.

"I'll put my copy of tonight's program in the mail after Maggie signs it. You've got a nice collection."

"I do so appreciate that." Lynne waved a business card. "And this contact information for my music."

"I'll tell him to expect that lyric notebook of yours." David reached for the door, and Evie joined him, stepped out. "Thank you for your time, Mrs. Benoit. Thanks, Lynne." They walked back down the drive.

Evie didn't say anything as David drove two blocks, then pulled to the side of the road and handed her his phone. "I didn't have to ask. Lynne thought Maggie might like to see her photo wall."

The spread was a classic homage to Maggie and the Triple M band. Maggie in multiple poses, magazine interviews, posters, photos from concerts, album covers turned into art. "It's beautifully arranged," Evie said as she scanned through the several shots he'd taken.

"Lynne's artistic in a way that seems innate," he said. "Her room itself is a display of past music memorabilia to modern-day lyrics, all visually fitting together. The poster I mentioned is the one above the desk, the first thing you see as you enter the room.

It's worth at least six thousand now, will be double that soon. The girl really does have value in what she's been collecting, a good eye for what to save." He leaned over to highlight one of the photos. "The center of the wall is Maggie in concert at the Music Hall."

Evie enlarged that portion, saw Maggie onstage in a lovely full-skirted gown. Photos from backstage, the dressing room with Maggie still in jeans and a sweatshirt, snapshots of her and Lynne mugging for the camera — that would have set this fixation and made it personal. Several photos of the concert in progress. One of Lynne later sitting on a white bedspread, displaying all the things she had acquired as she memorialized the night.

"The cassette player on the dresser — it's a recording Lynne made of people talking around the dressing room that night, Maggie's voice laughing as she got ready, doing her vocal exercises. Maggie knows she's being recorded, you hear her ask, 'Play it back, how do I sound?' I've seen Maggie prepping for a performance, she's gearing up to be vibrantly alive, and Lynne was getting two, almost three hours of that before Maggie went onstage. Lynne fixated for a reason that particular evening. She was predisposed to choose a favorite singer, and Maggie entered her life like a vibrant butterfly when Lynne was hungry for a role model. Lynne stuck to the honey."

Evie could see it as David put it into words. "And became an obsessed fan."

David nodded. "One who probably has a heart of gold trapped under the parts of her personality that haven't matured yet. Lynne wasn't nervous about talking with cops, and when you mention Jenna to her, it's sadness, but distant, in her face and voice. She coped with the stress by letting go of Jenna in her memory. Whatever happened, it wasn't Lynne."

"I ended up with the same conclusion but for other reasons. I'll talk you through my conversation with her mother as we drive. We need to talk to a boyfriend of Lynne's from back then, a Jim Ulin. His father owns a music store and adjoining coffee shop on Tailor Street." Evie found the address and tapped it in.

"What are you thinking?"

"Jenna had a habit of stealing boyfriends just because she could, and I've got Nancy describing Jim as one of those nice neighborhood guys who was good to Lynne. I'm wondering what kind of play Jenna made for him and when."

"Oh boy," David breathed.

Evie gave a sad smile. "This interview may still have solved the case. Let's go meet him."

TWENTY

A mannequin in a college-band uniform holding a trumpet looked about ready to destroy the hearing of another mannequin in mid-strum of an electric guitar. Evie gave them a second look, which she supposed was the whole point of a window display, then entered the music store. Two dozen guitars had been neatly hung across the south wall, a quick count came up with ten keyboards of various sophistications, and there was enough sheet music filling several racks to remind her that songs really were written down before they were played. It was a foreign world to her.

She glanced at David and caught an expression she hadn't seen before, a touch of joyful pleasure. He no doubt would be walking out of here with a gift for Maggie.

"Jim Ulin?" David was asking. The guy ringing up two music composition books pointed through the adjoining door to the coffee shop.

She turned that direction into a long, narrow room, a low stage with a *Karaoke Friday Night* sign in bright blue neon, tables and chairs arranged around a counter for food and drinks, neatly forming a U in the center of the room. Muffins, brownies, soda, coffees, and . . . pizzas, which apparently could bake in a stack of toaster ovens. Eight of them, Evie counted. If she ran a coffee shop near a college, she'd be serving pizza and staying open until midnight too. The popcorn was free and self-serve, pouring out of a carnival-style stirring kettle.

It was late for the lunch crowd, and since it was Friday, the six college students at a front table were watching people walk by, drinking coffee, and debating lamest movies, from the fragments of conversation picked up by Evie. The four at a back table were playing a card game, the remnants of a pizza cardboard on an adjoining table, and two who looked like brothers were perched on stools on the stage, dueling with guitars, mostly running riffs.

A nice place that has the feel of a college hangout, Evie mused. The guy behind the counter had finished cleaning the coffeemaker and turned her direction with a smile. She didn't need the nametag to know it was Jim from one of Jenna's pictures. "I'll take a black coffee and a brownie, and if you can spare it, a few minutes of your time on your next break." She put her card down beside a ten-dollar bill.

It got a second glance, along with a puzzled nod. "Sure. Choose a table, I'll bring your coffee and pour myself one."

The brownie was huge and chunky with chocolate chips. The coffee came in a ceramic mug rather than styrofoam cup — they were obviously going the green route, using dishwasher energy instead of taking up landfill space. She did prefer her coffee in something solid. She pocketed the change he brought over with her order. "Thanks."

Jim pulled out the opposite chair. "What can I do for you, Lieutenant?"

On the tall side, lanky, probably basketball if he was an athlete. Sandy hair and some freckles. Twenty-nine, she guessed, still looking young but for the eyes that indicated he was probably the wisest young man around here. He made a good first impression.

"I've been asking questions around campus about Jenna Greenhill. We have," she explained, nodding toward David, still in the music shop. "We were talking recently with Lynne Benoit and her mom."

That got a reaction, the kind of subtle response that made a relaxed hand twitch a finger and the knee stiffen, with the eyes shifting away to look at anything other than the cop.

"I was wondering how soon it was after Jenna showed up on campus that she began causing problems for you."

That turned his gaze back. Evie didn't know anything more than what she had just implied, but Jim just filled in the entire rest of the story in the memories that flitted across his face. "There are two versions of Jenna around campus," she added lightly. "One is kindness personified; the other wants to be the center of the universe and doesn't mind poaching other girls' boy-friends." Evie offered a sympathetic smile for the tension showing in him. "I'm going to guess I just found my second Candy, someone who described Jenna to me as a 'boyfriend-stealing cheater,' and turned similarly unflattering from there. You didn't like her, did you, Jim?"

"No. And to say that after she's missing just puts a spotlight on those words the wrong way."

"If it's the truth, it's just what was," Evie replied matter-of-factly.

Jim glanced around the coffee shop,

459

confirmed they weren't being overheard. He wrapped his hands around his warm mug and said, "Jenna was college and ambition. I was this place, the music store, my old man. I'm likely never leaving this neighborhood, and I'm okay with that. It pays the bills. The same folks have been around here for thirty years and they're good people. Dad and I are actually friends. But Jenna was looking and flirting and mostly, I think, bored. The fact Lynne was my choice startled her . . . I think it amused her.

"Maybe some of that with Lynne did start from familiarity — she's been around my world since she was six, and she grows on you. I've always liked her, even if you have to wince sometimes at how she doesn't understand people as they really are. Lynne's not perfect, but she's genuinely good. Jenna, well, the wrapper fools people. I'm not saying it's not flattering to have a good-looking, ambitious, and smart woman pause and take another look at you. But a wise man knows if you take a bite of that, you're going to get snapped by jaws that don't let go. I wasn't buying what she was dangling. And that annoyed her.

"She had other guys on her line. I was lower down her priority list, but she kept coming back. I started getting worried about how Jenna was going to play Lynne, cause problems from the other direction since I wasn't falling in line. Jenna was just starting to drop hints that direction when she disappeared. Had it gone on another few months, I would have been fighting a battle against the damage she was doing on that front. I can't say I wasn't relieved Jenna was gone, even as horrible as that sounds."

"Lynne's someone I imagine you instinctively want to protect," Evie remarked, "and you saw trouble coming. I've got no problem with your instincts, Jim. They were the right ones, given what I'm learning about Jenna."

"Thanks." He thoughtfully turned his coffee mug between his hands. "I may not be the smart college guy, but I can hold my own with your psychology-trained graduate. I've seen a lot of soap operas play out here, having spent my middle school years doing homework at the side table over there, and my high school after hours on the cash register. I've seen the college crowds come and go. Jenna was rare, unique — and not in a good way, I'm afraid. She was probably the most calculating for how to play a guy of anyone I ever saw up close.

"This is the coffee crowd," he explained, with a gesture to the room. "Come evenings, this place will be crowded and the music loud, and we'll be hauling in folding chairs so you're not sitting on the floor. The ones who drink the beers get emotional; that's the other side of campus. This is the subtle crowd, weighing tone of voice and choice of words. 'How do I want this next conversation to go?' Jenna had the good-girl wrapper. Didn't drink or smoke, cry about her weight, make a scene. She was smart, came with a pretty smile — and the guys fell over like bowling pins. I don't think many people noticed the real Jenna. Candy did. I did. And surprisingly, I think to some extent Steve did.

"He wouldn't say much, but he had her pegged and wasn't letting her set the agenda. Jenna wanted the proposal, the engagement ring, and Steve wasn't going to give in to her on when that should happen. She was subtly suggesting she might move on, lining up his possible replacements. She didn't get the fact Steve was the adult in the relationship, while she was still immaturely playing high school pecking order. My sense of it is he really loved her or he would have given her the shock of her life and let her go. He was willing to put in the time for her to grow up, but he had his work cut out for him. She was playing other guys right up until the day she vanished, and that has always left a queasy feeling in my gut."

"Did Lynne know Jenna was pushing your buttons?"

He recoiled, shaking his head. "No. No, she didn't realize what was going on. Lynne . . . well, she just doesn't catch on to subtle. Innuendos go right by her. Even actual rudeness often registers only as someone being abrupt. She hadn't known what Jenna was doing, and her true friends were sympathetic, patting my arm, doing what they could to edge Lynne's time away from Jenna. But most of them were state college, not Brighton, and weren't around as much as Jenna. On the surface, Jenna was Lynne's friend, and Lynne couldn't see deeper than that."

"When did you last see Jenna?"

"You mind if we shift to the music store? There's an office in back."

He wanted a smoke, she realized, fidgeting rippling his fingers. A good guy with a vice he'd want to hide from this very green, nothing-as-crass-as-nicotine college crowd. "No problem. Lead the way."

David had been deliberate in not making it seem like two on one. Evie caught his eye with a tiny shake of her head as she passed, and left him to fill the time spending more money on music for his girl.

The back office was a desk and two mostly comfortable chairs tucked in behind boxes neatly shelved floor to ceiling. "I saw Jenna the night she disappeared," Jim told her.

Evie sincerely hoped her phone recording in her pocket was doing its job. She settled into one of the chairs, forced herself to relax, and simply waited for what he might be willing to say next.

Jim opened a desk drawer, pulled out a pack of cigarettes, held it up till she shook her head with a smile, then lit one for himself. "It was after the concert. It's a huge, Mount Everest kind of Friday night for Lynne, with Triple M playing and Maggie herself in Lynne's dressing room. Lynne cleaned that dressing room and adjoining bathroom for a good six extra hours on her own time, fussed over every towel, hand-picked flowers for the bouquet on the dressing room table, polished every surface until it shone. She had to make sure everything was perfect for Maggie.

"Under normal circumstances I would have been in the audience that night because Triple M is solid music and Maggie's got an exceptional voice I enjoy hearing. But Lynne would be distracted — 'My boyfriend's here, I should introduce him to Maggie' — and she'd stew over how to do it without making Maggie uncomfortable, get stuck in a planning loop on what exact words to say and when . . ." Jim stopped and grinned. "I love that about Lynne, even as it causes no ends of problems, that true-north sense in her about how things are supposed to be. She's got a good heart.

"So instead of the concert, I worked the coffee-shop counter, let Lynne have her perfect night without distraction. I knew she'd be here by the time I was closing up at midnight to tell me about every — and I do mean truly *every* — minute of her special night. So I pushed off eating, figuring I'd put in a pizza and get a slice into her when she came — she wouldn't have thought of touching food once she went in to work about two that afternoon.

"The door chimes at two minutes to midnight as I'm turning chairs up, getting ready to mop." Jim blew out a steady stream of smoke. "It's not Lynne."

Evie could see the soap opera setting itself up. Lynne's most exciting night, and Jenna's timing for when to stir the pot playing out to perfection.

"I realized later that Steve was out of town. Had I caught there was an away game, I would have been braced and pre-pared. Instead, here's Jenna with her apologetic smile and her, 'Am I too late to get the last coffee in the pot? And can you add whipped cream?'

"It's been policy ever since the coffee shop opened that a customer even a minute before midnight gets served, and the full menu stays available. Doesn't matter if it's Dillon nursing a black eye after a fight with his wife and wanting a pizza, Officer Kelly looking for a refill for his thermos, or a group of eight students wanting specialty drinks. So I get Jenna her coffee and reopen the register to make change. Jenna's chatting away, and I'm not paying much attention. I'm finishing out closing and watching the door for Lynne. I don't notice Jenna's getting annoyed with my lack of attention."

Jim paused as he considered what came next, glanced over to see if Evie was still engaged, seemed relieved she looked relaxed. "Jenna never mentioned she'd been at the concert, never mentioned she'd been at her apartment only long enough to drop off her things and head back out. No, her spin for this is she's got an important paper to write, but she can't stand to be inside another minute, even if it's coming up on midnight; she just had to get in a walk. She'd just walk over here, stop for coffee, and if I was through for the night, I could be a gentleman and walk her back home.

"It wasn't the first time she'd done the late-night-stroll, I-walk-her-home pitch — it had become just something else to avoid with her. I'd started leaving Greg on the clock — the guy who covers nights on the music side — paying him the extra half hour so I could send him to walk Jenna home, given he lived two buildings down from her. It wasn't worth the grief I'd get from the women in my world when it got around — and Jenna would make sure it did — that I had told her to walk herself home."

Jim gave a pained smile. "Jenna was setting Lynne up to see us in a clinch. Only thing I can figure she was thinking. 'Steve's out of town, I'm bored, not ready to call it an evening, so let's make some mischief.' " He stubbed out the cigarette. "Lynne was going to walk in on a kiss or a slap to the face — I'm not sure which way Jenna had it planned. But Lynne doesn't show. Jenna's checking her watch, nursing that coffee to make it last, and I finally realize what the witch has in mind. Burns me good. The best night of Lynne's life, and Jenna's looking to cause her grief.

"So I move to the door, watching the street, ready to intercept Lynne, while Jenna takes her sweet time on the last sips. It would have worked. I'm sure Jenna had her cover story planned. She was waiting at the coffee shop because 'I just had to hear about how great your night with Maggie went. I had no idea Jim was going to get flirty,' and Lynne would have bought that in a heartbeat, even as she looked at me with crushed hurt for kissing someone else. Jenna was out to ruin Lynne's happy evening, use me to do the hurting.

"It's getting later than normal for Lynne, and I'm getting worried about her. Her agreement with her mom to 'settle somewhere by midnight' has always been pretty much gospel with Lynne. So I kill the lights at twelve-thirty, walk Jenna home mostly to get rid of her, who's stewing now and not talking. I figured I would meet up with Lynne, because if she's coming from either her home or the Music Hall, that's the street she'll take. I know she's going to be brimming to overflow about her night, wouldn't just decide she's tired and turn in for the night. But there's no sign of Lynne.

"It's twelve-fifty when Jenna enters her apartment building. This I know for certain because I'm standing on the sidewalk looking at the time, trying to decide if Lynne, running late, would have gone to my dad's place expecting to find me there, or if

Lynne's more likely at her parents', thinking it's too late to go out on her own, waiting for me to show up so she can tell me all about her big night. As her boyfriend, this is a serious problem, a real dilemma. If I text her, ask where she is, I'm saying I can't even figure out her mind on such a matter.

"So I walk over to Lynne's. But she's not home — she turns on the desk lamp in her room to let me know she's there. I reverse course and head home. Pop's asleep. Lynne isn't there either. She knows where the spare key is so she makes herself comfortable in the living room if I'm running late. Now I'm just plain worried. At one-fifteen I finally send a text and get one back saying *I'm busy.* In Lynne's shorthand that means her hands are full, she's doing something physical, and literally can't type right now."

Jim smiled at a memory. "Lynne's never done passive-aggressive in her life. When she's mad and doesn't want to talk with you, the text says *I don't want to talk to you. I'm mad about . . .* and you get the 'why' full barrel. So I plop down on my dad's couch and wait for Lynne to tell me where she is. Two hours and ten minutes later, she sends a text that says *It works! Maggie's a Genius!* But she still doesn't tell me where she is. It's becoming that kind of night. I text her back an all-caps *WHERE ARE YOU?* so I can get an actual call.

"Turns out she's writing songs, trying out Maggie's advice. She's at the twenty-four-hour FitClub, using one of their stair climbers. She'd done the treadmill, but running and thinking music was too involved. Free weights did better, but she thought steps might be the best. I won't tell you all the details she laid out in that call, but Lynne had turned Maggie's advice for how to write songs into her own method, and she's jazzed." He stopped for a moment, gave Evie a quizzical look. "I can do an edited version if this is too boring."

Evie chuckled. "No, no, Jim — having met Lynne, if you weren't giving me these details, it wouldn't be her and I'd wonder what you were fabricating. I appreciate the playback."

"Okay, so we finally end up over at a friend's house at four a.m. Lynne gives me the entire blow-by-blow of her night, shows me the lyrics she's already written while we help stuff circulars into the Saturday newspaper and slip on the rubber bands. Laura Pip's a teacher we've both known since grade school, she delivers Saturday and Sunday papers for extra money, and we help her prep when we can. Lynne talked non-

470

stop from the time we met up until I walked her home for a seven a.m. breakfast with her folks."

Jim shifted in the chair, and his voice took on a more matter-of-fact tone. "The crisis of the night averted, Lynne safely home and happy, I walked myself back, absolutely wiped, and hit the bed face-first. I worked two to midnight that Saturday, noon to midnight Sunday, and then I hear the news Jenna is missing Monday afternoon about three. It was my day off and I was painting a friend's garage to pick up some extra money. I packed up my stuff, got over to the apartment building shortly after four, found Jenna's friend Robin organizing a flyer distribution. Lynne's already out with a stack in her hands, papering every business window on her way toward the Music Hall. I mostly just walked with her, since Lynne was panicked and sounding desperate — like her dad. Letting her do it herself was probably better for her, I figured. We were out until one a.m. and on it again the next morning at six. I hung around Lynne nearly twenty-four seven those first few days, so her mom didn't have to worry about her."

He went to light another cigarette, needing something in his hands, Evie decided, as he mostly ignored it once lit.

"Lynne told me she'd heard the last thing Jenna did was send a text to her mom saying she was back at the apartment. I assumed that text was sent after I saw her walk into the building. It was weeks before I heard the time on that text, realized it was sent *before* midnight, *before* Jenna came to the coffee shop. By then it had also become clear this wasn't a casual mix-up or accident; someone had likely done her harm." He gave a long sigh. "And with a swarm of cops looking in every corner, I took the coward's way out, didn't raise my hand."

Jim stopped talking, but Evie knew the value of silence and simply waited.

"I was never interviewed, so I never lied." He blew out smoke. "And I know how that statement itself sounds, how it makes me look.

"Those first few days I was still angry at what Jenna had been preparing to do, and when conversations would come up about Jenna, most of the time I was standing right beside Lynne. Lynne didn't need to know her friendship with Jenna had been more a mirage than authentic, and she certainly didn't need cops grilling her, 'Tell me about your boyfriend and his relationship with your friend Jenna.'

"I always assumed the cops would eventually be at the coffee shop or the house to ask me about that night. I would have been seen walking Jenna home, what time was that, what had we been talking about, they'd want to see the texts with Lynne, put on extra pressure because I would have been one of last, if not *the* last, to see Jenna. But no cops came.

"At first I was relieved. Evidence had them looking at something that happened to Jenna Saturday morning, and they hadn't been around because they don't need my statement. Then I'm wondering maybe no one saw us that night or thought to mention it to the cops?

"So it's a couple of weeks later when I hear the time on Jenna's text to her mom is before midnight, before she came to the coffee shop. Cops had been working on the assumption Jenna was home at eleven-fifty p.m., and I knew Jenna got home exactly an hour later than that. If I'd thought that time difference was significant, I would have come forward. But by then everybody was hunting for blood, and I hadn't been involved. I'd re-created that walk in my mind numerous times. Had I seen anything out of place — a van, a car, a person who didn't belong? Except for the bright, near-full moon, I couldn't come up with one fact that distinguished that night from others.

"I got as far as the police station twice, but self-preservation turned me around. I wasn't sure who was going to believe me other than my dad, Lynne's parents, a few others who really knew me. It's a pricey college, and an arrest would have made people more comfortable — guilt or innocence wasn't going to play into it. The lawyer fees alone would have cost my dad the coffee shop, probably the music store, likely both."

Evie raised a palm to stop him there. "Is there anyone you can think of who might have seen you walk Jenna home that night, someone you know from the neighborhood who maybe kept quiet for the same reason? If so, I'd like the name."

Jim thought about it and shook his head. "I didn't notice anyone in particular that night. The close-at-midnight crowd — we pass each other, say a friendly good-night, but no one lingers to talk. And it was twelve-thirty before Jenna and I left the coffee shop that night. The streets were quiet by then.

"Those who live on that route, who would know me at a glance if they saw me, who might have been up at that time of night — there are a few. Paul Sanders waits up for his wife, Lisa, to get home. They sometimes sit on the porch and talk if it's a nice night. There's Jerry Verma — he owns the bakery and deli, sometimes goes in around midnight if he's catering a breakfast meeting. And the corner house is where Wilma Parks lives. She likes to read, and her living room light is often on until two or three a.m. The only other one I can think of would be Neva Timber. She works for the local paper, comes home after it's gone to the printer. Sometimes they hold off for a late-breaking story in which case she gets home after midnight. Those four might know a few more I haven't thought of."

"No dog owner taking a late-night walk, the dog wagging his entire body wanting to say hello to you?"

Jim faintly smiled as he shook his head. "No. Not on the night it would have helped me out."

Evie studied him. She'd formed a lot of impressions, opinions, thoughts while listening to him. Some of what she most wanted to know was likely lost to history and the passing years, but some of it remained. "Why tell *me*, Jim?"

"I've regretted the silence. It might have been the safe thing to do, even the wise thing given I was innocent, but it wasn't the right thing. I told myself if a cop ever showed up, I'd tell it like it was."

"You're the last one to see Jenna alive, other than who did this."

"I guess I am." He looked directly at her. "And I honestly don't have a clue what happened to her. I'm not hiding anything, Lieutenant. I'll answer any question, I'll take a lie-detector test if you like — not that it's going to be that useful after nine years, but it might. Put me through the ringer, I've earned it. But if you can spare Lynne, please do so. She doesn't deserve to have reporters hounding her for what she remembers. She's mostly been able to let go of what happened, move on with her life.

"I'd like you to believe me, but I know it's not your job to believe or not — it's your job to find out what happened to Jenna. Maybe what she was doing with me points to another guy she was playing. I wish I had even a glimmer of an idea to suggest. I don't. And it's not for lack of hours spent trying to figure it out, or lack of a few thousand innocent-sounding questions asked of those who drink my coffee."

Evie thought for a moment and went a different direction. "Why did you break up with Lynne? Her mom said that after you, Lynne went out with a Brad Nevery for a while."

Jim shifted uncomfortably in his chair.

"Come on. If you can't tell a cop, who can you tell?" Evie teased gently.

"I just confessed to being the last person to see Jenna alive, and the cop wants to know how come I broke up with my girl-friend." He gave a half laugh as he stubbed out the cigarette. "For the record, it was easier to tell you about Jenna than to tell you this, but yeah, you've got a good reason for asking.

"Lynne and I are both neighborhood kids. It's got its own code to it, when the college is right there and this place gets overrun nine months a year with people from every-where but here. Part of that code is you can't ever dump a neighborhood friend. You can have disagreements and disputes and even some bruises, but you can't break up and schism things, can't split your circle into factions.

"I had it out with a guy I went to high school with. He said some things, I said some things back, he shoves, I throw a punch. We don't shake hands at the end of it and settle the peace. Instead, we're walk-ing opposite sides of the street, our friends are having to choose. It gets back to Lynne. She's tied up tight with the guy's sister since second grade. And I'm like making her choose. So Lynne dumps me — she's hanging in with Kelly and by the unspoken rules, with Kelly's brother — because that's the code. I'm twenty-five and back in grade school with my girl in a huff over the fact I had a fight. Embarrassing is what it is, the mortifying kind. Lynne's not shy about making her decision known either. I pull out a chair at the table with her and Kelly to try to make peace, and Lynne picks up her coffee and finds herself another table.

"So you bite your tongue and go do what the code requires. Rick and I have a make-up meeting that degenerates into both of us throwing some more fists. Followed by another that is about as scorching. The third attempt we lay down enough peace we shake hands on the matter. Now Rick and I are fine. But Lynne's still got me stuck in some Siberian doghouse for disrespecting how things were, are, and ever shall be. And she puts a cherry on it by deciding she's going to see Brad Nevery for a while.

"I'm working on the problem. Lynne's type of anger is more a deep hurt and it's slow to cool off. She's at least not seeing Brad anymore. And she's back wrapping newspapers at Laura's come Saturday mornings — even when I'm there. The rest is pretty slow-going. I broke faith with what we are, which is a neighborhood that sticks together. That Lynne's perception isn't precisely reality, it's more a wishful hope, doesn't particularly weigh in on the matter. I shattered the confidence she had that I understood what matters. For Lynne, loyalty to friends is everything."

Evie considered that and found it fascinating. "What happens when a true friend breaks faith with Lynne?"

"Lynne gets bewildered. She applies the fault to herself, something she did, and it's painful to watch."

Evie could see that. "Anything more you want to tell me?"

Self-deprecating humor filled Jim's face as he shook his head. "No."

"You can't tell Lynne you told the truth to a cop today, maybe get back in her good graces by this brave act, because then you'd have to tell her what the truth was. So you actually did a selfless thing."

"Noble — that's me." Jim sighed and dumped the pack of cigarettes back into the drawer. "I started smoking after Lynne called it quits. Yet another reason she looks at me with pity in her eyes. For her there are only three vices in this neighborhood — drinking, smoking, and not loving music. Make that four and add disloyalty."

Evie couldn't help but laugh. She rose to her feet.

Jim asked, "How much is that truth going to cost me?"

It was a fair question, Evie thought. "It's going to be uncomfortable having cops looking at you, but if you're innocent, the truth is out there, and it's something a lot better than simply we couldn't prove you did it. Go talk to Lynne's mom, tell her what you told me. David or I will be in touch. There are going to be more questions. Just answer them truthfully, and to some extent, trust that we are good at our jobs. We will figure out what happened to Jenna Greenhill. I know for a fact the case is breaking and rolling toward an answer. And to the best of my knowledge, I've never arrested someone who wasn't guilty."

She set a second card on the table. "If there's a name from the past that strikes you as someone you did wonder about, call me."

"Thanks, Lieutenant." He stood, reached over to shake her hand, and tucked the card in his pocket.

David was sitting at a table in the coffee shop, a mug by his elbow, engrossed in a newspaper. Evie rapped knuckles lightly on the table as she passed to get a Diet Coke and then walked outside to David's SUV, waited for him to come with the key. *Nine years,* she thought as she idly watched Jim through the window. *He's cared about Lynne and held his secret for her sake all this time.*

Jim was speaking with the music store clerk, smiled at something he was told, bumped fists with the guy, then walked into the coffee shop. The girl who'd sold Evie the soda nodded at something Jim told her, took off her apron, slipped underneath the counter. Jim took her place, reached into the cooler and came up with a cold root beer for himself, drank half of it before picking up a towel and wiping down the counter. *Going back to work . . . after one of the more difficult conversations of his life.*

David clicked open the doors, and Evie settled into the passenger seat, twisted the cap off her soda. "So how much did you spend on Maggie, if I may be so bold?" she asked with a smile as she fastened her seat belt.

David smiled. "Not counting multiple coffees and the newspaper, eight thousand."

She choked and sputtered on her drink. "Next time lead a comment like that with 'A lot,' " she said through gasps.

"Sorry."

"Sure you are." She put the cap back on the soda bottle. If she drank the rest of it now, she would start hiccupping.

And she'd just recorded that whole sloppy episode. She slipped out her phone, closed the recording, sent the audio to her state account for safekeeping and a copy to David. She wasn't surprised to see her phone battery about dead. She plugged it into the car charger and returned to what David had told her. "Eight with triple zeros after it?"

"And two more for the change." He pulled carefully into traffic. "That particular keyboard would have set me back seventeen in New York, even with Maggie's professional discount. Some guy buys it on a lease plan, can't make payments after four months, it's back barely out of the box but they can't sell it as new, so the leasing company has to eat the difference. The store probably clears a thousand on each of the two sales, and I get more than a bargain. So it's close to a steal. That model's got a fifteen-year lifespan, even under concert conditions. Put it in Maggie's music room, our grandkids are going to be learning to play on it."

"You're thinking long term. Nice."

He shrugged. "Short term too. She doesn't need it, I could flip it next week to one of her friends for ten. Get Maggie to play a concert or two with it, it's worth fourteen. If nothing else, it's going to pay for landscaping at my new place — something better than geraniums in a pot."

She did like his practical side. "So spending eight thousand is a way to make money."

David laughed. "I'm good at it, you ever need some pointers."

"In spite of his wealth — or maybe it's the reason for it — Rob is good for those too. I handed Rob ten bucks one day, sort of a dare, and he gave me twenty-seven dollars and fifty-two cents back a week later. The two pennies he found on the street, but since he was doing business on my dare at the time, he considered it only fair to add them to my take. Rob had turned my ten into a box of very fine chocolates, asked the coffee-shop manager if he could try an experiment, put the open box on the counter next to the napkins with a Post-it note — *25 cents, your choice* — and an empty jar beside it. When the candy was gone, he collected the quarters, bought more chocolates. Repeated it again. He returned only a third of the profits to me. He'd earned another third for himself and gave the manager a third, though the sales tax he did pay out of the shop's take. Rob likes to say making money is mostly about spotting opportunities."

"He's right about that."

Evie could feel the tension draining out of her with the small talk, was grateful for it, even though a look at the time was ratcheting up the tension. She would likely be late for the charity event this evening. Her dress was at the hotel, and she was meeting Rob so she could ride with him. Lynne was probably already on her way into the city to get a good spot on the rope line. David would make it in time if she didn't hold him up any further.

David glanced over and said, "That must have been some conversation with Jim."

"He may be the last person to have seen Jenna alive. Jim walked her home from the coffee shop, watched her walk into her apartment building at twelve-fifty a.m."

"The original lie of omission. That is indeed a very interesting wrinkle."

"Jenna was trying to make mischief between Lynne and Jim, cause some turmoil on the day of Lynne's joyful meeting with Maggie, only it didn't go as planned. The audio is now in your account, so you can listen to the flow of it."

"Does what Jim said help us any?"

"When it comes down to it, only on the margins. Jenna's late-night walk is confirmed, but it was already on the theory list. She made a habit of stealing other girls' boyfriends — again, already known. The girl in this instance who would have motive to get even — Lynne — is cleared by her own conduct, her mother's comments, Jim's report on the timeline. Lynne simply hadn't realized what was going on. We now have Jim's word Jenna was alive at her apartment building an hour later than previously thought. That's about the substance."

"Did Jim kill Jenna? Take a crack at her to put a stop to this?"

"He easily could have. Lose his temper, strike out, Jenna's no more a problem. He's a local who could hide her body around here without it being discovered. He says she walked into the coffee shop at just minutes before midnight, and he walked her home, saw her enter her apartment at twelve-fifty in the morning. The first part of the statement could be true, the second part a lie if he's killed her and hid the body. Assume the confrontation takes place in the coffee shop, he's got hours to clean up the crime scene, make the evidence disappear. Everything he would need for a good cleaning job is in the janitor's closet. He's with Lynne and someone named Laura Pip at four a.m."

"Four hours is a decent enough murder window."

"Yeah. I've seen it done well in forty minutes, but that was with premeditation. Four hours when you didn't plan to kill someone, panic, 'What do I do now?' come up with a plan, then execute it — he would have been hustling. And from what I heard about her, I very much doubt Lynne would have noticed if Jim showed up at four a.m. unusually distracted. She was talking a mile a minute about the concert and Maggie's method of writing songs."

"Bottom-line it for me. Where are you, Evie?"

"I want him to be innocent. Jim and Lynne are like a hopeful love story that still might work out. But he's not innocent. He withheld information from the authorities when Jenna disappeared. It doesn't mean he caused Jenna's death, but we're going to have to find a way to clear him in order to take his name off the top of the list."

"Does he travel?"

"The conversation didn't get that far. He's not a Triple M fan beyond living in the shadow of someone who is. I doubt he recognized you in the brief glance he cast in your direction. He seems to be a homebody from what I picked up. If he snapped with

Jenna, it was for a personal reason. So, no, I'm all but certain he didn't head out to smother those other three girls." She lifted a hand to put an asterisk on that. "Jim's smart enough to do other crimes in an attempt to mask Jenna's murder. But since he didn't get on the investigation's radar in the months after Jenna, he wouldn't have risked another crime when he was getting away with this one. So, again, no. Jim would be lying low — not doing something else that might catch a cop's attention."

"I agree with that logic," David said. "If Jenna is tied by the missing driver's license to those other three women, it's likely Jim is in the clear. Did he say anything that might be helpful about someone else? The last person to see Jenna will also be the best witness for the scene that night."

"Jim didn't notice anything out of place. We'll have to push there again. Someone had to have been around if we've got the correct window for the crime."

"Murder is easier at night, but nothing says Jenna wasn't killed at, say, eight in the morning," David said.

"Exactly. That possibility is also on the theory list. It's something to come back to and reconsider. This could have been a Saturday crime."

David glanced over. "Let me ask you the hard question. Replay this for me. You sit down with Jim. You tell him we've just spoken with Lynne, with her mom."

"Yes?"

"Is Jim telling a fabricated story now to protect Lynne?"

Evie smiled. "I like working with you, David. That was my first reaction when Jim dropped the news he saw Jenna that night and he didn't tell the cops before. He's had nine years to work out a cover story that will protect Lynne. And that I could easily see him trying to do. Given how he told this story, it tells me five things are possibly true if Lynne was involved.

"It suggests Jenna died between midnight and one a.m., the time Jim is covering by saying Jenna was with him at the coffee shop. It suggests Lynne went to Jenna's apartment building after the concert to tell her about the night, and then trouble happened — Jenna hinting of something going on with Jim or speaking badly about Maggie?

"If Lynne did kill Jenna, Jim could be the one who took care of the body. Lynne could clean up a crime scene, erase any trace of it. There was more than forty-eight hours for the apartment air to clear of cleaning products. And she's good at putting things in their right place, could have easily restored order so it looked normal. Jim could have used the coffee shop's trash collection to get rid of any physical evidence. Things with blood on them, anything damaged, the murder weapon. They could have hidden the fact Jenna died that night if they worked at it together."

"If Lynne did it, talk to me more about the motive and why."

"The most likely trigger, Jenna tears down Lynne's illusions. 'The concert was okay, but I've heard better. Maggie didn't really like you; you're just the dressing room help. You're never going to be a singer, Lynne. Grow up and see reality, quit living in a fantasy world. Jim isn't even a faithful boyfriend, because he's flirting with me.' Jenna could slice into Lynne's soul with words in a bunch of ways. And if this happened after Jim had walked Jenna home, ignored her advances, and is choosing Lynne over her, Jenna is primed to be vicious. All it takes is Lynne pushing her back with a cry of 'No, that's not true!' — shoving her hard enough to send her into the corner of a table, and Jenna dies of a broken neck. Boyfriend covers it up, and now tries to protect Lynne years later. It's incredibly plausible given what I know about Jenna. I'm not sure it's in Lynne, but it's in Jenna."

David drummed fingers on the wheel. "If we didn't have other related remains, we'd have a hard time not bringing both of them in for formal questioning right now."

"Take your favorite theory. Jim did it. Or Lynne did it, and Jim is trying to help her. Or it's not a local crime, our concert traveler picked out Jenna and made her disappear, just like he's done others — and we're left with two locals who could look guilty — just like every other disappearance he's pulled off has been leaving someone local looking guilty."

"You liked Lynne."

"I did. And I like Jim. It's much easier to lay this crime on an unnamed traveling stranger. But odds say it's Lynne, if it really comes down to it, with Jenna provoking the scene that led to her death. Jim protecting Lynne by helping to cover it up is likely. And I do think that Jim is protective enough, cares deeply enough that he could have killed Jenna before she had a chance to rip into Lynne's illusions. Maybe it's not at the coffee shop, maybe Jenna is digging into Jim on that walk home and saying how she's going to tell Lynne how it really is. Jim is thinking about that, follows Jenna inside and pops her one, ends this at her apartment. Hiding the body is an easier problem than letting Jenna destroy Lynne."

She didn't want it to be Lynne, didn't want it to be Jim, but the truth was going to end up where it needed to be.

David held out a fist. Evie lightly tapped hers against it.

"We're days away from this being solved," Evie said.

"It's gonna be the traveler," David said. "Sometimes there are bad men who do show up and make someone disappear."

"I won't be disappointed if it is." Evie thought about tomorrow. "We're going to have a very full day taking apart Jim's life. He's not going to be sleeping much, wondering which way the case is going to roll. We might as well cut the uncertainty and pull him right into the misery of more questions, see if we can shake the story."

"Think he'll lawyer up?"

"Probably. Eventually. We're going to ask the questions that would have been asked nine years ago, and it's going to get very uncomfortable for him. I would like to keep this out of the news until we've sorted it out. The headline — *Man lied to police about missing student* — would just drown us in the politics of a wealthy college. We need the neighborhood on our side, or at least neutral, if we're going to get the facts. There's definitely a neighborhood versus college crowd line around here."

"We ask questions, we stay below the radar for as long as we can," David said. "Sharon and the others should be able to join us next week. We'll cover more ground then."

"Charity event tonight, rope line analysis tomorrow, focus on Jim. It's plenty for the weekend. You've got plans with Maggie?"

"She wants to see a couple of houses I'm considering for myself. And we'll spend time opening boxes as more of her belongings arrive in the morning. Mostly it will be Maggie on the relaxed side of a performance. She's wire tight right now. She has a love-hate relationship with performance days."

David pulled into the business park next to Evie's car. She disconnected her phone from the charger. "We'll keep an eye on Lynne, make sure she's where we expect. Anything else you want me to remember?"

David smiled. "Yes. Have a good time."

Evie laughed and stepped out. "I'll remember. See you tonight, David."

TWENTY-ONE

Evie scooped up the garment bag, purse, and box with her new dress shoes from the trunk, caught movement from the corner of her eye and realized Rob was coming out to meet her. She gave him a distracted smile as she tried to shut the trunk. "Thanks for letting me change here."

"Happy to be of service," he replied, then took the garment bag and shut the trunk while she locked the car.

She stood on tiptoe to kiss him. "Sorry I'm running so late."

"Nah, fashionably late is fashionable." He led the way inside.

"Your mother will notice, make some comment."

"She always has a comment. Case breaking open?"

"Sort of — I'll explain on the drive in." She took the bag and headed to the guest bathroom to change. She had chosen the dress for its color and simplicity, and she changed into it as quickly as she could, freshened her face with a touch of lipstick and mascara, combed her hair, tucked it behind her ears, took a last look in the mirror. *It'll have to do.*

Back in the living room, Rob looked great in his suit — he always made a statement without much effort. "What do you think?" she asked with a semi-dramatic twirl in front of him. "Too much?"

Rob tipped his head, smiled as he studied her. "You look lovely, especially in red."

" 'Bold and beautiful' is what the sales clerk said."

"She was underselling the reality. It becomes you, Evie."

"Five more minutes and I'll be finished."

"In that time I think I can find a tie to match. In case somebody can't figure out you are mine," he said over his shoulder.

She felt fresh nerves as she slipped simple gold studs into her earlobes and slipped on the black satin shoes. She took in a deep breath, slowly let it out again. She would handle his parents with tact and a smile. The evening was going to go fine. She rejoined Rob.

"You found more than just a tie." He'd swapped it out for one perfectly matching her dress's shade of red, adding a similar red square to his jacket's breast pocket. He was also holding a jewelry box. It was long and thin, *so not a ring,* she noted, relieved.

"I did. Why don't you try this?" He opened the box, and the necklace inside sparkled. Nearly six inches long by four inches wide, the five fine strands of gold latticed through a series of colored gemstones. She felt herself smiling as she carefully lifted it from the box, held it up, saw how the reds picked up the color of her dress. "It's perfect, Rob. Thank you." He always had exquisite taste yet didn't make it such a pricey gift that she felt she couldn't accept it.

He secured the clasp for her behind her neck. "I was expecting a safe 'little black dress,' " he quipped, "given we're joining my parents, and I thought to add some color. Instead, it becomes a good accent piece." He held her by the shoulders, looked into her eyes and said, "My parents will be blown away. I sure am."

She laughed, blushed. "Let's go find out." She picked up the matching bag with room for phone, comb, compact, Kleenex, and not much else.

Rob helped her on with her black dress coat and offered his arm. "To a good evening already begun."

"I'm all for that."

Rob's car, a dark sedan, was not flashy on the outside but was luxurious inside. He settled her in the passenger seat before circling to the driver's side. A nice habit, one of those courtesies whenever she was with him.

She was comfortable with this man, she realized as she watched him drive, calmly handling the heavy traffic. Rob was a contrast to the other men in her past, but he suited her in ways no one else did.

"You mentioned the case took a turn." Rob looked over at her with a question in his expression.

Evie pulled her thoughts back to her day. "I'll begin by mentioning the special guest singer tonight is Margaret May McDonald. She's a big deal in the world of music, and dedicated fans make sure to be at events like this. There's a guy I'm looking for, who might put in an appearance tonight at the rope line. And another of her fans from Ellis has appeared as a possible person of interest and will probably be there too. We'll be videotaping the crowds to review tomorrow. I met Maggie last night, and I like her a lot. David, the task-force cop I've been working with, he's her guy."

Rob smiled. "The world is indeed a very

small place."

"You'll like David when you meet him."

"He's the one who came back from New York to join the team?"

"Yes. Maggie's moving back to Chicago, which is why he made the shift."

"Anything you need me to watch out for tonight?"

"Security has a photo of the local fan and will keep track of her movements. I don't have a photo of the guy, so he would have to do something to attract attention, make him stand out in the crowd. I don't expect anything like that to happen tonight, I'm just aware it could."

Rob glanced over and looked her up and down. "I don't think that little bag is spacious enough for a badge and gun, and those shoes definitely aren't up for a foot chase."

She laughed. "The place will be full of security, uniform and plainclothes cops, given the mayor and so many political types will be present. If something needs attention, I plan to yell *police,* let someone else handle matters. I'm truly off duty for a change," she said, smiling her contentment.

"I'm noting this date, as that rarely happens," Rob replied with good humor. "And if you do yell for the police, I'll pretend I've never seen you before."

They laughed together, and Evie looked at the time. The program was beginning. "I'm truly sorry we're late again —"

"Don't worry about it. I can't imagine the day I care about that more than I do about you, Evie." He reached over to squeeze her hand. "I used to be punctual to everything, good manners and all that. Then I met you and saw what it's like for Dispatch to call you in the middle of dinner, urgently send you to the other end of the state. Or realized while I was waiting at a restaurant you were trying to disengage from a mother whose son had been murdered that afternoon. You don't control very much of your time, Evie. You try with care and kindness to carve out pieces of your life for me. So while you have your particular job, that's reality, and it's an adjustment I choose to make for us. I tell people who ask us to come to an event, a party, that we would be glad to come, but we may be arriving late, and they should start the meal or program without us. If we arrive on time, they are thrilled, and if we arrive midway through the evening, they feel honored we came by." Rob chuckled. "Without intending to, you've actually raised my stature simply by the fact I'm occasionally late to gatherings of important people. It harkens back to when only kings and queens dared be late."

"I wish there was a better reason for this delay. Interviews simply produced more leads than I had anticipated, and those conversations ran long."

"So you're making progress finding your missing student?"

"Good progress. Right now it's this big mix of competing theories and possibilities, but a few days of churn like this generally gets to that moment when a name rises to the surface and it's solved."

"I'm glad, Evie. This case matters, but it's also got to be a good step in the right direction to be that successful on a first case with the task force."

"Yes, for good press coverage and to give the governor political points for what could seem a personally motivated decision for this endeavor. We need cases solved to justify the investment."

"Well, I'm glad the governor chose you to serve on it. You're good at this work."

As it turned out, they weren't all that late. Rob let the hotel's valet park the car and pulled her arm through his as they made their way toward the hotel entrance. Evie was vividly aware of those behind the rope line straining to see each new vehicle's occupants emerging, hoping to see someone famous. She almost laughed at their disappointment when they recognized neither her nor her escort. She did a quick search of their faces but didn't see Lynne. Maggie should be backstage by this time, so her absence wasn't a surprise.

Evie tried to ignore the attention her red dress captured as they entered the ballroom. *Or more likely it's Rob,* she thought with a little smile at him. A hostess discreetly led them to the front of the packed room. They were getting extra attention, both because of their late arrival and all the guests who knew Rob. Evie stopped counting after several dozen raised a glass or said hello to him. She spotted David talking with a security official in the front of the room.

The round tables seated eight, and Rob's parents sat beside a state senator and his wife. Four empty chairs formed the other half circle, Evie's and Rob's names at two of them.

"I was afraid you weren't coming, even after having blocked in the tickets," his mother said, a bit of edge to her tone.

"Life happens, Mother. We're here now," Rob said calmly as he drew out Evie's chair next to her.

"Good evening, Elizabeth," Evie said with

a smile as she sat down. "Hello, Joshua." She was on easier terms with Rob's father than his mother.

His mother nodded to Evie, then quickly turned her attention toward the other couple. "Senator, I believe you've met our son, Robert?"

Waiters carrying large trays were bringing out salads and baskets of rolls. Evie gratefully went with the diversion, simply nodded hello with a smile when Rob introduced her to the senator and his wife. It was a delicious-looking salad, topped with caramelized apple slices and walnuts. She would have taken a quick cellphone photo to add to her collection of event dishes were his mother not sitting next to her.

She wasn't able to converse with the senator's wife since they weren't seated that close to each other, but she vaguely remembered having met the woman at a similar gathering last year and that Martha Davidson had an outgoing and large family. Evie felt Elizabeth's attention shift her direction, hoped she was able to keep up her end of the conversation.

"Evie, I'm glad you were free to join us this evening. Rob had said you might be working."

There was never a good way to handle that

question; she either offered too many details or not enough. "I'd hoped to be making an arrest before tonight," she said, "having discovered what happened to my long-missing Jenna Greenhill. But I often don't get my first wish. Sharing Rob's time and a wonderful meal with all of you isn't such a bad consolation prize."

She could feel Rob's hand resting lightly against her back, knew it carried his *You go, girl!* support.

"The . . . um, the task force Governor Bliss created is making progress?" Elizabeth asked.

Evie doubted Elizabeth was actually interested, it was more likely an indirect way to let the senator know the governor had made her appointment. It was politely asked so she tried to answer in kind. "The group has excellent detectives. I'm certain a number of cases will be resolved in the coming months." She needed out of this quicksand of her work, which never made good dinner conversation, so she changed topics. "May I ask which charity tonight has your greatest interest?"

"Joshua and I have long been supporters of the Children's Hospital Fund."

Evie glanced at Rob on her other side. "Do you have a favorite? I haven't heard you say."

"I'm an equal benefactor of them all, though I think I'll ask you at the end of the evening which has captured your heart. We can make another donation in both our names."

"I have a feeling it's going to be the House of Hope. Prostitutes don't get enough care and kindness," Evie replied, knowing the charity firsthand through Ann's involvement, and aware it happened to be one of the few religious charities being high-lighted this evening.

Evie caught a signal from David across the room and felt immense relief. "Actually, I am working briefly this evening. All these dignitaries at a single place, you understand." She gave the group a brief smile. "Would you excuse me a moment?"

Rob stood and held her chair as she slipped away to join David.

"His parents?" David asked when she joined him.

"Yes. Maggie must have put in a request — you're at the same table."

"I did at her request. I'll join you shortly so I can watch Maggie's performance from the audience."

"Elizabeth is likely to give you a polite third degree. How off duty are you?"

"Around Maggie I'm always additional security. I'm carrying credentials and a weapon, if that's what you're asking. You think I'm going to need them with his mother?" David asked, amused.

Evie couldn't help her laughter. "I couldn't figure how to easily carry mine in a handbag that matched my outfit. I figured I'd yell 'Police!' and let you handle anything that came up. You've seen Maggie?"

"I've been banished for the moment. She's in the dressing room with her hair and makeup people. Showing nerves, as you might have heard she still deals with. You're showing a few yourself. She's that difficult?"

"Elizabeth's a nice enough woman, and yet I always tense up around her. We had some minor collisions early on with the cop thing, and I've never been able to sort out how to handle her questions."

"Tactfully, truthfully."

"Trying my best."

"The rope line so far has been a lot of requests for autographs and selfies," David mentioned. "The back of the hotel has been getting some fan interest too — staff entrances, fans hoping to spot those who might try to slip into the hotel unnoticed. Security has been checking IDs for anyone entering the hotel throughout the day, so we'll have security camera footage to review for those areas too. Lynne has been moving between the two areas. She's at the back presently."

"I'm relieved to hear that. Thanks, David."

Evie walked back to her table, offered a small smiled apology to Rob. The entrée arriving gave her cover for avoiding further conversation. Evie settled in to enjoy the meal, listening to Rob's conversation with the senator about a business park development on the south side of Chicago. David slipped into the seat beside Rob some minutes later, and a waiter promptly brought him a dinner plate.

"All's quiet?" she leaned around to ask softly.

"We're good."

The mayor was just taking the podium, so Evie quickly introduced the two men.

"I've heard nice things," Rob said, offering a hand.

"The same," David replied with a smile.

After the mayor's welcome and introductory remarks, the lights dimmed for a video of the featured charities. The main speaker for the evening expanded on the work of the organizations represented in the video, and he closed with an impassioned and genuine plea for donations to continue the work of each. Baskets with envelopes had been distributed to each table to collect contributions, and a general stirring filled the room as checkbooks appeared and envelopes were stuffed and returned to the baskets.

The mayor shifted the program focus to the music for the evening. People turned their seats to better view the stage as he talked about their guest artist.

Applause grew as the curtain pulled back on Maggie in a shimmering pale-blue gown, flanked by tall vases of white roses. Two keyboards and two guitars comprised the musicians to either side, with a percussionist situated with his rhythm set in the back of the semicircle stage. She looked elegant and poised, comfortable before her audience.

Maggie waited as the sound filled the ballroom in a long lead-in, and Evie could feel the anticipation building. The slender woman before them was pulling the audience in with her infectious smile, a hand at her side tapping lightly to the beat. Because Evie was watching for it, she caught the extra joy in Maggie's expression when she located David. The accompanying music rose in volume, and Maggie's voice joined it with an energy that made the room come alive.

"Lover of mine, how great is your arrival,
Joy of my heart, how pleasant your smile,
Come and fill my heart, meet my every
    need,
Only with you, Beloved,
am I fully alive."

The voice behind the number-one song in the country soared up to the high ceiling. Evie noticed even the waitstaff stopping to listen. Having never been that near a performer before, it was a revelation as Maggie captured every guest in the ballroom with the power of her words and the charm of the music. By the end of the second song, the guests were transformed from interested onlookers to an involved audience. Increasingly enthusiastic applause broke out after each song.

The curtain closed on the final piece following Maggie's wave, and the mayor returned to the podium while the waitstaff hurried in with dessert.

"Very nice," Rob's mother said, looking specifically at David, and he smiled his thanks.

The mayor had been trying for some time

507

to get the crowd's attention, and after they finally quieted down, he said, "And now a final surprise guest for the evening." The room quieted further. "Please help me welcome" — the curtain behind him began to part once again — "our new governor, Governor Bliss!"

Applause filled the room to greet the man now striding toward the podium.

"Good evening, my friends. Wasn't that spectacular? I had to watch on a screen in the back, but Maggie of the Triple M band spoke to my head and to my heart tonight, folks. Let's give her another round of applause she'll be able to hear in the dressing room." The crowd cheered in response.

"I asked your gracious mayor here," he continued, "if I could add a few words tonight to underscore the enormous place charity has in our state and the work these wonderful organizations have accomplished for our citizens." He went on to list the impact felt across the state among children, families, schools, law enforcement, and others.

Movement at a side door caught Evie's attention. Maggie slipped into the ballroom wearing a simple blue dress, and not everyone immediately recognized her as she made her way between the tables. David stood and pulled out a seat for her. Rob slid his chair closer to Evie's to make room. The mayor went to the podium to thank the governor for coming, and again applause filled the room.

Maggie glanced around the table, read the situation, and before she sat she hugged Evie. "I'm so glad you were able to come tonight, Evie." Photographers working the room had spotted Maggie, their flashes going off in response. "Introductions, please?"

"Of course. Maggie," Evie said, "I'd like you to meet Senator Scott Mitchell and his wife, Martha. Also Mr. and Mrs. Joshua Turney, their son, Robert. David you obviously know well. May I introduce our guest singer for tonight, Margaret May McDonald, of the band Triple M."

"It's a pleasure to meet you all." Maggie smiled around the circle as she sat down by David, leaned her head on his shoulder. "I do know you pretty well," she said, and he chuckled. She leaned forward and added, "I've heard the name Rob Turney recently. Evie is smitten."

Rob grinned. "I'm glad to hear it, as it's mutual."

Evie didn't dare look at Elizabeth, but she was in awe of Maggie's understanding of the dynamics here.

Maggie nodded her approval, turned to David. "How was it, range of one to ten?"

"Wonderful, as always," he replied, offering a fork to share his dessert. "At least a solid eight, because the room acoustics could only go so far."

"I'll take it. Because I'm about to be outperformed." Maggie nodded to a children's choir now taking the stage. "Their soloist is an eight-year-old, and she's magnificent."

The mayor introduced the choir from one of the charities they had been highlighting. The children sang with all the energy they had, obviously having worked hard to memorize the words, clapping in rhythm at the same time. And the little girl, holding the mic like she'd done it all her life, brought the house down. Evie mostly watched Maggie, who was enjoying every bit of the performance.

When it was over, the socializing began. Many came to greet Rob and his parents. Politician types stopped by to speak with the senator and his wife. Maggie hurried to the stage to visit with the children before getting swarmed with autograph and selfie requests.

Evie had come to realize from past experience that it was the personal connections made before and after the program that was the real reason guests attended these events. It would be another hour before Rob was free to leave. She smiled a hello to those Rob introduced her to, stood quietly by his side listening to the conversations, offered a quiet remark to Rob in free moments between guests, until gestured over by his mother to be introduced to someone else. *My star must have risen with that hug from Maggie,* she thought, shaking hands with another woman Elizabeth thought she should know but likely would never remember.

The head of hotel security let her know the video surveillance would run until midnight and they could pick up copies in the morning for review. After nearly an hour, Evie sank into a chair, drank some water, and picked up a chocolate from a dish on the table.

Maggie joined her. "That's an absolutely beautiful necklace, Evie."

"Rob has very good taste . . . and the income to match it." They shared a laugh together.

"No more autographs?" Evie asked.

"It's a generational thing. The rest of the crowd doesn't realize their grandkids are going to be crushed tomorrow when they

511

find out they left without an autograph or photo. Have any plans with Rob for this weekend?"

"David and I have security footage to review tomorrow morning, but then I imagine Rob and I will spend most of it together."

"Dinner and a movie Saturday evening, church on Sunday, lunch with friends," Rob suggested from behind, kneading her shoulders. "We're going to make up for the last few weeks while our jobs are cooperating."

Evie thought it sounded wonderful, and leaned her head back to smile at him. "Perfect. Your parents get away okay?"

"They're going out for drinks with the city council president. Maggie, would you and David like to join us for a nightcap at my place?"

"Sure."

It couldn't have been scripted for a more memorable way to end a Friday night. Evie leaned into Rob as they said good-night beside her car. "Thanks for this, Rob. You had a very nice idea."

"You've got interesting friends, Evie. And I feel like David and Maggie are on the way to becoming my friends too."

She smiled. "Welcome to the worlds of

music and security." Maggie had taken them on a tour of her last few months via pictures on her phone, added stories from New York that only Maggie could have lived, David adding color by talking a bit about the complexities of keeping overly ardent fans from hounding her.

"I needed this non-work evening. We both did, right?"

He held her close and gently kissed her. "What do you say I pick you up around six tomorrow evening at your hotel, assuming your case hasn't moved to a solution before then? We'll have dinner, and you can choose the movie. I don't suppose I could get you to wear that red dress again?"

She laughed, lightly punched his arm. "Not a chance. But the rest of it is a deal."

She so wanted to find the courage to say yes to this man. His world wasn't hers, *but he was.* She thought she could learn to manage the occasional party and charity event because they were part of his life. He had already shown her he was comfortable with her friends, and seeing him with David and Maggie was reinforcing that. Tonight she felt the kind of peace she wanted for her life. God was showing her what a good thing felt like, and it seemed as though it was here.

She slipped into her car and buckled the seat belt, waved goodbye.

TWENTY-TWO

Evie mentally rearranged her work board as she drove to their ad hoc office early Saturday morning. Jim Ulin. Lynne Benoit. An unnamed concert traveler. One of those three held the probable answer to Jenna Greenhill's disappearance.

Today would be marked by interviews with people who knew Jim, finding those in the neighborhood who might be able to corroborate his story about walking Jenna home. He'd admitted to a fistfight with someone named Rick. She would chase that lead down, find out what had triggered the fight, understand when and how Jim reverted to violence. She would speak with adults who had watched Jim grow up, his friends, see if frustration with being stuck in the neighborhood, unable to attend college, had been gnawing at him. Jenna might have pushed Jim's buttons there if it was a sensitive point.

She wanted David with her when she sat down with Jim once more. If any part of his story was fabricated to protect himself, to protect Lynne, they should be able to find the weak spots. She couldn't help but like Jim, but that didn't mean he couldn't have killed Jenna or been involved in covering up what happened to help Lynne.

Focusing on the unnamed traveler mostly meant sifting through those on the rope line last night — isolate faces in the right age range, get the FBI to run facial recognition against DMV records, run those names against their multitude of other lists. It would mean hours of work on the video, though the task itself was straightforward. Looking at faces, coming up with names, running background checks, and then hoping somebody surfaced as a person of interest.

Satisfied with the plan for the day, she headed into the office, whistling under her breath. She had dinner and a movie with Rob to look forward to. Until then, she had a case to push to a conclusion.

"Hey, Evie. You're in early after a late night."

She nearly bobbled the box of muffins in her hands, not expecting to find David already here. "I didn't see your car."

David approached from the break room, coffee mug in hand. "I caught a cab over at four a.m. I didn't trust myself to drive. Had a crazy thought — or maybe dream — I wanted to run down."

"How crazy?" She opened the lid on the muffins and offered him breakfast.

He selected the blueberry one, nodded his thanks. "Do you think our traveler would select a new victim from that rope line? Consider it to be a Maggie event of significance, mark out his victim, pickpocket her driver's license?"

A dagger hit her heart as she winced. "It hadn't even crossed my mind that he might think that way. It's hard to lift a license when people are bundled up in coats and gloves . . . but yeah, to lift a wallet from a purse, that could happen."

"The thought hit me hard enough it wouldn't let me sleep. I've been looking at the security video." He motioned to the conference room.

"You should have called me. I would have come in and helped."

"No use both of us losing sleep if the idea didn't go anywhere. It was just crucial enough I wanted to check it quickly." He gestured to the projection screen, where tiled photos were on pause. "We've got four

517

camera angles from five p.m. to midnight. I ran one view at speed just to get a sense of how many people come and go, and most are there at the rope line for upwards of an hour. So I'm estimating the number of people is going to be around fifteen hundred. I've run it at three times speed, looking for a pickpocket, and come up empty — that dropped my stress level considerably. I'm in synchronized mode now, running all four camera angles together. I'm saving faces in the crowd, those who might be the right age — anyone mid-twenties to mid-thirties."

"Let's hope our traveler was there," Evie said. It would eliminate Jim or Lynne. She couldn't help but wish for that.

"I'm optimistic, if only because that's the only way to face hours of staring at video," David replied with a short laugh. "After this, there's the film from the back of the hotel. I scanned it, maybe a hundred fifty people, mostly dedicated fans who worked their way back there and stayed put for the whole evening. I've got Lynne moving between the two locations."

Evie unwrapped a muffin. "You want to swap places for a while — I watch the video, you dig into Jim's life?"

"Thanks for the offer, but I'll stay on it.

Once you start, it's like running a marathon. You don't want to let it beat you or stop until it's done. I'm sending the faces in batches to the FBI for those recognition checks with DMV. Some images aren't at a good angle, some people won't have Illinois drivers' licenses — could have been issued in Indiana or Wisconsin — but it'll make a solid start. As they feed names back, I'll send them to researchers for background checks."

"I appreciate this, David."

"The concert traveler I can handle. Put your focus on Jim."

"I'll be heading out for a long list of interviews once it's a reasonable hour to knock on doors."

"If I'm not here when you get back, I'll be at the hotel catching a few hours' sleep. Call if you get any leads and want me to join you."

"That I can promise." She settled at a desk to begin digging deeper into the life of Jim Ulin.

A day of productive interviews always put Evie in a good mood. It was coming up on two p.m. when she stopped in once more at the Benoit home, accepted Lynne's mother's offer of coffee. David was having a productive day as well, going by the number of messages she'd received. The FBI was having better success identifying people from the rope line photos than she'd expected.

Evie's phone dinged, and she looked at another face, now with a name, but didn't recognize the individual.

"Need to answer that?" Lynne's mother asked as she led the way to the kitchen.

Evie shook her head and pocketed the phone. "It can wait an hour." David would call if a background check said they had likely found the right guy. She accepted the coffee Nancy offered.

"Lynne should be getting home soon. I can text her for you, ask her whereabouts."

"No need, Nancy, but thanks. I just want to confirm something Jim said, but I can ask her another time. So Lynne had a good time at the concert last night?"

"She had a wonderful night. And before you ask, I can make a safe assumption she's probably with Jim right now, telling him all the details of the evening. They may not be dating anymore, but he's still important to her." Nancy hesitated. "Jim stopped by here last night while Lynne was at the concert. He shared with me his account of that night he told you."

Evie simply nodded and drank her coffee. She wasn't sure why she was sitting here with Lynne's mom, but maybe it was simply this — to get Nancy's read on what Jim had told her. "Did it surprise you?"

"That Jenna had caused him some problems, no. That he hadn't told the police the details back then — that did. I had no idea Jim had seen Jenna that night until he sat at this kitchen table and told me about that midnight coffee-shop visit." She twisted a napkin in her hands as she talked. "I'm concerned about what it's going to mean for Jim. He's the one you have to look at now, right?"

"Yes."

"Is there anything else I might be able to answer, Evie?"

"How did Jim change after Jenna went missing?"

"He was very worried about Lynne. She was searching the neighborhood and campus all hours of the day, looking for Jenna. In true Lynne fashion, she'd fixated on the possibility that if she looked hard enough, she could find her friend. Jim wasn't getting much sleep. He had good people working the music store and coffee shop, but he handled all the inventory, made up the work schedules, helped his dad run both places

521

— and he was needed. Within a week I was thinking this guy's going to make himself very ill if he keeps this up. I predicted that correctly. He spent close to a month fighting off a serious cough and bad bout of the flu. It's actually what got Lynne off her obsession with Jenna, the fact Jim was so sick. Lynne can be a pretty good 'mother' when it comes to fussing over someone who's ill. It probably embarrassed Jim to no end once he was feeling better, but Lynne doesn't offer much slack with her get-better rules. I suppose she learned that from me."

Evie smiled at Nancy's admission. "Have you had any concerns about Jim over the years? I've heard variations of the story about his fight with Rick."

"The one I heard from Rick's mother was they had a disagreement over Rick being back on marijuana. He'd made the mistake of handing off a joint to a friend at the coffee shop. Jim wasn't having the stuff anywhere around the place, insisted that Rick give up the habit."

Evie lifted an eyebrow. The variation she'd heard was of Rick insisting on driving after he'd been drinking. He refused to give his girlfriend the keys to let her drive. Jim had laid down the law, said he'd drive her home himself. And the sparks flew.

Nancy got up and arranged a plate of cookies. "Jim's had a few fights," she conceded as she brought the cookies over. "He tends to stand up for the people who are having difficulties taking care of themselves. It goes all the way back to fourth grade when he took on the playground bully and won that fight. And that characteristic doesn't play well when wondering how Jim would have handled Jenna. Not because of himself, but because of Lynne." She sighed, picked up a cookie, put it down again.

"But, honest truth," she said, looking straight at Evie, "the one thing I heard last night that I was most relieved about is this — Jim hadn't decided how to deal with the problem yet. He'd simply seen it clearly that night. Maybe he would have sought Steve's help, or he might have asked for mine. Maybe he would have had a talk with Lynne and found a way to break the news that Jenna wasn't being a true friend. But the one thing that seemed obvious to me as I listened was that he hadn't decided yet what to do. Jenna disappeared before Jim could figure out how to deal with it. I know how awkward that sounds, the timing of it, but for my part I'm sure of it. Whatever happened, Jim wasn't involved in Jenna's disappearance."

Evie nodded, said nothing.

"Common sense must tell you the same," Nancy said, almost imploring. "If something had snapped that night, if Jim had been involved, he wouldn't have said a word to you about seeing Jenna at the coffee shop at midnight or mentioned walking her home. No one has known that for the last nine years."

"Actually, I discovered this morning that two others in the neighborhood did see him walking with her," Evie mentioned. "They didn't tell anyone before this because they liked him, didn't want to jam him up on speculation. But the two were seen together."

Nancy bit her lip. "Surely there's more evidence to say what did happen to Jenna that night, other facts that will clear Jim?"

"The facts and theories on this case fill plenty of pages by now," Evie reassured. Her phone chimed with another photo match. She checked the photo and name — neither generated recognition. She pocketed the phone again, gave a small smile in apology. "Another angle being actively pursued right now."

Evie picked up a cookie, if only to keep the conversation going and on an informal level. "I'm looking for the truth in as many directions as it takes until I can find out what happened. I'm going to need to sit down with Lynne for an extended conversation in a day or two. It would help me to know what Jim talks to Lynne about today or tomorrow — if he tells her any of this or leaves the past alone."

"I doubt he mentions anything about Jenna to her, but if he does, I'll let you know how Lynne responds. I realize that conversation is going to have to happen. However I can help my daughter, it matters that you let me."

"I'll do my best not to surprise Lynne or you, Nancy, with the way the case unfolds. That's the best I can offer."

"I'll take it, and thank you."

Evie pushed back her chair and stood. "Thanks for your time." She held up the cookie. "These are great, by the way." She headed back out.

Evie wasn't surprised to find David had yet to retreat to the hotel for some sleep. "Are you swimming in caffeine yet?" she asked, leaning against the doorframe to the conference room.

He smiled. "The tiredness comes in waves. Another hour and I'll abandon you, crash at Maggie's for the evening."

Evie looked at the whiteboard, caught off guard by the running tally. "Two hundred sixty-three names? Are you kidding me?"

David laughed. "I've only sent you photos of those with backgrounds that look to be a match, those who lived around Ellis nine years ago, attended Brighton College, that kind of thing." He swiveled toward the board. "The rest of this is actually fascinating — the type of people who filled the rope line last night. Most were there to see the who's who of Chicago. I've been making educated guesses and categorizing them into groups as I pull up background info.

"Four are names I recognize, people known to be a problem for Maggie. Eighteen have criminal records, mostly car thefts and drug offenses. Twenty-six names went to the same college as one of our missing women. I'm digging into all those, looking for any sign one of them could be our concert traveler."

"You're making rapid progress."

"It feels like it, but it's going to take the weekend plus a few days to generate backgrounds on this many names. Once the bulk of the facial recognition is done, we'll want to step back and use all the data we have, develop a top-ten list to interview."

"I'm all over that," Evie agreed.

"How did your interviews go regarding Jim?"

"I confirmed part of his story, that he did walk Jenna home. It eliminates the coffee shop as the site of what happened, shifts it back to the apartment building. The rest of the conversations filled in how I see him. I still think it could be him even when I don't want it to be."

David's laptop chimed. "Another batch from the FBI — twenty-seven names I'll send to the printer."

"Where do you want me next?"

"Let me send the full list to your account. I haven't run the names against Maggie's database yet. If any of these people ordered tickets from the website or purchased other memorabilia, we can send their credit-card numbers through the big credit-card search."

"Perfect."

Evie moved to her desk, wished she hadn't run out of sweet-tarts, and made a mental note to at least buy some jelly beans. She could feel the case beginning to tip over like a wall of bricks. The pressure was doing its job.

"Evie."

At the urgent call, she looked over to see

David roll his chair back to rap on the glass, his other hand holding the receiver of the landline. She saved her file and hurried to join him.

He covered the mouthpiece. "The FBI team working the three smothered victims and the composite partial print just got a hit." He uncovered the receiver. "Tell me that name again."

"Andrew Timmets," he relayed, then spelled the last name. "Indiana license, 78 Mallard Road in Indianapolis. He's in the system because he's got a business license as a locksmith. He's twenty-seven. They just pinned his credit-card numbers to four of the five concert locations and dates. All but Tammy."

"They've got him!"

David grinned. "Yes, they do. So that means we do."

She spun his laptop on the conference table to face her and quickly ran the name against her favorite working lists.

David covered the receiver and said to her, "The FBI guys are now hollering over speakerphones with both Indiana and Ohio or I'd put this on speaker too."

"I'll take the relays. He's a Brighton music student who didn't graduate. That fits. And I've got him in Maggie's fan database.

There's a blue flag on the name with a four-digit number . . . what's that mean?"

David winced. "A photo was taken with Maggie. If she stands with someone at a public event for a quick shot by her photographer, a copy of that photo gets mailed to the fan."

"Can I access that photo so we have a picture of him?" Evie asked.

"The FBI is sending a photo over now." David pinned the phone against his shoulder as he swiveled to check incoming mail on the desktop computer. "And here it is." He clicked the image to full screen.

David broke in on the phone chatter. "Hey, guys, guys! He's in Chicago, not Indiana. Or was twenty-four hours ago. I can put him on the rope line here Friday night."

He pointed to the video feeds. "Run the video back to around six p.m., before the event starts, back of the hotel."

Evie searched for the guy around the time David remembered.

"There!"

She stopped the video.

"That's him."

David shifted back to the phone. "I'm looking at him on Friday night. We need a BOLO out on his car between Chicago and

Indiana. What's he driving? Odds are he spent the night here before traveling back. He attended Brighton College for a time, so I'm guessing he's got friends in this broader area. What's on his credit cards? Did we get lucky and he stayed at a hotel?"

"He drives a silver-and-gray Accord, sports model, license FST 616," David relayed. "There's a white van registered to the locksmith business, license BVR 3293."

Evie had grabbed a marker and was writing down the information on the whiteboard.

"No credit-card activity in the Chicago area," David continued. "Last charge was Thursday at a gas station two blocks from his home."

"Staying with friends? Traveling on cash? Prepaid credit cards?" Evie suggested. Her attention was now pinned to the security feeds — what he was doing, what he was paying attention to, who he was speaking with at the back of the hotel. He didn't look like a murderer, more like the college kid still living next door, young, neat haircut, clean-shaven, moving quietly through the crowd.

David got up and began pacing, the phone cord corralling him to within a dozen feet of his chair. "We need to get an APB out on

530

him, for the Chicago area as well as Indiana. The BOLO is going to be helpful, but it's the guy we want to hold on to. We need to figure out how to pick him up tonight. Can we ping his phone, get a location on that? Surely we've got enough to get a locate warrant."

"David, he's talking with Lynne."

David whipped around to view the streaming security footage.

Evie felt herself breaking out in a cold sweat. She saw no signs he was invading Lynne's personal space, trying to lift a wallet, but they were having a long and animated conversation. Lynne's smile flashed more than a few times at something he said. "Move away from her. Come on. Move on, speak with someone else," Evie whispered, her voice tight.

David's hand tightened on her shoulder. He sped up the video so they could see the length of the interaction.

Evie snatched up her phone, clicked on a phone number. "Mrs. Benoit, is Lynne home?" She shook her head at David. "It's important I find your daughter now. I have a photo I need to show her."

Evie silenced the phone. "She thinks Lynne's still with Jim at the coffee shop. She'll text to get that confirmed, ask her to stay put." David nodded.

"Yes, let me know, Nancy."

Evie watched the feed with her heart pounding. It wasn't good. He talked to Lynne for more than ten minutes, then moved on. But thirty minutes later, he was back talking with her again. Evie watched Lynne share what looked like a thermos of coffee with him — being herself, nice Lynne, not reading this guy properly. He walked out of range just after eight p.m., didn't reappear in the camera feeds.

Nancy's text confirmed Lynne was at the coffee shop with Jim, and Evie's heart rate settled.

"We need to know what those conversations were about." David ran back the video and froze the security-camera image of Andrew and Lynne talking together, sent the image to the printer. He also sent the FBI photo of Andrew to the printer. "Let's go find her."

"Thanks."

"Guys," he said into the receiver on his shoulder, "I'm changing phones. Patch me into the conference call on my cell."

David nudged her with his elbow, pulled out his keys and held them up. She smiled as she took them, not surprised he wanted the longer leg room of his vehicle over hers.

■ ■ ■ ■

Evie drove to the music store and coffee shop, not using the flashing lights because the situation didn't warrant it, but pushing the speed where she safely could.

"Indiana PD has an unmarked car at Andrew's house," David relayed. "There's no sign of his car, lights are off, mail still in the box — hasn't been home today."

"Can they get a warrant with the info they have?"

"Someone from the FBI team is vigorously arguing that question with a judge right now," David said.

He joined the ongoing conference call. "Let's knock on neighbors' doors, ask where he might be staying in Chicago, what hotel, which friends. Say there's an emergency. Just get officers to find someone who can place him. If you have to, get a neighbor to call his cell, invent a reason for the call — there's a gas leak in the neighborhood, a car hit a tree in his yard, something like that."

She scanned the street and adjacent lots for any sign of Andrew's car in case he'd followed Lynne.

The coffee shop was busy on a Saturday evening. Evie noted the full tables inside.

Dinner hour. *My dinner date with Rob . . .* As soon as she parked, she sent a quick text: *case breaking, sorry have to cancel.*

Jim was behind the coffee bar. *And there's Lynne.* Evie's heartbeat slowed into normal territory as she walked toward the young woman sitting on a stool near the popcorn maker. She was keeping the paper popcorn bags filled for the crowd.

It was Jim who spotted her first, spilling the iced coffee he was making. He shook the liquid off his hand, dumped it, and reached for a rag to clean up. He called something to the woman working with him. She nodded and started in on a new drink.

Jim ducked under the counter and came around, stopping beside Lynne, who was facing the other way and so hadn't seen them enter. Jim motioned toward the music store, and Evie diverted that direction, David following.

Wiping his hands on his apron, Jim stepped through the connecting doorway. Lynne was right behind him with a welcoming smile.

"I didn't recognize you yesterday," Jim commented to David, his expression calm, but his eyes looking wary. "You're Maggie's David, right? You really did buy that keyboard for her — they weren't joshing me?"

"Maggie's going to be composing on that keyboard as soon as the music room is ready at her home," David replied easily. "Hello, Lynne. I'm sorry your name wasn't drawn so you could attend the concert inside."

"You pointed me out to Maggie. I saw you do it. That was nice of you."

David smiled. "She remembers the tangelos you brought to the dressing room for her that night. That was nice of *you.*"

"Thanks. Mom sent me this weird message. I was supposed to stay put until you showed me a photo?"

"There's someone you met last night behind the hotel," David began. "I'd like you to take a look at the picture and tell me what you remember about your conversation."

"Sure."

David must have been recognized by someone in the coffee shop, as a couple of college students were now glancing his way and whispering together near the arched doorway leading into the music store. Evie shifted her jacket to show her badge, shook her head, and they left again.

David showed Lynne the first photo he'd printed.

"This is before the evening got started," Lynne said immediately. "See the empty spot here? That's where the bus parked with the choir kids. They arrived after the program started since they were the last ones onstage. And this space here, that's where the florist's van parked. Did you see the white roses for Maggie's concert? I stayed on the rope line until she arrived, then went to the back to watch the crew come and go."

David listened patiently until she stopped to take a breath, then tapped the photo of Lynne talking to Andrew Timmets. "It's good you dressed warmly for the evening. Do you remember what you two were talking about?"

Lynne wrinkled her forehead. "Just casual stuff."

"Can you remember some topics?" David asked. "Anything you said, he said?"

Lynne pointed out a woman in the background. "He was asking if that was Maggie's hairdresser. I told him no, that's Jessica Noland, who styles mostly politicians' and their wives' hair. She was probably there to help one of the platform guests. Maggie has her own stylist, and she was already inside. Not that there aren't good ones in Chicago she could use," Lynne said earnestly. "For music videos produced in Chicago, bands often use Kathy Gibson, Evelyn Marsh, or Tate Philips, while Maggie is loyal to Amy

Frond. And I'd seen Amy and her assistants arrive shortly after Ashley carried in Maggie's wardrobe box."

David tapped the photo of the man talking with Lynne again. "Did he say anything personal, his name or where he was from? Did he sound like someone from Chicago?"

"Indiana," Lynne said promptly. She patted her left wrist. "His watch was Indiana Bluedogs. That's basketball, and a collector's piece. It's exclusively for sale to alumni, or I suppose you could buy one from other alumni. Most people don't wear watches anymore, unless it's the smart kind, so the college must mean something to him. He wasn't old enough to have been out of college that many years."

"That's really helpful information, Lynne," David encouraged. "What else do you remember? It looks like he talked to you again about half an hour later."

"He was staying with friends and arrived late, missed Maggie coming in because he couldn't find a place to park. He wasn't a hotel guest and didn't qualify to use their parking lot. He finally found street parking in a neighborhood and walked a mile to the hotel. He wasn't dressed for the weather. He had a warm jacket and gloves, but not a decent hat or boots, only tennis shoes. I'd brought a big thermos along, so I shared my coffee with him. He made that face that says he's not accustomed to drinking it with so much sugar."

"Did he say anything about his friends, the people he was staying with?"

"I got the impression it was a married couple rather than college buddies, but he really didn't say much more. Just said 'she' when he mentioned being glad he was staying somewhere less costly than this hotel, and said, '*He* didn't warn me about the parking problems.' "

"Was he interested in anyone else who came or went?"

"No, but most people were already inside by six p.m."

"Did he comment on your Triple M sweatshirt?"

"He said something like 'a fellow fan' when he first walked up, like there weren't all that many of us in the crowd. It's hard to tell how many Triple M fans were there when everybody's bundled up, but I knew several from Maggie's local fan page who said they were going to be there. Some of us hung out and shared photos of Maggie while we waited for the program to conclude. We were getting tweets from a few lucky enough to be inside, which had a few pictures of Maggie, but no one had good sound so we could hear her."

David tapped the photo again. "Did you tell him much about yourself?"

"How do you mean?"

"Your name? How you met Maggie?"

"It would have been rude not to give my name when we're having a fairly long conversation. I said I was a fan of Maggie's, that it was wonderful to have her back in Chicago. Oh, and he said something about a long drive to see her." Lynne closed her eyes, pondering the wording. " 'It will be worth the long drive to see her.' Like that. He mostly seemed distracted to me — he was impatient for more activity, more coming and going, thought there would be a bigger crowd. You have to be patient if you want to capture the experience of a rope line. You need to wait for the action to come to you. He was all over the place, walking down past the vehicles, circling back to the front of the hotel, rejoining us at the back. You lose the best vantage points when you move around that way."

She thought for a long moment, shook her head. "He was nice enough but never said his name. He didn't stay to see Maggie leave. I told him she would use the back exit when the evening was over, she always does at events, but he must have thought she'd use the front and missed her leave like he missed her arrive. That would have totally bummed me out if I'd traveled a ways to see her." Lynne flashed David a smile. "Maggie looked great. She's been working out in New York, you can tell. She's gorgeous — her photos don't do her justice."

"I'd agree with you on that," David said. "Thank you, Lynne. What you told us helps."

"Okay." She shrugged. "But I don't see how."

"If you see him again, would you call me?" David handed her one of his cards.

"Sure." She looked at David, then Evie. "He must have done something."

"He maybe did. We need to talk to him. And you should consider him someone you don't want to be alone with."

"If I see him, I'll call." She carefully tucked David's card into her pocket. "I took your other advice. I sent my song notebook to Mr. Thomas with the cover letter you suggested. I copied all the pages first and then sent it registered mail because I didn't want it to get lost. I hope he won't think that too much trouble, that he has to sign for it."

"You did fine. It's a valuable notebook."

"It would be a really big break to have the same teacher as Maggie helping me fine-tune my lyrics."

"You've got a solid chance. He only takes on a few new songwriters a year, so if you hear back from him even with just a comment, consider that a real break. Submit again in six months to see if he selects you for the next opening."

"I'll persist," Lynne promised. "Maggie's voice coach was in Barrington. I asked if the woman could be my coach too, but she'd decided to retire. Maggie was her last."

David nodded. "Keep singing, Lynne. Your break is going to come — talent always wins with time and dedication."

"Thanks."

David looked to Jim. "Do me a favor and walk Lynne home tonight."

"Sure . . ."

Evie caught Jim's worried look and shook her head. They weren't about to explain further, even if Lynne hadn't been standing there.

Evie was feeling an urgency about what should come next. "We need to check out Maggie's hairdresser, makeup people, any support around Maggie at the event. Basically anyone who would know where she lives or have a way to find out."

"I'm on it," David replied, sending multiple texts as they returned to his car. "Maggie's band members left for New York this morning, but her hair and makeup people have hired new assistants for the Chicago area when Maggie is back here. We'll track down those names, make sure no one opens the door to an unfamiliar face tonight. I've already assigned security to cover the grounds at Maggie's home while she's in residence, just in case." He read replies coming in and nodded. "John is moving on getting that list of names, buttoning people up."

"Back to the office?" Evie asked, sliding the key into the ignition.

"Yes."

"As soon as we're there, I'll get the task force on a conference call, get them up to speed. We may need their help before tonight plays out. Sharon's assistance with the press is a given."

"Thanks." David dialed from the passenger seat. "I'm back, guys, talk to me. Tell me you've found something useful."

Evie used the wipers to brush off a fresh dusting of snow as she listened to David's side of the conversation. Road and traffic noise made putting the phone on speaker impractical.

"Nice!" David turned her way, relaying key points. "They located where Andrew Timmets stayed last night, have his background, just pulled up his social-media page under 'Tim Mets' — a play on his surname. But it's our guy."

Evie smiled. "That suggests he's posted something that could be worrisome to him if it was under his real name."

"I agree." David reached around for his briefcase. "Give me the rest of it, guys." He listened in while he opened the case and retrieved his electronic tablet, clicked it on.

"He grew up in Chicago," he relayed to Evie. "His parents are divorced, the father still here in Chicago, the mother now in Indiana. They've got a cop at the father's Chicago home, but the man hasn't seen his son in six years. The mother in Indiana isn't home."

"Where was Andrew last night?"

"Staying with college friends — a married couple, Judy and Jeffery Oakland. Andrew left at ten a.m., said he was heading back to Indiana."

"If he left at ten to go home, he would've been there by now with hours to spare,"

Evie said. "Either he's on the Interstate on his way home or he's still in the Chicago area."

"Indiana issued a locate warrant, but that search is coming up blank. Could be he's got his phone turned off, or he's not in their geographic area yet. They're having a hard time convincing a judge on the Illinois side to issue one. Cops are looking for other friends. They're trying to get his past phone records to help with their search."

"A long shot, but worth a try," Evie said.

"What's on his crime sheet?" David took notes as he listened on the phone. "Thanks, I appreciate the update. I'll be back in touch in about twenty minutes." He ended the call, pocketed his phone. "Andrew's got a pled-down B&E from when he was fifteen, which was sealed or he wouldn't have that locksmith license. Guys from that juvenile-hall era are suspected of running a robbery ring. Cops think Andrew is hopping over here and unlocking doors for them. He's been questioned by both Chicago and Indiana cops over the years, but no charges have been filed."

"He got into trouble young and never got out of it," Evie guessed.

David nodded. "Chicago cops are trying to track down those friends, but they aren't getting much cooperation from any wives or girlfriends at home. They're being warned not to tip Andrew off that cops are looking for him, yet as soon as the door closes, someone's going for the phone. He'll soon figure out he's got a welcome waiting for him in Indianapolis."

Evie glanced over as he brought up Tim Mets's social-media page. "I doubt he's heading home," she said. "Remember Lynne's quote? 'It will be worth the long drive to see her.' It's future. That bothers me. I don't think Lynne misquoted him, David. He drives from Indiana to see Maggie, misses her arriving at the event, misses her departure — maybe he's not leaving town until he does see her."

"Right," David said, his voice grim. "We can cut off the avenues to Maggie. She's not scheduled to make any public appearances, and we can lock down anybody with information about her home. But if we don't get traction on him in the coming hours, maybe Maggie spends tonight somewhere else. For now, a security guy is on the grounds — and it's a secure property. An address would get him only so far."

David scrolled through the photos and postings on Mets's page. "There's nothing particularly recent; a photo from a soccer match last weekend is the latest. He's a Maggie fan, all right — he's got quite a collection of concert photos under a Triple M tab. But he's also an ardent fan of what looks to be another half-dozen bands. He plays guitar, likes soccer . . . and is apparently rather vain given all the photos here of just him."

Evie smiled at his light assessment. She sincerely hoped they weren't still chasing this guy in a day or two. "It's going to be hard to live with if we ID him, then lose him, all within twenty-four hours."

"Let's hope he doesn't have that much cash on him," David said. "Nothing here looks to me like a smoking gun. There's no photo of one of the missing women, a group of postings that turn dark. Wait . . . hold on. I spoke too fast. This isn't good."

Evie glanced over. David turned the tablet toward her. "That's Maggie, there's her old Chicago home, and that's the sweatshirt I gave her for her twentieth birthday, which these days looks pretty faded."

Evie's interest spiked. "So he's met her that early on?"

He nodded, pulling back the tablet.

"We'll find him, David. There's really only three possibilities. He returns to Indiana and into the arms of the cops looking for him there, he keeps his head down and hides because he's heard we're looking for him, or he stays around Chicago because he wants to see Maggie."

"Play those out," said David. "If he's innocent, he pulls in the driveway of his house and says to the waiting cops, 'What's going on?' If he's guilty, but thinks he can get away with it, he pulls into the driveway and asks the cops, 'What's going on? Search my house? Sure, I've got nothing to hide.' It's that last option I'm worried about right now."

As Evie turned into the office park, the car suddenly filled with sharp electronic sounds. The phone in his pocket, the second phone in his briefcase, the tablet — notifications went off on all of them. Surprised, Evie nearly put the car into a snowplow drift.

"That's the perimeter alarm at Maggie's place!"

She hit the police lights, swung back into traffic, recalling the route they'd taken the last two trips, and added a siren to the noise.

TWENTY-THREE

Margaret May McDonald

Maggie used a glue stick to carefully re-secure a photo in an early concert album. She looked so young! There was Benjamin on drums, Paul still playing his original guitar. The memories flooded back from those early Triple M days. She turned to the last photos she had of David before he'd been hurt. She'd forgotten how much he had changed too. His entire presence was more solid now — he even stood differently, and his hair definitely included some gray strands. She smiled as she imagined his reaction if she said that to him. The man wasn't vain, but he was aware of the years passing.

She could make out faces to about eight rows back. The girl Evie was searching for might be in these photos. Maggie marked the page and carefully closed the album, placed it back in the box. David would take them to Evie when he came by later this evening.

She retrieved her songwriting box from the bedroom bookshelf. Filled with pastel paper, colored pens, and cutout pictures that had captured her imagination, it was her preferred way of working on new songs. A thick clip of pages rested atop the materials — lists of keywords, working titles, themes, lyrics half-formed to draw upon for further inspiration.

Maggie spread out the materials and stretched out on the carpet, started to develop the topic of moving to a new city, a new home, hopefully to capture her mix of emotions during the last month. She didn't want to lose this opportunity. She lived her life in many ways through her music, resolving what she felt, thought about, and wished for in lyrics she might one day share with others. The only straightforward part of a move was the packing and boxing, while the rest was about emotions. She wrote *Leaving* on one page, *Arriving* on another, and finally, *Settling In*. She started noting down everything that came to mind for each theme.

As she worked, she let her thoughts drift to the reasons that had brought her back to Chicago. She'd returned to be around those who knew her best, to spend time with Bryce and Charlotte, to have more hours in her schedule to be with David, to explore further the big question she still had to resolve for herself — David's faith. *Or do I mean my faith?* she mused.

She'd called a hiatus from David twice since this limbo began, when the pain rippled too strong to carry it, only to feel her heart shred even more. She was sure she didn't want to lose him. And so the subject of faith she was so tired of wrestling with rose again to the top. She hoped some talks with Bryce and Charlotte would spark something to break the impasse.

She could understand Christianity with her head. On the surface it wasn't hard to grasp, but the actual truth of it was like a rock she couldn't break open. She'd long since accepted the historical record — Jesus was no figment of someone's imagination. Jesus had lived over two thousand years ago in the area that was now Israel and Palestine. He'd been a carpenter, born in the city of Bethlehem, raised in Nazareth, and about age thirty he had become a prominent religious teacher in his Jewish society. He was crucified by Roman authorities with the agreement of Jewish religious leaders in AD 33.

People who had known Jesus had penned letters about him, recording what he said and did. When added to the letters written by his followers in the early church, and to the books written by the Jews about their God, it all comprised the Bible David read regularly.

Over the years, she had read portions of the Bible and mostly understood it. Christians believed Jesus to be the Son of God, that Jesus could forgive anyone for anything they'd ever done wrong because he had taken on himself the punishment for their sins. They believed in a loving God, who cared about people, helped them live a righteous life, and promised them a great future after they died. She had no problem with what Christians believed.

But their God had to be alive for their beliefs to be true. What she couldn't wrap her mind around was their faith's central tenant, that Jesus had walked out of a tomb three days after being crucified, and that two thousand years later he was still alive.

No matter how many times Maggie circled the question, it came down to the fact it couldn't be real — it was simply science fiction, wishful hoping. But her David, the sanest and most rational man she'd ever known, a cop with a cop's instinct to question and challenge *everything* to see how much was a lie and how much was truth, had come to believe Christianity — *Jesus* — was literally true.

She couldn't understand how *her David* had arrived at *yes,* and he seemed honestly puzzled by her inability to see that the answer was yes. Believing Christianity was true hadn't come together for her as it had for him, and she honestly thought she was right. *How can David believe something that can't be true?*

She didn't actually have a problem with his beliefs. David was a more loving, kind, and generous man *because* of his religion. Christians were taught to be kind to the poor, orphans and widows, to be honest, to live at peace with each other. The contributions David gave to the church were distributed to causes Maggie appreciated and could get behind too. The Christians she'd encountered were normal and nice, despite the few odd beliefs they held. She liked their music, thought most sermons she heard were full of good advice and challenges about how to live.

Accommodating David, living according to his religious views of the world, was an acceptable compromise as far as she was concerned. The weird stuff she could ignore.

David talked to Jesus every day — she heard him pray, talking to someone invisible just as clearly as he talked with her. A bit more difficult to deal with, David believed God's Spirit lived inside him, transforming his character to be like Jesus, which was tipping the credibility scale, in her opinion, but she could deal with it. If they could get married and simply believe different things, she was sure they would be okay.

But — and this was a big problem — his Christianity taught that he should only marry another believer.

She knew he held on to the hope that she would come to believe that Jesus was indeed alive. She could honestly say she *wanted* to believe that if only because she wanted their lives to move forward without this obstacle in their path. Her problem was deciding which world was reality. Either she did walk around among people who had God's Spirit dwelling inside them, who were in fact talking with a living Jesus and he with them, or she didn't. If they were right, if it was true, she was standing on the sidelines of one of the greatest unfolding miracles in human history, and she was missing out.

She didn't want to miss out. But she wanted whichever was *true*.

And she honestly thought David was wrong.

If only she could figure out *how to know*. David said it was as simple as saying, "Jesus, if you are real and alive, please make yourself real to me," that God was very personal and would communicate back in ways she could understand. If God was real, he had a vibrantly believing spokesperson in David. But so far all she had were more questions.

Even though she recognized David as a loyal, loving man, and she knew she was the person he valued the most on this earth, she also knew she was losing David to his religion in a way she couldn't put into words. The heart of David was with his God and would never return as totally hers. This had become a one-way journey for him.

David couldn't step back toward her and say, "I was wrong, this isn't true," for he honestly believed it was true. And she couldn't acknowledge it as true when she didn't believe it was. That impasse was unbridgeable. They literally needed a miracle.

As much as his decision had gotten them into this never-never land, it was her decision that was holding them there. This was the real reason she was back in Chicago — one last open and honest, heartfelt search for the truth. Either she came to believe or she let David go for his own good. She couldn't be the one holding David back from a wife and family. Not that she would tell him that. He'd simply continue to wait for her to change her mind. She wiped tears from her cheeks. Even thinking about it was breaking her heart. She'd have to somehow figure out how to believe. It couldn't be impossible if David had done so —

A loud crash, followed by two more in rapid succession shattered the quiet. Maggie swung around toward the noise. Something had hit the stone wall surrounding the property. Icy downhill road, more than one car . . . Another impact rattled the glass in the window as if struck by a hard fist.

Flashing strobe lights snapped on, and a piercing alarm rang out. She surged off the bedroom floor, scattering papers, Post-it notes, song fragments and lyrics in all directions. She knew security was in place — she'd said good-night to Bradley an hour before. A glance at the bedroom door told her the cameras had triggered on. *A crash, probably on the hill outside the property, ice complicating the speed and making the collision into the wall worse, multiple vehicles.* Bad, she told herself, but not that unexpected, living here rather than on the sixtieth floor of a high-rise.

Then she heard a sharp snap, an avalanche of glass striking tile like a high note shattering a crystal glass. *Patio door!* She bolted for the safe room, hit the mechanism in the closet as David had taught her, moving so quickly the door had barely opened before she was through. She turned to her right, reached hands toward the panel, punched it, and counterweights shifted to slide the door back with a *whoosh,* locking deep into matching grooves. The bolt of the lock dropping into place echoed like a deep-toned bell in the small space.

Battery-operated lights switched on automatically. On trembling limbs she slid to the floor, sucked in a deep breath. She was in a fortress of steel in an unreachable space. David had drilled the need for speed into her, and she had never been so grateful for something she'd only halfheartedly listened to at the time.

Someone has broken into my home — someone is inside. Bradley was on the grounds, local security would already have the alert, and the notification system in the safe room was linked directly to the police. A lot of responding officers would be helping out Bradley within minutes. Security cameras would already be showing them the intruder — who, how many, where they were.

She rubbed a shaking hand over her face. Her chest hurt. She forced a calming breath, and another, treating the panic attack as if simply stressing out before a concert — gaining control of her breathing and heart rate from long practice. She pressed her hands into the carpet, fisted them into the fibers.

How would someone know this is my home? That was so closely held information, it was virtually inaccessible. How many intruders were inside? What did they want? Were they after money? The lights were off downstairs, making it look like no one was at home. Break in, grab valuables, leave before the cops arrive. Not that much by way of furnishings had arrived yet. She wasn't one to collect coins or stamps or six-figure paintings. *Probably a garden-variety burglar in an upscale neighborhood.* It was easier for her to settle on that generic outcome than the possibility an irrational fan had found her.

Many in the music scene knew she'd left New York for Chicago. But today's internet made it possible for resourceful people to find out what they wanted. If this intruder knew it was her home, it could be an unhinged person who either hated her music or loved it too much. Both obsessions came with large numbers of people, some of them just plain nuts. Maggie gave a shaky laugh and wiped her eyes. "Some people are just nuts," she said aloud.

The deep quiet was almost as unsettling as the crashes had been. She couldn't see what was going on outside, couldn't make a call out. She understood why it was designed that way, but now the silence she could *feel* was thoroughly creeping her out. No phone. No video. Just a hidden fortress.

The security firm would have alerted David — it was set in stone with him. Anything happened, he was first in the loop. He'd probably be the one opening the door in a couple of hours. He'd warned her on that time delay, and now she hated that too.

Yet he wouldn't be quick to open the door, not until the threat had been dealt with, neutralized, cops were off the immediate scene, and a plan was in place to safely and securely move her out and away. And the press would likely assemble in droves, attracted to the commotion, then rumors it was her home. David would want her to remain in her fortress so police or security weren't hounding her with questions, complicating matters. He would make sure if and when she did give a statement, it would be at a neutral location, probably the home of a friend. She had understood it. Appreciated it. And now felt imprisoned by it.

She looked up and to her left. If she flipped the cover on that side panel and pressed the red button, David would respond instantly and get her out of this room. It was there to signal she was physically injured, needed immediate help.

She bit her lip, shook off the last of the panic, and carefully got to her feet. She turned to the back wall, lifted the cover mounted there, and pressed the green button. She watched it light, signaling she was inside and okay. "Do what you need to do, then come let me out ASAP," she whispered, trying for a smile.

Whoever was in her house, however many, and their reasons for breaking in, none of it particularly mattered. Nobody could get inside the safe room except David. "Come get me, David." Just saying his name helped to calm her further. Whatever was happening, it was on the outside of this room, and for now it wasn't her problem . . . couldn't be her problem if she wanted to keep her sanity.

Maggie looked at the shelves, turned on the battery-operated CD player, and surrounded herself with the soothing sounds of a Beethoven sonata. She pulled out a deck of cards, dropped two pillows to the floor for more comfortable seating, and settled in for a game of solitaire. Her hands shook as she turned the cards, adrenaline still rippling through her body.

Think about something else. Anything else . . .

She was looking for an idea for a new album cover. She needed to decide on a birthday gift for David.

She felt like throwing up. She glanced over at the trash can. *No, it's not going to get that bad. Think about the cards, listen to the music.* This was the worst kind of stress — not knowing, sitting atop panic that faded far too slowly.

I should have come to believe like David and married him years ago. She laughed softly at the unexpected thought, but felt more than a little comfort in it too. She occasionally wondered if initially it was the danger in David's job making faith easier for him than unbelief. It had to be comforting for him to know he was never alone. *So is that true, that he's never alone?* She could use some of that comfort right now.

Jesus, if you're real, please become real to me. I'm tired of this wondering, trying to get my mind around the question. I want to go to the side of the decision that is true, and I'm in the dark right now. She looked up at the light above her as it flickered once, twice, then steadied. She pulled in a deep breath and slowly let it out. The light burned on brightly. She was going to be okay. Everyone was going to be okay. David would be here soon. She reached over for a flashlight on the shelf, tested it, and left it on the floor beside her knee.

"Jesus, you could start by keeping the lights on," she whispered, and felt for the first time as though someone was listening.

David Marshal

David saw the blood first. A path on the carpet, the brightness of it under the lights, the destruction trailing toward the stairs and up, Maggie's framed record albums knocked from the wall, photos smashed where they impacted the railing. He looked at John Key.

"It's bad," John told him simply. "He's upstairs, dead."

"Maggie?"

"Inside the safe room. The green light came on about three minutes after the door closed and sealed. As far as we can tell, she's fine. And, thankfully, she didn't see any of this. Security feeds snapped on with the alarm — she'd been sitting on the bedroom floor, working on song lyrics. You see her look toward the window as the crashes happen, then back to the bedroom door when the patio glass shattered. She heard that and bolted."

"Thank you, God, for small blessings," David prayed, forced his heartbeat to settle. "He had help getting through the gate."

"It looks like three other guys. The dump truck struck first, the Caterpillar hauler second. We think our intruder was in the high-wheel truck that made it into the driveway and up to the garage. All we have on the first two drivers are black hoods, black sweats, black shoes — picked up by a dark blue or black Charger. Cameras that would have captured clear pictures for us got jarred out of position by the impacts — a fact we'll be correcting for the future. We learned that lesson the hard way."

"Bradley?"

"Got himself slightly clipped by the third vehicle and is on the way to the hospital with a banged-up shoulder. He would have stopped Number Three on his own, but we'd already seen the safe room door close by then and the area patrol was arriving on scene. I held Bradley in place so we didn't run up against possibly losing him in a situation that was becoming contained. They cleared the house as a group, found Number Three dead upstairs."

"Thanks, John. Maggie's going to have a hard enough time with this without one of her own getting killed." He examined the smashed patio door and the trail of blood caused by the flying glass, which probably sliced open his arm. "We need to know how he found her address."

"I've got a sinking feeling I already know," John replied. "We haven't been able to contact an assistant hairdresser Amy hired last week. Her phone isn't picking up. Her neighbor thinks she's out for dinner with her boyfriend."

"You'll let me know?"

"We've already pulled in some Chicago cops on it."

David looked over at Evie on the bench inside the front door, boots off, and now pulling on crime-scene booties. "Come up with me, Evie."

She knew what this was going to look like as well as he did. One of the good guys hadn't killed their intruder, meaning he'd done it himself.

They found the body in Maggie's bedroom, stretched out on her bed. The slice across the throat showed a self-inflicted angle — the knife still rested against his shoulder.

"It's hard to kill yourself that way," John said quietly. "Your hand wants to stop."

David looked over at John, noting the reflective way he said it, saw the man's military assessment along with the security guy who'd seen just about everything in his career.

Thank you, God was all he could think right then. That could have been Maggie.

"We've got it on video, not that the scene is going to need that much confirmation," John said. "Got a name for him?"

"Andrew Timmets, out of Indiana."

John glanced at Evie. "Is this the one who killed your college student?"

"He's linked to three murders; the chosen method was smothering. We hope he's also linked to Jenna. They were working on a search warrant for his home when the alarm here tripped."

"Any idea why he ended it like this?"

"Only a guess. I would have expected to see some kind of message if this was a suicide plan," Evie said, looking around.

"There's no obvious one. Video shows him rushing in, realized from the scattered materials that Maggie had been here just moments before, looks in the closet, the bathroom, starts to leave the room to search the rest of this floor, and abruptly comes back to the closet. There's no audio, but you can tell when he realizes he's dealing with a safe room. He's prying up the panel for it when he hears the security group arrive downstairs. He's looking around, considering a confrontation, barricading himself in here. Then his body obscures the gesture, but he probably gives Maggie the finger and drops back on the bed where he does what you see here."

David deliberately looked away to take in the rest of the room, seeing what Maggie had been working on when this happened. "We passed a lot of cops outside. How'd you keep them out there?"

"An understanding. The man in charge has been up to see the scene. They're now watching live video. We don't touch or move anything, we just figure out how to get Maggie out of this room without adding to the trauma she's going to deal with. I'm all for leaving her in there until the scene's clear, but they're saying it's going to be four hours minimum before they're ready to move the body."

"We'll keep it simple. You hold a sheet up between us and him, and I make sure she doesn't turn her head when she smells the blood, sees what's splattered on that wall. Even better, we use a blindfold to override her instinct to look."

John nodded. "Good. Let me see if we can get the stairwell debris cleared. It shouldn't take their photographer that long to document the chaos. We escort her out and straight down to my SUV."

"Where to from there?" David asked. John would have some options.

"I gave Bryce a call. She can stay with Charlotte and Bryce this evening, at least through the police statement. If she wants to go somewhere else after that, we'll figure it out then. I had her travel bags cleared to take with her, as they were still packed downstairs. She'll be comfortable for a few days."

"Thanks, John."

He left the room to make arrangements for her departure.

David sighed, considered the room again, avoided looking at the body. He wondered if Maggie would ever be able to live again in this home, and very much doubted it. "Evie, check the hall closet for sheets. If there's a pillowcase, a towel, we can use that as a blindfold."

She nodded and left.

There was no way to signal to Maggie he

was opening the door. The front surface was air-gapped to prevent sound transmission. He stepped into the master closet and looked down. The blood on the floor by the access panel was the worst of it. He could block what Maggie saw in the first few seconds by how he moved into the safe room, hopefully get her turned so she couldn't see directly into the bedroom. The smell of blood couldn't be covered, so he'd have to deal with that question quickly.

Evie returned with a sheet and a light-weight towel. David folded it into thirds, the idea to wrap it across Maggie's eyes. Evie offered the clip from her hair to fasten the towel in back.

John returned, and with Evie's help they held the sheet up in front of the bed.

David took a final look, nodded. "That's going to work. I'll come out with her and go straight down to the vehicle. Evie, if you could act as front guard, catch the doors for me — and John, if you could bring blankets from the safe room since she won't have a coat or any shoes. The car's going to have a chill to it. And if you could take a quick look around to see if there's anything she might have been writing on in the safe room she would want brought out with her, we then can leave the place to the cops."

"I'll do that," John agreed.

"Smile, David," Evie reminded him. "She needs to see all is well in that first glance."

He took a deep breath, let it out, smiled. "A good suggestion." He stepped into the closet and punched in the code known only to three people. The mechanism released, and the door smoothly moved to the side. Maggie was sitting on the floor, a deck of cards in hand. She'd been eating chocolate. A smudge of it was at one corner of her mouth.

"Hey," she said, her smile wobbly.

He made sure she couldn't see past him as he lowered himself to her level. "Hey back."

"You're early. It's been only an hour."

Her eyes shifted over his shoulder, tension rapidly returning to her posture.

"Someone died, Maggie." His hand covered hers. "We think we know who he is, a very bad guy from Indiana. We're going to get you out now so the cops can do their job."

"I didn't hear gunfire," she whispered.

"You wouldn't have heard even that in here. When we know for certain who he is and why he was here, I'll tell you."

He held up the blindfold. "I don't want you having this image in your mind. And

I'll carry you out to the car since there's broken glass lying around."

She closed his hand around the fabric. "I'll keep my eyes closed." She stood with him and kept her eyes fastened on his face. "It's no big deal, the decision about knowing."

"Then let's get out of here, Maggie."

He lifted her easily into his arms. She wrapped her arms around him tightly, tucked her head against his neck and closed her eyes. "Promise me something, David?"

"What's that?" He stepped out of the safe room, then out of the closet. He picked his way carefully across the room to avoid the blood.

"Let's restock with something other than chocolate. I'm sick of it."

He dropped a light kiss on her hair. "We'll do that, my Maggie."

TWENTY-FOUR

David Marshal

Maggie was nearly asleep, David's hand gently stroking the back of hers. Only when her breathing had turned deep and slow did he lift his hand and whisper, "Sleep calm, Maggie." He dropped a soft kiss on her forehead and eased away from the bedside, leaving the adjoining bathroom light on with the door cracked an inch.

He stepped into the hall where he could still see her, watched for any signs she might be falling into a difficult dream. Her thumb twitched occasionally. He hoped she was going to get at least a few hours of sleep. Charlotte and Bryce had a lovely home, quiet, peaceful, exactly what Maggie needed.

That Evie was leaning against the hallway wall quietly waiting — had been for more than forty minutes — didn't surprise him. She could be empathetic in a profound way when the situation required it. That Evie had also been working by phone and text, he didn't need to ask. "Tell me what else we've learned," he asked in a low voice without moving his gaze from Maggie just yet.

"First, Sharon wanted me to pass on her relief that Maggie got to the safe room in time. Sharon, Theo, and Taylor are available for anything you need — anything, anytime. They're just staying off your phone, as you're already drowning in more pressing priorities."

David felt himself relaxing as the bigger world settled itself around him. "Give my thanks to them when you can, Evie."

"Paul is at the scene to divert press attention toward his FBI team tracking down Andrew Timmets, avoiding headlines like *Maggie's boyfriend confronts Maggie's killer.*"

David smiled at the description. "I've got to appreciate friends who step in to take the bullets for me. I'm going to owe Paul at least a nice steak for standing in front of the media storm tonight. They'll have that headline or one like it before long, if there's a decent investigative journalist putting together the names of the smothered college students."

"It's more a counteroffensive. Give the

press something to write about with quotable sound bites, so that the more expansive story takes a few days to coalesce. The scene itself, with the vehicles smashing through the gate and wall, gives them dramatic visuals. They'll run with the stolen-vehicles angle as part of the lead."

The humor in her faded, and David knew why, simply nodded. "I appreciate the light touch, but it's okay. I know much of what happened to get us to this point. Lay out for me what's known."

Evie turned pages in her pad. "Andrew was tipped off by a friend in Indiana that cops were at his house looking for him, were asking about Virginia Fawn. That came from his phone texts. You want an answer for why this ended so dark, I'm guessing that's the reason. He wasn't going to get arrested for the girls' murders."

"Go on," he said.

"All three vehicles were stolen in the hour prior to the gate breach. Chicago cops have the driver of the dump truck in custody — one of Andrew's friends from his detention days. They're still looking for the other two. According to the friend in custody, a Tom Stanford, Andrew showed up just after five p.m. with an address and the idea of ramming the gate to get onto the property. He says they went along with the scheme because they were bored. They were in the middle of stealing the vehicles when Andrew, quote, 'got weird on them, angry about something on his phone.' The timing matches his getting tipped off about the Indiana cops.

"He changed plans, told the others not to come back for him, he'd leave his car nearby and walk away after he had photos of the evening's adventure. That's how he was referring to this — 'the evening's adventure.' He sent a rather cryptic text to his mother minutes before the gate was breached that could be read as a farewell. Chicago cops found the assistant hairdresser, Tina Newel, unconscious in the trunk of her car and with three broken fingers. Andrew would have gotten Maggie's address from her."

"Still alive?" David asked, surprised.

"Yes. It looks like he tried to smother her with a towel. He may have gotten interrupted or was in a hurry, but he didn't finish the job. She's in serious but stable condition, has a good chance of pulling through."

"Thanks for that blessing, God," David said quietly. Then to Evie, "Okay, what else?"

"They're serving the warrant on his home

in Indiana in about ten minutes. They've held off while this side sorted itself out, didn't want to walk into a possibly booby-trapped house if weapons or explosives were used here. If you want to see live video, the FBI can link us in."

He was tired enough that he didn't particularly care if he saw it or just read the report, but he had a feeling Evie wouldn't watch it unless he did also. They still didn't have evidence on connections to Jenna's death. They needed that house to yield useful information so Evie's case could move beyond simply reasoned speculation. "I'll watch it with you."

David heard footsteps on the stairs and glanced over as Charlotte Bishop came up to join them, carrying a large mug of the tea she favored. "I can sit with her, David. I promise, she won't wake up alone in a strange house." Her two golden Irish Setters had trailed behind her and now sat politely on either side, each studying him with solemn eyes.

Maggie would be in safe hands. "I'd appreciate it, Charlotte. An hour or so should clear away much of what I need to finish up."

"I'll text you when she wakes. Until then, go get the answers she'll want to hear. The more of her questions you can respond to when she asks them, the easier this will be."

David accepted the wisdom in her words. "Thanks again, Charlotte." He nodded toward the stairs, and Evie led the way down.

"How bad is the press situation?" he asked.

Evie stepped into the living room, picked up the remote, and turned on the national cable news channel.

David winced. "Aerial shots? Really?"

"They went live about two hours ago. The world now knows where Margaret May Mc-Donald lives." Evie left the commentary on mute. They knew far better than the anchorperson what had happened.

The three vehicles and the break-in through the stone wall and gate looked even more catastrophic from the air. Andrew had managed to get within feet of the garage with his truck, circled around the house on foot, and shattered the patio door to gain entry. "What's the elapsed time?"

"Two minutes, seven seconds from first impact to the patio door breaking. Figure another thirty seconds to cross the living room, run up the stairs and to the master bedroom. I'm glad Maggie didn't hesitate."

"That's the one thing Maggie promised

me — she'd act first, accept looking silly if it was a false alarm."

"I'm sorry she's losing such a beautiful place to live. John's still at the scene. He says things are slowing down with all the media underfoot. The medical examiner wants to do more review before the body's moved. It's going to be dawn before they haul away the vehicles. John's mostly negotiating the evidence — her phone gets looked at there, then returned to her, that kind of thing. He said to tell you Sam is outside here, will be wherever Maggie is until you say otherwise."

"If I can't have John himself, Sam's the guy I want. Thanks. I appreciate you playing messenger on the details. Where are we going to watch this video of the warrant being served on his property?"

"There's a secure laptop set up on the kitchen table." David turned that direction.

Charlotte's husband was dumping ice into a freshly brewed pitcher of tea. He glanced over as they entered. "Eat something," Bryce said.

There were fresh hamburger buns out, deli turkey, bologna, shaved ham, lettuce, American and Swiss cheese slices, mayonnaise. Any of that would do. David stacked himself a sandwich.

Bryce poured Evie a glass of the tea. "I'll be in my office if you need anything. David, the bedroom next to Maggie's has been made up for you. Give Gary your hotel room key. He'll pack your things, bring them over. Maggie is going to stay here with less fuss if you tell her this is where you're going to be too. The press can't bother either of you here."

"I appreciate that more than you know."

Bryce smiled. "We'll enjoy the company — I'm just sorry it's under these circumstances."

Evie brought up the video feed.

David pulled out the seat beside her and prepared to see what Andrew Timmets had left behind. It looked like four officers were doing the search, two with Indiana PD and two with the FBI. The video was being transmitted via the shoulder camera of a member of the FBI team. The audio was much like listening to a conversation on speakerphone, some voices clear and almost too loud, others hollowed out and difficult to understand.

The four first walked down a narrow hallway and took a left into the garage. Lights turned on to reveal two vans — a locksmith vehicle with business logo on the side, the other a plain white panel van.

"That answers one question," Evie said softly.

The white panel van looked clean inside, hand-vac marks still present in the direction of the carpet fabric. "Forensics will have a challenge, but maybe something is there," David offered.

The van was closed up and left for the crime lab to deal with. The four officers conferred and split up, one remaining to search the garage, one heading downstairs, another to the bedrooms, the last one to find any office area Andrew maintained.

David pulled off some blank sheets from Evie's notepad and began writing an official statement on events for the record.

An hour later, Evie laid a hand on his arm. David looked up to the video.

"We've found our smoking gun," a voice said, the person not yet on camera. "Look at this." The person shooting the video turned, and a figure came into view near a bed with a tall headboard. The cop was easing something out from behind it — a simple kitchen corkboard, a foot square, with a line of drivers' licenses stapled to it. "This is being ID'd as exhibit seventeen, found tucked behind the headboard of the bed in the master bedroom."

The board was shifted and held up to the

camera, each license centered for a dozen seconds so that the image was captured into the permanent record.

"That's Jenna's driver's license," Evie whispered, her voice tight. "Tammy. Virginia. Emily. Laura. He's claiming all five girls as his," she continued. Beneath each license was a Triple M concert ticket stub.

David watched the screen in silence as the board was slowly scanned by the camera again before being carefully placed in a large evidence bag.

"Anything else back there?" they heard someone ask.

The officer pulled the bed away from the wall to shine a light behind the headboard. "Nothing else in this location."

"Keep looking."

The video went back to the dresser as drawers were removed and checked for something taped behind or under them.

"I'm honestly surprised," David said. "We figured out the scope of his crimes without capturing him — that's rare. There are usually entire caverns of truth you haven't seen until you're actually looking at and talking with the person responsible."

"We still don't know how he abducted Jenna that night, or where he buried her body."

"He saved a few trophies. Maybe there's a journal or sketchbook, a marked-up map as his own keepsake . . . something else? Or we just accept the fact that Jenna's body will only be discovered when a curious dog or a backhoe crew locate the bones someday. We've seen any number of ways a gravesite gets opened up and made visible."

"I'll start taking your advice and pray about the problem in an actual faith-filled, God-will-answer-this kind of way," Evie remarked.

David smiled and glanced at his watch — two a.m. Sunday morning. No wonder he was blitzed. "You need to find a place to crash for a few hours, Evie."

"Rob is picking me up within the hour."

"Yeah?"

"I canceled dinner and a movie last night with a text, telling him 'the case is breaking open, sorry.' I owed him further explanation, so about midnight I sent one that said *Turn on TV.* Rob likes my pithy conversation starters."

David laughed, liking them too.

"He doesn't want me driving this tired, and I wouldn't mind twenty minutes with him just to put his mind at rest. His first reply was, *David, Maggie, you, okay?* I like his short and sweet notes too." She stood and stretched her arms. "I never want to drive on ice, siren and lights blazing, ever again either. That was idiotically scary."

He laughed once more. "I'm glad you were my wingman, Evie. We couldn't do much but follow in the wake of everyone else, but it mattered that we saw this all put to bed tonight."

"I'm sorry for the ending, that he's dead and we can't get all our questions answered, and that Maggie has to pay the highest price for everything. But I'm also stepping back enough to see the bigger picture. Only twelve days and we've run him to ground — it may be the best hit the task force does. It feels really nice."

"That it does." He looked at the video of officers finishing up at Andrew's home. "That it does."

Evie Blackwell

Evie slid into the passenger seat of Rob's warm car just after 2:30 Sunday morning, feeling disoriented from fatigue and from all the cups of coffee she'd downed in the last few hours. Her day was finally wrapped. Time for the hotel and ten hours of sleep.

Rob clicked on the interior lights, and his hand covered hers. "Look at me for a moment."

She did and found him studying her carefully.

"One dead, and you weren't involved in that, David and Maggie are okay, your case is wrapping up. On the scale of endings, how's this one?"

She appreciated his summary. "Compared to last fall and Carin County, this one's more sad than satisfying." She turned her hand to squeeze his. "I'm good, Rob, honestly. Most cases are like this. They end after finding the right name, catching the criminal — most of the time with an arrest rather than a call to the coroner — and then doing a lot of paperwork. That's the job . . . although this one had more tangles and personal ties than you would expect by the time it concluded."

"Your first case has made the national news."

Evie laughed at the way he said it, for they had indeed made a splash on all the cable networks. "I am so glad I'm not Sharon having to deal with the press tonight. She's welcome to that spotlight. Thanks for coming to give me a lift — this is nice."

"You're quite welcome." Rob clicked off the interior lights and backed out of the Bishops' driveway, lifted a hand to the security officer. "I wanted the pleasure of seeing you in person, and it doesn't hurt to have the firsthand story when people start calling, beginning with business, but mostly wanting to turn the conversation toward you, David, and Maggie and the case on the front page of the paper. You're making me famous merely by association since the charity event."

Evie leaned back against the headrest, amused by the fact he was right — her world was bumping squarely into his by how the case played out in the papers and television newscasts and among his friends. "How much would you like to know?" she asked.

"Whatever you feel like telling me now. The rest can wait."

She told him briefly about Andrew Timmets, those details that would already be on the news with the FBI's statement, but mostly she told him about Lynne and Jim, the story behind the story.

"I'm not at all surprised to find you sympathetic toward the two who might have been your leading suspects," Rob replied when she finished. "You've always liked the ones who've had the harder road to climb, and their relationship sounds as though it has potential to be something very special."

"I liked them," Evie said. "I would have

arrested them for murder if they were guilty, but still been sad the case had turned their way."

Traffic was light this time of night, and they would be at the hotel soon. Evie gathered her courage to ask Rob a question, knowing she was going to send into a tailspin what had been a comfortable conversation. "I'd like to ask you about something."

"Ask away."

"Ann said you smirked when I did the dramatic puppet conversation for kids at church after flight 174 crashed. Do you remember?"

Rob glanced over at her, looking stunned. "Is that how I got crosswise with your friend?"

"Did you? Do you remember the event?"

She saw an expression in the passing headlights that she'd never seen before, embarrassment certainly, but more than that.

"Evie, I do remember." He ran a hand behind his neck. "Guilty as charged," he added with a sigh, "but it wasn't as it might have appeared. I was listening to you, thinking about how positively and clearly you were able to explain even tragic death to the kids, and what life after death was like.

Then I jumped from that to a mental back-and-forth with my mother, if she'd been listening to the way you phrased it, and I remember thinking, *Evie's got you there, Mom,* felt myself smirk, and instantly regretted the dishonorable way I'd just thought about my mother. The Holy Spirit nailed me when I smirked. It's not something I'm going to easily forget. And Ann saw that?"

"It's made a lasting impression on her. She thought you were dismissing what I said or how I said it. Add to that the vast differences in our work lives, our personal lives, and she's always hesitated over whether we're a good long-term fit."

"Evie . . ." He glanced her way again. "I will be the first to admit that God is still working on me — in lots of areas, but particularly how I respond to my mother and some of her remarks. If I thought I'd ever be treating you the same way, Ann would have a very good point. But, trust me, God is correcting me on it now. You can count on Him for that, even if you're not sure of me. I won't ever be thinking disrespectful thoughts toward you, nor my mother in the present or future. I'm sorry for what Ann saw. But with God's help, it won't be happening again."

"I believe you." Evie smiled at her own

memories. "I know what it's like having that inner voice check you on something. It's reassuring to hear your explanation, Rob, and that you're close enough to God that He could get your attention. Thanks."

"It's an embarrassing memory — doubly so given that others witnessed it happen. But the problem is mostly dealt with, I think. I've been a remarkably better son around my mother." He sighed once more. "Any other questions?"

Evie shook her head, wishing she was as confident about how she herself was handling his mother. "We're good, Rob."

"Well, I'm glad you asked, rather than just wonder about it. And I will tell Ann what I just told you — I mean, if you think it would help."

"Let me think about it, but that's probably not necessary. As she gets to know you, she'll write it off as an out-of-character moment and let it go."

"Nothing else, then?"

There was nothing more she needed to ask, but there was something major she would need to tell him. But talking about her brother was not a simple topic to bring up. This wasn't the time. "No, we're good," she repeated.

Rob parked at the front of the hotel, came

around to her door, and slipped his arms around her for a long hug. Evie rubbed her hands along the back of his coat, leaning into the embrace. "Thank you. It means a lot that you came to get me at this time of night. I could have caught a ride with a cop, but this was better."

"Much better," Rob said with a smile. "Sleep in, then call me?"

"I will." Evie walked into the hotel lighter in heart because of their conversation. She was going to be sorting out her personal life in the next few weeks, *looking at those lists David made me start,* she thought with amusement, but now found herself looking forward to Valentine's Day. She would settle this by then in her heart.

TWENTY-FIVE

Evie munched on cinnamon toast and held her cell at an angle so David didn't have to listen to her eating a very late breakfast. He was still working out the press statement with Sharon, Evie listening in, mostly to enjoy the fact she didn't have to write it.

She picked up the large coffee she'd brought into the office with her and headed inside. Shifting the cellphone to her shoulder, she pushed open the door. "I'm fine, David," she said, "stay with Maggie. I'm just boxing things up today. John's going to take Maggie's fan mail, and the case boxes are returning to the archives. I need to finish up my final report, hand it off to the evidence clerk. Maggie needs you more than I do."

She figured if David stayed at the Bishops with Maggie, the man might get some sleep. He'd spent most of yesterday shuttling between there and Maggie's house to oversee shoring up the wall and getting the glass replaced in the patio door. The entrance was now blocked by vehicles intentionally obstructing the driveway, along with a group of men there to provide security.

"She's talking about wanting to go back to New York. Give me a day, Evie, and I'll be on the job again."

"If you hurry back right now, you've misjudged the women in your life. I'll keep you in the loop," she promised. "We're two weeks into the task force and we're both already due about four vacation days. I'll put aside anything you might want to see for when you come in." She said goodbye and tucked the phone into her pocket.

The flowers from Rob were showing their age, though they were still beautiful. She stopped to admire them, touched a few. She loved the guy who had sent them. *It feels good to admit that,* she thought. As mismatched as they might be in careers and even personalities, she loved him. He'd asked for an answer by Valentine's Day. She still had several weeks to sort out her personal life. That she was leaning toward yes and was getting comfortable with the idea suited her fine.

She dumped her backpack on a spare chair. She pulled out her now-ragged master list of facts and theories. Under *Facts* was a new entry:

21. Andrew Timmets killed Jenna Greenhill.

Under *Theories* she waffled between two competing ones:

27. He wanted something he saw in Jenna, to have her forever as only his.
28. Jenna annoyed him, and he wanted to have her gone.

She favored the second, given everything she suspected. Jenna had annoyed Andrew at the concert, said something snarky about Maggie or the band, gotten on his bad side, and he'd simply been in a position to react to someone who irritated him. He'd handled the problem by shutting her up for good. Lifted her wallet, and the rest was easy.

His dad being a locksmith, Andrew had learned those skills over a very long time. Get inside Jenna's apartment ahead of her, wait for her to go to bed, smother her once she was asleep, haul her body down the stairs and out at three or four a.m. when even a college neighborhood gets quiet. Use some common sense on where to hide the body and drive out of town.

Evie wouldn't tell that to Jenna's family. What she did want to do if possible was finish up the case completely. She took her coffee and walked over to the aerial maps of Brighton College and the surrounding area. She really had only one piece left: Jenna's remains, and one fairly decent clue.

Five rough sketches had been found in an envelope in Andrew's desk, along with his Last Will and Testament. They were obviously something he considered important. That they were maps seemed certain. Given there were five of them, it became a puzzle of geography. But with no method of orientation for the sketched lines, nothing as simple as a location marked with an X, the pages were a mystery.

A detective in Ohio had found the first answer early this morning, matching one of the pages to the Emily Close site by referencing the lines as gradients, not roads, turning the page into a topological sketch, the darkest line being a ditch and the only dashed line a bridge. With those marks providing units of distance, the sketch turned out to be accurate to within a few feet of where Emily's body was recovered.

Indiana quickly followed that format and picked out two of the remaining pages as directions to the remains of Virginia Fawn and Laura Ship. That left two pages and the question of which one was the map pointing to the remains of Jenna Greenhill and which to Tammy Preston.

Evie could live without the closure, but still she wanted it — for herself and for the families. She'd told herself she first would get the report finished, the case files stored, before making any educated guesses as to the geography. That plan lasted only as long as it took her to finish drinking her coffee while staring at the two sketches. She made half a dozen copies of both, modifying the scale with reductions and enlargements.

She took the aerial shots she had for the Brighton College area off the board, laid them out on the conference room table, and tried to get something — anything — to line up.

Two hours later, she separated the two versions of the sketch into neat stacks and considered again the problem. Part of it was fatigue. Even with the extra sleep, her eyes were tired and this was detail work. And she was working in the abstract with what were tangible facts. These were topology sketches reflecting how landscapes changed heights, nearly impossible to assess against an aerial map.

She grabbed folders, separated the two different sketches, stacked the aerial maps and carefully rolled them up. She put everything into a map tube and left the building. She needed a neighborhood expert's instincts to interpret the features on these pages. If there was anyone who knew the Brighton College area like the back of his hand, it would be the guy who'd grown up in the neighborhood.

"Since Saturday night, Lynne has been glued to the news. It was all I could do to keep her from going outside Maggie's house, stand there and cry. A puzzle like this will do her good," Jim insisted, "and no one knows this neighborhood like Lynne." Evie reluctantly followed him up the steps to the Benoit home. She wanted Jim's help, not to get pulled into a thousand and one questions about Maggie. She didn't know precisely those answers anyway, as she hadn't seen Maggie since early Sunday morning.

Lynne was the one who opened the door. "Oh. Hi."

"Lynne, this is one of those no-question times," Jim said firmly. He looked past her into the living room. "Nancy, can we use the kitchen table? The lieutenant here needs some help."

"Of course, Jim. Come in, both of you."

Evie knew immediately that Lynne was dying to ask at least a few questions, felt sorry for her when the girl promptly sealed her lips at Jim's remark. Evie followed them into the kitchen and said mostly for Lynne's benefit, "Maggie is fine. She's staying with friends. She didn't see what happened that night. Her home has one of those safe rooms where the door shuts and no one can open it. When her security sounded the alarm, she went inside the room and waited until David came to get her."

"She wasn't scared?" Lynne asked, her tone one of worry.

Evie gave her a reassuring smile. "It was quiet, she had music, some pillows to get comfortable. She was playing cards to keep herself occupied when David opened the door. I was there. I promise, she's okay."

"But she can't go back home, can she?"

"I imagine not, but Maggie's resilient. She'll find another great home to call her own."

"I made her a card. It's not much, just a sympathy card. Would one of you give it to her for me?"

"I can do that, Lynne," Evie said, thinking it might do Maggie good.

"I'll go get it and be right back." Lynne darted away.

Evie pulled out the materials she'd brought along. Nancy promptly put a plate of cookies on the table. "One good deed deserves another."

Evie picked one up with a smile. Jim pulled out a chair beside her, took a cookie, and began to arrange the aerial photos in order. Nancy came around to watch what he was doing. She put a finger on a house. "This is us."

"Yep."

"It's a very different view of the neighborhood looking at it from above," Nancy said. "You can see how large the yards really are compared to the houses."

Lynne returned with a light-blue envelope. "Thanks."

"Sure." Evie stored it in her backpack. "I'll see Maggie gets it as soon as I see her."

"You've brought a puzzle?" Lynne asked, looking curiously at the tabletop.

"I don't mean to be morbid, Lynne, but we might be able to find Jenna's remains if we can figure out these sketches," Evie explained. "These are topography sketches — the lines mark the way the land gets flatter or steeper. The lines aren't necessarily roads, trails, or landmarks. The man who drew these used other sketches like them to show where he put a body. We're assuming one of these two sketches might tell us where he buried Jenna. There might be a clue in the sketches, some feature in the landscape like a bridge, a culvert, a railroad crossing."

Lynne picked up one of the sketches, turned it several directions. "Okay, it's a land graph, like when you play a golf green and want to know how the land slopes and rises, it shows where to putt to reach the flag."

"Exactly," Jim replied, choosing a copy of the other sketch. "But it doesn't have a scale marked, so we can't put it beside the map and find the location. We have to *think* about the locations, see if we can see that land graph fitting the place we remember." He put his finger down near the first open area behind Jenna's apartment building. "Think about that tree behind Jacob's shed. Does this area match your sketch?"

"Too flat," Lynne said. "When it rains, that whole area is a puddle. This sketch looks like a round bowl." She glanced over his shoulder at the one he held. "That's closer, but you need long and narrow and steep at one end."

"Okay." Jim moved his finger south on the

aerial map to the next open area. "The bike trail by the drinking fountain. If you were to go toward the stream, that land falls off quickly."

Lynne shook her head. "It's too . . ." She made a gesture with her hand. "You slide on your butt to the bottom, but then it goes flat again. There's no curve. Yours needs a curve too."

Jim moved farther on the aerial map, and he and Lynne slowly took the neighborhood apart piece by piece, sharing memories and landmarks. They finished the first column of photos and moved closer to the college with the next column.

"Lynne, show me your sketch again," Jim said. She laid it on the table, and he nodded and put his finger on a spot. "The way these two lines intersect, they've got a defined corner. That can't be a natural feature; it has to be something man-made. You need a square corner and a big bowl."

"I know where this is!" Lynne said, excited, picking up the sketch. She grabbed Jim's hand and tugged. "Come on."

He laughed and resisted. "Where, Lynne?"

"Four squares twister — it's the spinner."

Jim pulled over another copy of the sketch Lynne had, put his finger on the intersecting lines, studied the sketch around his finger. "She's right."

Evie heard it in his voice, saw it in his face. He was seeing a place and its geography was matching up with the sketch.

"Let's *go,*" Lynne said, tugging again.

Jim grabbed his coat with one hand, pointed Lynne toward hers. "We're coming."

"Is it far?" Evie asked, wondering if it made sense to drive.

"Blocks rather than miles, south of the quad past the arts building," Jim replied. "We can walk it."

"I'll have coffee ready when you get back," Nancy said, wrapping a scarf around Lynne's neck, then kissing her cheek. "You did good, my girl."

Evie made a call as they headed out. "David, Lynne and Jim think they have figured out one of the maps. Come join us at the college if you like."

Evie answered David's call sixteen minutes later.

"I'm in the parking lot, south side of the quad. Where are you?" David asked.

Evie looked around for the tallest object she could describe. "Look north. See a tall, white marble column, kind of like a steeple?"

"Got it."

"I'm in its shadow."

"Be with you in a minute."

It was a rather serene place, still on campus and part of an outdoor art display of sculptures, memorial walls, plaques commemorating various events and graduating classes. It began where the quad ended and stretched about twenty feet wide along two blocks until it came to the cemetery behind one of the oldest churches in the neighborhood.

Lynne had stopped at a place midpoint, at an earthen sculpture meant to be experienced in a tangible way rather than just looked at. As kids, they had made up a game of twister in the bowl of earth, the four marble slabs of the monument providing reasonable distances to attempt to reach, while the sloped earth created a natural gravity well that made it impossible to play more than a move or two without falling over. The record, according to Lynne, was six moves, and she still held it.

The wind had cleared snow from the top of the sculpture, and Jim pushed the small drift inside away with the side of his boot. Evie saw with fascination that the four marble slabs had been etched with short music riffs, country and jazz, classic and rock.

Jim began sorting out the finer details of the sketch now that the reference point was set. Lynne paced off steps at his direction, carefully moved up the slope and back down, confirming the way the sketch had been drawn.

Jim nodded and made a final mark on the copy he held. "The unit of distance in this sketch is right at twenty inches. It holds no matter which direction you move away from the corner of that oblique."

"So where does that say Jenna should be found?" Lynne asked, spinning around in a circle while studying the ground.

David joined them as Jim reached out and quietly took Lynne's hand to stop her from getting dizzy.

"She's in the monument."

"What?" Lynne jumped sideways, away from the marble stones.

"There's no X to mark where the body is, just a bunch of contour lines to confirm you have the location, with the one man-made feature and a unit of distance you can use to calculate the rest. I don't think he buried her; I think he hid her." Jim pointed. "In there."

Evie looked at the solid bench sitting

adjacent to the four marble slabs set in the bowl of earth. The bench sat on a solid base. Jim walked over to the bench and put his weight against it, tipped it.

A bone tumbled out.

"Oh, put it back!" Lynne spun away with an anxious step as Jim eased the bench back down. A solid bench, hollow inside, keeping watch over an earthen bowl with four flat marble slabs marking the four directions. The plaque on the bench read, *Sit and overlook an eternal sea of music.*

Evie carefully rolled up the hand-drawn street maps of the area around Jenna's apartment building and returned them to the map tube. She took down the photos from the whiteboard, restored them to their original pages in Jenna's albums and scrapbooks, and stacked them all in a box to be returned to the family. She put the reports she had read back into order and stored them in another box, added the data sets of names she'd sourced and printed out while working the case. Her desk cleared rather swiftly when the decision was simply which folder to store the material in. She reluctantly dropped the last of her flowers, now wilted, into the trash.

Michael's byline had been on the front-page story today, the most complete of the reporting to date on what had happened with the missing women, at Maggie's home, and the search that had put the case together. She needed to call him, if only to say thanks for the fact he hadn't called her. He had quotes from Sharon, Paul, a nicely done insert on Jim and Lynne, comments from cops at the various scenes, and information on the recovery of Jenna's remains, including a statement from Jenna's family. He was an honorable man, who meant it when he'd said she was his friend, not a source.

Michael would have been under enormous pressure from his boss to make that call to her, and through her to reach out to David and Maggie. That he hadn't made the call impressed her. She'd debated calling him early on to share her own perspective, but the hierarchy of Sharon being the one to speak with the press protected the task force, and she wouldn't impose on her working relationship with David or use her knowledge of his relationship with Maggie for a news story. Michael had put together a great story without her help, just as she'd expected he would. He'd always been excellent at his job.

"Need some help?"

Evie smiled at Ann as her friend came in. "I'm about done. Jenna is a small case compared to some others we've worked."

She archived the electronic copies of the reports onto a flash drive and added it to the reference box. The Jenna Greenhill case would go back onto a shelf, only this time marked closed, once the medical examiner finished the final report on the remains.

Ann leaned in the conference room doorway. "Hey, David."

"Hey back."

Evie was glad Ann had come over. David had the fan mail Andrew Timmets sent to Maggie spread out on the conference room table, brooding a bit over it, trying to see if they could have picked out clues to what was going on before it had escalated so far. He needed to be interrupted, diverted to something else for a while. Evie had read the forty-two letters and emails. With hindsight she could see more than if she'd just read them as mail that came in over a stretch of years. She knew there was nothing that could have been done real-time just based on these letters, and David needed to get to that same conclusion.

"Maggie get away okay?" Ann asked.

David looked over to nod. "She's safely on a flight back to New York and away from the immediate press attention. She wants to finish up the songs for the next album and plans to use that as a distraction while I figure out where she's going to live in Chicago."

"Double house hunting," Evie called, and got the laugh she hoped for in reply.

David came out to join them. "I'm to find something equally as beautiful, and she still doesn't want a gated community." He leaned back against one of the empty desks. "While you're here, Ann, I thought I'd mention to you both — I had an interesting call from Detective Jenkins this morning. A letter arrived at the DA's office, written by Terrance L. Whitney — the real name of our Philip Granger — a man who entered WITSEC in 2014 and who died on the eighteenth of this month. The letter gives details regarding a body buried behind a wall in an Englewood building. The letter further stated he saw Blake Grayson shoot the man."

Evie grinned. The WITSEC death letter had shown up. She looked at Ann and found her friend was apparently fascinated by the pattern in the carpet.

"They can't prove murder with what they have," David continued. "The ballistics don't tie the gun to Blake, but to his bodyguard. And no one else so far is talking about what happened with Saul that night."

"It's not the first cold case solved where nothing could be done to bring justice," Evie mentioned.

"Been here before, will be here again," David agreed. "It just leaves a bad aftertaste."

Evie understood the sentiment. "You should tell Lori thanks for us, Ann," she teased, "and ask how she likes retirement. She must be living with a few hundred secrets like that of a guy being buried in a wall."

"She's not nearly as colorful as you're trying to paint her, Evie," Ann replied, amused.

"Uh-huh. That's like saying you don't have interesting friends. It doesn't hold given I've met a few of them." Evie slid a lid on the last box. "Sharon and the guys are coming this way for dinner. You want to join us? Taylor and Theo are now wrapped too. We're going to choose a new county and move on as a group."

"Sharon found her family?"

"A mother and two daughters, alive and well, with the case being closed simply as resolved. They don't need the press attention, and the only one who could be arrested over what happened to cause them to run is already doing jail time, enough he shouldn't get out even with early parole until after the girls have graduated college."

"A good ending."

"Five for five with one group alive is a nice opening set." Evie looked around the office space. "I already miss this place. The next county is likely going to find us working in some basement with florescent lights with a need for lots of air fresheners."

David laughed. "Isn't that the truth? You have a preference for where we go next, Evie?"

"Let's stay somewhere north — I'm getting resigned to all the snow. I wonder if there's something like a missing magician in those county summaries? That would be neat. Or maybe a missing chef? We'd enjoy working a foodie crowd of suspects."

Her phone rang in her pocket. She dug it out, noted the caller ID. "And this day was going so smoothly." She answered the state dispatcher, "Lieutenant Blackwell," then reached for a pen and wrote down an address. "Tell him an hour. I'm on my way." She slid the phone back in her pocket. "Huge favor, Ann — can you pack up my hotel room?"

"Sure."

She took out her hotel room key and

handed it over. "Cole thinks my arsonist just got caught by one of his own fires. I'm on my way to Hoffman Estates." She stuffed the address in her pocket and picked up her backpack, grabbed her coat and gloves. "Choose somewhere interesting for us, David. I can handle anything but a missing schoolteacher. I've had my fill of classrooms for a lifetime. I'll meet up with you in the next county."

"Done. I'll see you there, Evie."

She headed out. She liked working with him. They were wrapped with both cases before the end of January. That had a good feeling to it too. She'd landed on a successful team and planned to make the most of it. She was even optimistic she would sort out how to answer Rob and get her life in order in the coming month.

She was pulling keys from her coat pocket, hurrying to her car when her feet went out from under her. She stared up at the sky, stunned, then shifted to see if anything was injured but found her coat had padded the worst of the impact and started to laugh. Life had a way of tumbling her occasionally. She got carefully back to her feet, rescued her backpack. Still laughing a bit, she unlocked her car. She'd hurt her pride more than anything else. She could always count on life to throw her some surprises. She started the car, hoped the heat would kick in quickly. Then she drove to meet Cole at the fire scene, wondering what she would find waiting for her there.

ABOUT THE AUTHOR

Dee Henderson is the author of numerous novels, including *Traces of Guilt, Taken, Undetected, Jennifer: An O'Malley Love Story, Full Disclosure,* and the acclaimed O'MALLEY series. Her books have won or been nominated for several prestigious industry awards, such as the RITA Award, the Christy Award, and the ECPA Gold Medallion. Dee is a lifelong resident of Illinois. Learn more at DeeHenderson.com or facebook.com/DeeHendersonBooks.